A Trout in the Milk

When a clash of interests concerning a planning application results in a violent death, Senior Planning Officer, Arnold London, becomes embroiled in a chilling murder investigation.

Little does Arnold know that his assistant's secret attendance at an illegal auction will lead to a number of disparate clues, enabling him to pinpoint the murderer...

Men of Subtle Craft

Asked to assist a historian with research into a medieval mason, Arnold London is left in no doubt by his superiors that he is to keep his personal interests distinct from his planning work. But when local magistrate Patrick Yates is found dead in his own stableyard by means such as a medieval mason would have used, Arnold's research unlocks vital clues to the Yates murder – and he has to risk his own life to find the killer...

ROY LEWIS

A Trout in the Milk
Men of Subtle Craft

Diamond Books
An Imprint of HarperCollins*Publishers*
77–85 Fulham Palace Road
Hammersmith, London W6 8JB

This Diamond Crime Two-In-One edition
published 1994

A Trout in the Milk © Roy Lewis 1986
Men of Subtle Craft © Roy Lewis 1987

The Author asserts the moral right to
be identified as the author of this work

ISBN 0261 66257 0

Cover photography by Monique Le Luhandre

Printed in Great Britain

A Trout in the Milk

Some circumstantial evidence is very strong,
as when you find a trout in the milk.

THOREAU: *Journal*

CHAPTER 1

1

'Arnold,' the Senior Planning Officer intoned, 'we have a problem.'

The Senior Planning Officer was never precise in these situations, Arnold knew: what he really meant was that *Arnold* had a problem. He waited, as the Senior Planning Officer belched gently and considered the difficulty.

They were standing in the corridor by the coffee-vending machine, a monstrosity which had been installed just three months ago and which was already the subject of litigation, having attacked one of the cleaning ladies attending to it. The Authority defence was that it had leaned on her head, bruising it: the lady in question claimed it had leaped at her, and thrown her to the ground, pinning her down by its weight. She was claiming for inhibition of sexual enjoyment, consequently: her muscular husband reminded her of her ordeal by machine, and she could no longer enthuse over the sexual act. The Senior Planning Officer seemed unabashed by these events and visited the machine regularly, idling before it as though daring it to leap on him from its unsteady plinth. Perhaps he had problems with an over-enthusiastic wife. The only complaints he had voiced to Arnold to date concerned her cooking.

The Senior Planning Officer returned the plastic cup to the shelf beside the machine and beckoned Arnold towards his office. 'Mr Wilson and Mr Livingstone will be joining us soon. Shall we go in?'

Arnold nodded and followed the Senior Planning Officer. His room was quite different from Arnold's. Its desk was broad, modern and highly polished. The carpeting, a deep, royal blue in colour, reached the walls, except under the window where no one would notice. There were always two sharpened pencils on the desk set and Annigoni's portrait of the Queen—a print torn, Arnold suspected, from an old newspaper colour supplement and discreetly framed —gazed serenely out over Morpeth, towards the distant sea, from the office wall. Arnold envied the Senior Planning Officer his office but knew, resignedly, he could never aspire to such magnificence: he was under-qualified, in-experienced, and in the Senior Planning Officer's view, peculiarly subject to scandalous involvements with the police.

Publicity, in the Senior Planning Officer's eyes, was a Bad Thing.

'The problem?' Arnold inquired, sitting down gingerly on the edge of a chair as the Senior Planning Officer settled down behind his desk.

'Willington,' the Senior Planning Officer grunted. 'The Hall itself. And of course, its owner, Patrick Willington.'

'I'm afraid I'm not conversant . . .'

The Senior Planning Officer fixed him with a stern glance designed to wither. Arnold tried not to wither. Disappointed, the Senior Planning Officer scowled and said, 'From time to time there emerges what may only be described as a Trial for this planning office. I'm not talking about the infernal objectors to road widening schemes, the professional trouble-makers who turn up at inquiries and disrupt pro-ceedings. No, I'm describing the kind of person who con-stantly makes planning applications that either have no chance of success, or are so complex as to cause us untold hours of work, only to have them withdrawn at the last moment.'

'Mr Willington?'

'Precisely.' The Senior Planning Officer frowned. 'The file is on the table over there. Pick it up when you leave at the end of the meeting. Included among those papers are all the applications that Mr Willington has made over the last fifteen years. There were a number before that; before my time.' He belched lightly, caressing his stomach with a soothing hand. 'Some of them caused us real problems. A hopper, for instance which was on wheels but could not be moved about the yard. Did that constitute a "building" under the Acts?'

'Why couldn't it move?' Arnold asked.

'The weight of the hopper,' the Senior Planning Officer replied, 'had caused the wheels to sink into the soft ground. Can you believe it? And then there were the other applications, for the erection of loose-boxes and coach houses, the establishment of a caravan site, the restoration of a war-damaged building, the improvement of a private road . . . I tell you, they're endless.'

Arnold glanced towards the file; it seemed thick. 'Were any of the applications successful?'

'None. You would have assumed old Willington would have won *something*, wouldn't you? But half of them were withdrawn, anyway. Change of circumstances, he said. Change of mind, really. A grasshopper.'

The Senior Planning Officer had still not delineated the problem, Arnold considered. Almost as though he had caught the fleeting thought, the Senior Planning Officer scowled again. 'He's got another bloody application in. I want you to take it up. Get out there, find out what it's all about and—'

He had no time to say more. There was a discreet tap on the door, it opened, and a nervous clerk peeked around. She hesitated. 'Are you expecting two gentlemen . . .?'

'Mr Wilson and Mr Livingstone,' the Senior Planning Officer said and rose from his chair. The girl bobbed her head, disappeared and a few moments later two men were ushered into the room.

'Ah, Mr Wilson,' the Senior Planning Officer said, extending his hand, 'nice to see you again. This is my colleague, Mr Arnold Landon.'

Wilson was a middle-sized, middle-aged man in a grey, herringbone suit. His handclasp was hard and purposeful, with an element of curiosity in it as though testing for strength. There was a certain frostiness in his smile that suggested caution, and his eyes were as flat as a frozen lake, grey under an afternoon sky. 'Mr Landon,' he acknowledged briefly, and his tone was dismissive. In a few seconds he had summed up Arnold and concluded he would be of no interest. He would see only a lean, middle-aged man with thinning, greying hair and a wispy, ineffectual moustache dominated by a nose that jutted like a piece of weathered timber from a sunburned face. Arnold's baggy, worn brown suit was in sharp contrast to the Senior Planning Officer's neat grey smartness and he was a man to be discounted.

The Senior Planning Officer was turning with an ingratiating smile to the second man. 'You must be Mr Livingstone . . . I *presume?*'

There was a weary acceptance in Livingstone's intelligent eyes as he suffered the Senior Planning Officer's inane comment. He was taller, younger and more muscular than his companion. His reddish hair had receded at the temples, giving him the look of an academic, but there was a controlled force about his body that suggested much more athletic pursuits. He moved lightly on his feet, and his grip when he shook hands was light, noncommittal, as he made his own summaries. He stared at Arnold; his glance was vague, as though he was flicking over in his mind the pages of a book, concentrating not on the present, but on distant events. 'Landon,' he murmured. 'Haven't we met before? The name . . .'

'I think not,' Arnold said self-effacingly, aware of the displeased glance from the Senior Planning Officer. They could both guess what was coming, and neither welcomed it.

Livingstone's brow furrowed with thought, then slowly he nodded. 'No, we haven't met. But I've heard of you, I think. Aren't you the Arnold Landon who's an expert on mediæval buildings and that sort of thing?'

That sort of thing. It was, Arnold supposed, one way of explaining the passion in his life. Unqualified for work in planning as a result of a lack of formal education, he had ended eight boring years in the Town Clerk's Department simply because it had become known he was a queer chap who seemed to know everything there was to know about wood, and building materials . . . and things like that. It had been the decision of the Senior Planning Officer to arrange his transfer: there had been occasions since, as publicity had hummed about the Department, when the Senior Planning Officer had seriously regretted that decision.

Livingstone was still appraising him carefully. 'There was something fairly recently, wasn't there? In the papers, something to do with a killing, Oakham Manor in Northumberland, was that it?'

'Mr Landon,' the Senior Planning Officer intervened firmly, 'has had certain unfortunate experiences but they are nothing to do with the workings of this office. Please, gentlemen, won't you sit down? And some coffee? We have a vending machine in the corridor—'

Both men demurred, a trifle hastily. They were clearly used to something better than machine-made coffee. Or maybe, Arnold reflected, they wanted no involvement with the prime exhibit in a lawsuit.

The Senior Planning Officer was settling himself behind his desk once more. He steepled his hands, inspecting the fingertips, and smiled in mysterious fashion. 'I trust . . . ah . . . business is going well for both of you?'

'Well enough,' Wilson said.

'And actively enough to make us both wish to conclude business here with despatch,' Livingstone added coolly.

'Ah yes, of course,' the Senior Planning Officer said, flustered. 'I merely meant . . . the courtesies . . .' He collected himself, flushing slightly. 'Mr Landon, ah, the reason I've asked Mr Landon to be present here to meet you two gentlemen is because with pressure of work in the office it's necessary that I should hand over the responsibility for processing your application to him. It had been my intention to deal with it myself, but I have leave due to me, I am aware you wish early decisions to be made by the planning committee, and so it seemed to me that Mr Landon—'

'Fine,' Wilson cut in. 'So we've met your Mr Landon. He'll be handling the application. And now we've met. So . . .?'

The Senior Planning Officer unsteepled his hands. 'Ah. Well. Fact is, your papers are being processed, but in any application like this it's wise to have the . . . ah . . . background explained. Things can arise at the committee which are, shall we say, unexpected? Opposition can come from unlikely quarters. We don't enjoy . . . *difficult* meetings. The Chairman, for instance, he likes to have a *quiet* meeting. Things are so much more civilized that way. And it makes things so much smoother for us, as well. So, since Mr Landon will be handling the paperwork and, as responsible officer, will need to make recommendations to the committee, it would perhaps be wise . . .'

'I can fill him in on the background,' Livingstone said. He smiled. He had good teeth and the smile was easy, lending charm to his features. He knew it, of course, and Arnold was not fooled by it, but if it helped ease situations that was fine. Wilson remained tight-lipped and cautious, but his companion was clearly at ease.

'The situation is this,' Livingstone said, leaning forward in his chair and engaging Arnold with an earnest glance. 'Just north of Darras Hall, some twelve miles inside the boundary of the county, there's a place called Penbrook Farm.'

Arnold nodded slowly, considering in his mind's eye the map of the county he held in his office. 'I think I know it.'

'It's not up to much as a farm,' Livingstone went on. 'I guess in the old days, maybe thirty, forty years ago, it was a better proposition, but the old dear who holds it now, she's not really capable of developing it properly or even keeping it going. Most of the fields are fallow; there's very little livestock—a few sheep, I think—'

'None of your Chillingham herds and that sort of thing,' the Senior Planning Officer offered supportively.

Livingstone ignored him. 'The location of the farm is interesting. The main farmhouse—which is a bit ramshackle now—is built on a hillside overlooking some meadows, a meandering sort of stream, and then the ground rises to some fairly extensive woodland. Not valuable trees, you understand, just scrub, alder, a few Scots pine, rubbish really, but . . . environmentally attractive.'

The words had been used deliberately, and soothingly. The calculating Mr Livingstone, Arnold guessed, would be far more interested in profit than environment.

'Behind the trees there's something like another fifteen acres of land. Not worth much at all; granite outcrops, broken ground. You know the kind of area I mean.'

Arnold knew. Much of it was fast disappearing as housing demands spread out from Newcastle and Morpeth.

'Then, across the river, there's about another eighty acres of flat land and that's about the whole thing. That particular area doesn't form part of Penbrook Farm, though it does actually figure in our general plans.'

Arnold could already guess the answer but he asked the question anyway. 'Who owns that land?'

Livingstone shrugged. 'A business consortium.'

'And you have an interest?'

Livingstone hesitated, glanced at Wilson and then said stonily, 'Mr Wilson and I are shareholders, yes. There are others involved also.'

Arnold nodded. He was aware of the Senior Planning Officer watching him carefully. 'What exactly do your proposals comprise, then?'

'It's like this,' Livingstone replied. 'Penbrook Farm is worked out. It's never going to amount to anything again. The owner is an old lady who's never displayed much interest in the farm as a working proposition. We aim to . . . renovate the whole situation.'

'*Renovate?*'

Livingstone nodded. 'If you think about the situation you'll understand the possibilities. Penbrook Farm lies just north of one of the most expensive, stockbroker-type housing developments in the North-East. Not ten miles north-east of the farm is Morpeth, county headquarters. Okay, so the whole area of the North-East is tight in the middle of economic depression, but curiously enough it's also a place where there are still big pockets of real money.'

'I still don't see—'

'We're proposing to build an old people's home at Penbrook Farm.'

The intervention came, impatiently, from Wilson. His tone was cold and dispassionate. He took out a cigarette case from his inside pocket and lit a cigarette. In the silence Arnold stared at him disbelievingly. 'An old people's home?' he repeated.

'Just that.' Wilson's ice-cold eyes watched the smoke rise from his cigarette for a few seconds and then he stared at Arnold. The indifference was complete. 'We intend calling it the Minford Twilight Home.'

Arnold stared at Wilson for several seconds. Incomprehension had dulled his senses. Slowly, something cold crawled in his stomach as the name bit home. '*Minford?*'

'That's right.' Wilson was aware of the surprise in Arnold's tone but was unmoved by it. 'The Minford Twilight Home. You'll know Councillor Minford, I imagine.'

Arnold had never met Albert Minford but knew of him.

He had been active as a councillor for a decade or more. He had acquired sufficient wealth from the business his father had built to be able to regard politics as an appropriate substitute for a career. It was rumoured he was hungry for the accolade that had never yet come from Buckingham Palace; talk was he was still expecting an Honour, and this accounted for much of the charity work he was seen to be active in. He was not averse to accepting the odd local honour, however: when he did a stint as chairman of the local education committee he had been pleased to have a secondary school named after him, and there had also been the Minford Hospital Wing to be proud of after he had organized a charitable appeal some five years ago.

'I've heard of Councillor Minford. He's never served on Planning, so I've never actually met him. I wasn't aware he was active on Welfare, either.'

Wilson contemplated the glowing end of his cigarette. 'So?'

'Well, if there is a proposal to name the Home after him . . . unless . . . is he a member of your consortium?'

Livingstone stirred, Arnold thought somewhat uneasily, but Wilson merely looked at the Senior Planning Officer. Arnold's superior shook his head. 'No, that's not so. Perish the mere thought, Arnold. It would be . . . unethical, in my view, were that to be the case.'

Wilson smiled thinly. 'We have decided to name the new Home after Councillor Minford merely in admiration for the unstinting way in which he has served the community in his capacity as councillor. The county should be proud of his efforts, and it seems to us, as businessmen *involved* in the community, that the gesture would be an appropriate one.'

A short silence fell. Arnold felt as though he had been snubbed. The Senior Planning Officer contemplated his fingernails. Arnold cleared his throat. 'I see . . . May I ask, then, what the planning application comprises?'

Wilson's glance lingered over Arnold for a few moments, then slipped towards Livingstone. At the almost imperceptible nod of permission, Livingstone said, 'Clearly, you'll need to familiarize yourself with the situation.'

'Clearly.'

'There's a great deal of work to be done.'

'Of course.'

'We are aware there are certain members of the planning committee who will wish to go into matters in some detail,' Livingstone said. 'We are fairly certain there will be crucial questions concerning the location of the Home.'

'Opposition, you mean?'

A faint flush of annoyance stained Livingstone's features. 'We wouldn't say *opposition*. It's merely that certain members of the committee will, we guess, wish to be assured that there are no *problems* with regard to the location matter. It's as well that you should be aware—in case you are asked by the committee—of the *total* picture regarding the application. The Minford Home will be an ideal last resting-place for the elderly—peace, quiet, the Northumberland countryside, easy access to both Newcastle and Morpeth, with the sweep of the hinterland to enjoy, and distant scents of the sea . . . We are confident that Penbrook Farm, for these reasons, is the perfect location for such an enterprise.'

The presentation brief had already been prepared, Arnold thought cynically. 'Its location may be ideal, but I would have thought access was not *that* easy with winding country roads—'

'Ah, we have to admit,' Livingstone interrupted, smiling easily, 'there will be much work to be done. At considerable expense. *Our* expense. Road widening and improvement schemes will form part of the planning application. There's a diversion arrangement we'll need to have approved, a drainage scheme, a change of use for certain of the adjoining farm properties which are presently leased—but we've also built into the proposal certain conditions which we're quite happy to have imposed on us, relating to the preservation of trees and woodlands . . .' Livingstone smiled again, winningly. 'We've taken the best advice.'

Arnold hesitated, then took a deep breath. 'This all sounds . . . most philanthropic, but you'll forgive me for saying there must be a catch somewhere.'

The Senior Planning Officer frowned. 'Catch? Arnold, it's not our business to—'

'No, that's all right.' Livingstone held up a placatory hand, and twisted his smile into a grimace. 'We're businessmen, we admit it. Mr Wilson and I, and our associates, do have certain commitments here in this project—to old people, to the environment—but it would be less than honest to suggest we didn't have other irons in this particular fire as well. Service roads, access, the location itself, a fine place for a home for elderly people; but it's also a natural high class housing development which can serve the mobile business population of the area. We know already, for instance, that two of the major American companies who have executives in the district would be more than interested in acquiring high cost, easily saleable properties in such an area; there's the possibility of a country house because of the proximity of the moors, with shooting rights below the Cheviot; yes, we admit there are strong business considerations we have taken into account.'

The Senior Planning Officer had steepled his fingers again. His eyes were no longer on Arnold. He was contemplating his desk as though he had never seen it before. He was the independent, objective, uncommitted planning officer. All decisions in such matters were made by politicians: he was simply a servant.

'Such a development would need planning permission, for a change of use in agricultural land—'

'Which is at present largely derelict,' Livingstone supplied.

'And the farm—'

'It's possible a compulsory purchase order will have to be made against the owner of Penbrook Farm,' Wilson said harshly.

'These are high hurdles you've set yourselves,' Arnold suggested. 'A planning inquiry could be demanded, and the Minister—'

'Is unlikely to intervene,' Wilson said, shrugging.

'I beg to differ,' Arnold said warmly. 'In so many cases like these, public protests—'

Livingstone cleared his throat. 'In this *particular* situation we are fairly confident that the political will to carry through the proposals without a planning inquiry exists.'

'The price being an old people's home?' Arnold asked disbelievingly.

'The *Minford* Twilight Home,' Livingstone corrected him gently.

Arnold sat back in his chair. He stared at the two men facing him: Livingstone was still at ease, confident in his control of the situation; Wilson smoked his cigarette indifferently, aware there was nothing in this room to fear. Their plans had been made, their commitments determined, their paths cleared of possible debris, and Arnold was quite sure *they* were quite sure they could get what they wanted. He was not very happy about it. He glanced at the Senior Planning Officer for confirmation of any kind, but his superior merely shifted in his seat and gestured towards the manila folder in front of him. 'The details of the planning and compulsory purchase applications are here, Arnold. I think it's an appropriate time for us to go into these in some detail now. It will familiarize you with the whole situation before I go on leave. You can take it from there afterwards. Perhaps you'd like to start, Mr Livingstone? While you're settling the basic details with Mr Landon, I'll nip out and get us all a cup of coffee. Each.'

Before anyone could utter a word of protest, he drifted purposefully from the room.

2

Working in the Town Clerk's department had been stifling for a man who had been brought up in the Yorkshire Dales, with a father who had tramped with him through the valleys and across the fells, showed him the decayed villages, traced for him the remnants of a long-dead time.

In the Planning department it was different for he had reason and excuse to get out into the crisp morning air, travel the winding roads of Northumbria, smell the tang of the distant sea and in summertime watch the shimmering dance of the Cheviot, blue above Rothbury and the Coquet.

Three days after the meeting in the Senior Planning Offier's room, Arnold had got rid of enough paperwork to be able to undertake the tasks the Senior Planning Officer had left him before he took his leave, inevitably, in Scarborough. Arnold decided to make a day of it. The morning could be spent visiting Willington Hall; the afternoon, on a return journey that would take him not too far from his own home outside Morpeth, could be spent at Penbrook Farm.

The journey was deliberately planned. It meant that, since Willington Hall was located in the wild eastern hinterland of the county, close to the Cumbrian border, he could take the drive from Morpeth towards the old military road.

For Arnold, it was a perfect morning for such a drive. He left early, knowing that west of Housesteads he would have the autumn winds to cleanse his lungs while he contemplated the hard times the Roman sentries must have experienced as guardians of the northern frontier, Hadrian's Wall. He was early enough to be able to afford a halt at Crag Lough Wood. He sat on a granite outcrop and watched the wind shaking the pines as though it was desperate to hurl them into the lough below, where white horses danced against the reedy shores and a thin mist of spray drifted up over the heather slopes.

Those Roman soldiers and architects had been canny

men: it was easy to see why they built their wall here, across the frozen throat of Britain. The granite hills, rolling northwards, fell sheer at the stark, petrified wave of Whin Sill rock. The thin snake of the wall itself crawled over the crests—east over King's Hill to Carrawburgh, west by way of Cuddy's Crags to Steel Rigg and the Nine Nicks of Thirlwall.

But the Wilsons and the Livingstones of this modern time were canny men too, in their own way. They knew where they were driving, and they knew how to do it. They knew where the productive places were and they knew how to protect their backs against alien spears. But while Arnold felt he could relate to the empire-building Roman generals, he was entirely out of sympathy with the businessmen who were set to build their own little empires. It was a paradox; perhaps it was only distance and time that made the difference, and he guessed that it might be the same entrepreneurial drive that had motivated those long-dead generals and the new business captains. He could not tell.

Even so, the machinations of Wilson and Livingstone and the politicians in their pockets bothered him.

Such machinations, he reasoned as he left Crag Lough Wood, shouldn't really bother him. He should react as he was supposed to react, as a servant of the council, a humble Planning Officer. He had no hand in policy-making, no points of view to put that should be divorced from fact. An adviser on practical matters, nothing more.

Yet he knew, as he drove west, that he could not change. To the south, towards the Durham hills that served as a backdrop, he could see the last traces of General Wade's old military road. The shafts of sunlight that raked across the valley of the South Tyne were bleak and cheerless, presaging little other than a sequel of black cloud, squalling furiously across the valley slopes. A townsman might shiver deep into his raincoat, but Arnold saw only grandeur and the power of the air and the earth. Fanciful; yet realistic.

The Wilsons and the Livingstones came and went.

The problem was, while they lived, they could do so much damage.

Arnold drove on. The land lifted, rising until to the north he could see the dark distant cohorts of Forestry Commission pinewoods that had already altered the landscape of bracken and bentwoods that would otherwise have been recognizable to the Brigantians of fifteen hundred years ago. He glanced at his watch; he had calculated he would be at Willington Hall by ten o'clock. He should soon be reaching the cross-roads, and the sign that would direct him to Estley village and beyond, the Hall itself.

At last the road began to drop, carpeting pinewoods appearing ahead of him, and as it did so the sky lightened, patches of blue emerging against the grey, spreading, extending until the autumn sunshine was warm through the car window.

The tiny hamlet of Estley was passed; the church there was of little interest, dating from about 1500, except for the unusual ashlared hardstone used in its construction. The road narrowed thereafter, and its surface degenerated. The fields he passed through seemed exhausted; there was a general air of depression in the area, heightened by ruined barns, a weathered folly on the skyline, a tumbled sheep pen on the fern-withered slopes.

When he reached Willington Hall, Arnold was appalled.

He came upon it suddenly, unexpectedly.

It was the way the house would have been planned, perhaps three centuries ago. The shoulder of the hill curved away to the left and the road swung out of the trees to give a view across a small vale, sheltering under mist-shrouded hills. The Hall sat squarely at the base of the hill where at one time it might have twinkled in the sunshine, warm magnesian limestone sparkling after a shower of rain, fresh-hewn and crystalline. Its south front had been grand, the two wings curving slightly like bull's horns, protecting the broad terrace and the sweep of the steps, and the meadows below the terrace had sloped above the gently meandering stream to provide a smooth view to rising slopes beyond.

Now, all had changed.

The east wing had crumbled, taken on the appearance of a Victorian folly, its crenellations the result of depredations of rain and wind. At some time, repairs had been carried out but inferior stone had been used and the limestone had changed in colour to a dull, drab grey. Even from this distance Arnold could guess at the sponginess of the stone; along the east front it was worse, a flaky dust where the chemicals of the atmosphere had eaten into the surface of the stone.

He drove down into the vale and his heart sank.

The bridge across which he drove showed signs of senility: the handrails sagged, desperately clinging to their supports to avoid the plunge into a stream that had been fouled for years, weed-ridden and dank. The meadows beyond were rank, clotted with weed and unproductive, their richness dissipated, deserted even by summer butterflies. The broad steps that led up to the terrace were green with lichen; the limestone had been badly patched with sandstone and the consequent chemical reaction between the materials had led to rapid decay.

So it was with the Hall itself. The whole fabric of the building was at risk, *had been* at risk for two decades and more. The depredations of time, the weathering of wind and rain had destroyed the façade, eating into the stone and crumbling its splendour into decay.

Tears prickled at the back of Arnold Landon's eyes. He could not explain the emotion, and yet he was aware that the building still had a splendour that decay could not erase, a grandeur that the negligence of its owners could not destroy. Men had built it, but it had drawn around itself a mantle of history that, now, it would retain in spite of the erosion of time. It was an old man, clothed with dignity in spite of poverty and the beckoning of time.

And yet he could have cried.

The building was reflected in the man.

Patrick Willington was in his late sixties. He was a tall, desiccated individual whose hollowed eyes hinted at desperations he had thought he'd conquered forty years ago. His skin had a yellowed tinge, like parchment exposed to a light unfamiliar; his mouth was thin-lipped, so that the reedy voice came as no surprise. There was something in his nervous movements that suggested to Arnold the blind commitments of a fanatic, and his hands were as confident as an architect's, subtle in their movement, precise in their decision. He belonged to a time that was past in that he was gentle of speech, mannerly, concerned about the impressions he might convey. He was *genteel*.

And he had never known Willington Hall.

Arnold could not be certain at what point of time he had reached that conclusion. There was the evidence of the building itself, of course, quite apart from the grounds. But it was more subtle than that. Patrick Willington had lived at Willington Hall most of his life and yet he had never really *seen* it, never appreciated what it was and had been, never recognized what it had become. What existed in his own retinal conclusions was far divorced from the reality; perhaps his recollections of his family and its place in history were equally unreal.

'We have been here for a long time, of course, Mr Landon. You'll have heard of the Willingtons of Willington, naturally. Like so many of the landed gentry our origins are, shall we say, somewhat *scented*? Edward Willington was an administrator in Calcutta in the 1750s and did quite well, becoming a member of the council of Bengal. Warren Hastings's finances were in an appalling state of course, but old Edward helped out a lot there, organizing the opium revenue. He came back in 1784 quite a rich man. It was he who renovated the east wing of the Hall, you know: interesting to think opium paid for that. Passed the rest of his life at Willington Hall—he gave it the name—as a country gentleman.'

Standing at the long window of the library, he gestured vaguely, limp-wristed, towards the sour meadows below them. 'Old Edward was interested in it all, but there was trouble with his sons, and at the time of the Napoleonic Wars quite a lot of stuff was stripped out, for some obscure reason that escapes me. It was Charles Willington who extended the farmland in the 1840s, and his son William who changed the course of the stream in 1882. He was a lawyer, you know, and change was in the air for lawyers in the 1880s: he was infected by it. My father, sadly, was infected with something quite different: like my grandfather, he was addicted to chorus girls—though neither married one—and they tended to support their predilections by taking money from the property, and doing nothing to replace it.'

Patrick Willington was proud to explain to Arnold that his own attitudes to the estate had been quite different. 'I was a major in the war, you know, and saw some terrible things. Coming back to Willington was . . . like fulfilling a dream. I determined to stay here, build the place up again. There was a problem, of course.'

'The bad winter of 1947?' Arnold asked.

The old man glanced at him vaguely, turning away from the window. 'The winter? Oh no, I mean that was a blow, of course, decimated our sheep. No, there was a family problem. There were just the two of us, you see, my sister and I. I always thought we got on quite well, but she had a funny streak. Never realized her sense of . . . *position*, don't you know? There was a chap, lived down at the village . . . when I got back from the Army I heard she'd taken up with him, and we had some violent words about it and I forbade her. Anyway she took it all rather badly, and had the vapours, you know the way young women are.' His hollowed eyes clouded suddenly, misted by the passage of time and the vagueness of memory, and he seemed to be searching for something that eluded him after all these years. He shook his head. It eluded him still. 'Could never understand it, really. I mean, she took it so *actively*, you know what I mean? Refused to speak to me, sneaked off to meet the feller, all that sort of thing . . .'

His glance strayed to the windows and he paused. 'Out here, you know, with an estate like Willington, there are responsibilities. Family. They have to accept those kind of responsibilities. She didn't. Sneaking off like that. Henry now, my son, he's different. Always looked to the day when he would inherit Willington. In his blood. Longs for the day when he could get to manage it . . . bit headstrong, the young are, so I've kept him on a tight rein, admit it, but it's for the good, you know? But my sister, she was of a different vein. And when that feller came on the land, and I caught him, I did what any brother would do. Odd, that, she never forgave me. And she knew how to hurt; knew where to strike. Took from me my dearest possession . . .'

Arnold felt vaguely embarrassed. He had the impression that Patrick Willington was hardly aware of his presence any longer, but was contemplating a past that had become distant and unimportant, until dredged up by chance, as now.

'Still,' Patrick Willington said, as though picking up Arnold's thoughts, 'it's all of little consequence now. After that row she up and went, most surprisingly. Always thought her a mouse. But she left, went to Scotland or somewhere. She had some money of her own . . . Mother left it to her. I could have used that money . . . sunk it into the estate, maybe turned the place around with it. But she left, and somehow . . . there was a period when I looked for her, she'd taken to wandering . . . Europe . . .' His brow became furrowed, the desiccated skin stretched tight over his cheek-bones, as he foraged for reasons half forgotten. 'Never found her. Bad business. The wrong she did, it's never left me, but haven't seen hide nor hair of her since, so what's the odds?' His brow cleared as unpleasant memories departed. 'Bit of cash then would have made a difference, but I managed. Dragged the estate into the twentieth century. Tried to make the farms profitable. Improved the drainage in the lower fields. Upgraded stock. Brought in new strains.'

'Government subsidies—'

'Took advantage of those, naturally. Won't pretend it's not been hard work. But rewarding.'

Arnold thought about the sour fields he had seen on the approach to Willington Hall. He was fascinated by Patrick Willington's inability to perceive the reality about him. He seemed to feel all was well, and he had kept the estate going, but in Arnold's view, if the man could be applauded for his commitment to the land he could hardly be admired for his efficiency in managing it.

'We had appallingly bad luck, of course. I mean, the upkeep of the Hall itself has been crippling, and there was bad weather, the poor harvests, and the personnel . . . I mean, before Henry came home I had a young chap who was making a perfect hash of things, so I took over entirely from him, and when Henry's been long enough on the estate to *understand*, well, maybe I'll let him have a free hand.'

Not this side of the grave, Arnold thought.

The old man began to cough and his yellowish skin took on a transparency that emphasized his frailty. 'My new scheme, it will give us the chance to turn things around . . .'

It was to be a sawmill. Patrick Willington's application had seemed unrealistic when Arnold had looked at it in the office, but now the old man attempted to describe it and Arnold became more than ever convinced that the owner of Willington Hall had no more business sense than farming acumen. It seemed to Arnold that everything was against the project. As far as the estate itself was concerned, the woodland was thin and little that could be regarded as marketable grew there; much had been stripped away over the years. So a sawmill would have no immediate source of timber to start business. Secondly, the isolation of the Hall itself would surely mean that the likelihood of business coming to it would be remote: even if there was work in the area the access roads were hardly suitable for heavy traffic. Besides, to Arnold's knowledge there were at least two sawmills with spare capacity located within twenty miles of Willington Hall, and both were far more accessible, with main road situations.

'Are you sure this mill would be a paying proposition?' Arnold asked cautiously. He spoke with care because, strictly speaking, it was none of his business. As planning officer his concern was mainly with environmental matters, not with the likely profitability—or otherwise—of the scheme. As far as he could ascertain, Patrick Willington would be throwing money away over this scheme, money he could ill afford if one took into account the general state of Willington Hall.

'It will be a turning-point for the estate,' Patrick Willington enthused, 'and I look forward to the building once the application is approved. Now then, Mr Landon, a little dry sherry before you leave?'

Arnold left the crumbling terrace of Willington Hall with a feeling of despondency. The great estates of Northumberland still flourished, a High Tory fiefdom of ancestral parks and stately houses, discreetly hidden behind great avenues of sturdy trees. The farms were fat, the generous fields had still not lost their hedgerow oaks. But there were the Willington Halls too, the struggling manors where money had run out, where crippling death duties had taken their toll, and where mismanagement over decades had stripped the land of its richness until the houses themselves decayed, showed gaunt rib-trees to the sky and rain, and slipped into a graceless desuetude. Arnold bled for the waste and the sadness of it all.

He made his way back to the car, and was hardly aware of the man standing there until he was almost upon him.

''Morning.'

He was dressed in a leather-patched jacket and corduroy trousers and his boots were splashed with mud. The knotted scarf he wore at his throat had loosened and the skin there was as wind-tanned as his face and hands. He was about thirty-five years old but his fair hair was receding, thinning at the temples, and there were lines on his face that suggested he had concerns beyond his years. His eyes were a pale brown, lacking the softness of a darker hue, and somehow lacking in emotion: Arnold felt he was being subjected to a steady, cold appraisal and he found the thought disconcerting.

Arnold returned the greeting and began to unlock his car door. The man rested an arm on the roof of Arnold's car. 'You been to see my father?'

Young Henry, Patrick had called him. Arnold looked at the heir to Willington Hall with more interest. 'That's right. My name's Landon. I'm a planning officer, based at Morpeth.'

Henry Willington frowned vaguely. 'You come about the application regarding the sawmill?'

'That's right.'

'Bloody nonsense.'

Arnold was inclined to agree. He studied Henry Willington for a moment and then asked, 'Can't you persuade him to drop it?'

'Will it go through planning?'

'It's possible.'

Henry Willington grunted in dissatisfaction. 'No, I can't persuade him to drop it. He may be an old man but he's stubborn as hell as far as Willington is concerned. He thinks he *knows* what's best for the estate, in spite of all the evidence of his mismanagement that's staring him in the face. This isn't the first hare-brained scheme he's had, Mr Landon.'

'I understand,' Arnold said quietly, 'that there have been quite a few applications over the years.'

'A *few*!' Henry Willington snorted. 'That's an understatement. You know, the whole thing is crazy. I was eighteen when I was sent away—at some expense—to Seale Hayne Agricultural College. I came back with all the theory, and some good ideas. But my education was a waste of time. He never listened to a thing I said. Still doesn't. It would have been possible, maybe ten years ago, to turn this place around. Now, I'm not so sure. God knows why I still hang on.'

'You manage the estate, I understand.'

'Is that what he said?' Henry Willington said bitterly. 'Well, maybe it's so, in name. We've few staff anyway, and not much by way of stock, and the farms are leased out, so it's not much to manage at all. But he still does everything himself, even keeping the books, though I have to rewrite every damn one of them afterwards. He'll have told you how his father and grandfather ruined Willington. At least they had a purpose in their negligence, and they enjoyed themselves. But my father—he's just seeing the place down the drain. *Actively*. Can he get much pleasure out of that?'

Arnold hesitated. 'I think perhaps he isn't aware . . .'

'Damn right he isn't.' Henry Willington's fists clenched suddenly, and Arnold was aware of the frustration, coiled like a snake inside the man. 'And it's all gone too far now. Death duties will rip apart what's left of this place, and why the hell I stay on . . .'

Arnold could guess. Brought up at the Hall, Henry would find it difficult to tear himself away from the decaying estates. Hoping, perhaps, that there could be a retrieval of fortunes, a turn around of the finance, a return to better days. It would be a forlorn hope, and Henry Willington would know it. 'I'd better be going,' Arnold said.

Henry Willington's pale brown eyes were fixed on his. 'I don't want this application going through. If he spends— *wastes*—any more money on stupid schemes . . .'

'I don't really have much control over the matter.'

'You're the planning officer. You'll advise the committee.'

'That's all. Advice.'

'But you know it's crazy.'

Arnold nodded slowly. 'I don't think it'll work.'

Henry Willington held his glance for a long moment. Then he made a humphing sound, nodded, and stepped away from the car, apparently satisfied. And yet, Arnold thought, in the end nothing will satisfy Henry Willington other than the resurrection of the Willington estates as a manageable property. Which meant the likelihood of his ever being satisfied was remote.

Arnold's mood of despondencey did not fade until he had left Willington Hall way behind him. The morning was all but over now, but the sky had lightened, wintry patches of blue appearing above the hills. He had brought a Thermos flask of coffee and some sandwiches with him and he stopped on a piece of open ground, with a burn tumbling to his left, to have a sparse lunch.

A day out of the office like this was good. Willington Hall had been depressing, but at least Arnold was out in the open air, by himself. Penbrook Farm, his next point of call, was some thirty miles distant but it would be a pleasant drive over the looping fell road, and now the sky was brightening he would get splendid views across the North Tyne to the Durham hills.

He finished his lunch, relaxed for half an hour, just listening to the burn, and then he drove on. He arrived at Penbrook Farm in the early afternoon.

He entered the gate at the north end of the property and the fields lay spread below him. To his left was a copse of hazel with, to his surprise, a scattering of standard oaks. In front of him the land fell away, the fields neatly hedgerowed, and there was something about the pattern that affected him, a feeling of *déjà vu*, an emotion stirring inside him that reminded him of his childhood, walking in the broad-leaved woods with his father. He sat there, silent, looking at the fields, and the stream that straggled its way along the eastern boundary, the greening tiles of the roof of the farmhouse, the slow ascent of blue smoke from the chimney and the clump of the old barn beyond.

There was a lump in his throat, the prickle of tears at the back of his eyes and he could not understand why. Then he heard the tapping at the car window and he turned his head.

Inches from his face was the threatening muzzle of a double-barrelled shotgun.

3

The woman was in her early fifties. She had a woollen cap crammed on her head, from which a few greying, untidy curls escaped in a ragged fringe. A thick muffler protected her throat and the tweed jacket she wore had seen better days even before thorn and rain had further dilapidated it. Her woollen gloves had been cut off at the knuckles to leave her fingers free: they were red and wind-chapped, but the grip on the shotgun was fierce, and the pouched eyes in the heavy, folded face glittered with determined passion.

Arnold wound down the window with an exaggerated care.

'Don't get out, mister. You can reverse to the gate. Then I just want to see the back of you, going like hell down the road.'

There was a guttural Northumbrian catch in her throat, and her accent was Border Country, and yet there was something about it that suggested to Arnold not an affectation but a deliberate attempt to communicate. Her accent was adopted, but her intention was clear enough.

'Excuse me, but—'

'No excuse me. Just get off Penbrook.'

'You are . . .?'

'The hell with who I am. *Get off this property!*'

Arnold expelled his breath slowly. The wicked mouths of the twin barrels were pointed unwaveringly at his head, eager to explode, and his stomach seemed to have sunk, his legs beginning to tremble uncontrollably. He swallowed hard and said insistently, 'Are you the owner of Penbrook Farm?'

For a moment silence fell, and the gun barrels wavered slightly. The eyes were unremitting, however. 'No matter. I told you. Get off the farm.'

'I'm sorry, but I have a job to do.' Arnold's tone was firm even though his mouth was dry with fear. 'And I need to—'

'You hired by those bastards Wilson and Livingstone?'

The eyes darted suspicion and malice at him and the nose was wrinkled in distaste. Arnold blinked. 'Wilson and . . . er . . . Livingstone? Look, I'm employed by the local authority. I'm a planning officer, based at Morpeth, my name's Landon and I've come in respect of an application—'

He stopped as the barrels were suddenly lowered. The woman stepped back, uncertainly, staring at him with the same suspicion, but overlaid now with doubt. 'Planning? You come to weigh up cases?'

'Something like that,' Arnold replied in relief.

Silence fell between them. The woman took another step backwards. He could see her more clearly now, dumpy, middle-aged, clad in a calf-length black woollen skirt and gumboots, less menacing than previously, the shotgun drooping with uncertainty in her hands.

'Planning,' she said thoughtfully, then in a sharp action broke the barrel of the shotgun. 'You'll need to talk to

Sarah.' She paused, gestured down towards the farmhouse in the hollow. 'She's down there.'

'Thank you.'

The woman snorted impatiently and moved away towards the screen of hazel coppice from which she had earlier emerged. 'I'll see you down there . . . My name's Sauvage-Brown.'

She turned, making surprisingly little disturbance in the undergrowth as she ploughed her way into the trees. In seconds she had disappeared. Arnold sat silently in the car, staring after her.

Mildred Sauvage-Brown.

The Senior Planning Officer possessed language of considerable colour and invective. When he was disturbed he indulged in it. When he was deeply disturbed, and consistently disturbed, he controlled his language in that respect but the control was more effective for all that.

'Mildred Sauvage-Brown,' he had once said firmly to Arnold, 'is a violent pain in the backside.'

The conviction in the Senior Planning Officer's tone had persuaded Arnold that Miss Sauvage-Brown would be worth looking up. A view of the scattered files, and some discreet inquiries had given him the information he desired. She had never crossed Arnold's path, but most of the rest of the planning staff had bruises to prove the acquaintance.

She was a curiosity.

Her father had been a second-generation German immigrant in the United States. Her mother had been an English-woman of rather more than modest means. Mr Braun had anglicized his name upon his marriage and when Mildred was born in New York she had been endowed with a hyphenated surname that ensured remembrance of her mother's considerable social status in Hampshire, England.

Mildred had come to England in the last year of the war and had never returned. The clothing business run by Mr Braun and the money left to her by her mother had ensured she was well placed to indulge herself in England. Her indulgence had been supported by beliefs, nurtured by her mother, that old England was worth preserving, and by character, epitomized by Germano-American persistence and stubbornness, that broke through in numerous lawsuits, inquiries and tribunal hearings in Suffolk and Hampshire during the 1950s.

Evidently she had decided the South was, eventually, not worth preserving, for in the 'sixties she had come north, fallen in love with the Border Country and transplanted her affection. The roots had grown sturdy, deep and strong, and had, according to the Senior Planning Officer, strangled many a planning project at birth. He had grudgingly admitted that the country needed people like her, but not too often, and in not too great a number.

And Mildred Sauvage-Brown was here on Penbrook Farm.

For a moment, Arnold felt a twinge of sympathy for Mr Wilson and Mr Livingstone. Then he started the car and drove on down the hill.

The farm was interesting. On the hillside above the hollow there was a woodland of ash, elm and small-leaved lime trees. A spinney of thorn hung on the craggy edge of the hill and along to his right as he drove the twisting track he caught a glimpse of the squat stubs of old pollards. They would once have served as woodland boundary markers, and a small knot of warm excitement began to gather in his chest.

The track swung sharp left and he slowed as he came level with the barn, a fifteenth-century structure, he guessed. Beyond the barn was a pigsty, and then the farmhouse itself. It could not boast the lineage of the barn: there would probably have been an old farmhouse on the site but from its appearance Arnold guessed that the older building would have been demolished near the turn of the century because this structure was certainly no older than the 1890s.

He found difficulty parking his car; there was a muddy Range Rover parked across the track and a battered Austin in the yard beyond. Arnold reversed slowly, turned, and edged his way back up the track so that he would be able to leave the farm more easily after his interview with the owner. He cut the engine, got out of the car and locked it. He was parked some twenty yards from the pigsty.

It was a nondescript enough construction. The sty itself was squared, built of limestone which had weathered to a dull, drab grey, lichen-stained and crumbled badly in one corner. The pen beyond was perhaps five feet high, again of limestone, and part of the roof had fallen in, with the eastern corner repaired, badly enough, with corrugated iron. But enough of the original roof remained to interest Arnold. He walked across to the sty and looked at it more closely.

He was still standing there when Mildred Sauvage-Brown came down from the hill.

She stood glaring at him, the shotgun broken over her arm, a dumpy, scowling woman who resented his presence as an intrusion. 'You not gone in yet?'

Arnold shook his head. 'I was just looking at this.'

'The old pigsty?'

'That's it. *Very* old.'

'Rubbish.'

'True.'

Her head cocked on one side and she stared at him, summing him up. Perhaps there was something in the gravity of his tone that puzzled her, for after a moment she drew nearer and looked over the old sty, sniffing as she did so, as though odour would betray secrets not apparent to her.

'What do you mean, very old?'

Carefully Arnold said,' Well, not all of it. The outer walls, for instance, they'll have been erected maybe a hundred years ago.'

'And that's not very old?'

'Not in relation to the roof.'

She glanced at him unbelievingly and then turned again to gaze at the rusty corrugated iron, the tiles and the lichen-covered slates.

'So what's so old about the roof?'

Arnold pointed. 'The part that's collapsed, then the repaired section, that area isn't so old. But you see those slates? By my guess they'll be maybe three hundred years old.'

There was a long, stupefied silence. When Mildred Sauvage-Brown looked at him again her heavy face was dark as though she thought he was trying to insult her intelligence. 'How in the hell can you think that?'

Arnold smiled. He raised a hand, pointed carefully. 'Look at the top edge of those slates. You see the double line of holes? These days, when slates are used on roofs they use copper nails—better than iron nails because the iron rusts.'

'So?' Mildred Sauvage-Brown asked belligerently.

'Before they began to use copper nails, oak pegs were favoured. Too expensive now. But those nails holding those slates are rusted in—yet look at the smaller holes just beside them. Do you know what they once held?'

'You're going to tell me.' The Border Country accent was gone. Miss Sauvage-Brown was listening, concentrating, and a slight hint of her transatlantic tone was creeping in, even after all these years of English residence.

'The small leg-bones of sheep,' Arnold said confidently.

'What the hell are you talking about?'

'Believe me. It was a common practice in the North until well after Tudor times. Sheep bones—tough and cheaper than nails. Go take a look at Walworth Castle in County Durham sometime: they used to use the breast-bones of chicken there.'

Mildred Sauvage-Brown was saying something under her breath as Arnold walked away. It sounded like a string of vague obscenities.

*

Inside the farmhouse the air was warm with the blazing fire
in the eighteenth-century fireplace. The furniture was old,
the floor of the hallway and kitchen stone-flagged, and the
whole atmosphere was one of utility rather than comfort.
Yet the tea that was served to Arnold came from fine china
and the woman who served it was small, birdlike, gentle
and shy.

Sarah Ellis was no more than five feet tall and gave the
impression she had been built for domination. She fluttered
rather than moved, and she kept her grey head lowered,
unwilling to hold Arnold's glance for more than a few
seconds. Her voice was light, barely audible, and Arnold
guessed that she had spent most of her sixty years attempting
to escape confrontation. She wore a brown cardigan over a
high-buttoned blouse, long dark skirt and flat-heeled shoes.
She was nervous at his presence, yet struggled to contain
her nervousness, as though she had been trained to regard
politeness to guests as a duty. After Arnold had introduced
himself at the gate she had invited him inside to the parlour,
quickly produced a pot of tea and displayed some agitation
until Mildred Sauvage-Brown had joined them. Up till then
Arnold had managed only to elicit her name, the period she
had spent at Penbrook Farm—fifteen years—and explain
his own presence. Once her companion arrived Sarah Ellis
retreated gratefully over her cup of tea to listen rather than
to participate.

'So what is it you want to know from Sarah?' Mildred
Sauvage-Brown growled. She had removed the woollen cap
and the jacket: the grey sweater was baggy and her hair
tended to stick up wilfully from the crown of her head.

'I merely thought it would be appropriate to discuss
with you the proposals that are being made concerning the
establishment of an old people's home at the farm, the
purchase order—'

'They tell you they got plans to build over the hill?'

'I am aware of that—'

'It's all a fix, a deal they've made. Build the sop—the old folk's home—and then rake in the profits from a whole damned new village where no one but rich characters want it!'

'That's not quite the gist of their application—'

'Bet your ass it isn't!' Mildred Sauvage-Brown remarked balefully.

Arnold blinked, unused to the chameleon nature of the lady's language: the guttural Northumbrian sound had gone, and Americanisms were clearly creeping back. He wondered whether she adopted High Hampshire in planning tribunals.

'What I do wish to find out is the nature of the objections you'll wish to raise to the proposals,' he ventured.

'Objections?' Mildred Sauvage-Brown glared at Sarah Ellis. 'The first objection I'd be making on behalf of Sarah is that these bloody businessmen are seeking to turn a gentle old lady out of her home!'

'*You'll* be making?' Arnold asked. 'You have an interest in Penbrook Farm?'

'Interest?' To Arnold's alarm, Mildred Sauvage-Brown put down her cup, rose, walked to the fireplace, hawked and spat in the fire. 'What you really mean is do I qualify as an "aggrieved person" under your bloody ineffective Planning Acts. Well, I don't but Sarah sure as hell does as owner of the farm, and I'm preparing her case and I'll make damn sure she's not railroaded out of here. She's a sweet, gentle lady who's been put upon most of her life and I'm making sure it certainly don't happen this time.'

The sweet gentle lady made a gesture of feeble remonstration; it was ignored by the formidable Mildred. 'You know, I spent a few years in the south of England before I got sick of the whole attitude down there and came north. You damned English, you don't seem to know what you're doing with your heritage! Okay, the Romans didn't know better and carved a fair chunk of woodland out of the place, but by the Middle Ages woods were valuable property. It was a woodland economy, sure, and buildings were greedy for wood—'

'I understand it took six hundred and eighty oaks to build Norwich Cathedral's roof in the fifteenth century,' Arnold interrupted.

Mildred Sauvage-Brown stopped, glared at him, and opened her mouth silently. It was clear she was uncertain whether she was being mocked, and mockery of the kind that quoted supporting facts to her own obvious thesis was a ploy she had not previously met and was unable to cope with adequately. She snorted after a moment, and went on.

'In that economy, men learned to live with the woods. They managed them as a self-generating resource. They didn't clear-fell them: they raised sturdy new wood from the broad-leaved trees they'd put to the woodman's axe. Ash and hornbeam were cut in rotation—'

'I'm aware—'

'Coppicing extended the life of trees: there's a coppiced ash I found in Suffolk that must have taken root a hundred years before the Conquest. They dug it out, for a public lavatory! *That's* when I came north!'

'Miss Sauvage-Brown, I can assure you—'

'Assure me nothing! I know you clowns. Anything for a quiet life! You planning inspectors are all the same. I shouted my head off at fifty inquiries in Hampshire and Suffolk but all they were concerned with were *commuters*, for God's sake! So I came north, to the dales first, and then the Border Country where there was air, and hills, and a feeling of ancient times. But there are still attacks, and I've vowed I'll save you bastards from yourselves—protect the heritage you haven't the sense and guts to defend yourselves!'

'Please,' Arnold said firmly. 'I feel the same way you do. I think the heritage is important. But I'm here to discover

whether there are any sound reasons you can put forward
to overturn the planning application that's coming forward
from Messrs Wilson and Livingstone—with a certain political backing, I might add—'

'I might have guessed *that*!'

'But it would certainly help if you were to outline the case
you intend to raise,' Arnold went on. 'If there are matters
I can take into account I'll be able to raise them at the
inquiry, include recommendations in my report—'

'Mr Landon, we don't trust planning inspectors—'

'Mildred . . .' Sarah Ellis had raised a hand, meekly, as
though to remonstrate gently with her companion, calm
her down. Mildred Sauvage-Brown hesitated, then nodded,
patted the older woman's hand and returned to her seat.
Grumpily she said, 'All right, I can give you one matter
we'll be raising.'

'That is?'

She gestured with her thumb in the direction of the hillside
behind the farm. 'The woods, up there.'

'What about them?' Arnold asked.

'Not up to much for timber purposes. Oak, ash, some
beech and hazel. An *old* wood, Mr Landon. A wood that's
survived centuries because it grows on ground too poor to
be used for anything else. But the result is there's mediæval
banks and ditches up there. And more. There's yellow
archangel, bluebell, oxlip and herb paris, all the true species
of a primary woodland, slow to spread or regenerate, classic
indicators of a wood that may well have existed since Domes-
day. And don't tell me *that* word don't stir an Englishman.'

Sarah Ellis put out a soft, heavy-veined hand to touch
her companion's arm. 'Please, Mildred, don't get so excited.
I'm sure Mr Landon has come here to help.'

'So what's he got to say about the ancient woodland?'

Unhappily Sarah rose and drifted across to the other side
of the parlour. She picked up a small dark missal and
clutched it to herself as though seeking strength from it.

Arnold shook his head. 'I have to say, ladies, you'll not get much return out of that argument.'

'Why not?'

'Because the woodland you mention is not in danger. The plans cater for the retention of the woods. They'll be part of the . . . pleasing environment of the old people's home.'

Mildred Sauvage-Brown grunted triumphantly.

'Is there anything else?' Arnold asked.

'Nothing I'm prepared to discuss with *you*,' Mildred Sauvage-Brown snapped.

Arnold felt sad. He was aware that behind the woman's bitterness and awkwardness lay a real passion for the countryside—*his* countryside—but her aggressiveness made it difficult for him to explain his own feelings about the situation. He too was opposed to the Wilsons and the Livingstones of the modern world, but he was a planning officer and he had his duty to do. As Sarah Ellis, the ineffectual owner of Penbrook Farm, fluttered in the background he rose, and took his leave of the two ladies.

Mildred Sauvage-Brown followed him out as though she feared he would indulge in minor despoliations as he left. She stood staring at him thoughtfully as he unlocked his car, arms folded muscularly across her ample bosom and then, as he got in behind the driving wheel, she suddenly came across to him.

'When I was talking back there, doing my usual niggle about what you planning bastards have done to the country-side you gave me a brief impression—'

'Yes?'

'That maybe you . . . cared,' Mildred Sauvage-Brown said unwillingly.

'I do.'

'Why?'

'Do I need a reason?'

'Don't play games with me, mister.'

'I'm not playing games,' Arnold said seriously. 'Look,

I've got a job to do. That doesn't mean I'm not . . . sympathetic. I think some of your . . . aggression can cause damage to your case but that's up to you. But I was brought up in the Yorkshire dales by a father who was a craftsman, and he's passed on to me a lot of his knowledge and a lot of his love for wood, and stone. So I do understand. And I do care.'

'Enough to help?'

Arnold hesitated. 'It depends what you mean by help.'

Mildred Sauvage-Brown glowered, then jerked a beefy thumb over her shoulder. 'That pigsty.'

'Yes?'

'You say it's old . . . awful old.'

'Part of it is.'

'You can prove that?'

'If I were called to do so.'

She turned and inspected the slated roof from a distance. 'Those slates, whatever you say, they don't look so old to me. Clean, like they was almost machined.'

Arnold leaned out of the window. He shook his head. 'The old slaters, they used the best tool of all. Frost.'

'*Frost?*'

'That stone is laminated oolite. What you had to do was quarry it in the autumn, lay the slabs of stone on the ground and then water them every evening from December through to March, if necessary.'

'What the hell for?'

'It was essential the stone remained green—if the quarry sap dried out of the slabs the stone could be used only for dry walling, or road metalling, or burnt for quick-lime.'

'And the frost?'

'The force of even a single thaw, following a hard frost, could achieve in a few hours what it could take a man weeks to do. It would crack the stone into clean, flat layers of varying thickness. After that, the slatter would just cleave the stone along the fissures and trim each piece with a hammer.'

'Then hole the slate near the head,' the woman said thoughtfully.

'That's right, so it could be fixed to a batten.'

'With an oak peg, the leg bone of a sheep,' Mildred Sauvage-Brown said with a gleam in her eye, 'or even a measly little chicken bone.'

'Oh dear,' Arnold said to himself as he started the car, put it in gear and drove bumpily up over the hill and away from Penbrook Farm. The Senior Planning Officer wasn't going to like this: he wasn't going to like it one little bit.

CHAPTER 2

1

The fact that the Senior Planning Officer was leaving for his holiday in Scarborough in a few days meant that Arnold was not called upon to explain about Penbrook Farm when he returned to his office in Morpeth. A natural preoccupation with his intended east coast sojourn resulted in the Senior Planning Officer having little regard for anything still lying on his desk during those last few days before he escorted his wife southwards. They were travelling by train. His wife distrusted his driving skills.

It was an occasion, therefore, when Arnold was able to relax somewhat and not feel concerned that the files he was dealing with were likely at any moment to be whisked away and scrawled upon with a spidery hand; when discussions with architects were in no danger of interruption by a demand to be 'briefed'; and when Arnold could feel clear of the necessity to sit for an hour or more while the Senior

Planning Officer commented upon his wife's inferior cooking
and his resentment at Arnold's failure to take to himself a
similarly happy marital situation.

It meant Arnold was left more to his own devices, of
course, and was free within certain limits to make his own
decisions without fear of being countermanded immediately,
but this was not a situation he entirely relished: he was not
an ambitious man and had no desire for the acquisition of
the power wielded by the Senior Planning Officer. Nor did
he wish to be privileged by visits from councillors, wishing
to talk to the man in charge.

When councillors did come into his office, it was usually
by mistake. It was Arnold's habit to direct them quickly to
the office along the corridor. He did so that afternoon, when
the man in the neat grey suit entered his office.

'You'll want the Senior Planning Officer. Just along the
corridor.'

The man nodded, turned, then stopped at the door. He
glanced back thoughtfully at Arnold. He was perhaps six
feet tall, with a whipcord leanness to his body and a thin,
narrow face in which the eyes gleamed watchfully. He was
about forty years old, perhaps a little more.

'You're Landon, aren't you?'

'That's right. Mr . . .?'

'My name's Minford.' Councillor Minford. A youngish
man to have been so active in local politics during the last
ten years or so since his father's death and the closing down
of the family business. That Albert Minford was no pauper
as a result of the closure was evident from his dress: his shirt
was expensive, his shoes soft, rich leather. He moved quietly,
almost catlike in grace, and he made Arnold feel uneasy at
the insistence in his glance. It was full of calculation and
summaries, a polishing of opinions.

'We've not met before,' Minford said.

'That's right. I've heard of you, of course, Councillor.'

'And I of you, Mr Landon.' It was a casual statement,

and contained no obvious weight, yet Arnold felt his spine prickle uneasily. 'You have obtained a reputation for certain unusual . . . involvements during this last year or so.'

'My job—'

'Oh, no criticism of your work. Unusual interests, though. I like that.' His eyes said otherwise: they betrayed no real interest. 'Keeps a man . . . balanced, having other interests. I . . . ah . . . understand the Senior Planning Officer takes leave soon.'

'For a couple of weeks.'

'You'll be working at the planning hearing for Penbrook Farm.'

'I will.'

'You'll have reached conclusions.'

They were not questions, but statements, delivered in a flat, unemotional and yet oddly menacing tone. Arnold blinked, unsure of himself. 'I suppose you could say that.'

'And?'

Arnold hesitated, then shrugged. 'I'm not sure what you want to know, Councillor. I've been out to the farm, had a look around. I've read the papers prepared by the petitioners.'

'They have council support.'

'That's right.'

'So it should be straightforward.'

Reluctantly, Arnold nodded. He had in his mind a glimpse of a belligerent Mildred Sauvage-Brown, but he kept the image to himself. Albert Minford's eyes bored into him. Arnold waited.

At last, with a vaguely dissatisfied air, Councillor Minford turned away. At the door he paused, looked back towards Arnold thoughtfully and said, 'You've been with the department quite a while, Mr Landon.'

'Quite a while, Councillor.'

'Loyalty . . . to the department gets rewarded.'

Arnold said nothing. Albert Minford let the silence between them deepen: he had said nothing that was dangerous, made no commitment by way of an offer, and yet there lay between them something unspoken, a gift dangling, a reward to be grasped if only Arnold cared to stretch out his hand. Slowly, Minford nodded and left the room. He closed the door softly behind him. He would do everything softly, Arnold fancied, until he was crossed. Then the softness could well become merely the sheath for steel.

He sighed. It was all very well, the Senior Planning Officer going off like this, but it meant that Arnold was really snowed under with work. There was the Willington Hall file as well as Penbrook Farm: the Willington Hall application would have to be dealt with within the week at the same time as Penbrook was pending. And then there was the new application regarding Amble. Complicated: a new company, a development that was almost bound to raise objections, but something that the town itself might welcome in general to halt its gradual decline over the years.

And it would require a visit.

Arnold left the office at two in the afternoon. It was a bright day, and the early morning frost had disappeared from the roads although the hills towards the Cheviot were white-summited, sparkling in the bright air. Arnold drove north from Morpeth, taking the bypass towards Alnwick, and where the road dipped towards the ancient bridge at Felton he turned right and meandered through the winding road that led to the coast. Furrowed fields to his left glistened with frost and high above the hedgerow a sparrowhawk hovered, wings hardly quivering in the afternoon sun.

Warkworth Castle stood on the hillside overlooking the village, its ruined windows staring blankly downriver towards Amble. Arnold parked in the main street and walked back up the road towards the castle, crossed the moated bridge and entered the castle grounds. There was no keeper at the gate: tourists arrived only in the summer months and today there was no charge for entry. Arnold climbed the well-preserved walls and stood in the embrasure, looking out to the sea.

The breeze was keen at this height and he hunched in his overcoat. Below him the town lay warm in the hollow of the hill; the river crept in a slow half-circle around the town, under the old bridge where the martins nested, and then snaked seawards in a long, glittering coil. Two miles away he could see the first of the masted fishing-boats. They lay drawn up at the river edge, high and dry: when the tide came upstream, flooding the bar at Warkworth itself, they would ride gently on the swell. Beyond, as the river widened, the houses at Amble clustered at the bay. Church, warehouses, dark, decaying buildings of the waterfront. Arnold stared, and considered. A development there . . . it could pump summer life into Amble, even if winter would still be cold in the empty town.

Thoughtfully he made his way back to the high street.

He had parked on the steep hill above the market cross. A line of shops and offices ran opposite him and in one of the office doorways a man was standing. As Arnold began to unlock his car door the man raised his hand and walked across the street towards him.

'Arnold! What are you doing in Warkworth?'

Arnold Landon did not make friends easily. He lived alone and liked it, and his own personal interests tended to isolate him somewhat: few people were interested in discussing ancient wood and stone. His weekends were spent wandering in the villages and hills of Northumberland and Cumbria, seeking and identifying traces of lost worlds, mediæval, Norman, Saxon, Roman. Opportunities for social intercourse were few.

He did not exactly count Freddie Keeler as a friend, but the man's outgoing personality made it easy to talk to him when they met, and Keeler's own effusiveness was warming. He was an estate agent and auctioneer whom Arnold had

met some years earlier when he was working in the Town
Clerk's department. They had met from time to time in
Morpeth and for some curious reason Keeler had taken
Arnold under his wing socially, inviting him for a lunch-time
drink occasionally on Saturdays, when they had met in
town. Arnold hesitated now, and smiled lopsidedly.

'I might ask you the same,' he replied.

Freddie Keeler grinned, stopped, struck a pose and made
a theatrical gesture back towards the doorway he had left.
'Expanding!' he declaimed. 'Opened an office in Warkworth, haven't I?'

Keeler and Buckley. The sign was there; Arnold hadn't
noticed it.

'I thought you worked Northumberland from the Morpeth office,' Arnold said.

'Ah yes, but it's all a matter of confidence. You won't
realize it, but there's a hell of a lot of auction stuff goes
begging up here in the hinterland. Large houses, old folks,
they sell up and the sharks come up from London and
Manchester, but they don't like dealing with them. They
like a *local* dealer, someone they feel they can trust. And
that means you gotta be there, boy! Here, that is, if you
want to catch the stuff in the Border Country. Might even
have to set a place going in Jedburgh, eventually.'

Arnold nodded, smiling at Keeler's enthusiasm. He was
a tubby little man in his fifties, with sparse hair, a rolling
gait he claimed to have developed on the Tyne ferry as a
young man, and broad, red-knuckled hands. He wore a
tweed jacket and cavalry twill trousers as though he had
just discovered the fashion: there was something dated about
him, but it was an endearing quality. 'I've come up to take
a look at Amble,' Arnold explained.

'Amble?' Keeler knitted his brows. 'Planning business?
Oh yeah, wait a minute, didn't I see something in the local
rag?'

'It's possible.'

Keeler scratched his nose, glanced back over his shoulder and said, 'Tell you what, nothing much happening in the office, got a girl there anyway, I'll come down with you for a trip, hey? You can easily come back this way on the return, can't you? No need to go straight back to Morpeth. Might even be time for a swift half, if we wait till opening time!'

There seemed little Arnold could say by way of argument. Feebly he suggested Keeler might get a rush of business while he was away but the estate agent brushed the argument aside and clambered in beside Arnold. Together they drove down the river road towards Amble, leaving Warkworth at their backs.

Arnold had never liked the town particularly. It had grown rapidly in Victorian times with the growth of the fishing industry and the building of the coal staiths on the shoreline. The disappearance of the brigs hauling coal south, and the decline of first the coal and then the fishing industry had left the urban sprawl of red brick terraces without a reason for existence. The town centre had decayed and the shoreline itself had become a wasteland, the gaunt ribs of the old wooden gantries and coal staiths leaning with the sea gales against empty expanses of shale and coal slurry. A hundred years ago barges and brigs, proud-masted and heavy with cargo, had moored alongside the pier head, but the pier itself was now a rickety affair, planking and guardrails ravaged by wind and rain and exhaustion. Part of it had been fenced off with chicken-wire in an ineffectual warning ignored by schoolchildren; the staggering steps that were available alongside were still in use for the few pleasure boats that came alongside, and for the school training vessels that skirted the moonscaped land to brave the bar and the North Sea beyond.

Arnold stood alongside Freddie Keeler above the wooden railings. They stared out towards the bar and the white foam boiled in its surge as the wind shifted.

'Do you reckon they'll make a go of it?' Freddie Keeler asked.

'Of what?'

'The proposed marina.'

Arnold shrugged. 'I've no idea. I just look at these things in terms of planning applications. Whether they'll make it pay, that's another matter.'

'Local opinion says the whole scheme is farcical,' Keeler said. 'I mean, look at the coastline. Best beaches in the country, but empty because of inaccessibility and the damned wind that scours the sands on even the sunniest days. Fine harbours, but developed for a fishing industry that's all but disappeared. So who's going to come up here and start a yachting club? I mean, take the moors: shotguns are in plentiful supply along the rough shoots above Stanley in County Durham, and landowners from that moor right up through the length of Northumberland have made a packet by playing the market, raising grouse and pheasant, drawing in London businessmen and Saudi potentates. I mean, damn it, there's all sort of languages talked along the fells these days!'

'So I understand.'

Freddie Keeler wrinkled his nose, shrugged, and shoved his hands deep into the pockets of his overcoat. 'Saudis tired of hawking are one thing; can you imagine dhows racing on the Coquet? I tell you, man, the whole thing is crazy!'

'Is that the opinion of the Press?'

'There was a leader in the *Gazette* just the other day, Arnold. Said the scheme was a load of nonsense. To talk of boats returning to Amble is a pipe dream. There'll never be a return, hinny, no more than the coal will come back. What would be the point of mooring here at Amble, in this wasteland? Good harbour, sure, but there's facilities just up river, towards Warkworth. The castle to set the scene, a couple of decent pubs . . . who'd want to moor down here, with the wind whistling in from the North Sea straight up your backside?'

'Facilities could be improved,' Arnold suggested cautiously.

'So the Geordie Coast will compete with the Côte d'Azur?' Keeler scoffed. 'It's all a con, man, building a marina here. Waste of money. Unless . . .'

'Yes?'

'Unless it's someone else's money. Like yours and mine.'

Public money. It was a possibility that had already occurred to Arnold.

2

A week later the planning inquiry into the application regarding Penbrook Farm was convened at Morpeth. Wilson and Livingstone both arrived at the council chamber early, and Arnold was interested to note that they regarded the inquiry as an important one, since they had engaged the services of counsel to speak on their behalf and introduce the application. Arnold knew the man they had engaged: Arthur Sedleigh-Harmon, QC. He was a Chancery lawyer with a big London practice but a Northern circuit background, which enabled him to make forays north from time to time. It was hinted that he was a mean man, who undertook such briefs in order to be able, at his clients' expense, to indulge his passion, fly-fishing in the Border Country. Arnold had always thought him incapable of any passion: he was a tall, round-shouldered, dry stick of a man, hook-nosed, glazed-eyed, with a neat, trimmed moustache and a flat monotonous voice. But he was a successful lawyer, sharp-minded and incisive in his questions. He understood a witness's balance, or lack of it: he could topple a case with a question.

Mildred Sauvage-Brown was also in the council chamber, accompanying Sarah Ellis. Miss Ellis was dressed in brown, self-effacingly; Mildred Sauvage-Brown, on the other hand, had discarded her woollen cap, tweed jacket and black skirt but had dressed for the occasion in a heavy, mannish suit, belted at the waist, and a feathered Robin Hood hat was perched incongruously on her untidy grey curls. She had applied a red bow of lipstick to her mouth; it contrasted with powdered cheeks from which glared angry eyes, as though she dared mockery. Her glance slipped over Arnold dismissively. She watched Arthur Sedleigh-Harmon like a mongoose watching a snake.

The Queen's Counsel introduced the application in his flat monotone. Chairman of the Planning Committee was an elderly gentleman called Lansbury who claimed distant kin to the Labour politician of a bygone era; he was known to be ineffectual and inclined to doze. Sedleigh-Harmon's voice was conducive to an exaggeration of his inclination.

The application, Sedleigh-Harmon droned, would be one from which considerable benefit would accrue to the community, not least the elderly and infirm. The Twilight Home would be what it implied in its title: a haven for the old in which they would see out their days in quiet and comfort.

Mildred Sauvage-Brown snorted.

The monotone continued. Details of the layout of the home together with its configuration were appended in the schedule to the application; there would be minimal damage to the environment; service and access roads would be located in a fold in the land so as to cause the minimum disruption of the peace of the area.

Mildred Sauvage-Brown snorted again, and Sarah Ellis placed a timid hand on her companion's arm. Chairman Lansbury's eyelids grew heavy.

'And with that, Chairman, I will take my seat, although I am happy to take any queries at this stage,' Sedleigh-Harmon announced abruptly, and sat down.

Startled, Lansbury sat up, sniffing and scratching his cheeks in a sudden panic, until he remembered where he was and the purpose of the inquiry. An official at his elbow whispered to him. He coughed, cleared his throat. 'Ah . . . I understand there are objections to the proposals. Perhaps we could have a submission at this point?'

Formidably, Mildred Sauvage-Brown rose to her feet. Chairman Lansbury looked vaguely unhappy: clearly, he had met the lady at earlier hearings.

'Ah, Miss Sauvage-Brown. *You* are objecting to the application?'

'On behalf of the owner, Miss Sarah Ellis. We,' she intoned, sweeping a contemptuous glance over the group sitting across the room and comprising Wilson, Livingstone and Sedleigh-Harmon, 'cannot afford the services of eminent counsel.'

Arnold settled back. There was a nervous feeling in his stomach. Mildred Sauvage-Brown was not the kind of person to give up anything without a fight, and he had a feeling he was likely to end up right in the middle of her battlefield. It was not a prospect he viewed with any feeling of enjoyment.

'Chairman, in the beginning was the wildwood, the home of the wolf and brown bear,' Mildred Sauvage-Brown boomed. 'Even in the Stone Age three men with axes could fell an acre of forest in a morning—*stone* axes, Chairman! When the Celtic tribes arrived with iron tools and ploughs the rate of attrition was greater still. The Romans—'

'Chairman, may I interrupt?' Sedleigh-Harmon was rising to his feet, a bored expression on his hatchet features. 'The history of the wildwood in Britain is of no consequence to this hearing. Miss Sauvage-Brown is going to refer to an ancient woodland on the property, but the redevelopment of Penbrook Farm will not affect . . . this woodland, so we really do not need to waste time on this discourse.'

Mildred Sauvage-Brown expanded her formidable bosom. 'Waste time! When the heritage of England is being systematically destroyed by vandals like you! I insist—'

Chairman Lansbury raised sufficient nerve to lift a restraining hand. 'Please, Miss Sauvage-Brown, a moment.' When, reluctantly, she subsided, he turned to look at Arnold. 'Mr Landon, as Planning Officer involved you have studied this application?'

'Yes, Chairman,' Arnold replied, half-rising.

'Do you have any comment?'

'The development, as learned counsel suggests, does not affect the ancient woodlands on the hill, to which reference is probably being made.'

'Thank you.' The Chairman glanced nervously towards Miss Sauvage-Brown. 'No more wildwood, please. Will you continue?'

Mildred Sauvage-Brown ignored him for several seconds. Instead, she directed her glance towards Arnold. It was a compound of contempt and hatred: he should have been supporting her in her fight, but he was a craven coward. Arnold moved, wriggling uncomfortably in his seat. Satisfied, Mildred Sauvage-Brown returned to her task.

'Under protest, Chairman, I will say no more about the woodland, nor about the mediæval ditches and the coppices which mark it. I will say nothing about the deprivations of years; I will make no comment upon the damaging attitudes which have brought such woodlands to their knees, or the methods landowners have used to milk the tax system. I will say no more on these matters, important though they are, and even though I am far from certain that once this development is approved that woodland would *not* be at risk as a result of further depredations. No,' she cried triumphantly, 'I will draw attention to another matter entirely.' And she leaned forward, groped underneath her seat and raised aloft a rolled sheet of paper. 'Can I have a demonstration stand, Chairman?'

A rumbling consternation followed with the Chairman, wide awake, concerned to provide via his ushers an appropriate stand on which the objector, in the form of Mildred Sauvage-Brown, could obtain an adequate demonstration of her case. He wanted no appeal to a tribunal on the grounds of failure of natural justice, *audi alteram partem*, or any such nonsense. After several minutes' delay a sheepish county officer came in with the advice that the only item available was a blackboard.

It was brought in, without ceremony. It stood to one side of the council chamber while the formidable Miss Sauvage-Brown, who had had the foresight to arm herself in advance with a suitable number of drawing pins, proceeded to tack her rolled sheet of paper to the board.

It consisted of a neatly drawn sketch. As Mildred Sauvage-Brown began to explain, Arnold leaned forward, craning to read the legend on the sketch-map. *Penbrook Farm: where time stood still.*

As she spoke, he inspected the sketch.

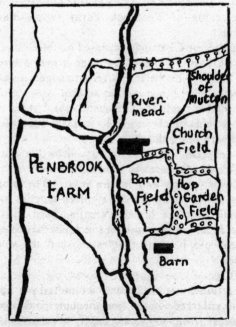

'One of the contentions in the planning application made by Mr Wilson and Mr Livingstone, and so *ably*,' she sneered, 'presented by eminent counsel, is that Penbrook Farm is not a going concern. I think the owner, my friend Sarah Ellis, for whom I am speaking, would agree. The farm itself cannot be seen as a profit-making business.'

She waved a hand towards the sketch, taking in the boundaries. 'The thirty acres or so that you see here provide little more than a modest hay crop, and perhaps enough winter grazing for a handful of sheep. But Sarah Ellis knew that when she bought Penbrook Farm fifteen years ago. It was never her intention to make it a "going concern". She came to it, fell in love with it, bought it, for reasons far divorced from the money-grubbing motivations of the Wilsons and the Livingstones of this world. The fact is, Chairman, the value of Penbrook Farm to naturalists is incalculable.'

'*Naturalists?*' the Chairman repeated doubtfully.

'Penbrook Farm,' Mildred Sauvage-Brown asserted, 'is that rare survivor in the intensively-managed countryside of the nineteen-eighties: a mediæval farm.'

'I don't understand,' the Chairman said, but the interest in Arnold's veins quickened as he inspected the sketch on the blackboard more closely.

'Let me explain,' Mildred Sauvage-Brown boomed confidently. 'Penbrook Farm is a mediæval farm with all its original fields, ponds and hedges intact. The farmhouse itself was pulled down in the eighteen-nineties and has been rebuilt, but the fifteenth-century barn still stands intact and I can tell you nothing much else has changed— even to the old pollards that established the woodland boundaries.'

'I don't see—'

'When farming was mechanized a hundred years ago and fields were enlarged for the new machines, Penbrook was saved because it was too small. Later, when new machines might have solved *that* problem, the property was bought by a man who was more interested in its possibilities as a rough shoot. As a consequence, it was still in a virginal state when bought by my friend Miss Ellis.'

'Mr Chairman,' Arthur Sedleigh-Harmon, QC, intoned, rising to his feet. 'All very interesting and ... ah ... emotional, but what has it to do with this inquiry? A *mediæval* farm?'

Mildred Sauvage-Brown bristled and the feather in her Robin Hood hat danced furiously. 'You clearly don't appreciate the situation as a *townsman* ... and a *Londoner* to boot! What we have at Penbrook is near to being unique! What Sarah Ellis bought fifteen years ago was a botanist's dream: Penbrook must be the largest surviving group of old flower-rich hay meadows in the north of England. Each of the fields is filled with the kinds of plants that have all but vanished elsewhere in the north—'

'Really, Chairman, I must ask for a ruling,' Sedleigh-Harmon protested.

'—yellow hay rattle, adder's tongue ferns—'

'Chairman!'

'—fantastic green winged orchids, so many wild orchids you could hardly walk without treading on them—'

'*Chairman!*' Sedleigh-Harmon insisted.

Mr Lansbury, pink-cheeked, banged his fist on the table. 'Will you just stop a moment, Miss Sauvage-Brown? What point is it you're trying to make?'

Mildred Sauvage-Brown stared at him, open-mouthed, as though she could hardly believe the question was directed towards her. 'Point? *Point?* Bloody hell, man, the point is if you let this development go forward you'll be destroying something it's taken seven centuries and maybe more to establish!'

Arnold knew it was always going to be an argument that would not hold water with Mr Lansbury. There were many reasons why planning applications were thrown out by the county council, but botany was not one of them. There was no doubt that the opinions held by Miss Sauvage-Brown were sincerely and worthily held, but the opinion of Chairman Lansbury was always going to be that modern progress should not be held back or stultified by amateur botanists chasing around fields with butterfly nets or grubbing tools.

'If that,' the Chairman said firmly when Miss Sauvage-Brown had protested at length, 'is the only objection you have to raise, I think we can bring this inquiry to a swift end.'

For a long moment Mildred Sauvage-Brown glared at him, then slowly, inevitably, she turned her head. She stared almost malevolently at Arnold Landon and he felt the courage drain slowly from his veins.

'No,' she said slowly and distinctly, 'it isn't the only objection I wish to raise. With your permission, I'd like to ask some questions of the Planning Officer, Mr Arnold Landon.'

The Senior Planning Officer would have been *far* from pleased.

3

Standing at his seat, Arnold felt completely exposed, naked and isolated. He was accustomed to giving evidence or making statements at hearings; he never enjoyed this kind of limelight but he had grown accustomed to it. On this occasion it was different, however: he felt forebodings that weakened his knees and made him unable to meet the fierce, demanding glance of Miss Mildred Sauvage-Brown.

'The old wildwood is gone for ever,' she said in a high penetrating voice. 'But would you agree that what remains is precious?'

Arnold moistened his lips with his tongue. 'I would say so, yes.'

'What does remain? A scattered mosaic of clumps and coppices, silent spinneys, lonely fox roosts, a few beech hangers, pagan groves of oak and yew—'

'Chairman, do we have to go through this again?' Sedleigh-Harmon protested flatly.

'—pocket woodlands where bluebells almost anæsthetize the senses, the miraculous depths of old, true forests—'

'Mr Chairman!'

Mr Lansbury banged his fist on the table in desperation. 'We've been through all this, Miss Sauvage-Brown. You said you wanted to ask the planning officer some questions. Will you do that, instead of eulogizing the vanished countryside?'

'So what of the works of man?' Mildred Sauvage-Brown snapped.

Silence fell in the council chamber. Arnold blinked, not certain whether a question had been directed at him or at the Chairman. Mr Lansbury also seemed somewhat taken aback.

'Miss Sauvage-Brown—'

'What of the works of man?' she repeated, stabbing a chunky finger in the air, in the general direction of Arnold Landon.

'I . . . I'm not quite certain what you mean,' he prevaricated, knowing perfectly well what she meant.

She glared at him and then moved to the attack. 'Tell me, Mr Landon, what were ancient roofs made of?'

'Obviously, wood, or thatch.'

'Stone?'

'Depends how far back you go,' Arnold replied cautiously. 'Stone as a material for roofing was still pretty rare, even in the Cotswolds, up to the thirteenth century.'

'But afterwards?'

Arnold swallowed hard. 'From the fourteenth century on, primarily to avoid the risk of fire, stone began to be used as a roofing material for churches and other public buildings.'

'And private houses?'

'And private houses. Indeed, from early Tudor times,' Arnold continued, almost forgetting the pressure of the questioning, 'stone became a favourite roofing material in Sussex, Surrey, the Cotswolds, the Welsh border counties—'

'And in the North?'

'Large parts of the northern counties, from Derbyshire to Northumberland.'

'You say stone,' Miss Sauvage-Brown said cunningly, 'but the layman would speak of *slate*?'

Inwardly Arnold groaned. 'That's right. Slate.'

'Tell us about this slate.'

Arnold told them. It was odd: even Sedleigh-Harmon, QC, who had seemed on the point of interruption several times now subsided as Arnold spoke to them of the slater's craft. He told the hearing of the sandstones and the oolites, of the splitting of laminated stone, and of the trimming into the approximate sizes, with their Lewis Carroll-sounding names: *muffities* and *wivetts*, *tants* and *cussems*. 'Very often no attempt was made to produce slates of uniform size and thickness—it's been said that in the north no two slates were ever identical anyway.'

Arnold paused; the room was silent. There was a glazed look in Sedleigh-Harmon's eyes but in the stocky bearing of Mildred Sauvage-Brown there was triumph.

'All right, Mr Landon, now let me hear you tell the Chairman here what it is you found when you visited Penbrook Farm the other week!'

'I . . .' Arnold hesitated, glancing at the Queen's Counsel, at Wilson, Livingstone and beyond them the triumphant Mildred, and there was a cold feeling in his stomach. 'I found . . . I found some roofing slates that are probably at least three hundred years old.'

'And *that*,' Mildred Sauvage-Brown almost shouted, 'is on the farm you want to tear apart for an old people's home!'

She sat down, abruptly, as though her case was made. There was an air of puzzlement and uncertainty in the council chamber, a vague rustling of voices as consideration was given to what Mildred Sauvage-Brown seemed to be saying. Destroy an ancient woodland; destroy a mediæval farm; destroy a three-hundred-year-old building—it was desecration.

Arthur Sedleigh-Harmon rose slowly to his feet. He stared at Arnold as though he were awakening from a long sleep, hooded eyes blinking, the suspicion of a yawn on his mouth. 'Mr ... er ... Landon. Planning officer?'

'That's right.'

'You visited the farm?'

Arnold nodded, undeceived by the passivity of the tone. 'Yes.'

'And found these ... inestimable, three-hundred-year-old slates?'

'Yes, sir.'

'Where?'

'I beg your pardon?'

'The question was clearly phrased. *Where* did you find the slates?'

'On ...' The words died in Arnold's mouth, and he glanced sorrowfully towards Mildred Sauvage-Brown. 'On a pigsty.'

There was a long, ominous silence. Arthur Sedleigh-Harmon traversed the courtroom with a slow, contemptuous, incredulous glance. At length it fastened on Arnold.

'A *pigsty*?'

'Yes, sir.'

'You *must* be joking!'

'No, sir.'

'Were our ancestors accustomed, then, to using expensive *slate* to roof so humble a dwelling as a ... *pigsty*?'

Someone in the council chamber laughed and anger touched Arnold's veins. 'Slate, Mr Sedleigh-Harmon, and three-hundred-year-old slate! Yes, our ancestors *did* use slate to roof humble dwellings! You can't go by modern ideas. There was a time, three hundred years ago, when every cottage, barn *and* pigsty had a slate roof—all were accorded the dignity of stone because they were important buildings. All right, the reverse is true nowadays: an old roof needs repair, the slates are stripped off and sold and replaced with tiles—often too red to blend—asbestos, corrugated iron, real misfortunes for a stone-built village. But even now the production of stone slates has not entirely ceased and—'

'Yes, yes,' Sedleigh-Harmon interrupted testily. He was annoyed; he realized he had made a mistake. He changed his tack, subtly, aware of a tide of sympathy that had welled up in the council chamber for days gone by, and he asked, 'How do you know the tiles . . . sorry, *slates*, are that old?'

'The peg holes—they are unique to the North.'

'How?'

'Size. They weren't made for the normal oak pegs or nails. They are much smaller.'

'So what kind of pegs were used?' Sedleigh-Harmon asked, carefully, his instinct telling him he was near something of importance.

'Bones, sir. Sheep . . . or chicken.'

'Well, well, well . . .' Sedleigh-Harmon expressed his astonishment flatly and stared at Arnold, one hand creeping up to caress the thin, pencil moustache he affected. 'You can, then, vouch for the age of these slates?'

'Yes, sir.'

'How?'

Arnold's heart sank. 'Because I've seen others like them.'

'In the North?'

'Yes, sir.'

'*Where?*' The question came like a snake striking.

'Walworth Castle, sir. Winchcombe Manor. Dene House—'

'How many examples can you name, say, in Durham and Northumberland?' Sedleigh-Harmon asked silkily.

Arnold hesitated. 'Perhaps . . . perhaps a dozen.'

'All in stately homes?'

Arnold shook his head dumbly. He was aware of the powerful form of Mildred Sauvage-Brown shaking with anger across to his left. 'No, sir.'

'Let me get the picture clearly then, Mr Landon. You aver there are ancient slates . . . on an ancient *pigsty* at Penbrook Farm. But these slates, and their . . . ah . . . location, are by no means unique in the North-East? There are several other, similar examples . . .?'

'That is so.'

'It follows, does it not, that if the development of Penbrook Farm were to go ahead, over the objections of Miss Sarah Ellis and her able companion Miss Mildred Sauvage-Brown, and this . . . *pigsty* were to be·destroyed, there would be no great loss to anyone, other than, perhaps . . . future generations of pigs?'

As laughter rippled around the council chamber Arnold inclined his head miserably. He had been dreading this moment for some time; he had known that Mildred Sauvage-Brown would have had expectations he had, foolishly, raised. He had hoped she would not have raised the issue, hoped desperately he would not be called upon to support her . . . and then fail her. 'There are . . . other examples,' he said. 'The pigsty at Penbrook Farm is not unique.'

And to his horror, Mildred Sauvage-Brown stood up in the council chamber and shouted wildly at him shaking her fist. '*Traitor!* You know that, Landon? You're a bloody traitor!'

4

The words echoed painfully in Arnold's mind for the rest of the day. It was not as though they had been unexpected: he had known from the moment he'd told Mildred Sauvage-Brown about the old slates on the pigsty that it was likely she'd use the information to try to oppose the development.

Equally, he had always known it would be an attempt doomed to frustration in that he would not have been able, in all conscience, to agree the find was of sufficient importance to support her case. She had seen him as a traitor—to her, to Sarah Ellis and to conservationists the length of England. But it had been inevitable.

The inevitability did not make it easier. He had felt great sympathy for her stand. He disliked her personally: she was the kind of upper class, meddling, aggressive personality he had no time for and instinctively distrusted, but he still understood and appreciated the cause she was standing for and fighting for. He wished he could have helped her more than he did, but it was not possible, not on the grounds she had wanted to use.

The scene had worsened, of course. Once she knew he would not be able to support her she had turned vicious, screamed at him in the courtroom, throwing off the restraining arm of her timid friend, and then she had turned her wrath on her real enemies, Wilson and Livingstone. It had brought a quick end to the hearing, with the Chairman deeming all objections answered. He had beat a hasty retreat, with Mr Sedleigh-Harmon, QC, uttering dire warnings that if Miss Mildred Sauvage-Brown did not desist in her scandalous and scurrilous remarks he would be advising his clients to take action for defamation.

Yet the words she had used and the claims she had made had bothered Arnold. It was unlikely there was anything in what she had said, but nevertheless he felt it was something he should be looking into. He would have done so, that afternoon, had he not had a visitor to his office.

Henry Willington had arrived unannounced. He tapped on the door, opened it and entered with a certain diffidence. 'Have you recovered somewhat now, Mr Landon?'

For a moment Arnold had been puzzled. Then, still sweating, he shook his head wryly. 'You saw the scene in the corridor.'

'I saw you coming out of the council chamber,' Willington remarked, 'all but pursued by that harridan. You'll forgive me for saying so, Mr Landon, but you shouldn't tangle with determined ladies twice your size!'

Arnold smiled, in spite of himself. 'She was somewhat . . . upset. I had been unable to support her in the planning inquiry and she wanted to vent her anger upon me.'

'It'll cost you—or her—a new shirt,' Willington said, gesturing towards Arnold's torn collar.

Arnold shook his head. 'She was . . . distraught. And in a way it was partly my own fault. A determined and forceful lady . . . and accustomed to demonstrating her point of view.'

'There wasn't much point in the other lady trying to stop her either. She was hanging on grimly, but it was like trying to hang on to a hurricane.'

'Miss Ellis. She actually owns Penbrook Farm. Mildred Sauvage-Brown is her companion. I think she was hugely embarrassed by the whole scene, but the fact is it was all being done for Miss Ellis's benefit, so I suppose she felt duty bound to save Miss Sauvage-Brown from the excesses of her own temper.'

'As you say, a very forceful lady. Companion to Miss Ellis . . .' Henry Willington frowned, and sat down near the door. He contemplated his hands for a few moments, still frowning, and then he said, 'I hope you don't mind me calling in like this, without an appointment.'

'The afternoon's almost over.' Arnold looked at the young man's bent head. The fair hair was thin on the crown, pink skin showing beneath. He was gripping his hands together tightly, as though concerned about something, holding tight rein on himself. 'I've no other appointments,' Arnold added.

'I was in town,' Willington said. He raised his head, his pale brown eyes cold. 'I thought I'd take the chance to call in, have a chat with you about that damned plan of my father's.'

'I'm available, Mr Willington.'

Henry Willington frowned. 'Is there any way I can quietly withdraw the application?'

'Your father is the owner of Willington Hall,' Arnold replied. 'You're his heir?'

'For what it's worth,' Willington replied bitterly. 'There'll be little enough left of the *patrimony* as it is; if the old man gets this application through and sinks more money into it . . . damn it, Mr Landon, you know the scheme is crazy!'

Arnold nodded. 'In my consideration it will be a waste of money. But the planning committee are unlikely to turn it down merely on that account. Patrick Willington may be a poor businessman, but that is of no account to them.'

'It's of damn serious account to me,' Henry Willington exclaimed with a flash of impatience. 'He's all but ruined the estate, what's left of it, and this bloody stupid scheme . . . He's a sick man, Mr Landon.'

Something cold touched Arnold's spine. Carefully he said, 'I saw no evidence of . . . sickness.'

'I could get him certified,' Henry Willington said and his pale eyes were cold.

'I don't think that's an area into which I could stray,' Arnold said hurriedly. 'As for the scheme—'

'He had a bit of a turn the other day,' Willington added, almost to himself. 'I wanted to call the doctor then, but the old fool wouldn't let me. One of these days . . . Anyway, you think there's little chance the committee will throw out the scheme?'

'I can't say. It will partly depend upon what objections may be raised to it. Will . . . er . . . will you be making any objections?'

'To my father's pet scheme to turn around the Willington fortunes?' Henry Willington's smile was bitter. 'No, I couldn't do that.' He stood up suddenly. 'A setback, some opposition like that . . . I mean, Mr Landon, it could kill him.'

It was meant as a joke, Arnold was certain, a black, humourless joke. But it left a nasty taste in Arnold's mouth. It also gave him another view of the heir to Willington Hall.

Now, the following morning, he thought back again over the final moments of the inquiry into the Penbrook Farm development. Certain things had been said, that bothered him.

Not by Sedleigh-Harmon, of course. He had risen to his feet to make some final comments regarding the environment. 'We have already made it clear that the ancient woodlands referred to by Miss Sauvage-Brown will not be affected. We have equally given assurances that, as can be seen from the plans, as little disruption as possible will be made, by the provision of access roads and service systems to the site when building commences beyond the ridge. The mediæval nature of Penbrook Farm, well, there is little we can do about that and surely, Chairman, you will agree that progress must be made: we cannot continue to exist in a mediæval society! And as for the pigsty slates commented upon so ably by the Planning Officer, and by which Miss Sauvage-Brown sets so much store, again I feel we can settle any problems there. If they are *so* important, my clients are prepared to preserve them *in situ*, properly fenced off, as a showplace. If this is not acceptable they are prepared to remove the whole sty, stone by stone, and re-erect it in a more suitable location. This way, the heritage will be preserved.'

'*Preserved?*' Mildred Sauvage-Brown's voice had risen to a hysterical yelp. 'You call that preservation? You and the rest of these bloody lunatics are throwing away the only things worth anything in modern society and you talk of preservation!'

Sarah Ellis had tapped at Mildred's arm, but the anger in her companion's veins would brook no control, and Sarah

Ellis had subsided, clutching to her bosom her little dark book and rocking sadly in her seat.

'Don't let's have this mealy-mouthed crap about the preservation of the environment from land-hungry clods like Wilson and Livingstone, and their mouthpiece Sedleigh-Harmon,' Mildred had shouted, as the pandemonium around her grew. 'They're after making money. That's all. And they'll stoop to every low deal, every dirty trick to do that. *The Minford Twilight Home!* Who'll really benefit from that? Bloody Albert Minford! And who'll be doing the building over the ridge once you *have* desecrated Penbrook Farm? Tell me that! And how many other deals are cooking to keep councillors sweet? The Alnwick drainage scheme! The Amble marina! That bloody bridge at Wark! There are the pies, but whose are the fingers dabbling in them! And who's plucking out the cherries?'

It was at that stage the Chairman had hastily called the hearing to a close and Mildred Sauvage-Brown had made her determined lunge in Arnold's direction. It had been unexpected: he had hardly expected to be designated as a major enemy, but perhaps she felt he was in some curious way worse than the others, because he had declared sympathy with her stand. He had tried to get out of the doors in the rush, but she had managed to coil her thick stubby fingers in his shirt collar, ripping it, before he managed to make good his escape.

But it was not that which really bothered Arnold. He felt guilty, and a sense of shame touched him for his inability to help Mildred Sauvage-Brown and Sarah Ellis more positively; at the same time he wondered whether he had entirely done his duty. Had he devoted enough time to the ramifications of the case before it was presented to the hearing? Had he really carried out a sound enough check on the *background* to the Penbrook Farm application?

He fished out three files from the cabinet in the office of the Senior Planning Officer. The first was the file concerning the bridge at Wark: expensive, some claimed unnecessary, and certainly an eyesore when placed immediately alongside the thirteenth-century stone bridge it would render redundant. The building firm was Corey and Fairhurst; architects, Glinson's.

Nothing untoward there. He checked the tenders: they seemed in order. He turned to the second file.

Mildred Sauvage-Brown had shouted about the Alnwick drainage scheme. He looked at the file: he knew very little about it. The details were there: the castle stood on the hill above the town and the land to the north-east fell away into meadows through which the Aln ran to the sea at Alnmouth. That particular spot was visually romantic: one could see days of chivalry mirrored in the scene. But just north of the castle there were drainage problems in winter and the Aln regularly burst its banks in the spring floods. The work was to divert part of the watercourse, raise banks and construct new sewers. Builders: Wellington Bros; architects, Samuel and Hines. Tenders in order.

That left Amble. Arnold had already dealt with the file personally and he had detected nothing unusual in it. The application was young yet; newspaper notices had been placed, inviting tenders. There were three tenders already in, and he had not paid much attention to them since he would expect others to emerge. Now he looked at them more closely.

Corey and Fairhurst, the contractors for the Wark bridge. That was all right: they were fairly big builders and well experienced in local authority contracts. The second bid was from a company he did not know. Floyd and Simson. He turned to the third tender. Again, a contracting firm with a pretty good record of local authority work—Nickerson's.

Arnold turned back to the second tender. Floyd and Simson. He stared at it, pondering. A limited company: managing director, E. Floyd; finance director, T. Simson. Something prickled at the back of his neck. A newspaper

cutting, or a photograph, some time ago, a few years back
. . . Floyd. There'd been a builder of that name in Newcastle,
but the firm had merged . . . with whom?

Arnold closed the file, walked out into the corridor and
obtained a cup of cool coffee from the vending machine. Its
days were numbered, he thought darkly. Any time now, it
would be brought to justice. He took the coffee back to his
office.

From his window he had a narrow view of the gardens
on the hill; above the gardens, wheeling against the morning sky, was a flock of fieldfares. Arnold watched them for
a while, sipping his coffee, and his mind drifted back,
sifting facts and memories . . . Floyd. A merger. It hadn't
worked.

But that was all he could remember. Irritated, Arnold
finished his coffee, replaced the files and then, hesitantly,
made his way along the corridor and up the stairs to the
Town Clerk's department. He still thought of it under that
title although it had long since been changed to Department
of Administration. He opened the door, walked in past the
serried rows of law books and law reports and headed for
the desk still occupied after thirty years by one Ned Keeton.
The man's shaggy head came up as Arnold approached and
the grey flyaway eyebrows twitched their surprise. 'Well,
well, Arnold, don't see much of you up here!'

'Having once escaped, Ned, I'm always reluctant to return.'

'In case they catch you again, hey?' Ned Keeton grinned
and shook his head. 'Me, I'll be escaping for good next
summer. Time to go.'

'You're sixty-five?'

'Sixty. Early retirement. Had enough, stuck in here. Not
like you, with the chance to get out and about. All I ever
see outside this office is the magistrates' courtrooms. Hardly
inspiring. But you didn't come up here to chat about my
future. What can I do for you?'

Arnold hesitated. 'Councillors. There's a rule about declaring interests, isn't there?'

'So there is with officers, like you and me. Local Government Act 1972. Have to declare any interest they have in contracts entered into, or proposed, with the council.'

'What's meant by interest?' Arnold asked.

'Financial, of course. Directors. Shareholders. And it covers members of their families too, in some cases.'

Slowly Arnold said, 'The declarations . . . they're contained in a register, of course.'

Ned Keeton scratched his head with his pen and gazed owlishly at Arnold. 'Oh yes, sniffing, are we? Fact is, in most cases the declaration is made in committee, so stated thereafter in the minutes, and provided the councillor hasn't voted on the issue that's the end of that. But a register . . . well, yes, there's a register. *Voluntary* register of interests. The canny ones who *think* they might be embarrassed in the future, they register their interests and that covers it. Of course,' he added slyly, 'people very rarely take a look at that register.'

'Do you think *I* could take a look?' Arnold asked.

'No reason why not,' Keeton replied with a wicked grin. 'Fully accredited, paid-up member, officer of the authority, all that kind of stuff. Access available. You want to tell me who you're looking for?'

'No.'

'Wise. Follow me.' Ned Keeton rose and shambled across the open-plan office, skirting the trailing plants that served as office dividers, until he reached the locked cabinet that stood outside the Chief Executive's office. 'Supposed to be highly confidential,' he said. 'But I got a key. Seniority, like. Help yourself, lad.'

Arnold helped himself.

There were only eight entries under the letter *M*. Albert Minford's entry dated back twelve years. Some of the interests noted had been excised as out of date, notably the interest he had held in his father's firm, since wound up. The more recent interests caught Arnold's attention.

Shareholder in Aln Enterprises, Ltd.

Director and shareholder in Ferrier, Glaze and Sharman, Ltd.

Shareholder in Corey and Fairhurst, Ltd.

Arnold closed the file and replaced it, locked the cabinet and went back to Ned Keeton. The grey-haired man cocked an inquisitive eyebrow. 'Find what you want?'

Arnold shrugged. 'Albert Minford is a shareholder in Corey and Fairhurst, the builders who tendered successfully for the Wark bridge.'

'He's declared the interest in the voluntary register?'

'He has.'

'Then that's it. All clean and above board. Can't be touched.'

'Did the planning committee know about his interest?' Arnold asked.

Keeton shook his head doubtfully. 'Doesn't matter whether they did or not. He wasn't on the planning committee. He declared his interest on the register. That's all he has to do other than not vote at council when the contract was ratified. Of course, it's a fact that people rarely *inspect* the register, and although the Chief Exec. is supposed to bring the attention of the council to such matters it's a task that is observed in the breach rather than in the act, and the likelihood is that few people on council would even have *known* Minford had an interest in the Wark scheme. Which means . . .?'

'You tell me.'

'Well, I'm leaving this dung heap soon, and you can't quote me, and I'll even deny the conversation, but there's always the possibility, isn't there? I mean, a councillor putting a word in, doing some lobbying with the right people, maybe for a certain buried kickback that emerges later in an entirely different field—and with most of the members not knowing what's going on at all because the bloke pushing the scheme has no personal interest on the face of things and the guy who *has* an interest has declared it, isn't *directly* involved in the decision, and so his interest isn't even noticed. Even if he *is* active behind the scenes.'

'Minford?'

'I didn't say that, Arnold, I didn't say that.'

Arnold was left with a vague sense of unease. Mildred Sauvage-Brown had made wild claims at the hearing; he had undertaken a check but had come up with mere suppositions that Ned Keeton would not support in practical terms. It left Arnold in limbo: he felt he should act positively to support Sarah Ellis and Mildred Sauvage-Brown, for theirs were feelings close to his own, but it was his duty as a responsible planning officer to process the applications expeditiously.

Yet both considerations led to the same decision: an expression of sympathy, and the need for more concrete evidence of corruption, demanded that he visit Penbrook Farm once again, and encounter the formidable Miss Sauvage-Brown.

He set off after lunch to drive the twenty miles or so to Penbrook Farm. The afternoon skies were heavy, mackerel clouds deadening the horizon, and the lanes were quiet as he drove across country. His head began to ache and he was filled with a sense of gloomy foreboding: somehow, he felt he was getting involved in matters that lay beyond his control. The Senior Planning Officer was right about these things: a quiet life was all that was needed—no alarums, no excursions.

But ahead of him waited Mildred Sauvage-Brown, a woman to whom causes, preferably lost ones and little ones, were life blood.

He passed Ogle and took the road west, skirting the

northern perimeter of Darras Hall until he neared Penbrook
Farm. He could see the outline of the ancient wood on the
hill and his heart was saddened: whatever Sedleigh-Harmon
might have claimed, that wood too would be at risk, in time,
as the old people's home, and the residential sprawl beyond
the ridge, became facts. He drove through the gateway,
down towards the farmhouse, past the Shoulder of Mutton
Mildred Sauvage-Brown had shown in her blackboard
sketch, across the stream and Rivermead field, and he
slowed as he reached the pigsty.

There were two cars parked near the farmhouse. Arnold
stopped the engine, got out of the car and then he saw
someone running up the lane towards the farmhouse.

She was wearing an elderly dress, the hem of which was
torn and muddy. Her shoes were caked with mud also, and
her grey hair straggled over her distraught features. To her
narrow bosom she clutched the inevitable little book, and
as he got out of the car she raised her hand to her face,
brushing back the wild straggles to see him more clearly.
There was a tear of relief in her voice when she called his
name. He hurried forward, reaching out for her as she came
to him, frail, weeping, terrified.

'Tell me,' Arnold demanded. 'What's happened?'

'Oh, I told her she shouldn't do it,' Sarah Ellis wailed,
hollow-eyed. 'I *told* her but she wouldn't listen, she's so
much stronger than me.'

'What's happened?' Arnold asked again.

'She's down at the barn. You must help, Mr Landon, you
must help!'

5

Arnold was nonplussed. He held Miss Ellis's shaking hands,
trying to calm her down while he got some sense out of her.
She was shaking violently, terrified and incoherent. She had
dropped her little book and Arnold picked it up, stuffed it

into his coat pocket, and tried to discover what had disturbed her.

'It's M—Mildred,' Sarah Ellis sobbed, leaning her head against Arnold's shoulder. 'She always overreacts so. I mean, I didn't know who he was, and there didn't seem to me to be any harm in it, but when Mildred came in she made me phone while she went down to the barn.'

'Is that where she is now?'

'Yes. But the way she's behaving . . . that poor man, it was awful, and Mildred was so rude, I just ran away again and cried, and then I saw you driving down the hill and I thought it was them and I came up to—'

'Them?'

'The Press. The *Journal*.'

'Mildred asked you to phone the *Journal*?'

'She said this was the way to get things sorted out.'

Inwardly Arnold groaned. He had the feeling that the events of the next few minutes could well mean publicity, newspaper coverage of the kind the Senior Planning Officer abhorred—and Arnold Landon, County Planning Officer of humble seniority, could well be right in the middle of it.

Instinct told Arnold he should stay well out of this situation; common humanity, on the other hand, dictated he should do something to assist the shaken Miss Ellis in her distress.

'The barn?' Arnold asked weakly.

'Oh, I'm *so* glad you'll help,' Sarah Ellis breathed. She grabbed his hand in a grasp surprisingly firm, and a moment later was trotting down the path with Arnold in tow like a reluctant lover. Sarah Ellis was a frail-looking old lady, but Arnold realized there were reserves of strength and steel in that elderly body.

They passed the first bend of the stream, crossed the narrow bridge below Barn Field, and above the hedge top Arnold could see the old timbers of the fifteenth-century barn, black and solid against the sky. From the spinney beyond, aware of the tension in the air, a great cloud of rooks swirled, clamouring their anger and distress, and darkening the sky like a smudge of smoke. The sound of their anxious cawing echoed from the craggy hill and found an answering chord in Arnold's chest. He could guess that trouble lay ahead.

They entered the gate and the path stretched ahead of them, muddied and difficult. Arnold dragged at Miss Ellis's hand. 'Do you think you need go any further?' he asked, aware that drama awaited at the barn.

'Please, Mr Landon, you *must* help!' she responded pinkly, panting in her anxiety. As though fearful he would desert her now, she gripped his hand even more tightly and Arnold was forced to squelch miserably behind her as she proceeded in her birdlike manner towards the dark barn looming ahead.

From this angle the barn had lost any charm it might have possessed for Arnold by virtue of its history. It seemed to lean against the hill, defying the ancient winds, and it was arrogant, fierce in its determination to survive.

As the path dipped in a fold in the field the barn rose higher in his vision to dominate the skyline and the arrogance became menace. Arnold could hear Sarah Ellis's breath tearing in her chest and her pace had slowed in spite of her quickening anxiety, but for himself there was a dull ache of presentiment.

The path curved, making its way with the contour of the slope towards the front entrance of the old barn. The door itself leaned crazily, broken on rusting hinges, and the timber of the construction gaped, wind-ravaged and weatherbeaten.

Projecting through the doorway were the shafts of an old cart. The shafts were made of hickory, and the cart itself lacked one wheel. It leaned to one side drunkenly, and the wheel it still possessed lacked spokes. But Arnold's attention was swiftly drawn from the ancient cart. Standing at its rear was Mildred Sauvage-Brown.

She was at her most belligerent. She stood squarely, a righteous colossus, legs braced apart and ruddy countenance aflame with determination. She was carrying the shotgun with which she had first introduced herself to Arnold, and his heart sank.

'What did you bring *him* here for?' Mildred Sauvage-Brown demanded indignantly of Sarah Ellis. 'I told you to phone the newspaper! Is there no sign of them yet?'

'Oh, Mildred—'

'Stop blabbing, Sarah! This is important! Media attention—'

Arnold stepped forward and the twin muzzles came up threateningly. 'Keep your distance, *traitor*!' she warned.

Arnold stared past her into the recesses of the barn. Just behind Miss Sauvage-Brown was a tripod, a theodolite lying on the ground. Beside the theodolite, his face contorted with terror and his hands locked together in supplication, was a man of small stature, on his knees, the eyes glaring wildly in his head. When he caught sight of Arnold he tried to speak but only a hissing sound came. 'Hell's flames,' Arnold said, shocked.

'I'll not warn you again, you traitor,' Mildred Sauvage-Brown snarled.

There was a gasping, choking sound from the man on his knees. He was wearing smart grey trousers tucked into green gumboots but they were stained with mud now and his hacking jacket was torn across the shoulder. His thin hair was plastered to his face in fear and his mouth was open, drooling terror. Arnold wet his lips. 'Who . . . who are you?'

The man tried to gasp a name but Mildred Sauvage-Brown spoke across the sound, contemptuously. 'His name's Carter. He's a surveyor. He's employed by those bloody rogues Wilson and Livingstone. You know what they had the gall to do? They sent him down here to Penbrook Farm with his damned instruments to make some preliminary calculations! If I'd been here at the time I'd have given him the boot! But Sarah—'

'Please, Mildred, this is all so unnecessary,' Sarah Ellis quavered, half-hiding behind Arnold.

'Now you leave this to me,' Mildred said. Her voice softened slightly, as she noted her companion's terror. 'You can go on back to the house if you like. I can handle all this.'

'What do you propose to do?' Arnold asked. 'Don't you think you can put that shotgun aside? Mr Carter is clearly . . . disturbed.'

'Damn right he's disturbed. But then, he came down here disturbing us, didn't he? Arrived when I was up on the hill, persuaded Sarah that he would do no harm, keep out of the way—'

'I was only . . . try . . . trying to do my job,' the little man broke in breathlessly.

'The hell with your job! Wheedled around Sarah, marched on down here with his bloody instruments and was all set up! I came down to the farmhouse, Sarah told me, and I realized the mileage we can get out of all this. Told her to phone the *Journal*, explain what I was going to do and then came down here to do it. What are *you* here for?'

Arnold thought the reasons for his presence irrelevant while Mildred Sauvage-Brown was still waving an armed shotgun in various directions. 'What are you going to do?'

'I'm going to make a statement to the Press,' Mildred announced triumphantly. 'I'm going to get the kind of publicity we didn't get as a result of the hearing. Do you know there wasn't a single mention of that hearing in any of the local newspapers?'

'It's not normal for them to report—'

'Not a single bloody mention of our case! That'll be

pressure, from Wilson and bloody Livingstone, I'm damned sure of it! All right, well, they've played their hand, and I'm going to play mine now.'

Arnold eyed the shotgun warily and the surveyor Carter whimpered as Arnold asked again, 'What do you intend to do?'

Mildred cleared her throat, hawked, spat, and ran the sleeve of her tweed jacket across her mouth, twitched the shotgun higher in the crook of her arm and grinned maliciously. 'I told you, I'm going to make a statement to the Press. I'm going to state our case, then I'm going to keep this miserable little whippersnapper here in the barn, locked up, with this muzzle trained on him until either that bastard Wilson or his trained poodle Livingstone gets down here and apologizes for the act of trespass this miserable worm has committed in their name.'

'He . . . er . . . he came on with Miss Ellis's permission,' Arnold suggested.

'She was conned. She didn't know what she was doing.'

The little man on his knees squirmed and appealed to Arnold, scrabbling in the dirty straw on the floor of the old barn. 'Hey, mister, get this crazy woman away from me, can't you? That gun—'

He subsided with a yelp as Mildred swung the shotgun in a dangerous arc, homing in on him. 'Shurrup, whippersnapper!' she commanded.

Arnold took a step forward, Sarah Ellis still clinging to his arm, weeping. 'Miss Sauvage-Brown, this is going too far.'

'The hell with that,' Mildred said confidently. 'We should have acted positively before now. Besides, it's too late for any arguing now. You hear?'

Arnold heard.

The rooks were creating bedlam in the spinney but on the distant wind he could hear the wail of a siren. It seemed that Sarah Ellis's phone call had had more than the desired effect. Perhaps alarmed by her tone, or concerned that this situation might develop into an even more newsworthy item if the police were involved, the *Journal* had clearly informed the local constabulary. They would be coming in force.

In a few minutes they came. Arnold groaned as the vehicles thundered down the lane and into Barn Field. There were four of them, two police cars and two others from which spilled three excited journalists and two photographers. The helmeted constables made a desultory attempt to keep them away from the approach to the barn but they eluded capture, running across the muddy field to get a better view—and better shots—of the dramatic scene unfolding at the entrance to the barn. One of the police officers was bareheaded, though in uniform. Clearly, he considered this was a method of defusing a dangerous situation. Equally clearly, he was in charge of the operation.

Mildred Sauvage-Brown cleared her throat and prepared for action. Arnold waited, helpless, aware that events had now gone far beyond his control, even if he had had any chance of controlling them earlier.

'Now then,' the bareheaded officer called as he strode purposefully towards the barn. 'What's going on?'

A photographer scrambled ahead of him, to one side, lugging his camera. He stopped to take a long shot of the scene and the officer scowled, waved an angry arm. 'Get the hell out of here!' He drew nearer to Arnold, scrutinized the sobbing Miss Ellis and asked, 'Who're you?'

Arnold completed the introductions, including the watchful Mildred Sauvage-Brown, and the bareheaded policeman nodded. 'I'm Chief Superintendent Fairbairn, I'm a blunt-speaking man, I don't like my afternoon off broken into like this and you better put that shotgun down, missus.'

The shotgun was waved negligently in his direction and the Chief Superintendent paled. 'Bloody hell,' he added.

'Don't want to talk to you, copper,' Mildred said coolly. 'But you better let those reporters come near and listen to

me, and let them photographers get a few shots or there'll
be shots of a different kind flying around this barn.'

As the Chief Superintendent's neck purpled Arnold intervened hastily to explain the situation. The reporters gathered close, scribbling away as they listened. 'The easiest
way, I think,' Arnold concluded,' 'is to let Miss Sauvage-
Brown have her say, and then maybe the whole thing can
be resolved peaceably.'

'I'll be wanting Wilson or Livingstone here,' Mildred
warned, 'or this little feller back here stays with me!'

Chief Superintendent Fairbairn considered the matter.
He raised a placatory hand. 'All right, we'll see what we
can do, and if you want to make a statement to the lads
here, well, you go ahead and do it, and then maybe we can
talk a bit more, all right?'

Slightly mollified, but still suspicious, Mildred Sauvage-
Brown nodded, and lifted the shotgun. The surveyor on his
knees groaned faintly. 'This is what I want you all to print,'
she said in a booming voice.

She proceeded to tell them. Arnold had heard it before,
at the inquiry. She reeled off the story of the woodland, of
the mediæval farm lands comprised in Barn Field and
Rivermead and The Shoulder of Mutton; she spoke of the
slated pigsty and if Arnold winced when she denounced him
as a traitor she clearly felt it was what he deserved. Arnold
observed the reporters: they began eagerly, taking notes,
but after a little while, as Mildred's rolling tones asserted the
unique nature of Penbrook Farm and painted the property
developers as villainous vandals the notes grew shorter,
attention wandered to take in the scene behind Mildred's
shotgun.

For the little surveyor, Carter, had decided to help himself.

Wrapped up in her demagoguery, Mildred had allowed
herself to be distracted, half-turning away from Carter,
declaiming to the reporters, and waving the gun towards

the entrance to the barn. Carter had decided to take his chance. As she spoke he had got quietly up off his knees and was beginning to edge into the deeper recesses of the barn. For a moment Arnold thought the little man was making a bad mistake, but then he realized there must be some other means of egress from the barn, which had caught Carter's attention. The two uniformed constables stood quietly beside Chief Superintendent Fairbairn, Mildred continued her attack upon Wilson and Livingstone, Sarah sobbed, and Arnold held his breath.

'And now, all that remains,' Mildred boomed, ending her peroration, 'is for one of those two bastards to get here and apologize. Or else,' she added, raising her woollen-capped head, 'I'll keep this miserable little man in this barn until they do!'

There was a sudden clattering sound from the back of the barn. Mildred whirled around in consternation and for one long second was transfixed by the emptiness before her. The Chief Superintendent bellowed some incomprehensible order and the two constables stepped nervously forward just as Mildred, realizing what was about to happen, dashed into the darkness of the barn.

From the back of the barn Arnold heard one more terrified yell, a cracking, rending sound and then the sharp report of the gun as one of the twin barrels was discharged. He ran forward involuntarily, releasing Sarah's hand but the policemen rushed past him, shouldering him aside. Next moment he was half shoved forward by the pressing reporters, eager in spite of the gunshot to get closer to events, witness them first hand. Within a trice they were retreating again as the policemen tumbled out.

Mildred Sauvage-Brown was almost beside herself with anger. Red in the face, woollen cap awry, she had reversed her grip on the shotgun and was now wielding it as a club, swinging it wildly in a wide arc, beating back the opposition, policemen and reporters, now that she had lost her prey.

Fairbairn was shouting again, but there was a note of panic in his voice; Arnold realized that Mildred had probably not fired the shotgun deliberately, but more by accident as she stumbled in frustration into the darkness of the barn. Even so, she was in no mood to be reasoned with now, as she obviously felt herself in danger of physical assault and was determined to defend herself to the end.

One of the reporters cannoned into Arnold. A flashlight lit up the scene with a garish white light. The shotgun stock hissed wickedly through the air. Arnold felt the wind of it and stumbled back out of range, lurched against the door of the barn and the old wood, already splintered and gnawed at by wind and rain, gave way with a groaning, cracking sound, as though it were finally despairing of survival. Arnold lost his balance and went crashing backwards. As he fell there was a catching at his shoulder, he felt something tear, and realized his coat had been ripped by a protruding nail. He lay on his back, angry, thrusting an exploring finger in the long ragged slit in his coat.

His acquaintance with Mildred Sauvage-Brown was proving to be expensive: first, a perfectly sound shirt; now a perfectly good overcoat.

He was out of range for the moment. Beleaguered, Mildred Sauvage-Brown was retreating and as she backed off, step by step, whirling her shotgun like a club, she was tiring. Arnold was reminded of an elderly bovine, taunted by snapping dogs, but Mildred would have seen herself in quite a different light. The breath whistled in her sagging bosom, her square stance plodded her back in front of the pressing group of policemen, and she would see herself as a heroine, fighting for the preservation of all she believed in, against the advancing tide of vandals. But she was middle-aged: a condition that did not make up for commitment. She was short of breath: a condition that did not support her determination. The shotgun still swung, dangerously, but the timing was erratic, the length of arc less regular, and her wrists were dropping, the shotgun stock now swinging at the level of the policemen's waists. They clearly thought themselves particularly vulnerable at this stage, but Chief Superintendent Fairbairn had the confidence of command. Standing back, he shouted '*Now! Get her!*'

Seeking citations, two of his constables dived in.

The shotgun completed its arc. Mildred Sauvage-Brown was unable, tired as she was, to haul the swing and she staggered, off-balance. A flashgun bulb exploded again and a shoulder took her in the midriff. The breath came out of her in a great gushing sound and as the second brave policeman came tumbling in like an over-eager puppy, Mildred Sauvage-Brown collapsed on her back, mouth wide open in silent passion as two red-faced constables straddled her, attempting to hold her down and avoid her flailing arms.

Chief Superintendent Fairbairn was almost dancing in rage as he tried desperately to prevent the two photographers from recording the scene. Valiant protectors of the peace when faced with a menacing shotgun was one thing: the public was equally awed by headlines which read, above appropriate photographs: *Further examples of police violence* or *Three brave coppers subdue one old lady*.

The one old lady, on the ground, emitted great gouts of suppressed air. She stared wildly at the roof of the barn, but Arnold thought he detected an element of triumph in those eyes. He felt sorry for her, but then, he felt sorry for himself too.

He surveyed his own condition. Coat torn, trousers muddied and stained. Nothing good would come out of this business; nothing good for anyone.

Sarah Ellis was crying, hands clutched over her tear-stained face. The red-faced constables, breathing heavily, hoisted the gasping Miss Sauvage-Brown to her feet. She seemed suddenly exhausted and her shoulders were hunched, so they handled her more gently, aware that most of the fight had been knocked out of her.

Arnold was standing at the door of the barn as they led her out, one arm locked behind her back. She glared at Arnold, but he could not be sure she recognized him. She was already contemplating a courtroom, and another opportunity to state her case for Penbrook Farm.

'Oh, your poor coat,' Sarah Ellis said to Arnold, clutching to him suddenly like a survivor to a waterlogged plank.

Arnold inspected the tear gloomily. 'It'll be all right,' he said in an unconvinced tone. 'Don't worry about it.' He turned, disengaging himself gently, having had enough of the Sarah Ellises and the Mildred Sauvage-Browns for the moment. 'You'd better go back with the constable.'

The policeman was large, sympathetic, and eager to make amends for assaulting her companion. 'Come on, lady, I'll take you back to the farm and you can tell me all about it.'

'What'll happen to Mildred?' she trembled.

The constable hesitated. He glanced at the forbidding back of his superior officer, but Chief Superintendent Fairbairn was still clucking at the photographers, warning them he'd be speaking to their editor. 'I shouldn't worry too much,' the constable offered. 'There'll be some accounting to do but, well, she didn't actually *shoot* anyone, did she? Look.'

Arnold and Sarah Ellis followed the direction of his pointed finger. The surveyor, Mr Carter, was a distant figure. He had decided not to wait around to press charges. Having shouldered his panic-stricken way out of the back of the barn, bursting through the rotten wood, he was now to be seen legging it across Barn Field, heading at pace for the lane and his car.

Arnold could hardly blame him.

The constable took Sarah Ellis's arm and marched along with her through the mud of the field, while the small platoon ahead escorted Mildred Sauvage-Brown towards the police car. Arnold trudged along behind Sarah Ellis, gloomy and despondent at the turn of events. The Senior

Planning Officer was bound to hear all about the fracas.

He shoved his hands in his pockets and became aware he still had something belonging to Miss Ellis. As they walked up the lane Arnold caught up with her, drew the little book from his pocket and looked at it. The book had a reddish-brown cover and seemed quite old. Some of the pages seemed to be loose.

'Miss Ellis, don't forget this.'

She clutched at it gratefully, managed a smile of thanks and the constable led her in through the gate of the farmhouse. Arnold walked towards his car, peeling off his damaged overcoat. He unlocked the car and threw the coat on to the back seat.

The first of the police cars was driving up the lane towards him, heading for the main road above. Mildred Sauvage-Brown was in the back seat, incarcerated between the two burly constables. There couldn't be much room on that seat, Arnold thought to himself. He stepped back as the car drew near.

Mildred Sauvage-Brown had recovered her wind and her enthusiasm. Undeterred by her arrest, she leaned forward, recognizing Arnold as the car drove past. 'We shall overcome!' she shouted at him. 'I'm not finished yet!'

Arnold did not doubt it.

'We shall overcome!' she repeated in a high voice. 'Those bastards will get Penbrook Farm only over my dead body!'

The police car picked up speed to master the rising ground in the lane. Mildred Sauvage-Brown was still shouting. Her words drifted back to Arnold, above the distance cawing of the disturbed rooks in the spinney beyond Barn Field.

'Only over my dead body . . .'

CHAPTER 3

1

The *Scarborough Advertiser* was not so insular that it did not carry national news; northern news tended to reach the front page, and so Arnold was not surprised when he received an irate telephone call from the Senior Planning Officer.

'I mean, what on earth is going on? What were you doing there at all—and getting *involved* in the situation!'

'It really was accidental,' Arnold replied weakly. 'I was just—'

'Just nothing! I have to make it clear, Arnold: we in the department must *not* get into controversial situations. We must be seen to be independent, *professional*, damn it! Let the politicians and their ilk rant and rave, we must maintain a discreet silence, maintain a dignified professionalism, give discreet advice—and have *nothing* to do with the Mildred Sauvage-Browns of this world!'

With the last sentiment, Arnold was in hearty agreement. The woman aroused feelings of annoyance and resentment in him: her aggressiveness, confidence and self-righteousness caused prickles of anger at the back of his neck and the mouthings she uttered about corruption in local government were of the kind that irritated him because they were so difficult to substantiate or dispute. He felt exposed: if there were any shady dealings on the part of people like Minford, Arnold felt he had to make them public as part of his moral duty, but he had no doubt that the Senior Planning Officer was not of the same mind. 'Circumspection,' the Senior Planning Officer warned. 'Circumspection.' It was another word for discretion, and shorthand for minding one's own business.

Mildred Sauvage-Brown possessed neither discretion, nor circumspection—and she intended minding everyone's business. Arnold groaned when he saw the news in the local newspaper the following evening. There had been a scene in the magistrates' court. Miss Sauvage-Brown had been hauled up before the local bench on a charge of disturbing the peace. Clearly, the police were hesitant about bringing a firearms charge against her, and the unfortunate surveyor, mindful of his own manly reputation, had obviously declined to press charges of assault and battery. It would have required only an assurance from the lady in question that she would refrain from further disturbances and she would have been bound over to keep the peace—which meant she would go free.

That was not Miss Sauvage-Brown's style. She had taken the opportunity to launch yet another attack on Wilson, Livingstone and Councillor Minford. She had repeated her vague statements about local government corruption. When the chairman of the bench had remonstrated, she had reminded him of his own involvement in the education committee scandal of two years previously and had called into question his moral obligations, one of which she suggested, should be resignation from his position as Justice of the Peace as being no fit and proper person to hold such a situation.

It was not a suggestion calculated to please the magistrate. He committed her to the cells for a month. After a hurried and nervous approach from the Clerk to the Court, the red-faced magistrate changed his verdict and bound her over for psychiatric reports. When she responded by telling him with some force what he could do with psychiatric reports, his face got redder and he committed her to prison for contempt of court in spite of the chalkiness of the Clerk of the Court's features.

Bail was eventually fixed at three hundred pounds. All in all, Arnold concluded, the proceedings seemed to have been confused and exciting. Any sensible woman would have backed down, taken the easy way out of court. Mildred Sauvage-Brown had not, and had made the kind of headlines she desired.

In the afternoon session, it seemed, the chairman of the bench had retired from the courtroom, saying he felt ill. There was a hint in the newspaper account that his legs were unsteady. Arnold did not blame him. In such trying circumstances, he too would have been tempted to take a few stiff whiskies at lunch-time.

She was still on his mind when he did the Saturday morning shopping in Morpeth. It caused him to forget several items and he was in a niggly frame of mind when he was forced to return twice to the little corner shop he frequented, for coffee, and later, some potatoes.

Accordingly, his normal equanimity was in short supply when he felt the hand buffeting his shoulder and he heard the booming voice behind him. '*Weel, are ye gangin' doon the yelhoose ter wet yer neb wi' yer marrer?*'

Arnold turned, coldly, but with fire in his veins. 'What I really can't stand,' he said, 'is people who are particularly careful about their accent and who would be annoyed if someone tried to imitate their rounded vowels, and yet who feel it's clever to try to use Geordie vernacular, and fail miserably at it!'

'Hey, hey, man,' Freddie Keeler stepped back, raising both hands in mock dismay. 'All I was doing was being a bit friendly, like. It's been a hard morning, plenty inquiries, no house sales, and I'm on my way for a pint. You want me to rephrase it? I'll do it, Arnold, just for you.' He struck a pose, left foot forward, left hand extended, head cocked on one side. 'Well, are you going down to the pub to have a drink with your friend?'

Arnold smiled, in spite of the simmering annoyance in

his veins. He knew the sharpness of his response had not really been the result of Freddie Keeler's request: there were other reasons, connected with Miss Sauvage-Brown's incarceration and yet generally undefined. 'I'm sorry, Freddie. You sort of caught me on the hop, then. You're going to The Black Bull?'

The tubby estate agent nodded. 'No better place.'

'I'll join you. Just let me lock up the car.'

It was only just after midday and the lounge bar was filling rapidly with Saturday lunch-time drinkers. As Keeler bought the drinks Arnold found some seats in the corner of the warm room, away from the droning of the horse race commentator on the television set suspended above the bar. Keeler stood there for a short while, watching the progress of the race; at its conclusion he came across to Arnold with an expression of disgust on his face. 'Typical,' he muttered. 'Never take a hot tip from a client. He knows you're trying to screw him on price, so he sets you up in revenge by giving you an also-ran as a dead cert.'

'Didn't know you were interested in horses.'

'Anything that'll make me money. Didn't you know that about estate agents? Anyway, you still got the glum face. Here's your beer. Drink up and smile.'

Arnold sipped at his beer. 'I'm sorry about that flare-up outside. I—'

'Say no more, dear boy. I can guess what brought it on. I saw the papers. I guess your boss ain't gonna be too pleased, as they say.'

Arnold grimaced. 'That's one way of putting it. And at the moment things don't seem to be dying down.'

Freddie Keeler caressed his nose, as though reminding himself of the red, broken veins that had started to accumulate under the skin. 'Mildred Sauvage-Brown. She seems quite a character.'

'She is.'

'And noisy.'

'How do you mean?'

Freddie Keeler grinned. 'Well, she certainly got the magistrate's goat, didn't she? Probably striking too close to home. You reckon he got stoned at lunch-time to recover?'

Arnold smiled. 'Seems like it. But you think she *was* getting near the truth?'

Keeler shrugged. 'There was a fuss a while back about him and some dinner lady at one of the schools . . . But she's just as noisy in your field, from all I can gather.'

Arnold hesitated. He had a feeling the Senior Planning Officer would not approve, but slowly, he asked, 'Do you think she's right about the other . . . allegations?'

Freddie Keeler sipped at his gin and tonic and then looked at Arnold carefully. He always gave an impression of being a cheerful, fun-loving man, a good drinking companion, one who viewed life as something to be enjoyed and not taken too seriously. But he was a good businessman, and Arnold had occasionally wondered whether Freddie Keeler was a deal more sagacious than he appeared. The bonhomie could be a front, a cover for shrewdness. 'Allegations . . . Smoke and fire, isn't it, Arnold?'

'I could also come back at you about old wives' tales.'

Keeler's eyes held hints of calculations. He rubbed at his balding pate. 'I don't know too much about what's been said by the good lady, but I do hear it involves a couple of businessmen.'

'Wilson and Livingstone,' Arnold supplied. 'Do you know them?'

'By reputation. Not exactly done much *business* with them but I've seen them work, and one of them at fairly close hand.'

'How do you mean?'

Keeler hesitated, uncertain suddenly whether to go on. Then he shrugged. 'Well, I'll tell you. I've always felt you're a bit . . . naïve about some things, so maybe it's time your eyes were opened to the wicked ways of the world. You ever heard of the Auction Act of 1969?'

'I'm not sure,' Arnold said cautiously.

'Its full title is the Auctions (Bidding Agreements) Act,' Keeler said, and added feelingly, 'I can quote it almost *verbatim*.'

'What's it say?'

'The Act says that if a dealer gives anyone a "consideration—" you know what consideration means?'

'Sort of payment.'

'Right. If a dealer gives anyone a consideration for abstaining from bidding at an auction sale a criminal offence is committed on the part of the dealer and the person receiving the consideration.'

'So?'

Keeler stroked his nose thoughtfully. 'Well, the Act has never been particularly popular with auctioneers and estate agents and dealers. You see, in the old days knock-out agreements weren't illegal.'

'Knock-out agreements?'

'An agreement between intending bidders not to bid against each other. The idea was,' Keeler explained, 'that a group of people got together at an auction, only one of them made a bid, the item got knocked down to him at a fairly low price and then the group could have a *private* auction among themselves later, when a higher price was likely to be gained. The difference in the price could be split between the bidders.'

'And the seller in the first place was cheated out of the proper sale price?'

Keeler shuffled uncomfortably. 'Well, he had his own remedy—he could always fix a reserve price on the article. Anyway, be that as it may, fact is the old legal position was changed, it's illegal to have such rings these days, but . . .'

'It still goes on?' Arnold asked after a short pause.

Keeler sipped at his gin. 'You can say that again. You

see, up around here, where you got so many big houses, with old ladies dying off all the time, there's a treasure house of antiques. Not too many people know their true value, and some of the London dealers are unscrupulous bastards. So there's more than a few people up here who've banded together to keep things quiet, keep the London mob away, and do our own private deals.'

'*Our?*'

Keeler waved his glass negligently. 'I been involved a few times.'

Arnold paused. 'What's this got to do with Mildred Sauvage-Brown's allegations?'

'Not a lot. But we were talking about Wilson and Livingstone.'

'They're involved?'

Freddie Keeler shook his head. 'Not centrally. They're just amateurs, if you like: fringe people. But they're on the circuit list, and they get invitations to the bidding rings.'

'Why?'

There was a roar from the end of the bar as another horse race ended. Keeler glanced back dolefully and shook his head. 'Suckers . . . Why do they get invited, you ask? I asked myself, some time back. And I got a theory. You see, I knew Livingstone way back. He's done well.'

'In what way?'

'He's a Byker lad, you know, though you wouldn't guess it now. He was a tearaway as a kid, quick to give you a *nasty dunch on the jaa*, and he talked like that, I'm telling you! Bright lad, though, and he left Tyneside for a few years, came back and moved upwards, rapidly.'

Arnold thought back to his first meeting with the tall, reddish-haired Livingstone. He remembered the athletic force of the man and could believe he could have been active in the Byker terraces. There was certainly no trace of a Geordie accent now, however: the man was controlled, and tough. 'His climb . . . was that in the property business?'

'That's right. I think he must have got going as a jobber builder down south, made a few thousand quid, expanded, then came back north and joined Wilson. That's when he really began to do well.'

Wilson, the frosty-eyed, middle-aged businessman and his younger, more muscular lieutenant. 'So what's the involvement with the auction rings?' Arnold asked.

'I told you. Just amateurs, really. And a couple of times I've had the feeling maybe they're conning us, using us to set up their own deals. Anyway, fact is, my personal contacts with them have been at the rings. Not that I attend many of them, of course, but either Wilson, or Livingstone, or on occasions both of them, tend to be there. Not spending much, generally, but once in a while . . .'

'A hobby for them?'

'For Wilson, I would guess. Livingstone . . . I'm not so sure. I think he takes it seriously. But I get the impression that character takes everything seriously. He's the kind who's got to win, you know? And maybe, if you take his Byker background into account, he'll do just about anything to do it.' He considered the matter for a moment, staring thoughtfully into the puddle of gin and tonic in his glass. 'Yes . . . old Wilson, he's a canny old buzzard and not above a bit of skulduggery, but it would be done at a distance, and smoothly, a knife between the shoulder-blades. Livingstone's a different kettle of fish. He'd do things *personally*, and he'd do it with a bludgeon. He'd like the sound of crunching bone . . . Mine's a gin and tonic again, Arnold.'

Arnold made his way to the bar. While he waited to catch the attention of the barman he was vaguely aware of the television discussion on the merits of various football teams. The Senior Planning Officer was a supporter of Newcastle United. It puzzled Arnold: association football was a mystery to him, as were most sporting activities. He assumed it was due to something missing in his genes.

He gave Freddie Keeler his gin and tonic, placed his own

half pint on the table and sat down. 'You read the newspaper accounts about the outburst from Miss Sauvage-Brown?'

Keeler nodded. 'The reports weren't very specific. Just making sure there was no libel suit, I reckon. It was easy to pick out Wilson and Livingstone, of course, but it looked to me like the local government corruption stuff had been edited out. Even so, I suppose it's Councillor Minford she's screaming about.'

'That's right. Have you had many dealings with him?'

Keeler shook his head. 'Not a lot. I mean, he's been in the building business way back, and I did a fair amount of work with his old man, but Minford closed down the business and went into politics. Had a fair bit of cash salted away: what his father had made, and he married someone who had her own cash.'

'Wasn't she involved in the building business as well?'

'Oh yes, I mean that's how they got together, the story goes. She was the daughter of that character who built up that Gateshead firm . . . what the hell was his name?'

'I can't say.'

'No matter. The company was a flourishing one—Jarrow Development Corporation—and they made a bomb in the 'sixties. He was a contemporary of old Minford and the two got together, decided upon a merger and it was about that time that Albert Minford got shacked up with his present wife. Eileen . . . damn it, what was her name? She'd been married before—she's more than a few years older than Minford so the story was he was as much interested in her cash as in her body—and she had a grown-up son. Her husband died a long time back, and she'd been working with her father . . .'

'I seem to recall something about it at the time,' Arnold admitted. 'Weren't they on the fringe of the Poulson scandals in some way?'

'Never brought to book, but there were a lot of fringe activities in *that* area,' Keeler said with emphasis. 'Thank

God I was never involved. Anyway, like I was saying, Jarrow Development and Minford's firm went into a merger arrangement, but something went sour and by the time the two old men had died the new company was falling apart. They cut their losses, went into liquidation, and the principals got out with enough cash to live on and more. Minford married his Eileen, with her grown-up son, walked into a political life, and she . . . damn it, that's right, she started another firm in her own right. Went into business with her son.'

Arnold frowned. Something stirred muddily at the back of his mind. He thought back, aware there was something he should remember but it escaped him. Annoyed, he put it aside.

'You've heard no rumours that would back up Miss Sauvage-Brown's allegations?'

'Don't really know what the allegations are,' Keeler confessed. 'But my guess would be she doesn't really know herself. I've had dealings from time to time with these conservationists. They see fascist pigs in every farmyard. They go for the jugular without much compunction and it's nothing to do with finesse. A slashing stroke, believe me, and the blood spurts everywhere. Difficult stains to remove. They know it. And they don't care. Bloody eccentrics. They'll do anything to save their bloody woodlands, hayricks and henhouses. Come across any old barns lately?'

Recognizing the mischief in the estate agent's tone, Arnold refused to rise to the bait.

Arnold was not sure what he had got out of his conversation with Freddie Keeler. He had been vaguely aware of the existence of auction rings: from time to time there had been reports of prosecutions, but everyone agreed that such arrangements were extremely difficult to prove. The only chance the police had was to find someone prepared to inform on the others; alternatively, there was the chancy business of following dealers when they left auctions and checking to discover whether they were meeting in secret as a group for the 'knock-out'. The trouble there was that if the meeting took place on private premises the police had no right of entry.

But even if Wilson and Livingstone were involved in such activity it could essentially have no bearing on the future of Penbrook Farm. Mildred Sauvage-Brown was making vague accusations but so far there was no factual basis for them to Arnold's knowledge. The Senior Planning Officer would advise him he was wasting his time; Freddie Keeler had characterized the lady's behaviour as eccentric, and perhaps deliberately vague because there was no basis for her claims.

As for Arnold himself, he was questioning his own motivation. He was sympathetic towards Sarah Ellis and the case made out by Mildred Sauvage-Brown for Penbrook Farm. But was that sympathy now causing him to go too far with his suspicions? Was he subconsciously taking the side of the two ladies, unjustly, when the two businessmen and the councillor in the case were doing nothing wrong?

He could not be certain and his own doubts made him depressed and unhappy. He drove home from his meeting with Freddie Keeler in a doubtful frame of mind. The skies had darkened, there was rain in the wind, and he suspected he would be able to do no work in the garden, as he had planned, that afternoon.

He made some lunch for himself and sat down in the small sitting-room of his bungalow. There was an old film on television: he watched it for a while and then drifted off into an uneasy sleep.

He woke with a start at four o' clock. The room was dim, and the black and white images of the film sent dancing shadows across the walls.

The files. He remembered looking at them; one in particular. A building firm, Floyd and Simson.

Freddie Keeler had been unable to remember the name of the man who had built up the Jarrow Development Corporation. But Arnold remembered now: Kenneth Floyd.

And his daughter had married a man called Simson.

A slow surge of anger crawled through Arnold's veins. He walked out into the hallway and put on his coat. He got the car out and drove down to Morpeth. He walked into the police station and got out his cheque-book.

Then he posted bail for Mildred Sauvage-Brown.

2

The trouble with Sunday newspapers was that they had time to devote to digging up further facts, embellishing them, and producing 'reasoned' articles, complete with the background to events. Arnold was horrified on the Sunday morning to find that his picture was in the paper.

It was not a good one, and a couple of years out of date. It had been taken, and used, at the time of the debate on the Old Barn at Rampton, when he had achieved a brief television fame. The photograph had not pleased him and it had rendered the Senior Planning Officer apoplectic. It was now reprinted, together with a rehashed account of the events at Penbrook Farm.

There was also a photograph of Penbrook Farm, taken from the old wildwood and showing the spread of the mediæval fields that Mildred Sauvage-Brown was attempting to save.

She appeared centrally, dominating the article itself. Arnold guessed the shot must have been taken at Penbrook Farm by one of the photographers present at the time: the man clearly had taken advantage of his presence to do some entrepreneurial shooting he had not submitted to his own newspaper.

It did not show Mildred Sauvage-Brown in a good light. Her mouth was open, roaring; a burly constable held her left arm, and she appeared to be swinging a right hook in the direction of Chief Superintendent Fairbairn. His features expressed alarm, but that could have been due to the poor focusing of the picture: in the excitement of the moment the photographer had probably got his focal lengths wrong.

There was also a print of Sarah Ellis. She appeared to be crying. She was standing in the front doorway of the farmhouse, raising one arm in protest to cover her features, unsuccessfully, and clutching in the other hand the inevitable book, as though it would save her.

Disturbed, Arnold took the phone off the hook in case the Senior Planning Officer was so moved as to ring him in high dudgeon, got himself his copy of *Archæologia Cantiana*, removed to the small bedroom he had furnished as a study and failed to concentrate for the next two hours.

The Senior Planning Officer finally contacted him at ten on Monday morning.

He was fairly polite, for the Senior Planning Officer. He was certainly succinct. And direct. In fact, Arnold could not remember when the Senior Planning Officer had made himself clearer. If there was any more trouble, any more publicity, any more *unseemly* involvement in matters scandalous, Arnold could expect a redeployment within the local authority.

And *then* there'd be no more gallivanting around the hills of Northumberland, to *everyone's* relief.

Nor did his philanthropic gesture—if that was how he could describe it to himself—regarding Mildred Sauvage-Brown, give him any satisfaction. At lunch-time a rather large and curious police sergeant visited his office at Morpeth. He eyed Arnold with some suspicion.

'Mr Landon?'

'That's right.'

'I'm Sergeant Entwistle. You . . . er . . . you posted bail on Saturday for a Miss Sauvage-Brown.'

Arnold hesitated. 'I did.'

'She wasn't too pleased.' The sergeant eyed Arnold again, curiously. 'She gave us quite a time when we told her she could leave. Said she had no intention of . . . how did she put it? Relinquishing her martyrdom. Yeh, that was it.'

'It sounds like her.'

'I brought your cheque around, sir. We . . . that is the Super thought you ought to have it back . . . with a word of warning.'

'About what?'

'About getting mixed up with funny people like Miss Sauvage-Brown.'

'She's not funny.'

'I think the Super meant . . . eccentric, sir.'

Arnold took the proffered cheque. 'I'm surprised you brought it round to me.'

'Not usual, but like the Super said, a word of warning.'

'Is the lady still in the cells?' Arnold asked.

The police sergeant shook his head. 'Naw. I think it was one thing to take a stand. Maybe she'd been reconsidering her position Saturday, except that the news that bail had been posted meant she got the idea someone was trying to interfere, take away her rights, sort of. But having taken the decision to stay . . . well, Saturday night ain't the same as Friday night, sir.'

'How do you mean?'

'Clientele gets a bit rougher. A few of the football crowd, one or two drunk and disorderly; noisy it gets, and smelly too. I think she kind of changed her mind about ten on Saturday night.'

'You mean she left?'

'Decided to pay her own recognizances. Paid up, cleared off, gone home, I shouldn't be surprised. But a gentleman like you, sir, you shouldn't get mixed up in things like this . . . people like her. So the Super reckons.'

It was a sentiment the Senior Planning Officer would have heartily endorsed.

The visit was not the last of the surprises Arnold faced that day, however. At four in the afternoon he received another visitor, just as he was despondently clearing his desk prior to going home. It was Henry Willington.

It was clear from the moment that the man walked into his office something was wrong. His wind-tanned skin seemed to have paled, and held a greenish look. Arnold remembered the lines on his face but they appeared to have deepened, cicatrices of doubt around his eyes and mouth. His pale brown eyes reflected that doubt: they seemed to be seeking something long since lost, the certainty of youth. At Arnold's invitation he sat down. His left hand was shaking slightly.

'Are you all right?'

'I think so.'

Arnold watched the man for a few minutes and then walked across to the filing cabinet. The Senior Planning Officer would not have approved, but Arnold kept a bottle of whisky among the files, for emergency purposes. There had only been a couple of occasions when he had felt the need to use the bottle: this was clearly one of them. He did not ask Willington: rather, he merely poured him a drink in the tumbler he kept in his desk and then sat down. 'You'd better tell me.'

'I've just been along the corridor.'

Arnold knew, suddenly, without being told.

'It can't have been a surprise, surely.'

'No, but when it happens . . .' The pale brown eyes tried to focus on Arnold but failed. Willington lifted the glass, sipped vaguely at the whisky, hardly aware of what he was doing. 'When it happens, it's unexpected, really, and the forms . . .' He sipped the whisky again. 'Seeing the forms, it sort of brings it home to you.'

'When did it happen?'

'Yesterday. He was going through his usual routine. Did the same thing every Sunday morning. He used to get up about seven, have some toast and coffee, fuss about in his study for a while and then sit down to read the papers. He called to me . . .'

His glance became dulled, introspective, and Arnold felt a vast sympathy for the man. He had been bitter about Patrick Willington, angry that his father had depleted the estate, wanted to get his hands on it to put things right, but now, when the opportunity was coming his way it had the taste of ashes. 'He was able to speak?' Arnold asked, to break the silence.

Henry Willington nodded. 'Oh yes, he was quite lucid for a while. But I . . . I knew there was something wrong. And then he choked, dropped the papers, and I ran to get some water . . . When I came back, he was dead.'

'Heart attack?'

The pale brown eyes were vague again. 'I called the doctor immediately. He was there before lunch-time. He said there'd probably have to be a post mortem . . . Mr Landon, he looked so *different*!'

'It wasn't necessary for you to come in today,' Arnold said gently. 'It could have waited . . .'

'No.' Henry Willington shook his head with a sudden vehemence. 'The things he said . . . I had to find out.' He paused again, distressed, and yet giving Arnold the impression he was almost standing outside himself, watching a shadow play—Patrick Willington, Henry Willington, Arnold Landon. 'I went through the papers in his study.'

Arnold hesitated. It was none of his business, but it was clear that Henry Willington wished to talk. 'Did you find that . . . his affairs were as bad as you feared?'

'I already knew they were bad. I merely found the confirmation.' He sighed, almost in despair. 'I knew his father before him had left the estate in a mess, but I think it could have been turned around, the whole situation, if only my father had possessed an ounce of business sense. Or even when I came back, an ounce of . . . he would never listen, you see.'

'The estate can't be saved?'

Henry Willington shrugged. 'There are still some properties to be sold, but it will be a long haul. I came in today to talk to the Registrar of Deaths, and to have a word with you about the planning application for the sawmill.'

'It can easily be withdrawn now,' Arnold said.

'That's good. It would never have worked, would it? He was so . . . *incompetent*.' The word had a sudden urgency that took Arnold by surprise. He had felt that Henry Willington's emotions were of sadness, loss and anxiety about the future. But now he knew there were still elements of the resentment he had detected that day at Willington Hall, when Henry had talked so bitterly of his father.

Henry Willington finished his whisky and set the glass down on the desk, regaining control of himself. 'You'll arrange for withdrawal of the application, then?'

'It's no problem. And if we can help in any way over the estate itself . . . as far as planning is concerned . . .' Arnold stumbled over the words, at a loss, but Henry Willington hardly seemed to hear him.

'There's no money of any consequence,' he said slowly. 'About thirty thousand in the bank. That'll not even cover the Hall's running expenses. What it requires is an injection of capital, wise investment . . .'

'Perhaps the sales you engender—'

'No.' The tone was positive, the eyes clearing, a little panicked wildness entering his glance as though the very thought of relinquishing Willington Hall terrified him. 'No. That won't be necessary. I'll find a way. There must be . . . there *will* be a way. The family have always rallied around in the past, in the old days, but Patrick was so stupid, so *criminally* stupid that he lost the chance, the only real chance there was at the time . . . And now . . .' Willington stared at Arnold with a sudden clarity, as though he were seeing him for the first time. Yet Arnold was left with the feeling that it was not Arnold that Henry Willington saw.

After the man had gone, instead of rushing home Arnold poured himself a drink and sat on in the darkened office. The rest of the staff had left, but he had a key, and he was disinclined to leave.

He sipped his whisky and thought of Henry Willington and Patrick Willington and a man who had died years ago in the Yorkshire dales. A man and his son . . . a difficult relationship. That between Patrick and Henry had certainly been soured, by the older man's fanciful dreams and incompetent bungling, and by the son's resentments, the knowledge that he could do better if only he were given the opportunity. Now that the chance had come it was probably too late; the old man was gone, leaving an unwelcome legacy.

It had been so different for Arnold. He would never lose the legacy his father had left him: of warmth, of caring; of the love for things that were disappearing, of traces of ancestors who had long since passed away. There had been no resentments, just a deep sense of loss when Arnold's father had died; yet even that loss was never to be deep, because his father had left so much of himself in Arnold.

The thought caused tears to prickle at the back of Arnold's eyes: the knowledge that he would never, really, be alone.

Arnold should have gone home at that point, but instead he reached for the bottle and poured himself another drink, unwilling to lose the moment and the memory. His mind drifted back over the days he had spent in the dales with his father, tramping through the disused farms and the dying villages. He was a child again, with a child's emotions, as he felt the whisper of a breeze on his cheek and saw the morning sun gild the hills.

He had had a sandwich at lunch-time and nothing since,

but the whisky was warming him, and he felt no hunger. A shaft of moonlight crept through the window and outside, he knew, there would be a hint of frost in the air.

At nine o' clock, the bottle empty, he rose unsteadily from his chair.

He had difficulty finding his keys to lock the door behind him. He had greater difficulty finding his car keys. Once inside the car, however, his confidence grew and with it came a strange sense of resentment.

He did not like Mildred Sauvage-Brown. She was the worst kind of conservationist: the noisy kind. She brayed her beliefs from the rooftops and antagonized people. She gloried in her eccentricity, claimed it as commitment, and gave a cause a bad name.

Moreover, she was arrogant. She was the kind of woman who would never take advice, who would always be certain she was right, who would override poor little mice like Sarah Ellis, and who would mercilessly use people like Arnold Landon to further her own ideas.

She was also insensitive, he concluded, refusing to accept a helping hand, too proud to allow Arnold Landon to salve his own conscience by posting her bail.

She needed to be told so, to her face.

Sober, Arnold knew, he would never be able to do it. Drunk, as he was, it was a different matter. Drunk, he could debate with philosophers, insult kings. And certainly put bloody Mildred Sauvage-Brown down a peg or two.

He started the car, drove away from headquarters and dared a police car to stop him as he swung out of the town, up the hill and across to the quiet country lanes that led towards Penbrook Farm.

The hedgerows seemed to lead him on whitely, and there was a gay sparkle of frost in the road. He passed one or two cars, and they dazzled him with their headlights, but the exhilaration in his blood gave him the confidence to continue, warmed him with the satisfaction of knowing that he

would be able to tell Mildred Sauvage-Brown what a fool
she had made of herself at the hearing and afterwards, and
particularly at the farm when she had so frightened the little
surveyor Carter. He would be able to say, loftily, that he
had been moved by the highest motives in dealing with the
matter of her bail, and she had showed crass and insensitive
stubbornness in refusing the gesture. And then he would
sweep out, back to the car, leaving her speechless.

The thought gave him a warm glow.

The gate to Penbrook Farm was open and Arnold nego-
tiated the track with confidence. The stream glittered in the
moonlight as he swung down past Rivermead Field and the
farmhouse was a dark, humped shape at the bottom of
the lane. He parked the car, killed the engine, switched off
the lights and got out of the driving seat.

There were no lights at the farm.

Arnold hesitated. No lights, no people, he reasoned, and
the glow inside him began to fade. He stood beside his car,
uncertain. The battered car was parked outside the house,
and the Land-Rover was also in the lane. It was possible
the two women had gone to bed, but on the other hand
there could be a room at the back of the farmhouse, where
he would see no light from the lane. He closed the car door
and walked towards the entrance.

The gate was open. Again Arnold paused. The warmth
he had experienced during the drive was evaporating at the
same rate as his confidence. He was not certain, now, that
he desired a confrontation with Mildred Sauvage-Brown: at
the same time, he would feel extremely foolish and cowardly
if he turned back, having come so far. He marched forward
with a sudden resolution and knocked on the door.

There was a hollowness about the sound that surprised
him. He waited, but there was no reply. He tried again,
knocking harder and then, without quite knowing why, he
turned the old-fashioned handle of the door and he realized
it was off the latch.

The door swung slowly open and Arnold stood framed in the entrance to the dark passageway beyond. There were no lights visible and although the moonlight penetrated the windows of the room on the left it gave little illumination to the stone-flagged passageway itself.

Arnold could not recall seeing the light switches when he had visited the farmhouse previously. He hesitated, not knowing what to do.

'Hallo?'

His voice echoed, fluttering through the rooms.

'*Hallo?*' he tried again, unable to control the slight tremor in his voice as his heart rate began to rise. The glow had now gone completely, to be replaced by a chilliness in his bones. He stepped forward, the flags ringing hollowly under his feet. He groped along the wall, seeking a light-switch near the door.

Something crunched under his feet.

Arnold stood still. Slowly he bent down, touched the stone flags, and he felt the slivers, sharp under his fingers. The light-bulb in the passageway had been shattered.

Alarmed, Arnold straightened, and called again. 'Miss Ellis? Miss Sauvage-Brown? Is there anyone here?'

He groped his way down the passageway, not waiting for an answer. Again there came the crunching sound under his feet—another light-bulb. They had been systematically smashed, of that he was now sure.

There was a pounding in Arnold's temples as he tried to recall the layout of the farmhouse. The passageway was cool, but he could feel warmth ahead of him, the kitchen probably, and even as he realized it he caught the dim glow under the door itself.

There was an open fire there: some light at least would be available.

He opened the door and the fire was low, turning to ash, and leaving only a dim light for the kitchen. It was enough for Arnold to see there was little sign of disturbance; a chair had been moved, leaning against the settee. But there was something that bothered Arnold, something that brought back unpleasant, half-recalled memories. An odour, a sickly, cloying odour that seemed to pervade the room.

Arnold swayed. He was drunker than he had realized, and although the tension and the thundering of his heart had sobered him somewhat, he was still left with uncoordinated muscles and muddled thought. He stood in the kitchen and tried to think straight.

A phone. There'd been a phone. Far corner of the room, in the angle of the old farmhouse kitchen. This was no business for him, an empty house with that disturbing smell. Police: he needed to call the police.

He moved towards the angle of the wall and immediately, in the dull glow of the firelight, he saw the huddled shape lying in the corner. He stopped dead, stared at it and recalled the odour and what it meant. Spilled blood.

His senses began to reel. He wanted to extend a hand, touch the body lying there, but he could not nerve himself to do so. His gorge rose, sickness threatening to choke him and, gagging, he stepped over the huddled body, reached for the phone and dialled 999.

He was able to gasp only, 'Police . . . Penbrook Farm,' before the phone dropped from his nerveless fingers and, retching, he staggered back into the centre of the room. He knelt in front of the settee, his stomach heaving, alcohol and distress combining to unman him completely.

His senses began to blur, but before the blackness descended upon him he recalled the police car in the lane, bearing Mildred Sauvage-Brown away from the farm. She had been calling out, triumphant and defiant.

They would never get the farm, she had insisted. Except one way.

Over her dead body.

3

'Just what in the hell were you doing there?'

It was a question that had hammered at Arnold for twenty-four hours. It had first been asked of him when the police had brought him out of the kitchen, still groggy, into the front room as arc lights had been set up and cars had driven up to the farmhouse and there had been much coming and going. Still hazy from his consumption of alcohol, he had been almost incoherent and was not surprised when the detective questioning him had expressed doubt about his answers and hinted he suspected the murderer of the woman in the kitchen was Arnold himself.

But everything had changed when Chief Superintendent Fairbairn had walked into the room, for he had brought a woman with him. At the sight of her Arnold had started to his feet as though a bomb had gone off. He cried out, choking, pointing an accusatory finger. '*You!*'

Dumpy, angry, shaking with suppressed emotion, Mildred Sauvage-Brown had snarled at him, 'You bastard!'

'But I thought it was you!' Arnold exclaimed, bewildered.

'And you killed her, thinking it was me!' Mildred Sauvage-Brown screamed, struggling to get at Arnold but held back by the Chief Superintendent. Two constables were called in to restrain her. Fairbairn looked at Arnold curiously. 'You thought it was Miss Sauvage-Brown who had been murdered?'

'I never thought of Miss Ellis,' Arnold replied, shaking his head, desperately trying to clear the fogs in his mind. 'The house was dark, the lights had been smashed, I wasn't thinking straight, and when I came into the kitchen . . . there was the blood, and the body in the corner, and I rang the police . . . and then passed out.'

'*Murderer!*' Mildred Sauvage-Brown hissed.

'Get that bloody woman out of here,' Chief Superintendent Fairbairn snapped, unfeelingly in Arnold's view. She would, after all, be much upset by the death of her companion, and she should be forgiven a degree of anger and passion. Fairbairn had then questioned Arnold closely, but had not got very far. Now, in Fairbairn's own office the following day, the man obviously hoped to get the facts a little straighter.

'I'd been drinking,' Arnold admitted.

'We know that. It was perfectly obvious. You'd been sick either from the drink, or from the sight of Sarah Ellis's corpse, or a combination, didn't matter too much. But why had you gone there?'

'I . . . I got drunk, and decided to have it out with Miss Sauvage-Brown.'

'Have what out?'

'Her . . . attitude.' Arnold was himself puzzled at his answer. The resentments he had felt had now faded; they had been inflamed by alcohol and they now seemed very trivial. He found it difficult to explain to the Chief Superintendent. 'You don't really suspect *me* of killing Miss Ellis, do you?'

'You're not ruled out,' Fairbairn said grudgingly, 'but there's no real signs you had much to do with it. No scratches, no signs of contact, no blood . . . And your behaviour, well, murderers don't usually ring us after they've croaked someone. Unless they're fiendishly clever. You don't seem to me to be fiendishly clever.'

'Miss Sauvage-Brown seems to think I did it.'

'Last night, she did.' Fairbairn shrugged. 'But this morning she'll have had time to reflect. But tell me—why did you think it was she who'd been killed?'

Arnold frowned. 'I suppose . . . well, it was partly that Miss Ellis was so . . . harmless.'

'Whereas the outspoken Miss Sauvage-Brown has spent most of her adult life making enemies of one sort or another.' The Chief Superintendent nodded. 'Anything else?'

'The words she used when you arrested her earlier. Over her dead body . . .'

'You thought them prophetic.'

'Something like that.'

Fairbairn watched Arnold closely for a little while. 'You puzzle me, Mr Landon. You say you went there to have a confrontation with Miss Sauvage-Brown. She clearly dislikes you—I'm told she attacked you after a planning inquiry recently. *Do* you so much dislike her?'

Arnold shrugged uncertainly. 'I was drunk—'

'Were you also drunk when you posted bail for her?' Fairbairn interrupted.

'No.'

'Funny thing to do, if you disliked her, wanted to confront her, been attacked by her . . .'

'She's . . . a difficult woman,' Arnold said weakly.

'And you're a funny feller,' Fairbairn said grumpily. 'All right, when you drove to the farm did you see any other cars on the road?'

'I passed a few, but—'

'Did you make out any of them?'

Arnold shook his head. 'Just dazzled by their lights, really.'

'You didn't see a Rover near the farm?'

'No, sir.'

Fairbairn scowled. 'We've had a report of a Rover being driven fast from that area. Complaint from a farmer who was almost knocked down. Like you, he was drunk. Unlike you, he was walking home. You didn't see the car?'

'No.'

'How long were you in the farmhouse before you found the body?'

'I would calculate a matter of minutes only.'

'Can you tell me what time you left your office?'

'About nine, I think.'

'Anyone to verify that?'

'I don't think so.'

'How long did it take you to drive to Penbrook Farm?'

'About an hour, I would calculate.'

Chief Superintendent Fairbairn grunted. 'I have to tell you, Mr Landon, that early reports from forensic would suggest—from body cooling times—that Sarah Ellis was killed close to nine-thirty, nine forty-five.'

Arnold stared at the Chief Superintendent, his mouth open. 'You mean . . . it happened only minutes before I got there?'

'Something like that,' Fairbairn said quietly. 'The person who killed her must have wanted to leave the house without being seen. Switching out the lights would have done that, but he—or she—must have panicked, smashed the light-bulbs, so the house could be left in darkness. Another reason for not holding you a *likely* suspect: no sign of glass slivers in your clothes.'

Arnold hesitated. 'How was she killed?'

'She was swung, with considerable violence, against the wall near the fireplace. Her head struck the wall—it crushed her head, lots of blood. She was pushed, or fell, in the corner near the phone.'

'The person who killed her . . . you said he—or she.'

Chief Superintendent Fairbairn regarded him blandly. 'We have still an open mind about the sex of the killer. I wonder . . . do you mind if I asked Miss Mildred Sauvage-Brown to join us at this point?'

She sat squarely in the chair to one side of Arnold, eyes smouldering dislike, anger and a deeper, more personal emotion that Arnold could not detect but could guess at. Chief Superintendent Fairbairn had called for cups of coffee and they waited for them in silence, the policeman obviously happy to allow the tension to grow between the two people facing him. Mildred Sauvage-Brown's dumpy face sagged at the jowls and there was an unwonted pallor in her cheeks;

the hands in her lap were twisted together, and Arnold shivered slightly at the thought she possibly wanted to get her fingers around his throat.

The coffee arrived at last.

Chief Superintendent Fairbairn smiled. 'Sugar?' he asked Miss Sauvage-Brown.

'Three spoons,' she replied balefully and glared at Arnold. 'Are you going to arrest him?'

'What for?' the Chief Superintendent inquired.

'He was there at the farm. What was he doing there? Didn't he kill poor Sarah?'

Arnold looked at his hands. There had been a spasm in the woman's voice, and although it was still bitter it seemed to have lost some of its positive aggression.

Fairbairn handed her the cup of coffee. She took it grudgingly. Fairbairn sipped his own coffee and said, 'There's little or no evidence to connect Mr Landon with the murder, although he seems to have doubtful motives for being there. I thought perhaps you might be able to help.'

'Why the hell should I know why he went to the farm?' she snapped. 'You got him here in your office. Why not ask *him*?'

'I have,' Fairbairn said blandly. 'He says he was there because of you.'

'*Me?*' Arnold's heart sank as Mildred Sauvage-Brown's voice rose in surprise. Her cup clattered on the desk. She glared at Arnold. 'What did *I* have to do with your going to Penbrook Farm?'

'I . . . I decided to have a word with you,' Arnold said weakly. It had seemed a good idea at the time. Sober, he had reviewed the situation with less confidence.

'About what?'

'Your attitude,' Fairbairn said with a smirk.

'*Attitude?*'

Arnold summoned his strength of mind and purpose. He was unable to meet the fury of her glance but he said,

'I have been . . . concerned about the way you've been behaving.'

'You've been *what*?'

'You've done the cause of Penbrook Farm no good. You've alienated magistrates, you've drawn bad publicity to yourself, you've behaved in an obstreperous manner and got yourself jailed—in fact, you've shown all the worst characteristics of so-called conservationists who give causes a bad name and as far as I'm concerned—'

'At least I don't go around killing old ladies!' Mildred Sauvage-Brown roared.

The words struck the room to silence. Arnold stared at her, shocked. He was aware of Chief Superintendent Fairbairn waiting behind his desk like a predatory bird, waiting to pounce, but Mildred Sauvage-Brown's face was drained of all colour and her hands were shaking. She had already come to terms with the death of her companion, of that Arnold was sure: Mildred Sauvage-Brown had a tough constitution, physically and emotionally. But it was another thing to handle words like *killing*, and to accuse, face to face, another human being.

Quietly Arnold said, 'I assure you, my presence at Penbrook Farm is accounted for by a drunken desire on my part to tell you what I've just told you now. When I got there, Miss Ellis was dead. I was . . . overcome. The next thing I remember was the arrival of the police.'

'What was the next thing *you* remember, Miss Sauvage-Brown?' Chief Superintendent Fairbairn asked in a silky, innocent tone.

'After what?' she asked, only half-understanding the question.

'After leaving the police station, having posted bail for yourself,' Fairbairn purred.

Mildred Sauvage-Brown stared at him, deep glints of anger moving in her eyes. 'What are you trying to say?'

'I'm not *trying* to say anything. Like Mr Landon here,

your behaviour is somewhat curious. First of all you seem to want to be shoved in jail; then you change your mind and want to get out. Having got out . . . where did you go?'

'I told you yesterday.'

'Not very satisfactorily. Tell me again.'

She shot a swift glance in Arnold's direction. Reluctantly she said, 'I decided to carry out certain investigations.'

'For what reason?'

'To support allegations I'd made in the courtroom.' Again she looked at Arnold. 'The fact is, after a few hours in the police cells I decided I wouldn't be getting very far. Not that way. I *know* what's been going on behind the purchase of Penbrook Farm, but until I come up with some facts there'll be no chance anyone will do anything about it. So I decided to get out of there. No one else is interested enough, or active enough to do it. I am. So I got out.'

'And . . .?'

'I made some inquiries.'

Fairbairn smiled. 'About what?'

'About certain business activities here in the North-East.'

'Did you come up with any answers?'

She hesitated. 'I *know* those bastards . . .'

'Any proofs?'

Chief Superintendent Fairbairn was treated to one of Mildred Sauvage-Brown's special glares. He seemed unaffected. 'No proofs,' he declared with satisfaction. 'And no record of where you went or to whom you spoke during this period.'

Mildred Sauvage-Brown's chin came up stubbornly.

Chief Superintendent Fairbairn turned to Arnold. 'The fact is, Mr Landon, we have something odd here. You turn up at the farm and phone us to tell us Miss Ellis is dead. Or something to that effect. Miss Sauvage-Brown does not.'

'I wasn't there.'

'Not at the farm? Not since your release from the cells?

Where did you go? You wandered, you say. Made *inquiries*.
Came up with nothing . . . or at least nothing you're prepared or able to divulge to us. No one you can name to say
where you've been. Until you *happen* to be approaching the
farm after we got there.'

'I was going home.'

'After Miss Ellis's death.'

'I didn't know—'

'If you *had* been there would it have happened?'

'How can I tell? If I had been there . . .' Her words
suddenly died away. She stared, stricken, at the Chief Superintendent, and the colour slowly came back to her face,
cheeks becoming ruddy as though she were embarrassed.
But it was not embarrassment, Arnold was sure. It was the
warmth of anger, the slow surge of fury as realization
dawned upon her, overcoming the blackness of her grief and
shock at the death of Sarah Ellis. 'Good God,' she said
harshly. 'It *was* me!'

'You?'

'It was me . . . *me* who should have been killed. It was
me they were after.'

'I hardly think—'

'But it's obvious! The bastard, he'll have heard I was
sniffing around. I'd shouted things out in the courtroom
and that was bad enough, but when I started making
inquiries around the coast, along the river, he heard about
it and he went out to that farm and he . . .'

Her words died away again. She sat dumbly, dully, introspective. Fairbairn waited. There was a tight feeling in
Arnold's chest. Her lips moved. 'Conspiracy,' she whispered. '*Murder* . . .'

'We're all aware a murder has been committed,' Fairbairn
said roughly. 'And your own activities and movements, still
unaccounted for, mean that you yourself are not entirely
cleared of suspicion. The natural thing would have been for
you to go home; you did not, and so . . .'

'But it was me he really meant to kill.'

'A motive—'

'The motive for killing me is obvious. I've been making too much noise,' she said wildly. 'I'm rocking too many boats. They went to the farm—'

'They?'

'That bastard Minford! Wilson maybe, or Livingstone— how the hell do I know? It's your job to work it out, your job to find the proof. I was interfering in their plans and they *conspired*—'

'Have you any proof of this?'

'Proof? Don't talk to me about proof. It's all so damned obvious, can't you see it? Wilson and Livingstone want to buy the farm. The spin-off for council support through Minford is the damned old people's home. The pair of them —Wilson and Livingstone—will get the building contracts in the area thereafter . . . It's so *obvious*.'

'And it leads to murder?'

'I had to be silenced. One of them went there—'

'Can you prove that?'

'*You* prove it, damn it! You're the bloody copper!'

'And you're a wild theorist who throws out allegations based on no fact!' Fairbairn snapped, reddening.

'I had to be silenced. One of them—Minford, check what he was up to. And Wilson, even though I doubt he'd do it himself. That Livingstone character, he's a hard bastard and I wouldn't trust him further than I could throw him and that's no distance. Yes, Livingstone, he could do it. He's hard, a nasty piece of work behind all that smoothness. Check on him, find out what he was up to—'

'Does he drive a Rover?'

She stared at him, taken aback. 'How the hell do I know?'

'I thought you'd made inquiries.'

'You still suspect *me*?'

Fairbairn glowered. 'I suspect anyone who makes wild

unsupported allegations, maybe to cover her own activities, against respectable businessmen—'

'*Respectable?*' Mildred Sauvage-Brown was almost beside herself with fury. 'They're raping the countryside, man. Is that respectable? They're subverting public morality. Is *that* respectable? They're making secret profits, using the cloak of democratic proceedings to feather their own nests—'

'Miss Sauvage-Brown, you say you've been making inquiries,' Chief Superintendent Fairbairn intervened, 'and you continue making these wild allegations, but I ask again, do you have any *proofs*?'

'But it's so *obvious*,' Mildred Sauvage-Brown almost screamed at him. 'What do you want? You want a *picture* of the man killing Sarah? You want a written confession that he thought it was me, that he intended killing me, that he killed her by mistake? You want a photostat record of the shady deals that are behind the whole situation? You want a tape-recording of the conspirators? You want a video show of their nefarious activities?'

'I want proofs, Miss Sauvage-Brown!' Chief Superintendent Fairbairn thundered.

'But can't you see the facts that lie in front of your face? You *stupid* man, can't you see the whole thing is so circumstantially obvious? Damn it, it's as obvious as a trout in the milk!'

At the look on Chief Superintendent Fairbairn's face Arnold closed his eyes and groaned.

Mentally.

When Miss Sauvage-Brown was led from the room she was still shouting. '*It's as obvious as a trout in the milk!*'

CHAPTER 4

1

One of the advantages of having a reputation for a mild eccentricity was that shopkeepers adopted a rather caring attitude towards you, Arnold concluded. They seemed to feel that you were to be protected, cosseted even. In the case of the lady in Morpeth who worked in the cleaning and repair shop, it was a fussiness towards him, in the way she folded the clothes he took for cleaning, and the manner in which she gently chided and admonished him as on this occasion, when he took in his coat for repair. 'I don't know, Mr Landon, what you need is a good woman.' She giggled. 'Or even a *bad* one. But a woman, any road, who'll look after you proper. Stop you getting yourself into scrapes. Make sure you're home at night when you should be. None of this going with bad companions like that Freddie Keeler. Too much money he has, not enough sense. I bet *he* had something to do with this tear in your coat!'

Arnold felt unable to disabuse her of her prejudices. He smiled patiently, bobbed his head a little to confirm her opinion of his helplessness and then took his car to the car wash, where the lady behind the desk always demonstrated her own view of his helplessness by actually driving his car through the wash for him. 'I know you don't like doing it,' she said. 'I remember the first time, when you got stuck in there with the window half way down and the brushes shoving water in all over you. Didn't you half come out like a drowned duck!'

Arnold recalled it all too well. It was the reason why he

was quite happy to allow her to look after him in this manner.

But there was another advantage to mild eccentricity. It was that one became accepted by people who were mildly eccentric themselves. Arnold's own peculiarity was harmless enough. Unmarried, he liked to live alone and devote his spare time to a study of the hills and ruined villages of the Northumberland hinterland. Stone and wood were his passions: where others saw them as dead, inanimate things, for him they spelled out history, lives, realities far divorced from the modern plastic world. And as his own eccentricity became known over the years, he had been drawn into a small circle of other enthusiasts. They were acquaintances rather than friends because their lives were bound up and circumscribed by their own enthusiasms. They could never become *close*: but they respected one another's feelings, and skills, and most of all, one another's knowledge.

One such was a man who lived in a tumbledown old presbytery in Felton. He had discovered a Victorian rubbish tip in his back garden and had excavated it lovingly for twenty years. His collection of bottles, Victorian bric-à-brac, samplers and irons was probably unique and certainly worth a considerable amount of money, but what was remarkable to Arnold and the rest of the world was the man's intensive knowledge of the minutiæ of the period, of the way their ancestors had lived, of what had been *unimportant* in their lives.

Another was Ben Gibson.

He looked like a decrepit frog. He had large, hooded eyes set in a fleshy, squat face. His back was bent, joints crippled by arthritis, so his small stature was rendered even smaller by his crouching gait. He was perhaps seventy years of age and had been a watchmaker until he was forced to close down his small business, from lack of custom and stiffening joints. He lived near Newcastle's Quayside, in the lower ground-floor rooms of a building that had once flourished in the old commercial days on the waterfront but which now echoed mustily to the feet of struggling entrepreneurs, starting new businesses in unsuitable premises, drifting into bankruptcy, and replaced by other, similarly hopeful, hopeless dreamers.

He always drank Earl Grey tea.

Arnold always enjoyed visiting Ben Gibson, not just for the tea he provided. There was a mustiness about the premises that was redolent of another age; he loved the echo in the stairwell when he stood there caressing the old oak balustrades and the whispers came down from the floors above; the light that filtered through the long rectangular windows was softened in its impact, heightening the impression that he had stepped back a hundred years.

And in some respects Ben's enthusiasms touched upon his own.

'Ah, Mr Landon, I'm delighted you've called on me. You'll be more than interested in the fact I've managed to get my hands on a rather battered but still complete copy of de Gheyn's *Croniques et Conquestes de Charlemaine* for, even though it is divorced from your own interests, the copy itself was wrapped in this . . .'

Ben Gibson knew all about Arnold's passions, and he cackled as Arnold handled with reverence the faded material that had once comprised an indenture between two carpenters and a builder.

'Amazing, is it not?' Ben Gibson said, his large frog eyes glowing with pleasure. 'Difficult to read of course. *Soudelet* . . .'

'Or *sondelet*, a saddle-bar,' Arnold offered.

'Yes, exactly, and *vertivel* . . .'

'It's sometimes printed as *vertinel*; it means a hinge-band,' Arnold explained.

'That's the trouble,' Ben Gibson said, rocking gently in his seat by the table as he nourished the thought, 'in most old handwritten manuscripts it's impossible to distinguish between *n*, *u* and *v*. It's only by tracing variant spellings that you can reach certainty.'

'There's also the point that the clerks who wrote these documents were liable to slips of the pen, naturally; and sometimes they were putting on parchment purely local terms of which they could give, at best, only a phonetic rendering.'

'Fascinating.'

'An interesting find.'

'One lives for such moments. More tea, Mr Landon?'

Arnold took some more Earl Grey tea. He sat quietly for a little while as Ben Gibson enthused over his find, and over his copy of de Gheyn. The man was entitled to his triumph and Arnold could understand the thrill that would be running through the old man's arthritic bones as he talked about it. He also knew that Gibson would, in a little while, recall his duty as a host, and make polite inquiry of Arnold's own interests.

'I see you've been in the news again,' the little man said with a sly grin, at last. 'I'm sure your superior officer will be getting nervous.'

Ben Gibson knew all about the Senior Planning Officer. Arnold sighed and nodded. 'He's due back next week. I'm pretty certain there'll be some harsh words.'

'But you'll have had the satisfaction of finding something interesting out at the farm you visited?'

Arnold nodded. 'Some mediæval tile work. But it's not that I've come to see you about. I'm aware of your deep knowledge of old manuscripts and papers of any antiquity. I've picked up something I'd like you to have a look at.'

The little man's eyes glowed again with interest. Arnold unzipped the leather filecase he had placed on the table between them and extracted the folder. Inside the folder was a single sheet of paper. In the filtered light of the room the colour of the initial letters seemed faded and tired, but the print itself, and the Latin words, were clear enough. Ben

Gibson took the folder, not touching the sheet, and he peered at it, inspected it closely, his lips soundlessly mouthing the words it contained.

'It's been treated roughly. There are stains . . . and dirt at the edges.' There was a hint of accusation in Ben Gibson's tone. 'The lower edge is torn.'

Arnold nodded. 'I'm afraid that might be my fault.'

'What's the provenance of the sheet?'

'I don't know.'

Ben Gibson raised his head, gazed almost accusingly at Arnold for a few seconds, before lowering his eyes to the sheet again, caressing the words with his glance, shaking his head slightly from side to side as he read. 'So where did you come across it, then?'

'I'm not sure.'

There was a short silence. Ben Gibson raised his head again, staring at Arnold, and then carefully put down the folder. 'I don't understand.'

Arnold shrugged helplessly. 'You must appreciate I live alone, and I collect all sorts of bits and pieces of paper, some connected with my interests, some not—ephemera, really, like articles in journals on architecture, that sort of thing.'

'Well?'

'Every so often I decide to have a clear out. The return of the Senior Planning Officer,' Arnold said sheepishly, 'affects me in a curious way. I take the car to the car wash; I clean it out; I get my clothes repaired; I empty the waste-paper baskets; I get together all the accumulation of paper in the house and give the place a springclean . . . I know it's nothing to do with the Senior Planning Officer, I mean he's never been to my bungalow, but I feel it necessary. *Compulsive.*'

Ben Gibson regarded him gravely. He touched the folder gently. 'And?'

'And I went out to the bin in the back yard,' Arnold said, 'and I tipped the rubbish out and just as I was turning away

I caught a glimpse of the Latin. I drew the sheet out—'

'Out of the *dustbin*?'

Shamefaced, Arnold nodded. 'I've no idea how it got there. I will have had it somewhere in the house, unwittingly. But once I saw it, inspected it . . . do you know what it is?'

Ben Gibson continued to stare at him thoughtfully for a full half-minute. Then his glance returned to the sheet. He shook his head in a slow doubt. 'I'm not sure. I can tell you it has a certain . . . antiquity. Its provenance . . . I'm not sure. I will need to check certain references, undertake some inquiries. Are you prepared to leave it with me, Mr Landon?'

'Of course.'

'Even if it is valuable?'

'Is it?'

'To me,' Ben Gibson said quietly, 'and men like me. To others, possibly not. But enthusiasts . . . they are sometimes unscrupulous.'

Arnold Landon smiled. 'Not *true* enthusiasts. I trust you, Mr Gibson. Besides, I brought it here out of interest, to see what it is. It's not my field. Once I know what it is I shall be happy to make a gift of it to you.'

'Perhaps not, Mr Landon, perhaps not.' Obviously pleased at the thought, the little man nevertheless seemed still a little concerned. 'One matter I would ask of you. Please consider again, try to think where you might have been keeping this sheet. I would certainly be interested to discover its provenance.'

'I'll do what I can,' Arnold promised.

He made a start that very evening. He began in his study upstairs. It was about time he started trying to bring order to the collection of papers, magazines, journals, books, maps and commentaries he had collected there over the years. The trouble was, once he started sifting through the material he quickly discovered that there was so much there he had intended to read but had not got around to reading that it was bedtime before he had even dented the surface of the problem.

It was going to be a long job, even if he disciplined himself not to follow every little interesting track disclosed as he turned over papers and books. He had to be systematic. He started to arrange the books in piles, and proceeded to leaf through them, carefully.

The following day he had to spend most of his time at a public inquiry in Morpeth. For much of the day he was barely occupied and was given the opportunity to let his thoughts wander, as the public inspector droned on in the report of his findings. Arnold's thoughts turned to Mildred Sauvage-Brown and her over-excitability. And what on earth was it she had shouted in Chief Superintendent Fairbairn's office?

A trout in the milk.

Curious. Arnold had no idea what she could possibly have meant.

It was still on his mind when the hearing was adjourned. He glanced at his watch: there was no need to return to the planning office and the library did not close until seven. He left his car where it was and walked across to the public library, entered the reference room and found a dictionary of quotations.

Oddly enough, he found it quickly, even though it was not a quotation familiar to him. Thoreau. *Some circumstantial evidence is very strong, as when you find a trout in the milk.*

What could Mildred Sauvage-Brown be trying to say in that context?

He spent another long evening looking through his books in the study. It was a fruitless search. There was another block of books on the shelves in the sitting-room but he felt too weary to go through them. They could wait until the following day.

Next morning he dealt with outstanding papers that

needed to be cleared before the Senior Planning Officer returned from Scarborough. One of them was the matter of Willington Hall. He had read in the newspaper that the funeral of Patrick Willington was to take place; now, he was able to close the matter of the planning application for the sawmill at the Hall.

He wondered vaguely how Henry Willington would cope. The man had seemed dazed, uncoordinated in a sense, shaken by the death of his father and by the enormity of the task facing him, even if it was something he had been waiting to undertake for years.

Previously, Henry had been able to blame Patrick Willington for the failure of the Willington estate. In future, he alone would have to bear the responsibility.

And, perhaps, the disappointing reality of knowing that Willington Hall could not be saved.

Arnold had a headache when he went home. For a while, after he had eaten a frugal meal of tuna fish and salad, he thought of simply watching television for the evening. Then he remembered the glow in Ben Gibson's eyes and decided he should carry on with his search.

At eight-thirty he was surrounded by a pile of books on the sitting-room floor, patiently working through each one, when the bell to the front door rang.

Arnold sat up on his heels, puzzled. He rarely had visitors at his bungalow, and never in the evening. There were no friends to call, no close relatives. Occasionally the newspaper boy called for his payment; once a month the milkman called. Frowning, Arnold went to the front door, switched on the porch light, and made out the vague form of one person, indistinguishable through the frosted glass of the door.

Cautiously Arnold opened the door.

It was Mildred Sauvage-Brown.

She stood squinting at him uncertainly, her pouched eyes

screwed up with doubt. She was wearing a dark overcoat, with a black band on the arm, sewed clumsily above the elbow. The folds in her face seemed to have sagged and her shoulders had lost their aggression: vulnerability seemed to have crept into her bearing and this woman was a long way distant from the one who had thrust a shotgun muzzle into Arnold's face at Penbrook Farm.

'Miss Sauvage-Brown!'

She had difficulty responding. She looked around her as though questioning her own presence; glanced at the sky as though sniffing the wind. She could not meet his glance, and she shuffled, her boots scuffing the stone and making a scraping sound.

Arnold cleared his throat. 'Can I . . . help you?'

She shot one quick glance at him and it was as full of pride as ever; then the uncertainty came again and she frowned, still saying nothing. Arnold stepped back. 'Perhaps you'd better come in.'

It was possible she detected the hesitancy in his tone, for she herself hesitated. He waited, and she made up her mind, ducking in an odd fashion as she entered the bungalow as though she expected to bang her head on the ceiling. Arnold led the way into the sitting-room. She stared at the piles of books.

'I'm sorry about the mess,' Arnold said inadequately.

She hardly seemed to hear him. She stared at the books without speaking and as the silence lengthened between them Arnold said nervously, 'Would you care for a glass of sherry?'

. She started slightly, and nodded. Arnold turned away thankful that at last she was responding in some way, and he poured two glasses of medium sherry. There was no choice: he catered only for his own tastes. When he turned round she was sitting down, the coat loosened at her throat.

'Thank you,' she said as he handed her the glass of sherry. 'You think I'm crazy, don't you?'

Arnold stared at her. 'I've never said that.'

'No. In your typically *British* way you'd understate it. You'd call me *over-enthusiastic*, or something like that.'

'Perhaps something like that,' Arnold agreed.

'Humph,' she said and sipped her sherry. It seemed to relax her somewhat, bring some confidence, the old aggressiveness back into her veins. 'You think I'm wrong, too, don't you?'

'About what?'

'Everything.'

'No. Not about the farm. You have a case . . . you had a case with which I'm in sympathy. I just felt . . .'

'That I went the wrong way about getting it put right.' The pouched eyes glittered suddenly. 'And you think I'm wrong about the rest of it?'

'The rest of it . . .' Arnold shrugged. 'You've made so many accusations . . . unbacked by facts . . . What did you mean by that trout in the milk remark?'

Contemptuously she said, 'You didn't get it?'

'No.'

'What's the natural habitat of the trout?'

'Water, of course.'

'So if you find a trout in the milk, it's circumstantial evidence that the bloody milk's been watered, isn't it?' she demanded. Gloomily she added, 'They used to do quite a bit of that in the old days. Watering milk to make it go further. Helped the spread of cholera.'

'I still don't understand the significance of the remark, as far as we're concerned,' Arnold ventured.

'Oh, I can't produce *evidence* of Minford's involvement in the shenanigans behind the Penbrook Farm deal, not the kind Fairbairn would call for. I tried hard enough, while Sarah . . . I tried hard enough, but I can't produce it, but damn it, Landon, the *facts* are there, the *circumstances*, and if the bloody police would only probe them, draw the conclusions from that circumstantial evidence . . .' She paused and eyed him warily, almost grumpily. 'You tried to go bail for me.'

Arnold sipped his sherry nervously.

'You tried to go bail for me and I wouldn't have it,' she insisted. 'Why did you do that? You don't even like me.'

'There were . . . circumstances . . . situations . . .'

'What?'

'I . . . I got angry.'

Her little eyes grew eager with interest. 'Angry? Because you guessed maybe I was right after all?'

'No. It wasn't like that. I . . . I'd been talking to some people. They reminded me, triggered something in my mind, and I checked.'

'What did you find?' Mildred Sauvage-Brown asked.

Arnold took a deep breath. 'A few years ago there was a company called Jarrow Development Corporation. It was run by a man called Floyd. He had a daughter called Eileen. She married a man called Simson, and they had a son.'

'So?'

'Simson died, Eileen Simson was widowed and her father's business began to run into problems. It was eventually the subject of a merger with a company run by Albert Minford's father.'

Mildred Sauvage-Brown straightened in her chair. 'Go on; this is getting interesting.'

Arnold shook his head. 'Don't read too much into all this. What happened was that the merger never really worked and the company was closed down, albeit leaving Albert Minford with a fair amount of money, enough to enable him to enter politics and make a living out of it.'

Mildred Sauvage-Brown growled something under her breath.

'In the meanwhile,' Arnold continued, 'Albert Minford and Eileen Simson decided to get married. With her husband in local politics and at a loose end, I suppose it was natural that she should go back to the kind of background she knew. She set up a building firm with her son: she used her maiden name in doing so, perhaps to make use of old contacts and goodwill, with her son coming in as a co-director in his own name. Floyd and Simson.'

The pouched eyes glittered. 'That's not the end of it.'

Arnold shrugged. 'The company has won a few local authority building contracts.'

'With Albert Minford pulling the strings.'

'There's no evidence of that,' Arnold said hurriedly. 'He had no interest to declare because he's no shares in the firm. He wasn't on the committee awarding the contracts. The agreements themselves were all the subject of appropriate tendering procedures and there's nothing there that can be raised in a court of law.'

'But Minford could have been pulling strings, doing the old boy thing, using a network of political friends to swing contracts, disclose tenders, all that sort of petty corruption.'

'There's no evidence of that,' Arnold insisted.

'But you went bail for me!'

Arnold took a deep breath. He finished his sherry. He wished there was some whisky in the bungalow. He poured himself another sherry, quite forgetting to offer one to Mildred Sauvage-Brown. 'I . . . I was shaken . . . upset. It was done on the spur of the moment.'

Mildred Sauvage-Brown shook her head. 'That doesn't explain such a committed action.'

'There is no real explanation. It was . . . a reaction.'

'No. You went bail for me for a very good reason. You knew I was right.'

'Miss Sauvage-Brown—'

'You knew I was right; knew what I said about that bastard Minford was true.'

'No.'

'You did it because you knew there was a financial fiddle going on behind the scenes.'

'No!'

Her eyes glittered triumphantly. 'You did it because—'

'No!' Arnold said desperately. 'I did it . . . I did it because I felt sorry for you.'

The words were out before he could stop them. The impact was immediate upon Mildred Sauvage-Brown. For several seconds she stared at him, bewildered, open-mouthed in astonishment. Slowly, her expression changed. The excitement, the flush of triumph that had been flooding her cheeks as she thought Arnold was on her side was fading. It was replaced by something else, a compound of puzzlement and embarrassment, disbelief and resistance. Then that too began to fade as she paled, her mouth tightening, her eyes slitting angrily. She looked away, glared at the empty sherry glass in her hand. Silence grew between them, painfully; her hand was shaking with suppressed tension. Arnold wished the words back; wished the earth would swallow him.

Mildred Sauvage-Brown looked up. Her glance was cold as death and as unrelenting. 'Don't ever say that to me again, Mr Landon.'

Arnold opened his mouth, but no words came. He had insulted her, shamed her, touched her at her most vulnerable point. She had built her character upon independence, and she was unable to accept that she should rely on sympathy, or kindness, from a man. She had refused the bail he had tendered. He understood why.

Silently he took the glass from her hand and poured her another drink. His hand was trembling slightly; she appeared not to notice as she took the glass from him. The atmosphere in the room was still tense; she turned away from him, and looked about her. 'Springcleaning,' she said.

Arnold took a deep breath, aware the moment was easing. 'Not really springcleaning. I'm just looking for something.'

'It's a mess.'

He agreed with the uncompromising statement. 'Yes.'

There was a short silence, and she relented somewhat.

'Much the same at Penbrook Farm. Nothing seems quite the same since . . . Things out of place. I'm . . . disorientated.'

'I can understand that.'

'Can you?' She shot a wary glance in his direction, still smarting. Arnold waited, and after a while she relaxed a little again. 'I came north for good reason,' she said.

'So I believe.'

'I knew little about the area. Oh, I'd read the romantic stuff about marauding Danes in the twelfth century, burned abbeys, plundered churches, the ever-present threat of the longships. And I saw the trickle of the new invaders, the different breed who merely plunder the silence of the dunes of Lindisfarne, the people who just want to see the pele towers, take a boat to watch the Farne lights blinking in the dusk, listen to *Johnnie Armstrong* played on the Northumbrian pipes. They are harmless . . . a nuisance perhaps to locals who don't need them for a living, but harmless generally. You know what I mean?'

'I do.'

'I didn't come up here *looking* for trouble,' she said doggedly. 'But when I saw it, I had to act. I could see the other, faceless men, the rape of the countryside, the destruction of a heritage . . . so many people won't *act*, Mr Landon. I *have* to.'

'I understand.'

'Then I met Sarah, and we settled at Penbrook Farm. She was such a gentle person, Mr Landon, she wouldn't harm anyone. And now, I think that if I'd been a different sort of person, if I hadn't been . . . what I am . . . Sarah would still be alive . . .'

She stared dully at the piled books on the carpet. 'You live alone, Mr Landon?'

'Yes.'

'You're used to it.'

'It's the way I like to live.' He managed a short laugh. 'Middle-aged bachelors are difficult people.'

'Middle-aged spinsters too. Perhaps more so. But I haven't lived alone for a long time. It'll take getting used to.' Her voice trembled slightly. 'I'm not sure how I'll manage.'

Arnold did not know what to say. He wanted to sympathize, extend condolences, but she had already rebuffed him when he had crassly suggested he had felt sorry for her. She had pride; she would not welcome any remark that was patronizing. It was a verbal tightrope Arnold was not prepared to walk.

'I've been going through her things,' Mildred Sauvage-Brown said almost dreamily, half-forgetting he was there, Arnold suspected. 'It's a strange thing. You live with someone for years and you think you know them, understand them, but then . . . it's a surprise. In her trunk, upstairs in the attic of the farmhouse, I found a bundle of letters. I didn't like to read them, but she had no one in the world, so in the end I looked at them. They were sad. She must have been a pretty little thing when she was young. And there was a young man.'

Arnold stood silently, hardly breathing, conscious he was intruding into a private world where Mildred Sauvage-Brown was temporarily lost.

'They were in love. The letters described his feelings. It was beautiful. He wanted to marry her. Something happened. The letters ceased abruptly. There was a lock of hair there; light brown, soft. Clearly, Sarah loved that young man and someone cruelly came between them. It must have been before she wandered in Europe—for there were cards, addresses in Italy and Holland. Poor Sarah . . .'

Mildred Sauvage-Brown was silent for a while, lost in thought, staring at the books littering the room. 'She left a will. Two wills, in fact. One was made, oh, twenty years ago. The second a couple of years ago. I'm her beneficiary, taking all her estate.' She stopped, and turned her head suddenly, as though remembering Arnold was there. 'I

suppose some people might see that as a motive for murder
—for *me* to murder her, wouldn't they?'

'I hardly believe so,' Arnold murmured.

'Poor Sarah. She's left me everything. I'll have to get
probate . . . but I've never needed money. And now . . .
Two wills . . . Funny thing, that. The wills were made in
different names.'

'How do you mean?'

Mildred Sauvage-Brown frowned. 'The second will, the
one in my favour, was made in her own name: Sarah Ellis.
But the earlier will, made twenty years ago, that was made
in the name of Sarah *Willis*.'

'Was it properly drawn?'

'By a solicitor. And she signed it Sarah Willis. Left all
she had to charity.'

'Perhaps she married, in spite of her early experience.
Someone called Willis.'

Mildred Sauvage-Brown shook her head. 'No. She told
me she'd never married. And the first will, it was drawn up
in old form, spinster of this parish, all that sort of stuff. Not
that it matters now. Not that any of it matters.'

'You'll miss her.'

Mildred Sauvage-Brown nodded her head and sniffed.
Arnold guessed she was near to tears. Perhaps his thought
was in some way communicated to her, for suddenly her
back stiffened and she snapped, 'Of course I'll miss her.
What a bloody silly thing to say.'

'Yes,' Arnold said awkwardly. 'I'm sorry.'

She sniffed again, finished her sherry and contemplated
the books on the carpet. 'You've got a lot of clearing up to
do there,' she said gloomily.

'It won't take me too long.'

'Humph,' she said, and sat there with her back to him.
He could see her face in half-profile and the dumpy, sagging
features seemed lost in thought. But the mouth was tightening again, and he gained the impression that her back was

straightening, resolution returning to her after the last, embarrassing few minutes when she had exposed her emotions to him, declared her grief at the loss of her companion, and displayed the vulnerability that he would not at one time have guessed lay behind her determined exterior. She stood up abruptly, setting down the glass.

She turned to face him, but she did not see him. He had the odd feeling that she had, indeed, forgotten where she was, or why she was here. She had come to get the answer to a question, and to have contact with a human being who at least had some sympathy with what drove her, and with whom she had in these last days become bound. Now, something else had happened to draw her away, bring back determination to her jaw, recall the glitter of her pouched eyes.

She walked past him, unseeingly. At the front door she paused, recalling old veneers that had not entirely deserted her. 'Thank you for the sherry, Mr Landon,' she said formally. But the glitter was still in her eyes, and the determination had a hint of angry excitement about it.

Arnold opened the door and she stepped out to the drive. There was a drizzle of rain in the air and Mildred Sauvage-Brown hesitated for a moment, some of her new-found commitment draining from her, perhaps at the darkness of the night, perhaps at its loneliness. She turned, and looked at Arnold. He could not see her eyes.

'Mr Landon . . .' She hesitated, perhaps startled at the plea that lay in her tone. She tested it, measured it against her own personality, and discarded it. The moment was gone.

She walked away, a dumpy, unattractive woman with an ungainly gait, missing the friend and companion of years, and the lump in Arnold's chest was leaden.

2

The return of the Senior Planning Officer from Scarborough was not an occasion for trumpets, eagles and the brazen neighing of warhorses, Arnold thought, but there was certainly an *atmosphere* in the office that morning. He felt the tingle of expectation the moment he entered the building and his spine remained sensitive until the moment when he was called into the Presence. The sensitivity then moved to his bowels.

The tirade that was visited upon Arnold was in the nature of what the Senior Planning Officer called a 'roasting'. There were adjectives used that were only vaguely familiar to Arnold, and in general, he conceded privately, the language was colourful and forceful, very much to the point.

The point being that the Senior Planning Officer was more than a little disturbed.

'I have made it clear, Mr Landon,' he finally summed up when he had regained control of his temper, 'and on more than one occasion, that this is a *planning* office where I expect levels of professionalism and objectivity, where we retain a distance from our clients and our political masters, where we do not get *involved* and where we stay out of scandalous and damaging situations. You have, over the last couple of years, failed to maintain the standards *we* demand.'

A regal turn of phrase, Arnold considered, that reflected the Senior Planning Officer's view of his own position.

'This, then, is a final warning.' The Senior Planning Officer puffed out his cheeks importantly. 'If you cannot curb the excesses of your enthusiasms and keep your head below the parapet of sensationalism, there is no place for you here in this office. You will be transferred.' His eyes glittered with portents of doom. '*Or worse.*'

He asked Arnold if he understood. Arnold admitted that he did and, must chastened, went back to his desk. He was summoned to the Senior Planning Officer's room again later that afternoon.

They were already seated around the miniature board-room table that the Senior Planning Officer kept for occasions such as these. The Senior Planning Officer suggested that Arnold already knew everyone present. He did.

Councillor Albert Minford sat at the Senior Planning Officer's left. He was in his usual uniform of neat grey and his eyes were as watchful as ever. His arm was draped carelessly over the back of the chair and he seemed at ease, but there was an inner tension in his body that was barely concealed.

Beside him was the building developer Wilson. He sat squarely in his seat, hands clasped over his spreading belly. He observed Arnold's entry with a mild curiosity, as though recent events had aroused a little more interest in him than he had previously considered possible, but the glance was still cold in its appraisal, and swift in its dismissiveness once again. Wilson was not a man who dealt with petty officials: he even resented the necessity to visit the Senior Planning Officer.

The visit had probably been at the suggestion of his colleague Livingstone. Arnold inspected the man more carefully now, after the comments made about him by Freddie Keeler. Maybe the man *would* like the sound of crunching bone: the ascetic look about his face was belied by the athleticism of his shoulders, and Arnold could easily imagine the man in a Byker rough-house, down by the river. It was likely his background had been left far behind him since his association with Wilson, but there were still hints of madness in his eyes, the kind of explosive promises that would be activated in the right kind of circumstances.

'I thought it would be useful if you were involved in these discussions, Arnold,' the Senior Planning Officer said coolly, 'since you stood in for me at the planning inquiry. At which, I understand, Miss Sauvage-Brown behaved so reprehensively.'

Wilson shot an impatient glance at the Senior Planning Officer. 'Do you think we can get on?'

'Of course, Mr Wilson. The fact is, gentlemen, the ... ah ... demise of Miss Ellis would seem to raise certain problems.'

'Such as?' Livingstone asked.

'Well, clearly, since she was a major objector to the scheme, her ... removal from the scene may well mean that the proceedings could be delayed.'

'I don't see why,' Livingstone said. His glance slipped towards Arnold and away again. 'She was a major objector; she's dead; I would have thought that meant the opposition would crumble anyway, and there would be no need for a continuation of the inquiry.'

'Things don't quite work like that,' the Senior Planning Officer demurred.

'It's important they *do* work like that,' Livingstone said softly, but behind the softness there was a cutting edge. He half-turned, to look at Albert Minford. 'There's been a considerable amount of effort, and ... consideration gone into the planning of this scheme. I wouldn't want to see it go awry now. Time is of the essence as far as we are concerned. If we are to proceed, we need to go ahead as quickly as possible.'

Albert Minford cleared his throat. He frowned slightly, staring at the table in front of him, and then he said, 'I see Mr Livingstone's point. I'm in agreement with it. The death of Sarah Ellis is ... sad, but it's really beside the point. It has no relevance to or bearing on the proceedings, and I feel we should get on with the matter immediately. The necessary orders should go out from this office at once.'

'Mr Sedleigh-Harmon—'

'Arthur Sedleigh-Harmon, QC,' Livingstone interrupted cuttingly, 'has given us an opinion. He feels we should act with despatch.'

'The Chairman—'

'Dick Lansbury.' It was Albert Minford who interrupted the Senior Planning Officer this time. 'He's a politician. He is aware of the pressing needs of this project. He will take the necessary steps.'

Arnold felt warm suddenly. 'By bowing to pressure?' he asked.

Albert Minford's glance was hostile. 'What's that supposed to mean?'

'It would seem to me that you're suggesting political pressure can be brought on Mr Lansbury so that the matter is dealt with quickly, in spite of the interests of the opposing parties.'

Minford's lips grew thin. 'I made no such suggestion. Dick Lansbury is a servant of the community. He will do what he thinks is right. I merely state I think I know how he'll react to the situation. The main opposer is dead. The project is of benefit to the community.'

'There are others—'

'Mildred Sauvage-Brown?' Livingstone queried. He twisted in his chair impatiently. 'The woman's a nut-case. She needs locking up.'

'*Kill* one. *Lock* the other up?'

Arnold's words turned the room to silence. All four men stared at him, the Senior Planning Officer's eyes widening nervously, the other three seemingly turned to stone momentarily. It was Livingstone who found his tongue first. 'Mr Landon,' he said softly, 'you have a loose mouth.'

Hurriedly the Senior Planning Officer interposed. 'Oh, I'm sure Mr Landon didn't mean—'

'What *did* he mean?' Wilson snapped, unclasping his hands and turning them into fists on the table.

'I wasn't implying anything,' Arnold replied. 'I was stating facts. One member of the opposition is killed. A suggestion that the other should be locked up to prevent further opposition—'

'It was a turn of phrase,' Minford said warningly. 'It wasn't a serious proposal.'

'It's just as well,' Arnold said. 'Because any action against Miss Sauvage-Brown would certainly cause eyebrows to be raised, in the circumstances.'

'What circumstances?'

They continued to stare at Arnold as he hesitated in the silence. He shrugged at last. 'Sarah Ellis's will,' he offered.

'Her *will*?' Albert Minford straightened in his seat, relinquishing the relaxed pose he had adopted. 'What about her will?'

'It leaves everything to Miss Sauvage-Brown. Including Penbrook Farm.'

'*The hell it does!*' Livingstone exploded.

The Senior Planning Officer stared thoughtfully at Arnold. 'How do you know this? It's too early for probate to have been granted.'

Uneasily Arnold admitted, 'She told me about it.'

'Who did?'

'Mildred Sauvage-Brown.'

Again there was a short silence. Wilson shifted ponderously in his chair and addressed the Senior Planning Officer. 'Your colleague seems to make odd *friendships*.'

'Arnold?'

'She's not a friend,' Arnold insisted. 'And I have no real connection with her. I don't even like her . . . But she . . . she's lonely after the death of her companion. She visited me. She told me about the will. And that leaves you with a problem, sir. I'm certain she'll fight tooth and nail to prevent the scheme going through, the more so now that Penbrook Farm is willed to her. She might even see it as a . . . monument to Sarah. She could be very . . . awkward.'

'You can bloody well say that again,' Livingstone said angrily. 'That damned woman's got to be stopped!'

Arnold looked at him curiously. 'I don't quite understand

the *urgency* of all this. The situation is more than a little delicate. A police investigation going on into the murder at Penbrook Farm. Probate of the will; Miss Sauvage-Brown's personal views, as the new owner of the farm about the scheme for development. I can't see that Mr Lansbury will want to hurry through the proposal . . .'

'Mr Bloody Lansbury!' Livingstone snarled. There were flecks of blood in his eyes, and he seemed to be losing control rapidly. 'He'll do what's right, and it's right to get this thing going!'

'Why?' Arnold asked.

The Senior Planning Officer shifted uneasily in his chair but it was Albert Minford who answered. 'You must accept, Mr Landon, that I have some experience of these matters, as a result of my background in the building industry, even though I left it for local politics some years ago. Matters such as the development scheme for Penbrook Farm cannot be set up overnight. They require a great deal of planning as I'm sure you'll be aware. Planning, scheduling, financing—'

'A lot of money can get locked up,' Wilson interrupted.

'Investments are made,' Livingstone said, 'and people expect a rate of return. If they don't get it, problems arise. Cash flow—'

'Charges on land, development costs—'

Albert Minford cleared his throat noisily. It was a warning. Wilson looked at his fists; Livingstone tried to relax, wash the tension from his veins as he still glared at Arnold. 'The fact is,' Minford said, 'delays of this kind cost money. Cost the business money. Cost the ratepayer money. So we have to find ways to . . . expedite matters.'

'There'll be talk,' Arnold advised. 'The Minford Twilight Home. Parcels of land for development beyond the mediæval woodland.'

'All agreed, with proper notices served,' Minford said smoothly.

'There'll be talk of corruption.'

'Nothing of the kind. All interests have been declared,' Minford insisted. 'And the business deals were agreed after suitable tenders were made.'

'There'll be suggestions that the whole thing must be seen against a wider background. Your wife's firm, Mr Minford. The Amble marina—'

A slow flush stained Minford's features. 'Wild words from Mildred Sauvage-Brown don't make cases, Mr Landon. You'd be well advised not to repeat them.'

'Mr Landon is only trying to ... advise,' the Senior Planning Officer interrupted hastily.

'His *advice*,' Minford demurred cuttingly, 'seems a trifle biased.'

Silence fell, uneasily. The two businessmen and the councillor avoided each other's eyes; they stared at the Senior Planning Officer as though he held some key to the whole situation. His skin was suddenly sallow, his eyes shadowed with nervousness. He wriggled slightly in his seat, and coughed drily. 'I think ...' He struggled with the thought. 'I think it'll be best ... in the circumstances ... Arnold, thank you for coming in. I'm grateful for your advice. We all are. I think now you've filled me in I can take the matter on from here.'

He was being dismissed. Arnold rose. He was vaguely relieved. It meant he need take no further concern in the matters of Penbrook Farm and the loneliness of Mildred Sauvage-Brown.

The conference between Livingstone, Wilson, Minford and the Senior Planning Officer went on for some time. Arnold tried to concentrate on the papers on his desk but his mind kept wandering away. There had been an odd atmosphere in the Senior Planning Officer's room: if he didn't know otherwise he would have described it as conspiratorial. The thought unsettled him, and edgily he left his desk and walked through the building until he found himself in the section used by the Department of Administration. Beyond the shelves of steel burdened with law reports he saw the shaggy head of Ned Keeton, bent over a heavy book on the desk.

'Ned?'

'Arnold! Can't keep away these days, hey? After my job? Fed up with the Senior Planning Officer?'

Arnold shrugged noncommittally. 'You busy?'

'Not enough to stop for a cup of tea. Sugar?'

'No, thanks.'

Arnold watched while the lawyer reached under the desk for the illegal kettle. Tea and coffee were served twice a day, and always available from the machines in the corridors, but Ned Keeton had long ago displayed his bloody-mindedness in face of authority and though there had been remonstrations from the Town Clerk, and later the Chief Executive, Ned had blithely ignored them and made his own tea, steaming the room occasionally when he was absent for a while as the kettle boiled on.

The two men sat silently, watching the kettle with a satisfied feeling. It was occasionally pleasant to feel one was bucking the system. When the kettle boiled, Ned Keeton produced a battered teapot from his desk, and made some tea. The mugs were ancient and chipped: Arnold didn't mind. His bore the legend *Lawyers are always appealing*.

'So,' Ned Keeton grunted. 'What's new?'

'Nothing much.'

'Rubbish. Two trips up here in a week or so when otherwise we wouldn't see you twice a year? Something's got on your tits.'

Arnold winced. 'I don't know . . .'

'You know. You want to tell me. Drink up.'

Arnold drank up.

'So now tell me.'

'Nothing I can put my finger on, Ned. Uneasy feeling, that's all.'

'This murder business? I bet the Senior Planning Officer is hopping. Doesn't like publicity.'

'Oh, it's that, of course, but there's something more. He always tells me we've got to be objective, but . . .'

'Well?'

'He's got a meeting with the developers and Councillor Minford. He seems inclined . . . to hurry through the inquiry. And I don't think that's right, Ned.'

'What's to stop it now the old lady's dead?'

'Mildred Sauvage-Brown.'

'She'll have no *locus standi*,' Ned Keeton said. 'Won't classify as an aggrieved person under the statutes.'

'She will if she's the owner. And she's going to be under Sarah Ellis's will.'

'Hah! So that's the situation.' Keeton scratched at his shaggy, greying thatch. 'Interesting. She could certainly oppose then, drag the whole thing out.'

'That's it. The developers want to move quickly. Maybe if they can settle matters before Mildred Sauvage-Brown gets probate . . .'

'Won't serve.' Ned Keeton frowned. 'A will speaks from death, as they say, and that means ownership will hark back —once the will is proved—to the moment of Sarah Ellis's death. No, if they want to hurry things . . . Remind me, these developers . . .'

'Wilson and Livingstone. Councillor Minford's backing them.'

'Oh aye, that bastard.' Keeton thrust out his lower lip thoughtfully. 'Wilson . . . Livingstone . . . Ah now, what was that last week . . .?'

Arnold sipped his tea while Keeton rummaged through the papers on his desk and then prowled impatiently among the shelves. Twice he struck himself on the forehead with the heel of his hand as though trying to beat memory back into his skull, but when he finally sat down again it was with an air of frustration. 'Time I retired, long past time, I tell you, kiddar. When your memory goes . . . Wilson, and Livingstone, one of them or both of them? They're major shareholders in Aspern International, the European trading firm. Bought in cheap.'

'So?'

'It's going down the tubes, man,' Keeton said blandly. 'It's the report I was looking for, can't bloody find. There's been an investigation, auditors called in, share-dealing frozen, listing suspended, and I'm damned sure those two characters you mention were reported in the *Journal* some time back as having pumped money in considerable quantities into Aspern.'

'I'm not sure I understand.'

'Simple, man. They got a cash flow problem. No wonder they want to get this Penbrook Farm development under way. They'll have investments tied up in Aspern, their bankers will be getting shirty, they need to show in their business plans a definite, uncluttered proposal to turn around lucrative business and delays is the last thing they'll want to contemplate.'

'You sure about this?'

'Sure?' Ned Keeton squinted up at Arnold. 'Sure enough. I tell you, if I was in their position financially I'd dump my own granny in the Tyne if she had a decent life insurance on her, man!'

Or maybe remove an old lady who stood in their way, by battering her to death in her own farm kitchen.

It was preposterous. It did not bear thinking about. But Arnold thought about it and could not expunge the picture from his mind when he got back to his office. The girl who worked partly as his secretary—he shared her with another planning officer—told him there had been a phone call for him while he had been with Ned Keeton, and he really should tell her where he was going to be in the building if she was to work efficiently. He took the number from her, and the request to phone back, but he barely noted it. His mind was full of other things.

Was it really conceivable that the financial pressures that Ned Keeton suggested were faced by Wilson and Livingstone would have led them to commit murder? Wilson certainly could not have killed Sarah Ellis himself: too middle-aged, too flabby, too *detached* to sully his hands personally with such an activity. Livingstone was another matter. The back streets of Byker had spawned him; the river lands had been his track. He had fought his way out of the area to become a businessman in the shadow of Wilson, but he still had the hands and the madness in his eyes to do the thing, if it was important enough to him. And money was important to him.

But could Albert Minford have any knowledge or understanding of all this? Arnold was half convinced that Minford had a corrupt streak. He had the gut feeling that the Amble project, and others, would have been the subject of subtle, indirect pressures from Councillor Minford, the kind that were not easily detectable but could result in favoured contracts for certain people. Blinds were drawn by declarations of interest, seemingly cleaning the activity. Behind the blinds more direct involvements could have occurred.

But it was still a far cry from murder.

Unhappily, Arnold paced around his room. He knew he would have an unsettled evening. He would not be able to concentrate, relax, for his mind would be filled with the churning possibilities that had been planted by the conversation with Ned Keeton.

He heard steps in the corridor, the murmur of voices. He hesitated, then walked across the room and opened the door. He saw the retreating forms of Wilson and Livingstone, the Senior Planning Officer leading them towards the lifts. The meeting was over. The fate of the inquiry into the Penbrook Farm scheme was probably sealed.

Arnold closed the door. He paced up and down, then

went to the window. A corner of the car park was visible; there was a Ford Escort, two Vauxhalls, and the roof of a bigger car, a Rover, visible.

Someone was getting into the Rover, as he watched. He could not see the driver as the car nosed forward, disappeared from his view to the car park exit.

Edgily Arnold went back to his desk. He sat down, stared blankly at the papers there. On top of the papers was the crumpled message sheet the girl had given him, with the telephone message.

In a little while his eyes focused again. He read the number, and the message. It was from Ben Gibson. He had tried to ring Arnold; would Arnold be kind enough to ring him back?

Arnold would do better than that. He would go to see him.

The lights on the Tyne bridge were bright against the darkening sky and their reflection glinted and danced in the black waters of the river below. The Quayside was deserted at this early hour although the traffic that thundered over the bridge was still heavy, running south for the motorway.

It would, of course, have been easier for Arnold to have phoned the antiquarian, but he had been reluctant to go home to the bungalow, with the dark thoughts still churning in his head concerning the death of Sarah Ellis. He had decided on the spur of the moment to make the journey south to Newcastle. A discussion with Ben Gibson would take his mind off the murder at Penbrook Farm, he would be able to enjoy the company of the amiable eccentric for a little while, and they he would be able to walk up Dog Leap Stairs to Grey Street and indulge himself a little by having a quiet meal in the Italian restaurant he had frequented occasionally on his visits to Newcastle.

But first he enjoyed the stroll along the darkening water-front. There were two freighters docked there: the timber loaded on the deck of the Norwegian vessel left a fresh smell in the evening air that reminded Arnold of his childhood: damp wood on summer evenings. The second vessel was bustling, preparing for a late evening tide that would take her down the winding river to the mouth of the Tyne and out to sea. Arnold thought he would like to be on her, sailing away from the niggling anxieties in his mind. For it was not only the thoughts of the possible guilts of Albert Minford and his acquaintances that were on his mind: oddly, Mildred Sauvage-Brown also bothered him.

He resented her presence in his thoughts. He had fixed her personality, determined what moved her, decided the kind of woman she was, some time ago, on the occasion of their early meetings. The image that had been presented at his bungalow had damaged that view. Her vulnerability, albeit a fleeting one, had disturbed him, cracked the edifice of personality he had constructed for her. And her loneliness had come too close to his own occasional feelings to be ignored. He had not suffered the loss she had, for Arnold had always been a solitary man; nevertheless, he was aware that the ache she felt was not one unfamiliar to himself. He had known empty, yawning evenings and the quiet darkness that seemed endless.

But her emotions were matters she could struggle with and overcome herself: she was strong enough to cope. He wanted no part of it all, so was annoyed that she still crept into his mind, an image, a dumpy, unattractive woman with a barbed tongue and an aggressive personality. The Quayside, he hoped, would dispel that image. Instead, strangely, it enhanced it.

He decided to go to Ben Gibson's house.

There were no lights in the upper floor windows: business, clearly, did not demand a burning of late electricity to fulfil small orders. Arnold rang the bell at the top of the stone stairs and then descended the short flight to stand in the doorway as a light flicked on behind the door. The steps shuffled along; the door opened and Ben Gibson stood hunched in the doorway, carrying a shotgun over his arm and peering suspiciously out at Arnold.

'It's me. Arnold Landon.'

Gibson coughed deep in his throat, an embarrassed sound, and lowered the muzzle. There was an expression of confusion on his ugly, squat features and he bobbed his head in apology. 'I'm sorry, Mr Landon. You should've said you were calling to see me. We get trouble around here from time to time. I can usually tell when; there's motorbikes tearing up and down the waterfront. But you can never be certain.'

He backed away, his arthritic bones making him shuffle like a crab. Arnold followed him into the passageway. 'That's the second time I've had a shotgun pointed at me in my life, and the first time was only a couple of weeks ago.'

'Oh?'

The tone did not imply Ben Gibson wanted to hear any more about shotguns; his embarrassment was such he wanted the incident forgotten. 'There's no shells in the gun,' he explained. 'It's just to frighten them away. They're only kids, really. And I'm an old man.'

It was as though he meant injuring an old man would be a matter of little consequence to the world. Perhaps, Arnold thought, he was right.

Ben Gibson broke the shotgun and set it down in a corner of the room where it was easily accessible. Clearly it wasn't the first time he had had occasion to take it up. He motioned Arnold to a chair and said, 'Visits in the early evening are unusual for me. I find them a little disturbing. It requires a little Armagnac to steady my nerves thereafter. Would you care to join me?'

'I'm sorry I disturbed you. I should have returned your call. However, a little sherry if you have any . . .?'

The gnarled little man poured himself a drink and then

opened a bottle of dark-coloured sherry. It was sweet and rich in taste. Arnold liked it. Ben Gibson's frog eyes observed him gently above his glass. He smiled. 'I'm pleased you called, Mr Landon, in spite of my nervousness. Your visits are few, but always welcome.'

Arnold was slightly embarrassed at the compliment. He nodded, smiled, and said, 'I got your message at the office, but thought it was time I took another trip to Newcastle. I presume your call concerned the sheet I left you?'

Ben Gibson nodded. He turned, walked across to the handsome mahogany bureau that stood against the far wall and fumbled for a key in the pocket of his faded waistcoat. He unlocked the bureau and from one of the pigeonholes extracted the sheet which Arnold had given him. He stared at it for several seconds with his back to Arnold: when he turned around Arnold could detect a certain sadness in the old man's face.

'It's been a pleasure to handle this sheet,' Ben Gibson said.

Arnold looked at him in surprise. 'It's valuable?'

Ben Gibson lifted a shoulder in a gesture of doubt. 'What is meant by the word? The sheet I hold here is rare. Its rarity makes it valuable. But do you measure value in currency of the realm? I think not. True values are held in the heart and in the mind, but especially in the heart.'

Arnold knew what he meant. He felt the same way. He had seen things in decayed villages that were treasures to him but were intrinsically of little value. 'What is the sheet, Mr Gibson?'

The old man did not answer him immediately. He sat down, handling the sheet with care, still gazing at it lovingly. Then he lifted his glass, sipped slowly at the Armagnac, and asked, 'You still cannot recall where you came upon this sheet?'

'No.'

'You know nothing of its provenance?'

'I'm afraid not.'

'A pity. A great pity.'

'Why?'

'It is very old.'

'And rare, you said.'

Ben Gibson nodded slowly. 'That is so. You see, the history of printing in England is such that by the end of the seventeenth century there were perhaps one hundred thousand titles printed. In the next hundred years that number leapt to some four hundred thousand: in other words, after 1695 there was an immense explosion of printing.'

'Why was that?'

'It was the result of the repeal of the Licensing Act.' Ben Gibson sipped his Armagnac. 'Under the Licensing Act books could be printed only by members of the Stationers' Company. Members of the company had enjoyed that monopoly since 1555. The printing of books was in fact restricted to London, Oxford, Cambridge and York. But once the Act was repealed the monopoly was destroyed and printing became possible in cities other than those towns.'

'And what does that mean as far as this sheet is concerned?' Arnold asked.

Ben Gibson frowned. 'I can't be sure, not precisely, but I can make an educated guess. Let's be clear about one thing. This sheet was not printed before 1695, but it's old. And rare. And there's a clue buried in it that interests me.'

'Clue?'

'It was perhaps natural that once the monopoly was removed from the Stationers' Company, other cathedral cities should establish their own presses. After all, printing was largely confined to the production of religious materials. One of the earliest attempts to found a new press was in the cathedral city of Durham. They used foreign knowhow, naturally enough. A man called Gyseght, I believe. A Belgian. He established a press in Durham, under the auspices of the cathedral itself: they were enlightened enough in

Durham not to believe the press the invention of the devil.'

'You think there's a connection between this sheet and the Durham cathedral press?'

Ben Gibson nodded. 'The press was established round about 1696. Gyseght was a vain man, proud of his skills and insistent on leaving his mark on all he printed. Accordingly, he marked the lower case *g* in the materials he printed, so that the work could be recognized as emanating from him, and his press.'

'It appears on this sheet?'

'I think it does,' Ben Gibson said gravely. 'Look.' He pointed to the crooked *g* in the third line of the Latin. 'I've inspected it closely with a magnifying-glass. I'm pretty sure —sure as my old eyes can make me—that this sheet comes from a work printed by Gyseght in Durham.'

'When?' Arnold asked, a feeling of tight excitement rising in his chest.

'Ah, well, there you are,' Gibson replied. 'Fact is, the span of years during which Gyseght worked and the press flourished was narrow. The establishment at Durham was not a success. We can't be certain why, but the likelihood is Gyseght died without properly training a successor. Whatever happened, within eight years of its foundation the Durham press foundered. It was followed later, of course, by other presses, but the *original* establishment, the Gyseght foundation, lasted for just eight years.'

'And so, if this sheet comes from a book printed by Gyseght—'

'Its rarity value is high,' Gibson announced gravely. 'You must consider. A press founded after the repeal of the Licensing Act. One of only a few. It ended after only eight years—turn of the century. Its output would not have been great; the number of volumes that would have remained for twentieth-century eyes to see would inevitably have been few and located in the great museums: the British Museum, the Bodleian . . .'

'And this sheet—'

'Extremely rare.'

'And valuable.'

Ben Gibson was silent for a moment. Then he nodded, leaned forward and handed the sheet to Arnold. He looked sad.

'I told you,' Arnold said after a short silence, 'that you could keep it if you wished. I was only curious about it. For you—'

'Things would be different. I know,' Gibson said, his eyes large and luminous as he gazed at Arnold. 'I have made the study of such materials my life's blood. But a rarity of this kind . . . I would love to accept such an offer, if only of the single sheet. But—there is more.'

Arnold looked up from the sheet. 'What do you mean?'

'You still cannot recall where it was you found this sheet? How it came into your possession?'

Arnold shook his head. 'I'm at a loss. I've looked through all the books in my bungalow. I just can't recall . . .'

'It's important that you do recall. Try hard . . .'

The *spaghetti carbonara* was delicious. Arnold ordered a bottle of Valpolicella to wash it down, and then treated himself to a rare steak. He took no vegetables because the spaghetti had been filling, but as he toyed with the steak his mind was not really on the meal. He was still puzzled about the provenance of the sheet he had discussed with Ben Gibson.

The old man had refused Arnold's invitation to join him at the restaurant in Grey Street and Arnold had not been displeased for he wanted to think over the past days, consider deeply where he possibly could have found the sheet.

'It's clearly from a religious work,' Gibson had explained, 'a psalter, or a missal. And I have to tell you, the sheet itself is valuable. It would certainly bring you in a large sum from an enthusiastic collector. I can't name a figure: much depends upon whether there was an American bid. They rather ... overvalue history sometimes. But if you could lay your hands on the whole book ... if you have it on your shelves just waiting for this sheet to be returned to it, then we are talking not merely of a large sum of money, we are talking of a fortune ...'

The trouble was, Arnold could not remember that there was anything on his shelves that remotely resembled an old missal. The books he had patiently sifted through in his sitting-room had been wide-ranging, but most were his own collection of materials that reflected his own passions: wood, stone, ancient buildings. There were old prints there, books of some rarity, but this sheet was something else again, a puzzle.

A puzzle to add to the other Ben Gibson had presented to him.

'It's important that you do recall. For there's more. It may well be that in your own interests you find few to talk to—an interest in old buildings among amateurs usually tends to be restricted to archways and configurations, local stone and steeples. I imagine your detailed knowledge and understanding is rare ... It's not quite the same in my world. Antiquarian books ... it's a passion that is shared by many, on a worldwide basis. And, inevitably, there is a network, a web of contacts that extends throughout this country and others. One has connections ... we never meet, but information travels along the lines of communications like whispers over a telephone.'

'What sort of information?' Arnold had asked.

'Provenance, sometimes. More rarely, a ripple of excitement, a whisper that something unusual is coming on the market. And this is what has happened, literally within the last forty-eight hours. It has been whispered that a Gyseght book has been found and is to be auctioned.' The old man had paused dramatically. 'A Gyseght book ... not *perfect*, but a find of huge value.'

'And you think—'

'Who can tell? Coincidence is the mainstay of existence. Whose life or career is truly planned? All I can say is two things: a Gyseght book is on the market at the time you find in your own home a sheet printed by the same man. Secondly, the whisper that a Gyseght is for sale was a whisper that was suddenly snuffed out.'

'You mean the work was withdrawn, or sold?'

'Those are two possibilities.'

'There is another?' Arnold had asked, half-guessing.

'There is.'

But it did not solve the puzzle that niggled away in Arnold's mind. He simply could not identify any of his books that might have a connection with the missal sheet, and he could not recall ever having seen the sheet, as a bookmark in any of his books, or in his house at all.

He had never seen it in his home. Arnold frowned, ordered a *cappucino* and observed his image in the window of the restaurant. Tall, hunched, lean, his prominent nose shadowed by the overhead light . . . what had he actually *done* that particular day, the day he had found the sheet?

There had been his overcoat to repair: he had taken it to the cleaners. It had been crumpled on the back seat of his car since he had thrown it there after the arrest of Mildred Sauvage-Brown at Penbrook Farm.

Then there had been the compulsive need to clean the car inside and out. He had taken it to the car wash, aware of the impending return of the Senior Planning Officer.

And that had led him to the springcleaning of his bungalow: gathering together the accumulation of newspapers and other clutter, emptying waste-paper baskets, throwing the lot in the dustbin and then . . . finding the sheet.

He shook his head. The coffee arrived. He stirred the chocolate gently into the coffee, still frowning. Dark streaks appeared in the creamy froth, uncertain, muddied as his mind. Muddied as Mildred Sauvage-Brown's campaign strategy. Mildred Sauvage-Brown . . .

He had never thought his mind could tingle. The feeling was one which he would have expected possible, physiologically, only at his nerve ends, under the skin. But he *felt* his mind tingle, was aware of something happening in his head, a dancing image that was just out of reach and yet sufficiently frightening to raise the short hairs on the back of his head.

Mildred Sauvage-Brown . . .

Mildred Sauvage-Brown at the inquiry before Mr Lansbury; tearing at his shoulder in the corridor; swinging her shotgun in a vain attempt to repel the police at Penbrook Farm. Images, pictures tumbling over and over in his brain . . . he closed his eyes tightly, until spots floated against a black background and when he opened them again the image reflected in the window shimmered and danced.

But Arnold hardly saw the mirror image; instead, he saw something else, a photograph, a group. He groaned. He thought of the photograph, and he thought of the events and the incidents and as the Italian waiter hovered with the bill he fitted them together, the photograph, the pictures in his mind, the tumbling events of the last few weeks.

And he worked out in his mind the provenance of the sheet from the Gyseght missal. More important perhaps, he worked out the implications of it all upon recent events.

CHAPTER 5

1

Arnold found the next two days agonizing.

The Senior Planning Officer had taken back the conduct of the Penbrook Farm application and Arnold was more than a little disturbed to learn that an approach had been made to the chairman of the Planning Committee, Mr Lansbury, to have matters expedited. Arnold considered it dangerous: it would seem that the Senior Planning Officer was bowing to the pressures of big business and there were almost certainly going to be further whispers of local government chicanery current around Morpeth.

Surprisingly, there was no reaction from Mildred Sauvage-Brown. Arnold had expected she would come tearing into his office, or the Senior Planning Officer's, with loud and vociferous complaints about Lansbury's decision. Perhaps the death of Sarah Ellis had affected her deeply, so deeply that she had temporarily lost course, become unable to direct her thoughts positively towards the saving of Penbrook Farm. Or maybe she was, literally, defeated, her loneliness and loss destroying all sense of purpose.

There was nothing Arnold could do about it. He was no longer involved in the Penbrook Farm issues, and he had his own work to get on with. There were three new applications to process and the Willington Hall matter finally to set to rest. He phoned Henry Willington to tell him the sawmill development was now formally withdrawn and was not surprised at the reserved manner with which the heir to Willington received the news: Henry would have more on his plate than he had perhaps bargained for, with the estates inevitably having to be parcelled out for sale, merely to keep the house itself going.

But what really distressed Arnold was his inability to contact Freddie Keeler.

He had tried to reach him several times by phone. At first the girl in the office had been noncommittal: Mr Keeler was not available. Later, after the third call, she had reluctantly got through to the Warkworth office to make her own inquiries. She had called back to say that Mr Keeler was away on business.

Late the following afternoon Arnold called at Keeler's Newcastle office personally. The girl was darkly attractive but disinclined to be helpful. She was in no position to let Arnold have details of Mr Keeler's movements. Was he a tax inspector or something? Mr Keeler was certainly away on business, and it involved the sale of certain properties in Cleveland, *that* much she could divulge, but beyond that business ethics would not allow her to go, and Mr Landon shouldn't ask. 'I mean, if you're really a planning officer I might be giving away confidential information that would be damaging to Mr Keeler's business, mightn't I?'

So Arnold was left with the churning in his mind, the fear in his chest, and the gnawing anxiety that he should perhaps go to the police. But with what? Half-baked theories, a sheet of paper that a Quayside eccentric said was valuable, and a conglomeration of wild accusations from a woman who had already spent a night in jail because of the violence of her behaviour.

That, and a Rover leaving the car park of the planning office at Morpeth.

It was hardly enough to bring anything but a rebuff from the police, and Arnold had already had a few of those in the last two years. So he kept his counsel and worried about the whereabouts of Freddie Keeler.

'Guisborough, man!' When Arnold finally reached the estate agent by phone the next morning there was exultation in the man's voice. 'I been staying in Guisborough, and I got a sweet deal all set up! There's a country house up there on the Cleveland Hills with about eighteen acres of prime land. The possibilities are ginormous—'

'Freddie, I need to see you.'

'Aye, man, so I gather, with all these phone calls and the pestering you been giving the girl here in the office. But I had to stay incognito, like, down in Guisborough because there's more than a few sharks prowling around, and I had this deal all set up and there was no way—'

'Freddie, where can we meet? It's *urgent!*'

They decided upon The Duke of Wellington.

It was a convenient enough meeting place. It meant that Arnold could get there easily in his lunch break from the office, driving south along the winding country roads that snaked their way towards the sea, while Keeler could sensibly undertake the journey en route for his Warkworth office, which he had apparently neglected for some ten days.

The pub itself was on a rise, commanding views across the countryside and the sea; somewhat isolated for daily traffic, it nevertheless had a good catering reputation in the evenings and tended to draw numerous clients from the Alnwick and Morpeth areas. Today, the car park was almost empty and the lounge bar was quiet. Arnold sat there with a glass of lager in front of him and waited for Freddie Keeler to arrive.

He was fifteen minutes late when he breezed in, ordered himself a gin and tonic and swaggered across to join Arnold. 'Hey, what a day, man! Finally got rid of two houses up on the Town Moor, and clinched the Guisborough deal as well as shifting a couple of farms up Rothbury way. I tell you, life's looking good at the moment.'

He shrugged himself out of his trench coat and sat down, looking pleased with himself. 'Now then, laddie, what's the trouble? How can Uncle Freddie help?'

Now that he was face to face with the estate agent, Arnold found it difficult to explain. 'I . . . I want some information,' he began lamely.

Keeler looked at him with a cautious air. 'Now hold on, bonny lad. You're a planning officer; I'm an estate agent. There's not going to be any sort of *confidential* stuff you want to prise out of me, is there? About my mates in the business, that sort of thing?'

'It's got nothing to do with your business . . . not the house purchase side, at least.'

Keeler looked puzzled. He sipped his gin and tonic. 'Well,

let's have it out, lad. I'm not a mind-reader. What is it you want from me, hey?'

'We talked, recently,' Arnold began cautiously.

'Aye.'

'About the auction rings.'

Keeler frowned, and stared for a few moments at his gin. 'I recall. But that's . . . well . . .'

'There's no threat in this, Freddie,' Arnold hastened to say.

'That's as may be. But the auctions, well, they're a bit delicate, you know, Arnold? I wouldn't want you to be asking around about them too much. I mean, I said a bit more than I should have, and there are some heavy lads among the interested parties, you know? They're not above lifting the odd boot if they feel they've been shopped.'

'Believe me—'

'All right, just so long as you know the score,' Keeler said heavily. 'What do you want to know?'

'I want to know whether there's an auction ring arranged soon.'

Keeler frowned. 'A ring? You mean, is there anything planned for a knock-out agreement?' He shook his head. 'Not to my knowledge, Arnold. I mean, there's been no decent sale on for the last month or so. There's one planned in about six weeks that'll bring in the sharks. Furniture mainly, but there's a couple of pieces that the lads will be working on, I reckon.'

Arnold hesitated. 'I'm not thinking so much of a knock-out agreement operating after a sale. I want to know whether there's likely to be a *private* auction occurring, just with dealers involved and no publicity.'

Freddie Keeler stared at him for several seconds, then slowly shook his head. 'I think you got things wrong, Arnold. A *private* deal? No, things don't work like that in the rings. A private deal of the kind I think you're talking about comes about only when there's specialist stuff on the market, and when its provenance is ... shall we say, a bit doubtful? Then, the word goes out on the grapevine, and the dealers gather. They're a bit like vultures, I tell you,' he added feelingly, 'and the whole thing's a bit too rich for *my* blood. I mean, there's *real* money flowing around on those occasions.'

'Are you in touch with that kind of grapevine?' Arnold asked.

Freddie Keeler finished his drink, rose and walked to the bar. He ordered another drink for himself and one for Arnold, but there was a slightly truculent air about him as he sat down again. 'Look, I told you this was a specialized sort of operation. The links are different—depend on what the items are. And, well, outsiders ain't exactly welcome. Arrivals at the rings, they're by invitation only, you know what I mean? So you got to be careful. Me, I can't say any more unless I know what it's all about.'

Arnold hesitated. 'What do you need to know?'

Keeler leaned forward conspiratorially. 'First of all, the nature of the items.'

'There's only one.'

'*One?*' Keeler's eyes widened. 'So what is it?'

'A book.'

Keeler was about to snort in derision but the noise died. He sat back, eyeing Arnold carefully. 'One item. A book. It's got to be bloody old, then.'

'That's right.'

Keeler screwed up his features in thought and contemplated the ceiling. 'Yeah, all right, I got a few connections I could sound out, but I'm not certain they'll come through. Not unless I had a good story.'

'What kind of story?'

'To explain your interest.'

Again Arnold hesitated. He was not certain how much to tell Freddie Keeler; uncertain how much he had yet even substantiated in his own mind. He shook his head reluctantly. 'It's a delicate matter, Freddie.'

'Most business deals are.'

'Business?'

'Oh, come on, Arnold. You're not really interested in *books*. Not unless they're about bloody stone or wood. And I have a gut feeling, from the way you've been sweating after me that this isn't interest, it's *business*!'

'Well . . .'

'I'm the soul of discretion,' Keeler said, 'and I love the idea of you coming down from your bloody pedestal to dirty your hands in the commercial market.'

'The book is an old one, Freddie.'

'So you tell me.'

'It's worth a great deal of money.'

'A *great* deal?'

'That's right.'

Freddie Keeler's eyes shone wetly. 'And where do you come in, Arnold?'

'The book . . . it's an old missal, or psalter, printed in Durham at the end of the seventeenth century. It's worth a lot of money, even though it's not perfect.'

'*Perfect?*'

'It's been damaged. Pages missing. Maybe only one page.'

'And?'

'I can lay my hands on that page, I think.'

Freddie Keeler whistled, then smiled broadly. 'You cunning old bugger! I always had you marked for the character who'd hand over any find to what they call the *proper authorities*! But you're not above making a few bob yourself, then! What's the pitch?'

'The sheet came into my possession,' Arnold said. 'I need not explain how.'

'Mum's the word, boy,' Keeler cackled delightedly.

'I discovered what it was, but was told that the book itself was being made available for sale..Almost immediately, the sale went underground.'

'That's the pattern, boy, that's the pattern. They'll have valued the thing, realized questions might be asked, the bloody *heritage* merchants will be sniffing around, so they'll go to private auction, invite them with rich blood, and the book will quietly disappear into some collection and a lot of money will change hands. With no export licences being called for!'

Arnold was still vague about what best to tell the estate agent, but the line he was pursuing seemed fruitful so he plunged on. 'What you have to realize, Freddie, is that while the book is extremely valuable—even imperfect—its value will increase significantly if it were a perfect copy.'

'I'm ahead of you, bonny lad, I'm streets ahead of you. There's no way you'd be in the market for buying a book like that, but you're in the market for *selling*!' Keeler chortled happily. 'What a turn-up! A single bloody sheet and you can make a bomb, just playing the buggers off against each other, and you end up with a tidy sum and no risks while they pay you through the nose in order to heighten their own profit margins. Arnold, you're on a winner!'

'If I can reach the auction,' Arnold reminded him.

Keeler frowned darkly, his excitement evaporating. 'Aye, point taken. Well, look, old son, tell you what I'll do. I said I had a few contacts. I'll try them; have to be discreet, of course, and if I come up with anything . . . well, it'll be up to you. Dicey business getting you into the ring. They'd be too suspicious. And I got my own reputation to consider. Don't want to be seen as unreliable, like. But if I do get the word, it's yours. And my best advice would be to find out who the buyer is, then approach *him*. Won't get the best deal that way—playing them all might be better, because they're greedy sods, but it's safer. Suss out who's the buyer.'

'It was something like that,' Arnold admitted, 'I was considering.'

'Arnold, my friend, leave it to me. So drink up: there's time for another!'

2

Arnold always felt that the further north he drove, the greater became the raw flavour of frontier country. It seemed to hang in the wind as he drove along the looping road, rising over the fells with the Cheviot menacing to his left and distant sea views to his right. He dipped down to cross winding streams and rose to pass craggy outcrops of rock where sixteenth-century Scottish pirates had camped, while the distinctive sea tang drifted in from the shores beyond Bamburgh and the hoary old sea-castle built by King Ida the Flamebearer.

'Lindisfarne,' Freddie Keeler had said to him over the phone. 'For God's sake don't ask me why; all I can suggest is that the guy who's selling the book wants the transaction in as out of the way place as possible. All right, it's common practice for the auction rings to go to some quiet place, well away from snoopers and possible police activity, but this character must be really shy if he's chosen Lindisfarne! But you nail 'em, Arnold; nail 'em for every penny they got!'

He had taken a day's leave from work. The Senior Planning Officer had raised no objection: Arnold had some leave due to him. Moreover, he had kept a low profile during the days since the Senior Planning Officer's return, and perhaps had given the impression he had been chastened by the tongue-lashing he had received.

Had the Senior Planning Officer been aware of Arnold's intentions he would have been apoplectic.

Arnold was not sure of his intentions himself. He had not been entirely honest with Freddie Keeler, of course: he had no intention of selling the sheet from the missal, or of trying to set bidders at each other's throats. Nor was he particularly interested in who was going to buy the book; rather, he was interested in the name of the person *selling* it. The thought itself caused a cold prickle at the back of his neck. He was half-hoping he was making a bad mistake over the missal, but he had to find out. If his suspicions were justified, on the other hand, he was not sure what he would do. *One step at a time*, he muttered to himself, *one step at a time*.

He had planned his day carefully. He rose at nine and made himself a good breakfast, to quell the nervousness in his stomach as much as anything else. Then he chose warm clothing, for he had the feeling he might be in for a long, cold wait.

He set off at ten-thirty, armed with two flasks of hot coffee, safely stowed in the back of the car. He had dawdled into Warkworth and had a light lunch at The George, then taken the A1 north again, past the scattered pele towers on the road to Bamburgh.

It was early afternoon when the country had opened out and the signs beckoned him to Berwick; he turned off, took the road beyond Dunstanburgh castle and travelled parallel to the main road—a longer route, but one he felt safer on in his nervous state.

The narrow roads twisted their way northwards and he thought about the old Lindisfarne, the austerity of which must have suited Aidan and his band of Irish monks who had settled there in the seventh century to establish the Celtic church and evangelize the North. Things were different now: the abbey had been destroyed centuries ago and remained only as a gaunt, ribbed tourist attraction, the castle had a fairytale appearance crowning the rock above the island in its Lutyens restoration and under the care of the National Trust, and it was bric-à-brac and Lindisfarne Mead, a rugged coastline and the feeling of isolation from the mainland, that brought the tourist throngs in the summer.

But for Arnold, some things would never change. Only sixty miles from Newcastle, Lindisfarne, the Holy Island, nevertheless had retained its remoteness, closed off as it was for three hours either side of each high tide. Arnold drove across the narrow causeway in the late afternoon as a pale sun glistened on the sinisterly named sands—the Swad, and the Slakes—and the stone causeway was still wet and smelling of the sea as the dark water lapped at its edge. He could imagine it as little different from the days when the Danes had marauded ashore to burn the abbey, and the day in 875 when the monks, fearful for their precious relics, had finally departed to the south and Durham, with their priceless Lindisfarne Gospels.

Arnold shivered, and carefully drove his car off the causeway into the sheltering dunes, piled high by the wind from the Farne Islands. He turned off his engine and the silence drifted in upon him. He would have to wait now, he guessed, until the Farne lights were blinking in the dusk above the sea.

He had no plan of action as such. The word from Freddie Keeler had been that the meeting was to be held at Lindisfarne at a pub, The Dog and Whistle. He could not tell Arnold of the scheduled time: his informant had given him basic information but had Freddie pressed for more detail suspicion would have crept in. Nor could Freddie discover who had been invited to the auction, but it was not due to start until about eight in the evening.

Arnold had decided to arrive early for one simple reason: he wanted to have a view of who might be driving across the causeway to the auction.

From his parking spot he could see a stretch of some fifty yards of the causeway, while the shoulder of the dune hid his own car from the drivers on the road: they would be sweeping past before they could see him and it was unlikely they would even notice him. And if they did, he would probably be dismissed as a birdwatcher, or a courting couple. He waited, opened his first flask, found the coffee hot and watched the glistening Slake as a cold wind came in from the sea to carry the unearthly crooning of eider ducks, floating on the dark sea below the grassy cliffs of the distant Heugh.

Two cars drove across the causeway but they were of little interest to Arnold: small and battered, they probably belonged to local families, gone for the day to Berwick, perhaps. The men Arnold expected would come in bigger vehicles than these.

He considered again the warning words Freddie Keeler had uttered on the phone. 'And let's get one thing straight, Arnold—I don't know anything about all this. I don't *want* to know. Things can get rough with some of these merchants —they're not exactly Debrett.'

'I'll remember that,' Arnold had assured him.

'And one more thing, my son. Keep your eyes peeled, because you're not alone, kiddar.'

'How do you mean?'

'I told you. I had to tread careful when I was asking around. All right, I got the information in the end but it wasn't easy, especially since I wasn't the only one asking questions.'

'I don't understand.'

'Neither do I. But I'm telling you. You haven't been the first asking questions about the auction.'

'You mean a possible bidder?'

'No. Not so. I told you: auctions like this are by invitation *only*. You don't ask your way in. I been asking around to find out where and when; it seems someone else has been doing the same thing. And that makes people edgy. What about your own informant?'

'Informant?'

'The guy who identified the sheet for you.'

Ben Gibson. 'No, I hardly think he'd make inquiries.'

'Well, I'm telling you facts, old son. So go canny.'

Arnold waited. Dusk was falling and the lights were twinkling on in the scattered houses on the island. A gash of red glinted across the sky, outlining the castle on its rock, towering gauntly over the village, and high in the night sky an intermittent flashing heralded a jet plane flying north.

Seabirds and seals, wild geese, dunes, deep shining sands. An unearthly place, and the coughing roar of a vehicle approaching at speed across the causeway. Arnold wound down his window in the gathering dusk and peered out, smelling the sea tang and feeling the cold wind bite at his cheek.

It was a Land-Rover. Driven at speed, probably a local again, hurrying home before dark. Arnold checked his watch: it was near seven. Soon, he guessed, they would come.

They did, at last, some forty minutes later, not in convoy but at short intervals. Deep-throated cars, big cars, bright headlights lancing along the Slake and past the dunes towards the quiet village.

Arnold counted them.

Eight, before the silence swept in from the sea again, and it was time he himself moved.

Arnold started his car and drove carefully out of the dunes towards the lights of the village.

He parked at the top end of the village, near the area reserved for tourists queuing for their ration of free Lindisfarne Mead before they bought a bottle. The streets near the tiny village square were quiet enough, curtains drawn at the windows, and Arnold walked slowly down the main road, past the Land-Rover parked awkwardly, half on the pavement, until he came to the top of the hill.

The evening was not dark; a crescent moon silvered the sea beyond Lindisfarne Castle, where the black ribs of the old staiths jutted out starkly against the twisting ripples. The abbey stood to his right, its ruined walls lurching against the sky, but just below the abbey, where the lane started, twisting down towards the shoreline, several cars were parked.

Arnold hesitated. It would be impossible for him to gain entry to the auction, and he did not know the man—or woman—he was looking for. The cars—big and powerful —would be owned by the men he sought, but when they finally left how was he to distinguish one from another?

Thoughtfully he walked down towards the cars. As he drew near he saw that among them was a Porsche and two Rovers: the moneymen were here. He looked about him, gazed towards the abbey and the small burial ground on the hill and then he walked back to his car. When he returned to the abbey lane he was carrying his binoculars.

He would see little in the evening light, but the lens of the binoculars might help. Carefully he made his way up to the cemetery on the hill, his feet crunching lightly on the sandy track, until he reached a vantage-point near the abbey walls. He stood uncertainly for a while, and then found a convenient gravestone against which to lean. He focused the binoculars and began a slow sweep of all the houses in the vicinity of the parked cars.

The cottages, their doors and windows, crept darkly into his view. There were occasional lights, a few lit windows, but nothing of interest. He reached the doors of the pub, The Dog and Whistle, and there was a scattering of cars in the narrow park, lights blazing in the bar and lounge, but the frosted windows gave him no insight. Then, almost as an afterthought, Arnold elevated the binoculars to the upstairs windows.

They had been careless.

Although the group had parked their cars in the lane, well away from the pub, and walked along the road, one by one, they had felt themselves secure in the private upstairs room of the Dog and Whistle and had drawn no curtains. The hill on which Arnold had positioned himself, however, gave him an advantage: with the aid of the binoculars he could see into the room.

Not that he could see a great deal. A few heads and

shoulders, a certain movement as men walked about, talking to acquaintances, a general casual movement which suggested to Arnold they had not got down to serious business yet.

Then one familiar head came into view; Arnold struggled with the focusing, to sharpen the image, but he already knew who the man was. Freddie Keeler had told him previously that Wilson was interested in the auction rings, and now the evidence lay before Arnold. Wilson was at the upstairs gathering in the Dog and Whistle.

They seemed to be settling down as he watched, drawing up chairs, arranging themselves in a more formal fashion. One man sat with his back to the window, and again Arnold considered the set of the shoulders familiar but he could not be certain. And there was one man standing. He appeared to be speaking to the gathering. Desperately Arnold tried to make out who he was, guessing that the man would be the seller, the person putting up the missal for bids. In an attempt to get a better angle, away from the obstruction of the man near the window, Arnold moved, stepping away from his vantage-point. His shoes crunched on gravel; at the same moment he heard something away to his left.

Arnold stopped, gazed around carefully, but among the shadowed, leaning tombstones nothing moved and gradually the prickling feeling at the back of his neck subsided. Graveyards at night were not exactly the most soothing places to be, he considered. He took up a new position, near a stunted tree, and applied the binoculars again to the upstairs room of the Dog and Whistle.

The man was someone he had never seen before.

He was a thin, small man, bald, with glasses. He was dressed in a dark suit and he made much use of his hands. There was no doubt in Arnold's mind that the man was conducting the sale; equally, there was no doubt that he was a professional. His gestures, his movements told Arnold the man had done this before.

The seller was using an agent.

It meant further problems for Arnold. He could not be certain the seller was in the room at the Dog and Whistle now. He might be, and Arnold had counted on that event, but using an agent meant the seller might be in the room, incognito, or he might be elsewhere, awaiting the moment when the agent could report the sale completed.

The situation seemed to be slowing in the upstairs room. The little bald man was more hesitant, less frenetic in his gestures. They were nearing the market price. Even as Arnold realized it, the little bald man suddenly clapped his hands together, was smiling broadly and then bobbed his head as he reached forward to pick something up. It was a glass. He raised it, drank.

The sale had been completed.

Arnold lowered the binoculars. He leaned back against the weathered bark of the tree and the blood began to pound in his head. He was not sure that he should be here at all. He should have gone to the police. But with what? For that matter, what did he have now? Precious little. A face—a small, bald man with glasses. And a theory.

He waited.

He checked his watch in the faint light. The group would be forced to break up within the next ten minutes or so if they were to be absolutely certain of making it back to the mainland. From the information he had received, the tide would be on the turn and within half an hour the causeway at the Slakes would be awash, impassable for cars. It was always best to give the tide a good twenty minutes either side before its run, for when the water did cut off Lindisfarne from the mainland it came in at the speed of a racehorse.

Someone was leaving the Dog and Whistle. A tall man, he walked confidently and quickly, down towards the cars parked in the lane below the ruined abbey. Arnold focused on him as he drew near, passing the lighted window of one of the cottages below. The face was unfamiliar. The man entered the Porsche: in two minutes its rear lights were glowing on the hill as he braked at the bend. A moment later he was lost to sight and the thunder of his engine was a distant sound.

A second man left the inn. His head was lowered and he walked quickly, as though seeking to avoid recognition. Arnold could not make out his face and when he entered one of the Rovers Arnold became agitated, craning forward to try to make out the man's features.

When the Rover manœuvred out of the lane Arnold was in a quandary. There had been a Rover in the car park at Morpeth; a Rover had been spotted the night Sarah Ellis had been battered to death. Anxiously Arnold watched as the car accelerated away up the hill, then he swung his binoculars back to the upstairs room in the Dog and Whistle. He drew in his breath sharply: the man whose head and shoulders he had thought familiar was now standing, stretching lithely. It was Livingstone.

And even as he watched, Wilson came back into the line of sight. It was not he who had left in the Rover. Both Wilson and Livingstone had been present at the auction; both were still there, and there was still one Rover left parked in the lane.

Arnold waited, glancing anxiously at his watch. They would be cutting things fine. Unless they had decided to stay for the night on the island. Even as he thought so, he realized the party in the upstairs room was breaking up. Another two men emerged from the inn and started to walk down towards the lane. Arnold bobbed about, trying to get a better line of sight and away to his left he heard a rushing, rustling noise, as though he had disturbed something, a sheep perhaps, or a nocturnal animal. He focused on the small group, but could not make out whether Wilson or Livingstone were included. Car doors were being banged, as two more men came down the hill, headlights flashed on and car engines coughed into life.

Arnold realized he was in an impossible situation. He could not sensibly see who was leaving; he had no idea which of these men the auctioneer would have been working for; and even if he could identify him, unless he actually *recognized* him he would be unable to give effectual chase because his own car lay in the park at the top end of the village.

He started to hurry forward, through the graveyard, dodging his way through a scattering of leaning headstones until he reached the grassy knoll above the lane. He slowed, cautiously, and checked the cars. The second Rover had left the lane in the interval while he had been scrambling forward.

But the little man with the bald head was walking past the lane, down towards the gate leading to Lindisfarne Castle.

Arnold hesitated. The man was walking purposefully, his bald head glistening in the faint light of the crescent moon, and he had his head down, scuttling along as though he were in a hurry. He was some twenty yards past Arnold before Arnold took the decision to follow him.

It was easy enough.

Beyond the lane the road ended. A rough track, worn and rutted from the cars that drove there in the summer months to park along the shoreline, led to the National Trust gateway which barred casual visitors. The gate was open now, and the auctioneer was hurrying through it, but Arnold made little sound as he followed him, keeping to the grass verge and moving swiftly.

Ahead of them loomed the turreted castle on its black, craggy rock.

Once the auctioneer had moved along the track to the right of the castle he would be climbing on rising ground. It was possible then for Arnold to throw aside caution and hurry around the left side of the crag, climb over the rocky base until he reached the bank that led down to the shoreline and come up behind the auctioneer and the person he was meeting.

As he hurried along Arnold recalled he had seen neither Wilson nor Livingstone go to the cars in the lane, and it would have been easy for either—or both of them—to leave the inn unseen from a side entrance and make it to the headland before the auctioneer arrived.

Arnold reached the foot of the crag and scrambled over the rough rocks, grabbing at the tussocky grass to pull himself up swiftly. He was in the shadow of the castle now and made no attempt to quieten his progress: the auctioneer would be unable to hear him from the other side of the crag.

Twenty yards above him the moonlight gleamed faintly on the rock and as he drew near the top of the bank Arnold moved more cautiously. To the left of the crag, and some thirty yards from the track that wound up along the side of the rock to the castle gateway there were three humped structures. They were the hulls of fishing boats, Arnold recalled, which had been turned over, had doorways fashioned in them, and were now used as storage huts. Arnold moved towards them carefully, and the faint sound of voices drifted to him on the night air.

He crouched, uncertain how far to proceed, and then the matter was resolved for him. A car engine coughed into life and headlights whitened the crag below the castle. The light swung, moved across the crag and lit up the track leading back towards the village. As the engine roared in the darkness Arnold stood upright, realizing he had made a bad miscalculation.

Wildly he scrambled up the last few yards of the bank, reached the side of the inverted hulls and burst past them to the path beyond. The little auctioneer had not heard his approach and as Arnold rushed out from behind the hulls he gave a startled yelp, raised his hands in alarm and then shot off like a startled rabbit towards the headland.

Arnold ignored him. He was interested only in the vehicle

and it was already at the top of the track. All he could see of it was the rear lights, glowing as the vehicle dipped over the ridge. Angrily Arnold ran forward as the driver disappeared over the ridge.

When Arnold had followed the little auctioneer he had made a mistake. He had never considered that the man selling the missal might have arranged to meet the auctioneer privately, on the headland; and he had certainly not guessed that the man would have kept his car parked near the hulls below the castle. Arnold should have considered it, thought of it earlier, but it was too late now as he ran after the car, shouting desperately.

At the top of the ridge Arnold stopped for a moment, breathing hard as anger and frustration seized him. He was not thinking straight; in his excitement he had not considered the auctioneer: he should have grabbed the man, questioned him, forced from him the identity of the man who had instructed him in the sale of the missal. Arnold looked back but he could see only the rocky coastline and the darkness of the sky. The startled auctioneer had fled beyond the hulls and would already be half way back to the safety of the village lights, a mile away. Either that, or he would be out there on the shoreline, hiding.

Arnold turned again, to glare after the receding lights of the car. He knew there was no chance of catching it now, but even as he told himself so he gained the impression that the vehicle was slowing below him on the track. Arnold hestitated, puzzled, and then he guessed what was happening.

On the rutted track progress would be difficult. Perhaps the driver had gone too quickly in his eagerness; wheelspin might have slowed him, even brought him to a halt on the broken, rutted ground. There might yet be the opportunity to catch up with him and excitement surged again in Arnold's chest. He began to run down from the ridge.

The sandy loam crunched under his feet and as he came

down the slope he felt almost that he was flying. The track curved away below him, rounding the shoulder of the crag, and the vehicle ahead still seemed to be in difficulty, struggling across the bumpy ruts, its engine whining away in the night air. Arnold hurried down the slope and reached the bottom of the crag but then he too found the going far from easy. The ruts were difficult to make out in the darkness, the uneven surface was dangerous underfoot and he fell, twice, losing his rhythm and lurching along the rutted track, until he took the precaution of stepping aside to the grassy verge where he was able to pick up speed.

Ahead of him, the vehicle was nearing the gateway to the road. Arnold could smell exhaust fumes in the air and the engine was roaring desperately as the driver fought the wheel, bucking the car across the furrows, sliding it nearer the entrance. Arnold tried to increase his own speed but the breath was whistling in his chest and his lungs were aching at the unaccustomed exercise and excitement. He was still some thirty yards from the car when the engine roar became steadier, throaty, the rear lights swung wildly, then straightened, and the driver forced his vehicle through the gateway, colliding with the gate as he did so.

Arnold knew he was finished. He could never catch the car now. Furious with himself for his lack of foresight and for his incompetence, he watched helplessly as the vehicle gathered speed, headlights flickering up as it reached the lane at the bottom of the hill and wound its way past the abbey and up the hill.

Arnold slowed to a gentle trot. It was hopeless. He was reluctant to give up the chase and doggedly he kept going, but it was with a sense of angry despair. He lurched along the track to the gate and the lights of the car disappeared around the bend above, heading into the village. Arnold trotted past the lane, and the vantage-point he had held in the graveyard, but there were no cars parked at this end of the track now.

The Dog and Whistle was still ablaze with light and someone was singing in the bar, a broken version of *The Keel Row*, but Arnold staggered past the inn door, feeling the leadenness of his legs increase as he turned into the hill to make his way past the stretch of cottages leading up to the main square.

At the top of the rise someone was starting a car. Its headlights glowed fiercely at him for a few moments, then the vehicle was reversed into a side street, to come out again in a charging rush, swinging wildly into the street. Arnold had his head down, gasping as he toiled up the hill. The blood was pounding in his head and there was a lancing pain in his chest. He slowed to a walk; to continue running was stupid. The chase was over.

His chest heaving, he walked quietly through the village towards the square, where he had left his car. When he reached it he stood there for several minutes, leaning against it, waiting for the pounding of his blood to subside and his breathing to return to normal. Then, painfully, he unlocked the car and climbed inside.

He felt completely dispirited. His journey to Lindisfarne had been wasted. He had discovered nothing beyond the fact that both Wilson and Livingstone had been at the auction. He had no idea who the auctioneer was, and he had no idea which of the two men had instructed him in the sale of the missal. Arnold had misjudged the whole situation, made a fool of himself, and run the risk of breaking his neck in the darkness of the rutted track.

Despondently he started the car.

His clothing was stained with mud and there was a damp patch on his knee where he had fallen in the wet, tussocky grass. He felt stupid, and as he drove along the lane out of the village, back towards the Slakes, he cast over the events of the last hour gloomily, hardly aware of the road ahead of him, contemplating miserably the incompetent manner in which he had conducted himself. Now, he could not imagine what on earth had possessed him, trying to discover for himself the man who had sold the missal. He was not suited to the role of detective: there were professionals who did this sort of thing, and did it far more efficiently.

There was a rushing sound under the wheels of the car, and Arnold blinked. For several seconds he was puzzled, as the noise increased and he felt the car slow, not responding properly to the accelerator. Then his eyes widened as he saw the black stretch of water in his headlights, and he realized how he had compounded all the foolishness of the last few hours in a dangerous fashion.

He had forgotten the tide and the causeway.

He took his foot off the accelerator in panic and braked; a moment later, he surged the car forward again. He had no idea what to do. The water was lifting in a bow spray in front of him, he could not see the road ahead and he knew that if he tried to turn he ran the risk of plunging off the road itself into the soft sand. There was no turning back, even though he was only a hundred yards or so along the causeway, and he knew he stood no chance of getting right across to the mainland. His hands were frozen to the steering-wheel and his mind spun in wild panic as he drove on, helplessly, until the car engine coughed and spluttered, sea water drenching the plugs and killing the ignition.

The car shuddered to a stop. Arnold stared helplessly out of the window. The water looked black now, spreading all about him, marooned on the causeway. Desperately he tried to calm himself, think what best to do. Chances were that as the tide came racing in it would lift the car, deposit it in the deeper water and he would be forced to climb . . .

Climb.

Of course. In his panic, he had forgotten. Marooned vehicles were not an uncommon experience on the causeway. Particularly during the summer months, tourists were constantly being trapped on the causeway, ignorant of the speed with which the tide came in, risking the trip back to the mainland even though they could see part of the causeway under water. Arnold should never have attempted the drive, would not have attempted it but for his gloomy introspection, but though he was trapped he recalled now that provision had been made for fools such as he. Half way across the causeway there was a refuge, a hut built on stilts to keep it well above the tidewater. In the summer it was a regular occurrence for helicopters to be called out to lift off stranded motorists. There would be no helicopter tonight, but the refuge was there.

If Arnold could reach it in time.

He got out of the car, stepping gingerly down to the roadway. The black water swirled around his legs, reaching almost to his knees and he felt the panic rise in his chest again, for he had no idea how far he might be from the refuge. The moonlight had faded and the sky darkened; he could make out dimly a stake driven into the sand at the side of the roadway and he knew that there would be a succession of these, marking out the causeway itself. He needed to move from one to the next, taking care not to step off the roadway into the treacherous sand of the Slakes.

He could feel the drag of the tide against his calves as he began to walk, quickly, thrusting through the water with a long stride. His movements caused the water to swirl higher against his knees and as he progressed from one stake to the next he realized that the tide was truly ripping in across the sands at speed. Moreover, the causeway dipped slightly as it reached the halfway point and the water would be deeper there. He had to hurry.

He hurried. The drag grew stronger against his legs and as he struggled from one stake to the next in line the splashing surge soaked his thighs. Two minutes later he was aware of the increased depth as the coldness seeped across his hips. He knew he could not be far from the refuge but he still could not see it in the dim light.

To make matters worse it began to rain, a light drifting

wetness that rapidly soaked his hair and began to drip down his face. He could see no lights ahead of him on the mainland and none behind him from the village. He was aware of the distant sound of sea surge beyond the dunes, but closer at hand the lapping rush of the tide panicked him, as he seemed to be trapped in a dark, wet world where the coldness reached up towards his chest.

Walking was more difficult now. The tide was running in fast and the water was up to his waist so that he had to throw his arms wide to retain balance as he forced himself along the causeway. He tried to keep the fear in check; the refuge could not be far distant, but he still could see nothing and his heart was beginning to pound uncomfortably.

He had been a fool to ever attempt the crossing; he had been a bigger fool ever to come north to Holy Island.

Something dark loomed up in front of him and Arnold stopped.

For a moment he thought it was the refuge and then realized it could not be, for it was not high enough, or bulky enough. He peered ahead, waded a few more steps, and then realized that he was not the only person trapped on the causeway. He remembered now, when he was struggling up the hill, a vehicle had started up in the village, hurried out into the lane. The driver had been trying to beat the tide and now, like Arnold, was trapped. It was a relief to know there was more than one fool in the world, Arnold considered, and thrust his way forward towards the vehicle.

It was a Land-Rover. He had expected it to be empty, but it was not. As he drew level with it, a window was wound down. Arnold looked up, peering incredulously at the face staring down at him.

'What on earth are you doing here?' he asked.

'I'm scared,' said Mildred Sauvage-Brown.

3

The rain had increased in intensity and the sky had darkened even further as Arnold persuaded Mildred Sauvage-Brown to step down from the vehicle. She tried to argue at first, complaining that she would be safe from the tide in the Land-Rover, but Arnold insisted she come with him, for neither of them was certain how high the tide would rise, and they would be completely safe only in the refuge.

She came splashing down beside him and she clung to his arm in a manner distinctly unlike the usual Mildred. He felt her fingers biting into the muscle of his arm and she was shuddering, perhaps with the coldness of the water, but possibly out of sheer fear. Arnold half dragged her forward as the blackness surged coldly about them and her fear caused his own to ebb as he concentrated on pulling her along with him. It was clear in moments, however, that she had stalled the Land-Rover only a matter of twenty yards from the refuge, for it loomed out of the darkness on its long stilts, only a short distance ahead of them.

Arnold raised his face against the rain. 'You should have gone straight to the refuge, instead of huddling there in the Land-Rover.'

She shook her head, saying nothing, and the fingers were still fierce on his arm as he dragged her towards the ladder that reached up to the haven above.

She seemed unwilling to go up first, but Arnold insisted short-temperedly, pushing her to the rungs and shoving her from below when she seemed reluctant to step upwards. It was unreasonable, he felt, with the cold black water swirling around his hips, for her to argue silently in this manner against taking what was the obvious step, and reach for the safety of the refuge. 'Get on,' he shouted. 'Hurry up there before we catch our death of cold, let alone drown!'

She began to climb the ladder. Arnold grabbed at the

rungs, began to lift himself out of the water, his head butting against her leg and he shouted at her again, in exasperation. 'There's nothing to be scared of! Get on! I tell you there's nothing to be scared of!'

But there was. Arnold realized it at once when the voice came to them from the darkness above.

'Come on,' the man said, 'I'll give you a hand.'

And Arnold knew why Mildred Sauvage-Brown had been scared.

The refuge was small and dark. It smelled of wet timber, and it was unfurnished, with no heating, but then, it was not intended as anything other than a temporary refuge.

'There is a phone,' the man said, 'to be used for emergency purposes. Bloody thing's broken, isn't it! Typical. Anyway, we're safe enough, as long as we don't succumb to pneumonia. You smoke?'

Neither Arnold nor Mildred Sauvage-Brown replied. They were standing close together, huddled near the doorway, and the other occupant of the refuge was leaning against the wall, some six feet away. In the darkness it was impossible to make out his features, but Arnold could hear him fumbling in his pocket for cigarettes.

'Can't imagine how you two came to take the chance on the causeway. I just wasn't thinking. I had to get back to the mainland, and when I started on the causeway I thought I could still make it. But that damned tide comes in at a hell of a lick. I got past the refuge all right, maybe half a mile on but the car just died on me. I thought it best to make it back here, rather than struggle to the mainland. I mean, you can't take the chance, can you? But didn't you two see the water coming in? I mean, you must have been several minutes behind me.'

There was an odd, excited tension in his voice as though he was slightly inebriated. Neither Arnold nor Mildred Sauvage-Brown made any reply and the silence that fell became edgy. The man facing them sensed the tension in the hut and he stopped fumbling for his cigarettes. His breath began to rasp in the darkness and he shuffled, turned away, to pull something from his jacket pocket. There was a clicking sound; it came again, and at the third attempt the cigarette-lighter flared, was held out at arm's length. Arnold could see the man's face only dimly, but the flame of the lighter illuminated his own and Miss Sauvage-Brown's.

'Hell's damnation,' the man whispered raggedly. The flame died and there was a long, uncomfortable silence. At last, the man said, 'Mr Landon.'

'That's right.'

'An odd . . . coincidence.'

'I doubt that.'

Mildred Sauvage-Brown cleared her throat. She touched Arnold's shoulder. 'Do . . . do you know this man?'

Arnold nodded in the darkness. 'We've met.'

'Is he the man you've been looking for?'

Arnold's skin prickled. He turned his head, to stare at her in the darkness. He could just make out the line of her sagging features but he could not make out her expression. 'What do you mean? Why do you think I'm looking for someone?'

She was silent for a few moments. She came closer to him, half-whispering, even though the other occupant of the refuge could clearly hear all she said. 'I reached the island before you. I too was up in the graveyard, watching the inn. I saw you come up, and I hid behind the headstones to your left.'

Be careful, Freddie Keeler had warned him. Someone else had been making inquiries about the auction, before him. Arnold now understood why inquiries had been made, and who had made them.

'I was still in the graveyard when you went down. I couldn't follow you, for you'd have seen me, and I just didn't know what to do. Then I saw you walk down the lane after the auctioneer, making your way out towards the headland.'

The man clucked his tongue in the darkness, a nervous reaction based on surprise. But he said nothing, and when Mildred Sauvage-Brown went on her voice had strengthened, courage seeping back into her as she spoke, remembering why she had come here to Lindisfarne.

'I didn't know what to do. I guessed you were looking for the man I was, but I had no idea how to proceed when you walked down the lane. So I decided to go back to my Land-Rover and wait. It was parked on top of the hill, in the village street. It gave me a good view of the village, the castle, and the headland. Then, a few minutes later, I saw the car come down from behind the castle.'

Arnold glanced across to the other occupant of the refuge. He seemed to be standing stiffly in the darkness, hands clenched at his sides, listening intently and almost holding his breath.

'The car came past me,' Mildred Sauvage-Brown grumbled, 'but I didn't know what you were up to, and what was happening. It drove out of the village very fast, I couldn't see who was driving, and although I thought I heard some shouting I couldn't be sure. After a little while I saw you, Mr Landon. You'd been running, but you had begun to stagger. It was then that I guessed what had happened.'

Arnold remembered the vehicle starting up as he climbed the hill in the village, the headlights flashing over him, the acceleration out of the village.

'I just didn't think,' Mildred Sauvage-Brown admitted. 'When I saw you, realized you'd been running after the car, I guessed what had happened and I just drove straight out of the village. After . . . after him.'

She shuddered violently, and Arnold remembered her fear in the car. 'Did you know he was up here?' Arnold asked gently. 'Is that why you wanted to stay in the Land-Rover?'

'I couldn't be sure,' she replied. 'There was just the one car left the village before mine—no one else had gone for some time. And when I found that I couldn't go on, with the tide coming in, I realized that he would probably have been stopped as well, with the water coming in so fast. There was the *possibility* that he might have made it to the mainland but I couldn't be sure, and I . . . I was afraid that he might be up here. I didn't *know*, but I didn't want to take the chance.'

'What is this all about?' said the man against the far wall. 'What are you talking about? What have you been doing on Lindisfarne?'

'Looking for you,' Arnold said simply.

The man was silent for a little while. 'I don't understand,' he said finally.

'I think you do.'

'Looking for me? Why should you do that? You know where I live.'

'Yes, I know where you live,' Arnold replied, 'but when I came to Lindisfarne I didn't know *you* were the person I was seeking.'

'You're talking in riddles.'

'No. And *you* don't believe that either. You know why I've been looking for you.'

The man in the shadows cleared his throat nervously. He rubbed his hands against his thighs as though he were suddenly cold. 'This is stupid. I don't know what you're talking about. I don't know why you're on Lindisfarne, and all this talk about searching for me . . . How can you be sure I'm the person you seek?'

'It's obvious,' Arnold replied. 'Three cars left this island after the tide started to run. The first was driven by a man eager to leave Holy Island after he'd received the report he wanted from the auctioneer acting for him in the sale at the Dog and Whistle. The second vehicle was Miss Sauvage-Brown's Land-Rover. I was in the third.'

'Yes, but—'

'You've already told us you were heading for the mainland. There's no one else in this refuge. You have to be the man who drove away from the headland. That means you're the man I'm looking for.'

'Headlands, auctioneers . . . I don't know what you're talking about.' There was a tremor of desperation in the man's voice. 'I've no idea—'

'You know.'

'I swear—'

'You were at the headland, talking to the auctioneer—'

'For what reason, dammit?'

'To discover whether the sale of the Durham missal had been successfully completed!'

There was a long silence, broken only by the rhythm of the rain on the roof of the refuge. The man facing them shifted uncomfortably. At last he said quietly, 'I know nothing about any Durham missal.'

'Don't be a fool,' Arnold said. 'To deny it is a waste of time. It will be no difficult task to trace the auctioneer, eventually. He'll be able to identify you as the person who commissioned him to arrange the sale on Lindisfarne, quietly, among a selected group of persons interested in exclusive, expensive possessions. He'll be able to identify you, and I'll be able to testify you met him at the headland, and found you here later, at the refuge, stranded like us by the rising tide . . .'

'And I,' Mildred Sauvage-Brown added in a harsh whisper, 'will be able to point the finger at the murderer of Sarah Ellis.'

'Murder?'

'You killed her!'

'Listen—'

'You murdered Sarah for that missal!'

'That's *crazy!*'

*

The words had crackled out with a fierce desperation and were followed by a complete silence. Startled by the vehemence in the man's tone, Mildred Sauvage-Brown had stepped back, stumbling against Arnold. Now she stood close to him and she was trembling. Arnold himself felt cold, uncertain what to do or say. They had come this far but the man with them in the refuge had killed once, and the passion in his tone meant that he could be capable of killing again.

'You've got it all wrong,' the man said at last, in a quiet, reasoning tone.

'So tell us.'

The three of them stood still, and the darkness closed around them as the wind rose, beating rain against the roof of the hut in a gentle tattoo. Mildred Sauvage-Brown was shivering: she seemed to have lost all her self-assertiveness and aggression. She had made the same guess as Arnold, linked the missal to the death of Sarah Ellis, and had started making inquiries about its sale. She had set out, like Arnold, to find out who was selling the missal, but now she had found him her nerve had failed, the anger and desire to revenge Sarah had faded, and she was frightened.

So was Arnold.

'This suggestion,' said the man in front of them, 'it's ridiculous. Even if you can show that I had a missal for sale, it doesn't mean anything. I'll be able to prove to you, and to anyone you tell, that the item I sold was an old family heirloom. I'll be able to demonstrate its provenance—'

'Then why did you find it necessary to sell it secretly, out her on Lindisfarne, away from prying eyes?' Arnold asked.

'I haven't admitted I did sell it yet,' the man replied. 'But if I did . . . there's nothing wrong in dealing with a small group—'

'Unless you stole the missal in the first instance.'

'I didn't steal it!'

'First you say you didn't *sell* it, then you say you didn't *steal* it—you're getting confused,' Arnold said.

'No,' the man said flatly. '*You're* confused. I need say nothing. I need admit nothing. I've done nothing wrong. You have no proof of my involvement in anything, and as far as this Sarah Ellis thing is concerned—'

'What if I were able to prove that the missal you sold belonged to Sarah Ellis?' Arnold asked.

'I haven't *admitted* selling anything yet,' the man said shakily. 'But proof . . . what proof are you talking about?'

'In the morning, when we go to the police, maybe we can put it to the test.'

'Police? Test? What are you talking about?' The man moved restlessly away from the wall, but coming no nearer to them. Nevertheless, Mildred Sauvage-Brown tightened her grip on Arnold's arm.

'It was I who found Sarah Ellis's body at the farm,' Arnold said. 'I was shaken. When I went in, I thought it had been Miss Sauvage-Brown who had been killed. It was only when she arrived with the police that I realized it was Miss Ellis who had been lying there. But the experience coloured my thinking, and my judgment.'

'What's that supposed to mean?'

'I assumed Sarah Ellis had been killed by mistake. I thought the intention might have been to assault and perhaps kill Miss Sauvage-Brown, because of her attempts to prevent the development of Penbrook Farm. As a result, I never thought of other motives, or other intentions.'

Mildred Sauvage-Brown stirred beside him. 'I thought the same thing for a while,' she whispered. 'Oddly, it didn't frighten me. I was enraged. I was determined to find out who had killed poor Sarah.'

'It was some time later,' Arnold went on, 'before I found a sheet of paper at my home. I had been cleaning the place out, cleaning the car, getting my coat repaired—and there was this sheet in the waste-paper bin. I didn't know how it got there, but when I took it to a friend of mine, an antiquarian, he told me it was valuable. Part of a missal printed in Durham. Old, and valuable.'

'So?' The man leaned back against the wall, seeking support. 'What's that got to do with anything here on Lindisfarne?'

'A great deal.' Arnold paused. 'I puzzled for a long time; I could not think how that sheet came into my possession. I went through all my books—'

'I didn't know about all this,' Miss Sauvage-Brown said wonderingly.

'But it wasn't until I saw the photograph in the paper that everything clicked into place.'

'Photograph?' the man said hoarsely.

Arnold nodded. 'The previous occasion when I visited Penbrook Farm a certain . . . altercation ensued. Miss Sauvage-Brown had arrested a surveyor in the barn and was threatening him with a shotgun. The police arrived, and so did reporters and a photographer from the *Journal*. He took a number of shots; one of them was taken when Miss Sauvage-Brown herself was arrested. It was published in the Sunday newspapers. It wasn't a very flattering photograph . . . but in the background was Sarah Ellis. She was clutching something in her hand. Something she always carrried with her.'

'All her life she carried it,' Mildred Sauvage-Brown muttered sadly.

'An old missal,' Arnold said.

Silence fell. The man against the wall seemed frozen, incapable of speech, and Arnold waited, the blood beginning to pound in his temples. The man shifted uneasily, and cleared his throat. 'You said something about *proof* . . .'

'A sheet broke loose from that missal. It came into my possession.' Arnold paused. 'When I heard from my anti-quarian friend that a missal—a Durham missal—was up for sale and that it was not in *perfect* condition I put the facts together. Maybe the sheet I held was part of the missal for sale. If it was ... maybe Sarah Ellis was killed for the missal, *not* in mistake for Mildred Sauvage-Brown ...'

'I came to the same conclusion myself,' Miss Sauvage-Brown muttered, 'that time I was up at your bungalow. I was standing there, thinking about Sarah, and I saw all those books of yours scattered around in the sitting-room, and I recalled how Sarah had always loved that old missal, took such comfort from it ... *and it was no longer at the farm.* The police had asked me if anything was missing, but I had been too shaken to think straight, and I'd forgotten, never told them ...' She stirred, turned her face to stare at Arnold. 'But how did the sheet get into your possession?'

'It took me a long time to work out,' Arnold replied. 'But it happened that day at Penbrook Farm. It was all very confusing. While you were being taken into custody, and everyone was running around the place, I almost forgot about it. The fact is, when you trapped the surveyor in the barn Miss Ellis went running up the lane for help and found me. Her dress was stained and muddy, and she was in such a state she dropped her book. I picked it up, stuffed it in the pocket of my coat while I tried to soothe her and find out what the problem was. I returned it to her when I was leaving Penbrook Farm but one of the pages had worked loose, and remained caught in my pocket. My coat was torn, so I threw it in the back of the car.'

'But you said you found the sheet in the waste-paper basket,' Mildred Sauvage-Brown reminded him.

'That's right. But what happened was that it must have fallen from my coat pocket when the coat was bundled on to the back seat. A few days later I took the car to be washed; I cleaned inside and collected bits and pieces of paper from the car and dumped them in the basket. I didn't *notice* it until later, when I had started clearing junk out of the house. By then, the chain of events had become blurred ... I didn't make the connection.'

'All this ...' began the man in front of Arnold.

'Can be proved,' Arnold interrupted. 'And if you've sold a damaged missal today, a missal with a page missing, and the page I have with a friend in Newcastle turns out to be the page from the missal, you'll have some explaining to do. You'll have to explain how you got your hands on the book, after the page had been lost, and about the same time that Sarah Ellis died.'

'Circumstantial evidence, that's all it would be,' the man demurred, 'merely circumstantial evidence—'

'Sometimes,' Mildred Sauvage-Brown snapped triumphantly, 'it can be very strong, like finding a trout in the milk!'

'What?' the man said in puzzlement but Mildred Sauvage-Brown made no reply.

'The fact is,' Arnold said, 'if the page fits, it brands you as a murderer. You killed Sarah Ellis to steal that missal.'

The man was shaking his head, as though weary of the accusations being made against him. 'You don't understand. You just don't understand any of it. That missal . . . I didn't steal it. The damned thing has been in my family for generations. It was mine; I sold it today, yes, but it was always mine to sell. And that,' Henry Willington added with a sigh, 'is probably the irony of it all.'

4

Arnold stared at the heir to Willington Hall in amazement. He shook his head. 'I don't understand.'

'Why should you?' Henry Willington said wearily. 'The story goes back a long time. Sarah . . . she wasn't called Ellis at all. Her name was really Willington. She was my father's sister. Sarah Ellis was my aunt.'

'Your *aunt*?' Mildred Sauvage-Brown bristled. '*Willington?* That's not possible! She . . .' Her grip slackened on Arnold's arm and she stood up straighter. She peered at Henry Willington across the dark-shadowed room. 'And yet . . .

she was odd about names. I told you, Mr Landon, that time I came to your bungalow. She'd made a will years ago, but the name she used then was *Willis*. When I met her she called herself *Ellis*.'

'But originally she was called Willington, believe me,' Henry Willington asserted. 'But I can understand her not wanting to use it. She hated it; hated the family—'

'But how long have you known she was living at Penbrook Farm?' Arnold asked.

'I didn't know at all—neither did my father. I'd never even seen her—I thought she was probably dead, and my father certainly thought so. It was quite a shock that Sunday morning, when he saw her photograph in the newspaper.' Henry Willington was silent for a little while. 'The shock, and the anger it generated brought on his stroke, I think. He died the same day.'

'Anger?' Mildred Sauvage-Brown queried.

'I told you,' Henry Willington said in a tired voice. 'It all goes back a long, long time. My father was an autocratic bastard when he wanted to be. And he caused her trouble, when she was about twenty or so.'

'What sort of trouble?' Arnold asked.

'Oh, I don't really know the details of it. And I only heard my father's side of it, and he'd have been biased, of course. In a nutshell, it seems that his young sister Sarah conceived an affection for one of the local lads around Willington Hall. Sarah fell in love, head over heels, but my father—her brother—wasn't pleased. I understand he felt she was lowering herself, going below her station in life. He could be incredibly Victorian at times.'

'So what happened?'

'Not sure, exactly. He busted it up, that's for certain. How, I don't know, but he waded in, interfered, made sure that Sarah and this friend of hers would never get together. But the result couldn't have been what my father expected.'

'How do you mean?' Mildred Sauvage-Brown asked.

'She didn't take it lying down, did young Sarah. She up and left Willington Hall and my father never saw her again. He made some inquiries, and discovered she had gone to the Continent under an assumed name. He did trace her a couple of times, but then she disappeared for good and he gave up. She had money of her own, that had come to her from her mother's side of the family, and she was independent, she could afford to live well enough all those years. He didn't care, anyway. There was just one thing that rankled—it was the reason why he had tried to find her at all.'

'Reason?' Arnold asked.

Henry Willington was silent for a while. He seemed to be thinking, dredging up the past and inspecting it, not liking, perhaps, what he saw, of his father, his aunt and himself. 'Well,' he said, 'when she left, she didn't go empty-handed.'

'How do you mean?'

'She hated my father; hated him for what he had done to her life, in destroying her chance of happiness with the man she had fallen for. She clearly decided to leave Willington Hall and never return, and she took all her personal possessions—'

'Including love-letters,' Mildred Sauvage-Brown said in a sad tight voice. 'Love-letters she kept for half a century.'

'—but she also wanted to get her revenge on her brother. So she took something of his. Something he valued highly. An item he cherished, even though he might have had to sell it to support the Hall in later years. She took it to hurt him as much as she could—'

'Good for her,' Mildred Sauvage-Brown muttered.

'The missal,' Arnold said quietly.

'That's right. It had been willed to my father. It was a prized possession. Sarah's taking it with her made him mad as hell. It's why he pursued her to the Continent. It's why she changed her name.'

'And it must have given her great satisfaction to have

returned, years later, to live in the same county as her brother, with the missal, knowing he would always bleed over its loss,' Mildred Sauvage-Brown said. '*Good* for you, Sarah!'

'So you'll understand,' Henry Willington said in a flat voice, 'just how great a shock it was for my father when he saw the photograph. He recognized her. *My God,* he said, *that's Sarah. And she's got the missal with her still!*' Henry Willington paused. 'He was apoplectic with rage. He started to cough. Then he had a stroke. I called the doctor, but he wasn't long in dying.'

'Sarah obtained her revenge at the end,' Mildred Sauvage-Brown said.

'And you got Willington Hall,' Arnold said to Henry Willington.

The man shuffled. He stepped forward, shaking his head. 'It wasn't intentional . . . I hadn't planned it that way . . . But when my father died, imagine the position! For years I'd tried to persuade him to let me have the managing of the estate. Instead of that, he persisted in his hare-brained schemes, dragging the estate down. And when he died, and I received control and ownership of the Hall, what was left for me? A decaying property, worn-out farms, a situation that was all but beyond redemption. He'd left me *nothing*! Like his own father before him, he'd *bled* the estate, in his own way.'

'But there was the photograph,' Arnold said, the hairs prickling on the back of his neck as he saw the inexorable logic of the thoughts that would have gone through Henry Willington's mind.

'That's right. The photograph. It had killed my father— in a sense it had given me Willington Hall. But it also gave me something else. A lifeline. A chance to save the estate. That missal didn't belong to my aunt Sarah. It was my *father's*. And on his death, it belonged to *me*. And it could help me bring Willington Hall back into shape! If I could retrieve it, sell it, I could use the money to rejuvenate Willington!'

'So you went to Penbrook Farm?' Mildred Sauvage-Brown asked. 'You went there that day, when I hadn't returned from Morpeth?'

'Her address was there in the news item. I went there,' Henry Willington said, his voice faltering slightly, 'but nothing went the way I'd planned. I'd hoped to persuade her, thought that she'd be pleased to meet her nephew after all these years, and I hoped we could come to some kind of accommodation . . . But it wasn't like that.'

'Sarah could be a very determined lady,' Mildred Sauvage-Brown said sadly.

'When I told her who I was she told me she had always hated my father, and had certainly taken the missal to revenge herself on him, but now she regarded it as her own. It never left her possession; it was as though it was a reminder of the man she had lost as a young woman, and nothing would now induce her to part with it. She would never give it to me. Perhaps when she died . . .'

'You tried to take it from her,' Arnold said flatly.

'But it was mine! And I could use it to save the Hall!' The rain increased, the pattering sound turning to a drumming on the wooden roof of the refuge. 'I went there, introduced myself and tried to explain. She was unreasonable; she simply wouldn't listen, or even try to understand! All right, maybe we were two of a kind apart from the blood link—I with my obsession, she with hers. But what *use* was the missal to her? What good was it doing?'

'She cherished it,' Mildred Sauvage-Brown said fiercely.

'But its sale could make an immense difference to the future of Willington Hall!' Henry Willington glared at her for several seconds, before adding angrily, 'And it was mine after all. *Legally*, it was mine!'

'So what happened?' Arnold asked.

'She refused to give it to me. She was holding it, clutched

to her. I can't be sure what happened then, really. I suppose I lost control . . . the frustrations of all the years with my father blocking every attempt to bring order to the chaos . . . and now this old woman insisting on clinging to something that didn't belong to her when the reason for her revenge was already dead . . .'

'You tried to take it from her.'

'She was surprisingly strong,' Henry Willington said. 'Determined. She held on . . . I was afraid the thing would get damaged . . . I didn't hit her, or anything like that. I got hold of the missal, I swung her away from me, and suddenly, when she lost her grip, the determination seemed to disappear and she was light as a bird . . . She crashed against the wall. She didn't make a sound after that, and I saw the blood, and I didn't know what to do. I pulled her into the corner . . .'

His breathing was laboured in the silence of the room. Above them the rain drummed with increasing intensity and in the distance there was the low growl of thunder. 'I was frightened,' Willington went on quietly. 'I was afraid I might be seen leaving the farm entrance so I smashed the light-bulbs . . . I imagine that will be seen as evidence of deliberation . . . but it wasn't like that.'

He moved across to the window and stared out into the blackness, the rain streaming down the glass.

Beside Arnold, Mildred Sauvage-Brown shifted uneasily. 'What now?' she asked.

Arnold felt wet and cold and despondent. The fear that had touched him, the prickling at the back of his neck when he had heard Henry Willington's voice above them on the ladder, all that had gone. Misery gripped him and he wished fervently he had not come to Lindisfarne and never heard of Penbrook Farm, but was lying warm in his bed at Morpeth.

'What do we do now?' Mildred Sauvage-Brown insisted.

'We wait,' Arnold replied. 'We wait for morning.'

5

'Early retirement?' Arnold repeated in astonishment.

The Chief Executive grimaced, exposing his perfectly aligned teeth in an unconscious attempt to demonstrate their perfection. 'That's right. We couldn't follow up suggestions of redundancy for the Senior Planning Officer, because clearly we'll need to fill the post. So I had a chat with him, and we decided upon a . . . er . . . strategy.'

'But he's only in his early fifties,' Arnold protested.

'Age, in these circumstances, is irrelevant.'

'Circumstances?'

The Chief Executive thought for a moment, considering matters of great portent, then reluctantly waved Arnold to a chair. It was leather, and deeply comfortable: only in the office of the Chief Executive were such chairs to be found. The Chief Executive grimaced again, raised his eyes to the ceiling, steepled his fingers and decided. 'In part, Mr Landon, *you* are responsible.'

'For the Senior Planning Officer's decision?'

'One might say so.'

'How?'

'I run a pretty tight ship, Mr Landon. I was not in command here when you were employed in this department so you won't have had occasion to come under my controls. But my petty officers, they tell me things, keep me informed.'

Arnold had heard about the Chief Executive's 'controls'. One of them was nicknamed 'Sniveller' Samson. A clerk in the legal section, he had the ear of the Chief Executive, and used it.

'It followed that when information reached me concerning your visits to my department I arranged to have a few questions asked. Certain issues then came to light.'

'Issues?'

'Precisely. I was told you'd been asking questions, looking at files . . . on certain matters and about certain people.'

'Like Councillor Minford.'

'And Mrs Minford, and her firm of building contractors.' The Chief Executive sighed. 'Command can be a lonely, and quite precarious business, Mr Landon. To protect my own frigate I found it necessary to send out my own reconnaissance units. After all, if there *had* been any corruption, and I hadn't investigated it . . .'

'And *has* there been?'

'I didn't say that.'

'But the Senior Planning Officer—'

'Is retiring *early*,' the Chief Executive interrupted, 'and at his own request. He agrees that he . . . ah . . . became rather too closely *involved* with certain business interests. Early retirement would seem to be the most appropriate solution.'

'What about the business interests you mention? I take it you're talking about Wilson and Livingstone?'

The Chief Executive's glance came down from the ceiling in irritation. 'I mentioned no names. Suffice it to say that I have had a discreet word with the Leader of the Council and certain suggestions have been made in certain quarters. Thereafter, it's nothing to do with me. I have done my duty. Beyond that, it's a matter for your own department. Planning, after all, does lie there. I merely command the whole ship. Which brings me to the reason for my calling you here. Your future . . .'

'*I* hadn't contemplated early retirement, Chief Executive—'

'No, no,' the Chief Executive said hastily, 'I wasn't about to discuss that kind of proposal with you. Not at all. I mean, if you *and* the Senior Planning Officer were to retire from the department at the same time the Press would smell a witch-hunt and who knows what wild allegations might be made about council and business activities!'

'Then—'

'We shall have to bring in someone new, of course, to succeed the Senior Planning Officer. It's clear we cannot offer the post to you, for you have no qualifications to support your application, and there are certain other matters . . .'

'I've no wish to apply,' Arnold said. 'I'm quite happy where I am.'

'I'm pleased to hear that,' the Chief Executive murmured unconvincingly. 'So we'll advertise, and a new head of the department will be appointed. Which brings me to the other matters. They can be summed up in one word, Mr Landon. Attitude.'

'Chief Executive?'

'*Attitude*. I'm sure you do good work, in the planning department. But this . . . leaning towards the extraordinary, this . . . peculiarity of interest you have, can you promise me it will become somewhat more . . . muted in future? Concentrate on your job, Mr Landon, please do.'

'I'm not conscious that my interests interfere with my work, Chief Executive, but I take your words in the spirit they are meant.'

'That's good,' the Chief Executive said, hooding his eyes in satisfaction. 'Rather more *muted*, that's the answer.'

As he left the room, Arnold was almost certain he heard the Chief Executive add under his breath, 'And then maybe we'll have rather fewer corpses around the place . . .'

Two days after the advertisement for the Senior Planning Officer's successor was placed, Mildred Sauvage-Brown came to see Arnold. She made no appointment, but simply barged unannounced into his room. Clearly, she considered that as a public servant he had no right to expect courtesies from members of the public.

'It's a cover-up,' she announced, 'and I won't stand for it.'

'What's a cover-up?'

'Minford. Wilson. Livingstone.'

Patiently, Arnold said, 'But it's what you've been campaigning for! The public inquiry has been cancelled. The development application for Penbrook Farm has been withdrawn. The plans for the Minford Twilight Home have now been changed: the home will be built on the outskirts of Morpeth, and Minford's name will not be associated with it. Haven't you won everything you've been fighting for?'

'As far as all *that* is concerned,' she said breathlessly, 'of course! But it's the way it's been done that I simply can't countenance. No scandal has been uncovered; no corruption unearthed! You know as well as I do that my allegations about Wilson and Livingstone and Minford and all the chicanery of the contracts behind the Penbrook Farm were true.'

'But difficult, if not impossible, to prove.'

'And the solution is quietly to advise those bastards to withdraw, there's no mud-slinging, and it's all dealt with behind closed doors? That's not my way, Mr Landon!'

'It's the way of politics, Miss Sauvage-Brown.'

'Humph.'

'You've got your way. And you live to fight another day.'

'Humph.' Some of the anger died in her eyes and she sat down, uninvited, a dumpy, vaguely unhappy middle-aged woman in a hacking jacket and tweed skirt. 'Sarah didn't live to fight any more battles.'

Arnold made no reply. There seemed nothing to say.

'Henry Willington's up for trial soon,' she said. 'What do you think he'll get?'

'I think he'll be found guilty of manslaughter. The term of imprisonment . . .' Arnold shrugged.

'What about the missal?'

'It was legally his. There's no question of confiscation on the grounds of a killer not being allowed to profit from his crime.'

'But what'll happen to the money he got from the sale?'

'Most of it will go to pay off accumulated debts on Willington Hall. The rest will be waiting for him, I imagine, when he gets out of jail. I'm not sure he'll enjoy it much.'

'Perhaps not.' Mildred Sauvage-Brown frowned. 'Poor Sarah . . . it was all so unnecessary.' She rose abruptly. 'But I have the farm and I shall run it as Sarah and I had decided. I shall save that mediæval woodland, *and* the tiles on the pigsty . . .' She paused, jutted out her lower lip in thought, looked back reluctantly. Her brow was thunderous with uncertainty and her tone was uneasy. 'I suppose I ought to thank you, Mr Landon.'

Equally uneasy, Arnold replied, 'It's not necessary.'

'You *did* help, in your way.'

'I was doing my job.'

'Yes . . . But perhaps I was a bit . . . over the top, accusing you at the inquiry of being a traitor.'

'It's all over and done with, Miss Sauvage-Brown.'

'Even so . . .' Mildred Sauvage-Brown shuffled in discomfort. She was not used to making apologies and she was equally nervous about developing relationships. 'Fact is, with your job and my . . . interests, our paths are likely to cross from time to time.'

Arnold hoped not.

'There's the Amble thing, for instance,' she went on. 'The marina. Quite wrong. No one wants it.'

'You'll have no status at that inquiry, Miss Sauvage-Brown,' Arnold said, alarmed.

'No, but I'll have to speak out! I mean, there *must* be some sort of fiddle going on there. Public money involved. Corruption!'

'Miss Sauvage-Brown—'

She was walking out into the corridor. Over her shoulder, reluctantly, she was muttering, 'If I do get a bit . . . well . . . you know, excited, and say things that are a bit . . . *extreme*, I hope you won't take offence. It won't be that I don't respect your point of view . . . or your professionalism.'

He followed her into the corridor. She was stepping into the lift. Her face was faintly flushed as she looked at him, the doors closing upon her. 'I just hope you won't take it personally,' she said.

The doors sighed and she was gone. There were workmen in the corridor, taking away the coffee machine. When it had 'leaned' upon the office cleaner it probably hadn't intended the unfortunate lady to take it personally, either, Arnold thought gloomily.

He hoped the successor to the Senior Planning Officer would be appointed before the Amble inquiry started. He went back to his office and made himself an illegal, but infinitely superior, cup of coffee.

At the weekend he'd drive out to the Nine Nicks of Thirlwall. There were always compensations.

Men of Subtle Craft

CHAPTER 1

1

The twig cracked, with a light snapping sound. The doe's head came up sharply, her body tense, muscles ready to surge into action.

The eyes made out nothing to cause the animal further alarm. She was unable to distinguish the form of the hunter in the trees: the camouflaged shirt and stained jeans enabled the motionless figure to merge into the background. Wind direction had been gauged, woollen socks had been pulled over stout leather boots to muffle the sound underfoot, and there had been only the mishap of the broken twig to raise the alarm.

In a little while the doe, satisfied, resumed feeding, her hide dappled by the early evening sun that filtered low through the trees and cast long shadows down towards the stream fifty feet below. It was towards that burn the deer made their way as dusk fell.

Across the stream the hill rose, open farmland stretching away beyond the deer fence to the hazy, craggy outlines of Cheviot. A blue haze of smoke rose lazily in the air from a distant wood fire and the road that crossed the bridge over the stream was empty, a dusty track winding its way over the ridge to the lonely farm on the hill.

The hunter paid no attention to the view across the stream. The arrow was sliding gently from the quiver and was set, nock against bowstring.

This arrow was utterly unlike the mediæval clothyard shafts that had been used on ancient battlefields. It was a fine-tuned missile of drawn aluminium, made in the United

States. There were no grey goose feathers in the fletching of the tubular shaft: flexible waterproof nylon vanes gave it an almost silent accuracy.

The doe's head was down, snuffling, as the bow slowly came up.

Aerospace technology had spawned this weapon: this was no traditional longbow of solid yew or hickory. The cam bow was a sinister-looking contraption with a diecast magnesium alloy handle and polished limbs of laminated graphite and epoxy resins. Cables and aluminium cams took the strain until the bow was fully drawn, and the arrow, with its multi-bladed broadhead of shatterproof stainless steel was designed to be released at an explosive speed of one hundred and ninety feet per second, its razor-sharp cutting edges capable of slicing through the toughest hide like butter.

At the last second the doe raised her head. Perhaps it was some instinctive feeling that presaged danger; perhaps she had heard the slight hiss of breath from the hunter as the full draw-weight of the bow was taken. The animal stared straight at the hunter, poised for flight, but it was too late. The arrow sang, there was a blur of light, a flash as the sun caught the flight of the missile, and then the doe was gone, collapsing sideways as the arrow thudded home behind the shoulder.

The hunter was aware that it was virtually impossible to kill cleanly with one flight. The thrashing of the animal in the undergrowth was noisy, mixed with a coughing sound as the doe spat streams of blood and kicked, trying to rise against the missile that had half paralysed her.

She was still kicking when the hunter finally stood above her, staring down dispassionately. The first arrow had broken a rib, sliced through the lung, lodged in the spleen. The doe was still quivering after the second arrow slashed through the belly and pierced the liver, but the eyes were glazing coldly.

The hunter was breathing lightly, but quickly, as though

excited by the thrashing and the blood. But like the animal just killed, the hunter's senses were also keen, sharpened to the environment and the intimation of danger.

There was someone nearby.

Bowhunting in England was an illegal activity. Local magistrates could be hard on offenders, particularly up here in the Cheviots. The hunter remained still for several seconds, then moved smoothly and quietly through the ferns beneath the trees to a vantage-point, screened by pines, above the road.

The man standing on the track below seemed to have emerged from nowhere. He was stockily built and wore a tweed jacket with patched elbows, hands thrust in his pockets. He had taken off his hat, and the early evening sun gleamed on the scalp that showed through his thinning hair. He was standing, feet braced apart, staring up the slope directly towards the spot where the deer had died, moments ago.

The hunter glanced around carefully. The man below was alone. It was likely he had come down from the farm on the hill, or had walked up along the burn, below the fold of the ridge where he would have been invisible to anyone in the trees, until he reached the track where he now stood, glaring suspiciously in the direction of the hunter.

The man hesitated, half turned to walk away along the track and then stopped again, swinging his head to scan the treeline. His face was tanned, his eyebrows heavy and black, a contrast to his thinning hair, and the hunter recognized him, knew him.

He was a man who deserved to die.

It would be a long shot, but not a difficult one. The man standing on the track would never know what had hit him. That would be a pity . . . and it would be a pity he would never know who had released the arrow in his direction.

With studied care the hunter in the trees slid an arrow out of the quiver. The broadhead was fine-edged under a questing thumb: it would be capable, at this distance, of punching a hole four inches square in the target on the roadway.

The hunter nocked the arrow, raised the bow and the first pull raised the sophisticated sights with their calibrated tracks until the hunter could pick out the lapels of the tweed jacket. The sights moved fractionally; the centre of the man's chest was targeted and the cables and aluminium cams began to take the strain as the hunter drew smoothly, left arm rigid against the cable guard, gloved right hand holding the tense bowstring.

An expelling of breath, a light, long drawing in of air, a holding, a savouring of the moment before the deadly broadhead would skim through the air on its lethal mission . . .

A coughing sound broke the silence of the hillside, a rumbling noise, an approaching car from the right where the road swung around past the screening trees. The hunter froze, instinct calling for a release of the bowstring, inclination urging the destruction of the man in the roadway, but an innate caution holding back the action, calling for control. If the car came around the bend, and the man was lying stricken in the roadway . . .

It was a small Ford, silver-grey in colour, and it came rumbling around the hill, slowing as the driver caught sight of the man in the roadway. The hunter could make out the driver as a woman, and it was obvious the opportunity was gone unless two people were to die on the evening hillside. The gloved hand lost some of its tension; as the hunter breathed out again the cables smoothly took up the relaxing strain and the aluminium speed cams whirred silently to rest.

The car had slowed, was stopping, and the woman behind the wheel was leaning out to call to the man in the roadway. The words were indistinguishable, but clearly the driver had come out to meet the man in the roadway, bring him back from his evening walk. After a short discussion the man, somewhat bad-temperedly, got into the car. The woman found it difficult to reverse the vehicle and a stream of blue exhaust stained the air before she managed to swing the car around on the narrow track and head it back the way she had come.

The hunter was silent on the hill, shadowed completely by the trees, watching, with an ache of disappointment. The crags that rose to Cheviot were purpling now, and the sky above was darkening from its pale blue to a deeper hue. From the distant farm there was the sound of a dog barking, and as the car vanished around the bend the sound of its engine rapidly faded.

A soft silence returned to the hill. There was no movement from the doe now, but her death seemed to have affected the woods. There was no birdsong, no movement in the undergrowth, and the Cheviot itself seemed stricken, waiting for danger to pass and death to reach out to nothing else on the hill.

The hunter replaced the arrow in the quiver. There were two more arrows to recover from the still warm, quivering body of the deer. They would be cleaned in the grass as darkness gathered under the trees, and then the body of the dead beast would have to be dragged down the hill to the car hidden in the dry gully some three hundred yards away. The exercise was not to be relished: it was an anti-climax after the smooth, quiet efficiency of the stalking and the kill.

Therein lay the excitement: the long waiting when nothing seemed about to happen; the quick heartbeat at the first signs, the first sounds of movement in the undergrowth; then the stalking, silent under the trees until the pent-up, heart-stopping tension in those seconds before the arrow exploded into flight.

That moment was almost orgasmic. Now, there remained only a vague irritation at the thought of hauling the carcase down to the car.

But this day there had been that other moment to savour, a moment that could be weighed and enjoyed for its tension, its bunching of hate and muscle, commitment and excitement. The bowsight had been concentrated on the centre of the target's chest and the hunter could still envision the blood-soaked image that had been relayed: a hole punched in a man's chest, life blood pulsing out to stain the ground as sightless eyes stared skywards.

Not the eyes of a doe; the eyes of a man.

The hunter stared down the empty road. It had been close. Seconds . . . a second, and the act would have been done. If the woman in the silver-grey Ford had not appeared to call away her employer it would have happened, it would have been done. As it *needed* to be done. The man down there deserved to die.

The hunter smiled reflectively.

He deserved to die, and it could be done. But this would not necessarily be the only opportunity.

There would be another time: perhaps soon.

But now, there was the deer. The hunter moved, to retrieve the arrows, and then stopped, hair rising at the nape of the neck. Some thirty yards away, crouched against a tussock of grass, was a dog. It was lean, alert and watchful, its body tensed as though ready to spring and the hunter stared at it as the low rumbling came from the animal's throat.

The adrenalin began to pump again in the hunter's veins. Thirty yards: swift mental calculations, and the dog crouched lower, belly against the ground, its sheepdog frame quivering as it bared its teeth at the smell of blood, and the threat it sensed as the hunter's tension was communicated to it. Its eyes glistened as the hunter's hand moved slowly towards the quiver, and it heard the smooth hiss of the arrow sliding from its home.

The hunter moved slowly, precisely, eyes fixed on those of the dog, hands and arms moving gently, engaging the nock, raising the bow until the arrowhead rose, its needle point lining up with the black and white shoulder of the dog. The animal rose slightly, the rumbling threatening in its throat and the hunter breathed in, gently, waiting for the moment.

The twig cracked loudly, snapping like a dry bone in the silence of the woods. The arrowhead dropped, wavering as the hunter glanced around, quickly and nervously. When the rustling came from among the trees it was followed by movement, a dark frame thrusting its way through the undergrowth behind the dog.

The hunter lowered the bow as the tall man came walking down the hillside, snapping his fingers to the dog. It responded, hackles lowering immediately, even though it kept its eyes fixed on the threat of the longbow.

The man was lean. He moved with a long, patient stride that showed he walked these hills regularly, and his tanned skin made it obvious that he spent much time in the open. His dark jacket was elderly and patched at cuffs and elbows and his battered hat was pulled low across his forehead, pinning the thick grey hair into place.

He reached the dog and stood there for several seconds, staring at the hunter with the lowered bow. He creased his eyes, and his glance was sharp, weighing up the situation, aware of the tension, and something angry danced in those eyes as he stared at the hunter, anger and disgust mixed in a shadow of dislike.

Then the glance slipped away, almost inadvertently, to take in the silent road below, before returning to the dog, and the bow, and the hunter. It was then that the hunter knew that this man had seen all that had occurred—the death of the deer, the arrival of the man in the road below, the moment when that arrow had almost been loosened. There was one, slow moment when fear prickled against the hunter's skin, and then it was gone.

The man with the dog had his own reasons to hate. If the

arrow *had* exploded towards its mark he might even have melted away over the hill. He would have his own reasons to want the man in the roadway dead, and he would not interfere with the hunter now.

The dog rose, to nuzzle against the owner's leg. The hunter moved too, sneeringly, replacing the arrow in the quiver, moving to pick up the other shafts.

When they had been cleaned in the long grass the hunter looked up. The man with the dog had gone.

2

In the courtyard in front of the Newcastle University History Faculty building two young students sat with their backs to the wall and their arms around each other. As he walked past them Arnold Landon felt vaguely uneasy. At moments like this he definitely felt his age. It was not that he objected to public expression of affection by the young; far from it. He considered the irreverence young people always showed for their elders was a healthy sign, a signal that they would not accept the *mores* of a previous generation as gospel. At the same time he felt uneasy, for he was not exactly sure what the sex of either of the two lovers on the lawn might be. The permutations were, admittedly, limited in their possibilities, but some of them left him uneasy. And feeling his age.

He entered the wide doors, admiring the entrance hall, and approached the desk behind which the porter, corpulent in a slightly shabby uniform, sat reading a tabloid newspaper.

'Excuse me. I'd like to see Professor Evesham.'

'He expecting you, sir?'

'At ten.'

The porter inspected the clock on the wall behind him. It was just two minutes before the hour. He seemed pleased with such punctuality and smiled vaguely at Arnold, put down his newspaper and reached for the telephone.

As he called Professor Evesham's office Arnold looked about him. He had not entered these buildings before. The hallway had some interesting features. The archway leading to the offices on the right was built of stone of a light creamy-yellow colour. Clipsham stone, he guessed, although it might have been part of an old consignment of Caen stone that had found its way northward in the vogue for using such stone that had occurred in the 'thirties, when much of the present university building had taken place. Odd, that; a thirteenth-century fad for Caen stone being repeated in the nineteen-thirties. Not least when there was perfectly good local stone that looked much the same available from Beer or Clipsham.

'Mr Landon?' The porter dragged Arnold back to the present. 'Professor Evesham is able to see you in his room. It's straight up the stairs, around to the right through the swing doors, and third on the left.'

Arnold followed the directions given. He found himself in a narrow corridor, facing a half-open door labelled with a dog-eared card bearing the legend *Alan Evesham*. Arnold tapped on the door and it swung wide quickly, as though the occupant had been waiting behind it.

'Landon? Good. I'll be back in a minute.'

The man was gone before Arnold could reply. Arnold hesitated, then entered the room. It was a complete clutter. The table below the mullioned window was scattered with papers, some of a certain antiquity. Arnold wondered for their safety as a light breeze rustled through the open window, lifting them.

A cigarette smouldered in the ashtray and Arnold stubbed it out, self-consciously, fearing for the papers. He looked around: leaning against the wall was a mediæval pike; on the floor behind the desk was a fourteenth-century crossbow with a butt inlaid with chased metal. The waste-paper bin had been used as a makeshift quiver, ugly-looking bolts stuffed into it.

One wall was dominated by an ornately scrolled oak bookcase. As Arnold admired the workmanship he noted that Evesham's interests seemed warlike: the bookcase was packed with volumes ranging from Second World War tactics to an account of Agincourt, with French military manœuvres, Crimean histories and the Mexican war of the 1840s thrown in for good measure.

'Military history.'

Professor Alan Evesham was closing the door behind him with his left foot. He held his arms out stiffly, carrying two cups of coffee. One of the paper cups was already stained by a dribble of spilled liquid. Arnold nodded towards the books.

'Quite a collection. Your hobby, or simply what you teach at the university?'

'Hobby, work, passion,' Alan Evesham replied and slipped past Arnold through the clutter of the room. He kicked aside a dull-metalled breastplate and swore under his breath. Arnold waited.

Evesham put down a paper cup on his desk, finding the only free corner, handed the other to Arnold, wiped his right hand on the seat of his jeans and then stuck it out in welcome. 'Alan Evesham.'

'I'm pleased to meet you,' Arnold said warily.

Alan Evesham was not the kind of man he had expected to meet. When he had received a phone call from the university, with a request that he find time to call in to see a history professor, he had had a mental image of grey, middle-aged sobriety. But Alan Evesham was hardly more than thirty years old, with a shock of sandy hair, and narrow, bad-tempered eyes that would swing in expression from glittering enthusiasm, Arnold guessed, to virulent annoyance. The mouth too was the kind that would express impatience in a man who would be given to hasty judgements and eternal dislikes. Few students would like him, perhaps, though his professorial post suggested that the university authorities respected him for his knowledge and ability.

'I've heard about you,' Evesham said sharply, and tugged at the hairy sweater he affected as though he disliked hearing about anyone other than himself. 'You're reckoned to be quite an authority in certain fields.'

'I wouldn't put it quite like that.'

Evesham slumped in the chair behind his desk. After a moment Arnold took the seat facing him, noting that Evesham had made no pretence to politeness.

'Gifted amateur, then, is that it?'

There was a thinly veiled belligerence in his tone that was not unfamiliar to Arnold. He was used to meeting a certain resistance whenever he was called upon for consultation with the academic world. His reputation of recent years had grown because of his love for wood and stone—and the understanding of the past that had grown out of this obsession. There had been occasions when he had confounded the experts: this had endeared him neither to the Establishment nor to his own Senior Planning Officer, who regarded such activity as vaguely open to suspicion.

'I'm not sure I care to classify myself in any way,' Arnold responded mildly. 'I'm a planning officer, employed by Northumberland—'

'But you claim to know a lot about mediæval times.'

'Claim, no—'

'Professor Agnew suggested I should enlist your help.'

So that was it. Arnold stared soberly at Alan Evesham. The man had not shaved that morning and there was a fine ginger stubble of beard on his chin. He cared little for appearances, that was certain; what he did care about was being told by a respected senior professor in the university that he might usefully turn for help and advice to a humble planning officer with no academic background.

'Professor Agnew has probably over-estimated my abilities.'

'Quite likely. But Professor Agnew is responsible for the allocation of certain grants . . .' Evesham glowered, then reached for his paper cup and sipped his coffee. 'You've seen the books on my shelves. You'll have realized I'm a military historian. At present I'm conducting an inquiry into the Middle Ages. Twelfth century, in fact.'

'Interesting.'

'Very. Agnew reckons I could consult you with advantage.'

'About military history? I'm afraid that's not quite—'

'Not your scene?' Evesham's brow furrowed impatiently. 'So what *is* your . . . field?'

Arnold hesitated. 'I'm not sure I'd claim one. I have a certain . . . knowledge about the use of stone in the Middle Ages, and I have been successful in dating various structures from the joints used in the timber—'

'So what do you know about master masons in the twelfth century?'

Arnold blinked. 'It depends what you want to know. I mean, it's common enough knowledge that stone buildings in the Middle Ages were erected by professional workmen. There is a large number of accounts which demonstrate that the work they undertook was under the control of a chief, or master, mason. The actual mason in charge might change from time to time, naturally, during the course of the work—'

'Do you know the names of any of these master masons?' Evesham interrupted.

'Well, a large proportion of these chief masons have left their names only in single building accounts. On the other hand, some of them can be traced in a succession of jobs in different parts of the country—'

'Ahhh.'

'I beg your pardon?'

Evesham shook his head impatiently, but his eyes were

less hostile than previously, and there was an edge of surprised satisfaction to his mouth. 'Go on.'

Deliberately, Arnold took a sip of his coffee. It was weak and milky and he disliked the taste of it. He also resented the fact that he seemed to be in a situation where he was being called upon to prove something to Professor Alan Evesham.

'I'm not sure how you want me to go on, or why. If you want to know about the old master masons, well, some of them obtained official positions, of course.'

'Would you regard them as architects?'

Arnold shrugged. 'Not exactly, not in the modern sense. But they were responsible for the design and details of the buildings upon which they worked—'

'And so should be regarded as the architects of the Middle Ages, surely,' Evesham said testily.

'If you say so.'

'And the *ingeniatores*?'

Arnold raised his eyebrows.

'The *engineers*,' Evesham sneered.

'I was aware—'

'One such engineer was employed by Bishop Hugh Pudsey at Norham Castle. He described him as *vir artificiosus . . . et prudens architectus*.' Evesham smiled. 'The good bishop thought of the engineer in question as a prudent *architect*.'

'But he was talking about Ailnoth,' Arnold said quietly.

He had been unable to resist the temptation and the reaction was satisfying. Evesham's head came up and his mouth dropped open. He put down his paper cup, and his hand strayed to his mouth as though to rearrange his surprise. His mean little eyes had widened too, and respect was creeping into them together with astonishment. '*Ailnoth!* How do *you* know about him?'

'You don't have to have a university pedigree to be interested in and read about architecture,' Arnold remonstrated mildly. Now he had made his point he could afford to be generous. 'I have read . . . a little about the builders in the Middle Ages. While I work from a knowledge and an understanding of wood and stone I've also found it necessary to read . . . the experts.'

Evesham frowned, as though he was not quite sure if he was being mocked. He shook his head. 'All right, so you've heard about Ailnoth. What do you know about him?'

Arnold took a deep breath, nettled again by Evesham's manner. 'Well, I suppose I know a fair bit about him, really. In 1157, I know, he was surveyor of the King's buildings at Westminster—'

'—and the Tower.'

'He was paid the not insubstantial sum of seven pence per day—'

'—an annual salary of £10. 12s. 11d.'

'He supervised the purchase of stone and lead for work at Windsor Castle—'

'—between 1167 and 1173—'

'And after the rebellion of 1174 he was in charge of the dismantling of Framlingham and Walton Castles.'

Evesham sniffed. 'He also supervised work at Westminster Abbey when the *frater* had been burnt.'

'I didn't think this was going to be set as an examination, Professor Evesham, nor as a competition. I don't see what either of us is getting out of this conversation.' Arnold hesitated. 'Professor Agnew suggested we talk. You seem to be satisfying yourself as to my . . . credentials. I don't really have any. And I certainly don't see how I can help you in any way, as far as military history is concerned.'

Evesham bit his lip in thought. Several seconds passed in silence before he nodded, forcing out the words. 'I'm sorry.'

Arnold shrugged. 'That's all right.'

Evesham eyed him silently for a little while. 'You seem,' he said reluctantly, 'to know about master masons . . . and more importantly, about Ailnoth. But you've missed one obvious fact.'

'What's that?'

'How most of them really spent their time.'

'I don't understand,' Arnold said slowly.

Evesham glanced at the papers on his desk, and scratched his nose thoughtfully. 'The mediæval age was a great church and cathedral building time. But it was notable for something else as well. It was a time of war.'

'So?'

'My interest isn't in church building or the erection of cathedrals. So why am I interested in what you know about masons? The truth is, masons in those days didn't spend most of their time on religious buildings. Think about it: Wulfric at Carlisle in 1172, Maurice at Newcastle in 1174, Richard at Bowes and Walton—they weren't concerned with churches. They were building *castles*.'

'I understand that.'

'But what you don't seem to have grasped, Landon, is that military works were the *primary* concern of these architects, these engineers. They were mainly concerned with military engines, with mangonels, catapults, trebuchets and so on. It was their job to design the defences which would allow them to use the artillery they possessed themselves and resist the weapons brought up by the besiegers. Look at the records again: when the existing west wall of the lower bailey of Windsor Castle was built with its three towers in 1228, the *master trebucheter* was one of the two persons appointed to supervise the work.'

'It's a point of view—and a fact—that had not come to my attention,' Arnold said slowly.

'Hmmm.' Alan Evesham was silent again for a little while. 'I suppose I have to credit Professor Agnew with more sense than I have done,' he said grumpily. 'Just as you won't have appreciated the significance of military history in ancient building operations, so my obsession with military history hasn't left me with time or inclination to look at the purely *building* implications surrounding the facts I seek. And that's why it occurred to Agnew to throw the two of us together.'

Arnold hesitated. 'I can understand the logic of Professor Agnew's suggestion, even if I feel I probably have little to offer. But what's the purpose of the . . . collaboration?'

The word collaboration drew dark colours of protest in Evesham's eyes; he quelled them as he came to terms with the fact that even this discussion was a collaboration, in a sense. He shrugged unwillingly. 'I mentioned earlier that Agnew is in charge of certain research allocations in the Faculty. I've been working on a theory for some years, and I believe I've got conclusions which are valid, but which require proof, a certain verification, before I can publish. I think Agnew is quite keen for me to publish . . . but he insists that money is short. Bloody cuts . . .' he added gloomily.

'But where do I come in?'

'I went to Agnew when I learned he was going to phase out the research support grant. I explained, and I *know* he's interested, but . . . well, to cut a long story short, he said he didn't have the money to support the research. I'd have to take short cuts. One of them, he suggested, would be to pass up the opportunity to undertake my own research. Instead, I should use skills and knowledge already available to us in the North. You.'

'Me?'

'You,' Evesham repeated, scowling. 'It's question of a marriage of minds. You might bring a certain objective understanding to the situation, to supplement what I've learned and what I believe to be the truth.'

'It's very flattering—'

'No doubt,' Evesham said brusquely. 'But time is short. We have a couple of weeks only, before I'm committed to a Scandinavian conference. I have to pick your brains at speed.'

'I see. At least,' Arnold added cautiously, 'I *think* I see. You questioned me about chief masons—'

'But specifically I'm interested in Ailnoth.'

'Ahh.'

'How much more do you know about him?'

Arnold shook his head. 'Not a great deal. I've only really come across his work in Framlingham and seen some of his building accounts. I was . . . er . . . boasting a little, really.'

'A shot in the dark, is it?' Evesham said gloomily. 'Well, no matter. I've been able to trace the movements of Ailnoth the *ingeniator*. He certainly got around a bit.'

'It was a common experience for masons,' Arnold suggested. 'Prominent masters of the craft were often employed at various locations in the country as consultants, and sometimes as architects to supply the design from which the work was carried out.'

'It certainly happened with our friend Ailnoth,' Evesham agreed. 'He was sent with one Martin Simon, a carpenter, to view the site for a new castle the King wanted to build in York and within two months he was back at Westminster, having taken in on the way a job at Beverley.'

'In my own observations I've been able to trace work which was started by a mason from Exeter being completed by one from Stafford,' Arnold interrupted. 'And the work itself is in Durham.'

'Quite,' Evesham said rather crossly. 'The point is, I've managed to trace Ailnoth's career fairly clearly until about 1181. There's a hint he might have been involved at Dover Castle in 1181–2, but it's not absolutely clear, and after that date he seems to have dropped out of sight completely. At least, that's what scholarship would have you believe.'

'You've found evidence to the contrary?'

Evesham leaned forward in his chair, pushed aside the half-empty paper cup and began to rummage in his papers. 'Yes, here's my note. There's a couple of documents I rooted out in Canterbury; they lead me to believe there was some sort of scandal. Maybe corrupt practices of some kind.'

'That was not particularly uncommon.'

'I believe it. Things haven't changed. Anyway, I came across this document. It's the evidence of the Master of Works:

> There was removal of timber, stone and lime. I know not where it went. The roofing of the church and the stone-work suffer injury through lack of care. The outer pilasters which are also called botraces have for the most part perished for defect of covering . . .

The thing is, the works in question were under the control of Ailnoth. And I think he was disgraced by the inquiry that went on. But he didn't just drop out of sight.'

'What did he do?' asked Arnold curiously.

'The next best thing. Turned his hand to other aspects of the trade. More lowly, but still remunerative. I think he started doing repairs—maybe the ones at Baynard's Castle in 1183. He became a supplier of plaster, stones and tiles.'

'You've got evidence for this?'

'Sketchy,' Evesham admitted.

'So where do I come in?'

Evesham hesitated. 'I'm really only interested in Ailnoth as a military *ingeniator*. I've been studying military installations in the North, dating back to the twelfth century. And I have a feeling . . . a gut reaction, if you like. I think Ailnoth came north after his disgrace. I think he worked as a supplier of materials, but from time to time, when requested, he threw in his abilities as a mason and an *ingeniator* as part of the deal he struck. I'm sure I can trace the movements of a man called Ailnoth in the North after 1182 —as a *supplier*. But was it the same Ailnoth?'

'You want *me* to try to find out?'

'Agnew says you've got an eye. No academic background, but an eye. And luck.'

Arnold wasn't sure whether he should feel pleased or

slighted. 'I don't even know what you want me to look for.'

'You've heard of the disputes regarding Langton Castle?'

Arnold had been vaguely aware of academic discussions regarding the ruined castle north of Morpeth; they had been reported skimpily in the popular press. 'It's the ruins near Langton village in Northumberland. A thirteenth-century castle which was laid waste by the border raiders in the fifteenth century and was never rebuilt.'

'Thirteenth century, but with some walls possibly dating to the tenth.'

'In the tenth century buildings were made of timber.'

'But some stone.'

'Occasionally.'

'And maybe at Langton.'

'It's possible. But what do you want me to do? Inspect Langton Castle? I don't think I can do much—'

'I've already inspected it. As a military historian. I'd like you to look, from a building point of view. But first, I'd like you to meet me at the village itself. Or more precisely, at its church.'

'Why?'

'To show you what I think is the last resting-place of Ailnoth the *ingeniator*.'

As far as Arnold could make out it was a pretty thin thesis—and one not particularly important anyway. Alan Evesham was obsessed with the idea that the military architect he saw in Ailnoth had returned to the North after his work on the great castles, and in relative obscurity had continued his work, exercising his skills in Northumberland. But he had to admit he had no hard evidence of the work, although he was told by the vicar of the tiny church at Langton that the parish records contained some reference to the supplier of plaster and stone that Evesham sought. That the military historian was urgent in his need to discover the evidence to support the thesis was clear to Arnold: the

Professor would never have turned to a 'gifted amateur' in other circumstances. But Arnold still doubted whether he truly had anything to offer.

The Senior Planning Officer was of like opinion.

Not that he was prepared to say so directly to Arnold. His predecessor had left the planning department under a cloud, and the new Senior Planning Officer seemed to feel that he had a cautious path to tread, one mined by subordinates who were disloyal, incompetent and unreliable. His solution to the problem had been to interview each of them in turn upon his arrival, make snap judgements, and then retire into the safety of his office, emerging rarely, and issuing instructions from time to time. They were usually succinct, to avoid misunderstanding, and precise to avoid responsibility.

Arnold had had his interview with the new Senior Planning Officer and he had been left in no doubt that his interests were regarded as bizarre and his experiences unsettling. He was to keep his personal activities clearly separate from his work for the department.

He had had his interview, and now he received his instructions.

'Report to Mr Sanders. University activity only in spare time. Relieve Mr Sanders of Kilgour House file.'

It did not take Arnold long to realize the quandary the Senior Planning Officer had found himself in: he would have been inclined in the first instance to turn down the request from Professor Agnew that Arnold be consulted by Alan Evesham. But that immediate reaction would have been tempered by a more considered reflection. There were other matters to take into account: the fact that Professor Agnew's brother was a councillor; the Professor's reputation and the consultancy work he undertook for the Morpeth Trust; the public image of the Planning Department after the little-lamented departure of the previous Senior Planning Officer. So, the decision had been hedged. Arnold should be allowed a token activity—time off to meet Professor Evesham, but after that, work only in his own time, on whatever project Evesham was committed to. And try to bog Arnold down with work, so he would have neither opportunity nor inclination to spend much time digging away in the ruins of Northumberland's past.

'I thought you already had a pretty fair case-load,' George Sanders said. He was nicknamed 'Hollywood', but had no resemblance to the old actor whose name he bore. He was a balding individual of some thirty years of age, inclined towards gloom, and addicted to pinball machines which he attacked with ferocious concentration each evening in a local public house. He sat in his office now, scowling at the manila folder on the desk in front of him.

'I'd have said hefty, rather than fair,' Arnold suggested.

'Old Iron-Knickers trying to tie you down, I guess. He's come into this department like a breath of hydrogen sulphide.'

Arnold had no idea what hydrogen sulphide might be, but he could guess at the sentiment behind the remark. 'Is this the file on Kilgour Estates?'

'It is,' Sanders fingered the curling edge of the folder gloomily. 'Wouldn't have minded a few trips up into that area myself.'

'It'll require a visit?'

'More than that. A few, more's likely. You've got a purler here, Arnold, a real purler.'

'In what way?'

Sanders grimaced, displaying stained, tobacco-abused teeth. 'Like I said, I wouldn't have minded the trips out, but I was in no way keen to start. On the face of it, the application's more or less straightforward . . .'

'But . . . ?'

'There are problems.' Sanders sniffed noisily. 'To start with, there are several letters in the file. There's people up there who aren't too happy about Patrick Yates.'

'Is he the applicant?'

'That's right. The owner of Kilgour Estates. Local magistrate, all that jazz, behaves like a country squire, you know what I mean. Hasn't gone down too well with some people . . . and with others, well they claim he's acted in a fashion you can argue is cavalier. I followed up one of the letter-writers . . .'

'Have you put a note on the file?'

Sanders wriggled dolefully. 'No, I didn't. The conversation became kind of . . . personal. I think, now you're taking the file, maybe you ought to see these people. There's certainly something weird about the whole thing.'

'Weird?'

'That's right. Maybe it's just me, but I get the impression that this guy Yates creates reactions in people that become a bit out of hand. I mean, from one source you hear he's got such a reputation for carnal pleasures that it won't be long before he needs to get fitted for plastic kneecaps; but someone else will tell you he's a raging queer.'

'And this is relevant to the planning application?' Arnold asked in wonderment.

'It is in so far as it tells you something about this character's personality and the effect he can have upon people. The whole business is a can of worms and better you in than me.'

'What worms have you teased out so far?'

'A fat one. A lawsuit.'

'Oh dear.'

'Right.' Sanders clucked his tongue thoughtfully. 'One of the things exercising me was how I was to deal with a planning application from Yates when there was a lawsuit pending about his ownership of Kilgour Estates.'

'His ownership is in question?'

'He's got the deeds. But there's some guy who claims he's the rightful heir to Kilgour who's screaming about undue influence and wants the will that left Kilgour to Yates set aside.'

'How long has Yates held the property, then? Is this a recent development?'

Sanders gtrunted, and pushed the file across the desk towards Arnold. 'He's been living on the property for about twenty years, and has owned it—if that's the right word— for about three years. The claimant—he's called Bob Francis—also lives in the area now, but he emerged from the bush somewhere about eighteen months ago. A writer. Been out of touch, he says. And comes home to expectations and no realities. So he's trying the courts.'

Arnold picked up the file and weighed it thoughtfully in his left hand. 'How far has the lawsuit proceeded?'

'I think you're going to be lucky. My worries were to some extent unfounded. Chances are there'll be a decision within the next few weeks. This guy Francis, he had no money and it was going to be difficult to get legal aid. As far as I understand it, Francis would have had to take it to a judge in chambers who would pronounce on the likelihood of success. If the judge thought it was remote, Francis's case would have been thrown out. Poor Bob would then have had to slink back to his romantic hovel on the fell.'

'So what happened?'

'Ah, well, rather interesting. Suddenly poor Bob had money. Not quite certain where it came from. A mysterious benefactor. There's a village whisper that his wife is . . . shall we say . . . somewhat disenchanted and not willing to shell out any more of her own money to support his legal tantrums. But he's come up with the readies, even so, though exactly who the guardian angel might be . . . well, it's just rumour. Anyway, it all comes around to the fact that there *will* be a court hearing, full panoply of the law and all that jazz.'

Arnold frowned doubtfully. 'Do you think Francis has a case?'

'How the hell can *I* say?' Hollywood Sanders shook his head. 'I'm no lawyer. What I can say is I'm glad to get rid of the thing. Believe me, the whole business has something . . . *sniffy* about it, you know what I mean? So as far as I'm concerned, it's goodbye Charlie and good night.'

Which was little satisfaction to Arnold since he was left holding the file and the responsibilities that went with it.

3

It may well have been because of Sanders's concern about the 'sniffiness' of the Kilgour Estates business that Arnold seemed to find little time to start looking into the file. Sanders had injected a certain reluctance into Arnold as a result of his comments. Apart from that, however, while Arnold might normally have been tempted to take a quick look at the file over the first weekend—for he had rather too much on his desk for comfort at the moment—he also had Professor Evesham to think about. If he was to offer any serious assistance to the historian it would be as well if he placed his knowledge of Ailnoth the engineer on a sound footing.

Accordingly, Arnold visited the libraries in Durham and Newcastle Universities. He read all he could on the mediæval masons and engineers. In Newcastle he managed to read—or at least, skim through—two of Evesham's own books on military history. At Durham he spent a few hours in the library at Castle Green and then afterwards mused upon mediæval building as he strolled alongside the river under the towering crag on which the university and castle stood.

It was buildings such as these that Ailnoth had built, in his peculiar pattern of endeavour: places of learning, locations for prayer, and symbols of strength, and power, and war.

But he had learned little new about Ailnoth: there was

certainly no published link drawn between the engineer and the building supplier in the north of England.

He tried to get through his backlog of work in the early part of the following week. It was Thursday before he found time to pick up the Kilgour file. It was soon apparent that Sanders was right: there were several letters in the file that raised protestations which had little to do with the planning application itself. Rather, they were concerned with issues Arnold regarded as peripheral. There were letters regarding the state of the tenant farms, and in particular there was one very abusive, occasionally obscene, and excessively bitter missive from a man called Enwright.

There was also one from the claimant to Kilgour Estates. The filed letter from Robert Francis was more moderate in tone. It was carefully typed, and merely stated that since he had an interest in the estate through the lawsuit against Patrick Yates he contended no application for development at Kilgour should be contemplated by the planning authority. There was a long, rambling letter from someone called Winfield, detailing real or imagined grievances against the 'squire', but seemingly confusing the present owner Yates with the previous owner, Colonel Edridge. And there was the anonymous letter.

After Arnold read it he had doubts whether it should have been placed upon the file at all. It was scurrilous and in parts obscene. It was partly written, in a hand obviously disguised, and partly made up of printed words cut from magazines and newspapers. The accusations it contained ranged from under-age defloration to bestiality. The writer clearly did not like Patrick Yates.

It was not clear whether the writer disapproved of the planning application.

There was a map attached to the filed application, Kilgour House lay north of Morpeth, in the Cheviots. It comprised some three and a half thousand acres. The sun was shining in Morpeth and Arnold decided it was time he went out to inspect the ground, and discuss the application with Mr Yates if that was possible.

The phone rang, unanswered. Arnold decided to drive out to Kilgour anyway, without an appointment fixed.

He left the car park at ten in the morning and took the A1 north, branching off after a few miles to plunge into the heart of the Northumbrian countryside. The route he took led him towards the towering mass of Cheviot, while to his right, as he crested rising foothills, he caught blue flashes of the seascape towards Bamburgh, distant pele towers crowning nearby crests, and a faint tang of salt in the wind from the coast.

For the next half-hour he drove through countryside familiar enough to him. There were the developed villages of thatched and stone-roofed cottages bordered by trim gardens hedged with box, still within commuting distance of Morpeth and Newcastle. Thereafter the hills loomed up ahead of him, the road twisted and turned back on itself and only when he breasted the next rise and saw the rich farmlands spread out along the lower slopes of Cheviot did the changes begin.

He had consulted the map and undertaken the detour from roads he knew well. The road dropped and a valley opened out ahead, dominated by a ridge outlined starkly against the backdrop of Northumberland hills crowned with fir and aspen and echoing to the cackling of black grouse. A stream ran through the valley, and the road followed its meandering; rich fields spread either side of the road for some two miles but then Arnold passed a dilapidated sign that seemed out of place. It bore the legend ASH FARM, but the chain supporting it was broken and it hung at an angle. The track diverting from the main road seemed overgrown and ill cared for. Half a mile further on he passed two cottages: trees grew against the base of the first and its crumbling walls seemed supported only by the strangling ivy that overran it.

MEN OF SUBTLE CRAFT

The second cottage had been badly roofed with corrugated iron, rusted and flapping, and its wooden front door gaped on rusted hinges, windows broken under the eaves above.

Arnold drove on, puzzled. The valley seemed prosperous enough, the land rich and capable of effective cultivation. He had caught a few glimpses of livestock, and there had been a tractor at work beyond the trees, yet as he drove further into the valley the signs of dilapidation and decay seemed to increase. He recalled the letter written by the man called Enwright: it had been abusive and Arnold had skimmed quickly through it for that reason. But the letter had been right about one thing: it had referred to the bad husbandry of the owner of Kilgour House, ascribing certain motivations to it, and while that was something Arnold could as yet have no views about, one thing was certainly clear: Enwright's remarks had some ring of truth. The tenant farms seemed run down, decayed and abandoned.

It was an odd way for a prosperous estate with rich farming lands to be managed.

The village itself was tiny: a collection of ironstone cottages and a public house that looked large enough to serve the needs only of the village itself. There was an air of rural contentment about the place as it slumbered in the morning sunshine and the road that swung left, signposted KILGOUR HOUSE, was well metalled and the hedges were neatly shorn.

A half-mile on Arnold caught his first glimpse of the house itself. It lay at the foot of a steep bank crowned with larch and alder. The main building, built of warm brown and yellow sandstone, quarried in the West Midlands, testified to a Victorian builder who had wanted something different from the tough gritstones of the northern hills for his home. The main entrance was fronted with imposing steps and colonnades, a trifle flamboyant for Arnold's taste, but architecturally in keeping with the style and taste of the period in which it had been constructed. The west wing of Kilgour

House was recessed, fronted by an ornamental garden which curved pleasingly towards an old carriage drive that must have been the main access point to the house a hundred years ago. At the end of the drive was an imposing set of wrought-iron gates, and beyond those the archway of Jacobean stables in a fine state of preservation.

The green lawns in front of the main house were bright and trim and the gardens were ablaze with colour. The stream cut through the trees on the right and fell into a natural basin fronting the house. A short distance away, overshadowed by an ancient oak whose mighty branches were supported by timber buttresses, there was an ornamental pool, half covered with lilies. The house was in no need of renovation: whatever decisions might have been taken with regard to the tenant farms further up the valley, they had had no application here. Kilgour House was in no need of repair: it had been well maintained, and sensitively repaired. Arnold's eye was keen but he could detect no unwise short cuts in the manner in which facings had been repaired, and no lack of vision in the way the entrance had been renovated.

Overall, Arnold approved.

He drove up to the house, swung towards the driveway and parked near the great oak in a spot he guessed would cause no obstruction. The sun was warm on his back as he walked up the steps to the main entrance, and on the grey slate roof of Kilgour House a blackbird sang a full-throated song.

The entrance was imposing, the bell a replica of an older Victorian iron version. The sound echoed inside and there was a short wait before the door was opened and a woman looked out.

She was in her mid-forties. Her hair was drawn back severely from her handsome features and lightly dusted with grey. Her eyes were of a startling blue, intense in colour and perception: the glance flicked over him and became dismissive. Arnold was not unused to making such early impressions. She stepped forward and the sunlight caught her skin: she was pale, as though she avoided the sun so that best advantage was gained of the blue tracery of veins under her skin. But such delicacy of impression was not echoed in her mouth: it held a marked determination, a conviction about what was right and wrong in her world. She was a handsome woman, and would have been a beautiful one but for the element of ruthlessness in her make-up which would always have deterred some men.

She frightened Arnold.

'Good morning,' he managed. 'My name's Landon. Is Mr Yates at home?'

'What is it you want with him?' The tone was cool, not impolite, but controlling events.

'I work for the planning authority. I thought it was time I came out to see him about it, and carry out a first inspection. I did phone in advance, but there was no answer.'

'No.' She considered Arnold, and the problem, her eyebrows drawing together delicately in a little frown of annoyance. She glanced around towards his car, and then nodded slowly, before stepping back into the hallway. 'You'd better come in.'

The hallway was magnificent. The oak panels were burnished gold; the echoing stone beneath their feet was polished, reflective of the high roof with its curved beams and the gallery that ran the length of one side of it. The woman was walking ahead of him, towards a room that would have once served as a morning-room, Arnold guessed: he wondered what use this manor house would now have for such accommodation. The woman was wondering about other things: she paused in front of a full-length mirror against the morning-room entrance and inspected herself. Arnold gained the impression it was a calculated inspection that had little to do with female vanity: it was a checking that all was in order.

'Wait here,' she ordered, and entered the room after a light tap on the door. She closed the door behind her, leaving Arnold to contemplate the sun streaming in through the high latticed windows at the far end of the hall.

He walked towards the stairs. The timber was old and splendidly carved, curving up along the flight of stone steps to the first floor of the manor house. He guessed it predated the building of the house by perhaps a century: someone had cared for this house, enough to use the best materials, sensitively chosen. Now he thought about it, there had been a Newcastle builder called Connaught who had often undertaken commissions in the Northumbrian hinterland . . .

'Mr Landon.' Her voice was quiet, but positive. 'Mr Yates will see you.'

She stepped back into the room as Arnold approached hurriedly. She closed the door behind him and stood near it as Arnold advanced towards the man who had risen from the easy chair near the window where he had been taking advantage of the sunlight and the view over the hills.

'Mr Landon? I'm Patrick Yates.' He was extending his hand, his voice was courteous, but already Arnold was beginning to dislike him.

It was a condition in which he found himself rarely. Arnold was not given to making hasty judgements: long walks with his father in the northern hills, visiting ruined villages on the Yorkshire moors, being encouraged to look and touch, feel and think, had moulded his character in such a way that he tended to suspend judgements.

'Wait,' his father had suggested. 'Never jump to confusions.' The pun had been deliberate, and it was a precept that Arnold himself still held.

Yet there was something that he found immediately dislikeable in Patrick Yates.

In the fleeting moments of this meeting he tried swiftly to analyse what it might be. Yates was a stocky, well-built man with thinning hair and an elegantly tanned skin. His eyes were brown and gave the impression of warmth, though the warmth was somehow *skilled*, holding elements of professionalism that detracted from their apparent honesty. His heavy eyebrows were relaxed but his mouth was controlled: smiling now with an easy charm, but with a hint of doggedness at the corners that might mean Patrick Yates would brook no opposition to things he had decided upon.

His handshake was firm, his manners practised, and though Arnold could not be certain what had caused his hackles to rise instinctively, he wondered whether it was because Yates's handsome features held something of the Dorian Gray about them. He was in his late fifties, Arnold guessed, yet there was something *younger* about him, an indefinable air that would make him attractive to young women and the despair of older ones who would wish for their own forgotten youth to return.

It might simply have been envy, but Arnold could not be sure.

'Pauline, is there any coffee available?' Yates asked.

The woman near the door nodded. There was a small table at her side. It supported a gleaming silver coffee-pot. She poured Arnold a black coffee at his request and brought it across to him, as Yates waved Arnold to the second easy chair near the window. He took it, and the coffee, vaguely aware that the cushion on the chair had been plumped up as though someone had recently been sitting there. Yates observed him coolly for a moment and then smiled. 'You won't really have been introduced to Pauline.'

'No.' Arnold struggled, wondering whether to rise.

'Pauline Callington. No, don't bother to get up, Mr Landon. She's my housekeeper.'

There was a tiny, bitten precision about the way he pronounced *housekeeper*. Inadvertently, Arnold looked up at the woman. She was staring at Patrick Yates. Her mouth was rigid and a muscle tensed briefly in her cheek before she brought it under control. There was a short silence as they looked at each other, Yates smiling softly, charmingly, the woman unmollified as the word hung in the air between them. The tension was palpable and Arnold could not guess at its cause. It was the man who held the whip hand, nevertheless. 'I don't think you need stay, Pauline. But thank you for the coffee.'

It was made to sound like an insult. She was unable to control the slow flush that stained her mouth and cheek. But there was iron in the woman. She inclined her head slightly, and without a word or a glance in Arnold's direction she turned and walked from the room. The door closed gently behind her.

Patrick Yates sighed. 'It's necessary, if one is to maintain relationships on an even keel, that certain things are made clear from time to time. Do you find that in your own circumstances, Mr Landon?'

Arnold sipped his black coffee. He was unwilling to be drawn, partly because he was not certain what the basic relationship between Yates and his housekeeper might be, and also because he was inclined to suggest there were ways of dealing with people other than insulting or humiliating them. But Yates's manners were not his business. Planning applications were. 'I've come to discuss your application, Mr Yates.'

'So I gathered. Do you see any problems?'

'In essence, no. Your proposals are to build an ornamental lake—'

'To replace that rather vulgar little pond in front of the house,' Yates said easily. 'It hardly sets off Kilgour, does it? Such a lovely house needs an appropriate setting.'

'Indeed. And the house *is* lovely.' If Yates thought so, he couldn't be all bad, Arnold thought. 'You also want to build a tennis court—'

'At the back of the house, that's right. It won't affect

the outlook, or the external façade or the environs.'

'And certain improvements to the stables. The Jacobean stables—'

'Will be unaffected,' Yates interrupted, obviously slightly bored at the necessity to explain something that would have already appeared in the plans he had submitted. 'I want to undertake improvements in some new stable blocks, and upgrade those I made available some five years ago.'

'They were cottages at the time.'

'That's right.'

'You obtained no planning permission.'

'I was not the owner, then.'

There was a curious, challenging inflection in Yates's last words, as though he was resisting an attack already repulsed once before. Arnold nodded. 'I don't wish to imply we'll be looking at that situation now. The fact is merely noted. I will need to look at the plans on the ground, however, and there are certain objections—'

'I'm aware of them. Under planning law, I don't see you need to take any notice of them.'

'Aggrieved parties—'

'The Enwrights of this world don't classify as aggrieved parties,' Yates said sharply.

'There is also the matter of the lawsuit,' Arnold suggested quietly.

Yates's coffee cup clattered on the table as the man rose abruptly to stand in front of the window. He locked his hands behind his back and glared out across the lower meadow and the stream in front of the house to the rise of the hazy hills beyond.

'The lawsuit is rubbish. It doesn't stand a chance.'

'The lawyers—'

'Mr Landon, I was trained as a lawyer and I know what I'm talking about. The claim doesn't stand a cat in hell's chance!'

He brooded silently for a little while as Arnold sipped his

coffee uneasily. 'You don't know much about this place, do you, Mr Landon?'

'No,' Arnold replied, subdued by the submerged ferocity in Yates's tone.

'It was built in the early years of the nineteenth century. The land was purchased by the Edridge family: industrialists from Staffordshire who sought the life of landed gentry for themselves and their sons up here in northern farming country.'

'There are worse places to live.'

Yates hardly seemed to hear him. 'They built the cottages to make the village about 1815, and they built this house. They cared for the place. They started a tradition, and their children followed that tradition. Life was placid, controlled, and good for more than a hundred years. But times change, Mr Landon, times change.'

'They do,' Arnold agreed unhappily and put down his empty cup.

'Colonel Edridge, as a young man, was keen to follow that tradition. He nurtured the idea and ideal of a continuous and protective ownership. I met him when he was about to retire from the Coldstream Guards. He wanted legal advice. We became friends. Eventually he asked me to become his estate manager. It was an attractive offer. I came twenty years ago. Kilgour House became my home.'

'It's a beautiful place.'

'Charles Edridge was an immensely sociable man who had a certain vision. He saw himself as part of a tradition in which a rural community of rural workers could flourish. His function was to form a link in a long chain. He'd hoped to found a dynasty, too. He married. A Swedish girl he'd met during the war. It didn't work. She was utterly incapable of providing him with the sort of love he needed, and they were divorced. Desertion.'

Arnold hardly cared to listen to the story: it was not relevant to his visit. But Yates was telling it as though there was some point he needed to make.

'The problem was,' Yates continued, 'if he could have no children of his own, how was he to deal with the estate?'

'Remarriage?'

'His experience with his wife had scarred him,' Yates said dismissively. 'But there was a first cousin, who had a son. They started a correspondence, and it seemed there was the chance that . . . You've got to understand, Landon, how a man like Charles could feel, if he was let down. There was a Trust, you see. Certain financial problems arose in the late 'fifties. Charles borrowed against that trust. It was not, perhaps, wise. When I met Charles, I advised him how to put it right. He had money available in the late 'sixties and it could be managed . . . but the cousin, he raised Cain. Caused problems. It cost Charles fifteen thousand pounds to settle, but worse than that, it embittered him against his own family. He wanted nothing more to do with them.'

'So the friendship with his cousin's son—'

'Ended,' Yates announced sharply. 'If Charles ever had seriously considered naming him as his heir, he certainly gave that up as an idea in the late 'sixties. They were not in touch. There was no correspondence. The man himself, once he grew up, made no attempt to get in touch.'

'We're talking of . . . Robert Francis,' Arnold suggested.

'The self-styled heir to Kilgour,' Yates sneered. 'He dropped out for years, a *writer* he called himself. He only crawled out of the woodwork again when he heard that the Colonel had died.'

'Leaving the estate to you?'

Yates turned his eyes in Arnold's direction. The glance was now cold. 'This has been my home for twenty years. I was Charles Edridge's closest friend. He had no other family. To whom else should he leave the estate? To a branch of the family that had let him down, abandoned him, *sued* him? I tell you, the man is a fortune-hunter, an impecunious rogue who wants to walk into a fortune he's never earned.'

'But which you have.' Arnold regretted the words as soon

as he had spoken them, but Yates barely reacted. It was as though a personal, bitter anger was uncoiling inside him. Controlled normally, it was now moving like a slow deadly snake of hatred, taking over, directing the man's passions down a single, obsessive path that made him largely oblivious of his surroundings.

Arnold rose to his feet uncertainly. 'If we could have a word about the planning application—'

'I think maybe he's also behind the recent niggling about Ash Farm,' Yates interrupted, hardly seeming to have heard him. 'But when you get down to it, these people, they just don't know what farming is about, do they? Charles Edridge was not the greatest of farmers. When I came, the estate needed *managing*. And I turned it around. The basic problem was that the estate was too heavily tenanted. And the rents were uneconomic. So it makes sense—any sensible person would agree. What is necessary is to face reality, accept that a heavily tenanted estate is less productive than one where the owner takes the farms in hand. Do you know that in 1985 three-quarters of the let land put on the market in this country failed to find a buyer?'

'I wasn't—'

'Damn it all! It's far more profitable to allow a vacant tenanted farm to fall into ruin. What's the point of re-letting it and charging an uneconomic rent? Larger agricultural units are more cost-effective!'

And there was another reason which no doubt would have influenced the owner of Kilgour House—Edridge or Yates. If a tenancy was not re-let, once the tenants had gone the underlying value of the freehold property could rise at a considerable speed. The capacity of the owner to raise money on the vacant property would be greatly enhanced.

It was a policy that could help raise finance to build an ornamental lake, and renovate old stables. But Arnold did not say so, for Patrick Yates was glaring at him and his mouth was set like a steel trap.

Arnold reminded himself he was at Kilgour to consider

and investigate a planning application, not to take sides in an agricultural dispute.

Yates seemed disinclined to allow the conversation to end, however. 'I know what the story is, spread by people who are lazy, incompetent, and think the world at large owes them a living merely because they exist in it. I see enough of them when I'm sitting on the bench. When I was chosen as a magistrate some years ago I had views about life here in the country, and those views haven't changed. The North needs regeneration; the estates like Kilgour need hard work put into them. But it needs to be *unsentimental* work. On the bench I crack down hard on poaching: I know my views are unpopular—but I'm enforcing the law! Equally, if I'm to turn the estate around, make it the kind of place the Colonel always dreamed of, and bring it back to the prosperity it once enjoyed under the Edridge family, I have to make realistic decisions.'

Arnold rose unsteadily. He didn't want to be on the receiving end of this harangue: he suspected that while he might agree with the motives, he would not care for the consequential actions. 'The tenants—'

'A-hah! The tenants!' Yates's eyes gleamed angrily and his mouth was edged with a hard bitterness. 'I can guess what some of them will have been saying. They'll be pointing to the capital improvements that used to be made to their farms—and which have ceased during the last ten years or so. They'll be pointing to the three-year rent reviews I've instituted over that period, and they'll be saying that the rents have risen significantly each time. What *I* would say to you, Mr Landon, is: look at those rents. Compare them with the average nationally. And I challenge you to show me where Kilgour rents are above the national average. It's nothing more than the whining, bleating noises of a bunch of incompetents who have battened off this land for decades and are unwilling to face the harsh realities of the modern economy!'

The challenge was one Arnold was unwilling to accept. 'I'm sorry, Mr Yates, but all this is hardly my business. I'm here merely to carry out an inspection related to the planning application you've submitted.'

He had been unable to prevent the coolness entering his tone; Yates recognized it as a mark of disapproval, and his lip curled contemptuously. He was clearly beginning to regard Arnold as a member of the other camp. 'You'll have received letters, nevertheless, from the tenants. You'll need to give fair weight to my side of the story.'

'Letters have been received,' Arnold agreed cautiously, 'but as far as I can see they bear little relevance to the planning application and our powers in that respect. To that extent they will play no part in the decision—and it follows that our own discussion becomes . . . to that extent . . . tautological.'

Alarmed at his own boldness suddenly, Arnold ducked his head, mumbled that he needed now to carry out his inspection and requested Yates's permission to walk around the premises. Yates stared at him for several seconds, a frown marking his brow as he weighed up in his own mind the possible barriers that the planning officer from Morpeth might raise to his own view of the world. Then he nodded. 'Walk where you will. I'll say goodbye. There's no need for further conversation. If there's anything further you need to ask, it can be done by letter, I presume.'

Arnold was happy to escape the coldness of the room.

The housekeeper, Pauline Callington, was standing in the hallway, fussing with a bowl of flowers. She didn't look the type to go in for extensive flower-arranging. Her eyes fixed on Arnold as he walked forward; they were hesitant, but calculating, and he thought she was going to let him walk past to the front doors without speaking, but at the last moment, she called his name.

'Mr Landon.'

'Mrs Callington?'

'I wouldn't want you to think . . .' She seemed flustered suddenly. It was as though she had something important to say to him, but could not bring herself to say it. He waited. She shook her head, puzzled with herself. 'It's no matter . . .

Arnold walked out into the warm sunshine. The blackbird had moved to a hedge of hawthorn but was still singing lustily. Behind the house a spreading chestnut was alive with creamy candles. The air was soft and warm, the hill was green and around Kilgour House there was an air of peace and quietude.

Arnold enjoyed his brief tour of the property. He looked at the Jacobean stables, inspected the ruined cottages that were to be converted, admired the sweep of the ornamental lake on the plans and checked where it would actually be built above the weedy, overgrown pond.

It was a beautiful location, here under the hill, with the fells rising green and brown and fading to a distant blue in the distance, and Kilgour House and its estates should have been a haven, a jewel in the northern farmlands.

The fact that it was edged with bitterness, plagued with quarrels and scarred with a long-standing dispute, based in ancient differences and conflicting viewpoints could not be ignored, however. Arnold sighed. It was a pity, a great pity.

But it was none of his business.

CHAPTER 2

1

The arrangement Arnold had made with Alan Evesham to visit the village of Langton and its ruined castle had been somewhat indeterminate. On the Saturday morning, therefore, Arnold was surprised to receive a phone call from Evesham.

'What time will you pick me up?' Evesham asked abruptly.

'Pick you up?'

'To go to Langton. It won't take you far out of your way. I have a cottage in Ogle.'

Far out of my way, Arnold thought. Only about fifteen miles. 'I thought we'd be meeting at Langton itself,' he demurred.

'Can't. Dodgy motor. And old Agnew won't pick me up; says he's already up in the area overnight. Can give me a lift back, though, if *you* can manage to take me out with you.'

Reluctantly, feeling he had been cornered, Arnold agreed to pick up the Newcastle professor within the hour. He was not in the best of tempers when he drove away from his bungalow to make the cross-country run to Ogle. On the other hand, there was a certain curiosity stirring in him as he wondered what sort of cottage Evesham might have in Ogle.

It was a delightful surprise. At the end of the small village a narrow pack-horse bridge of some antiquity crossed the clear, stony stream and the track beyond, barely metalled, ran through hawthorn hedges to end in a small cluster of three cottages. All were old. One had certainly been originally constructed at the turn of the eighteenth century; in both of the others there were hints of earlier construction, and the timber braces in Evesham's cottage suggested to Arnold that it must have been the first cottage built in the tiny hamlet. He hadn't even been aware of the lane's existence at the end of Ogle village.

He told Evesham so.

The young professor seemed unimpressed. 'Swine of a place to live in. Have to have my own generator. No gas. Would never have lived here, but the place was left to me by a decrepit aunt, and it's cheap, commutable to Newcastle. When the bloody car's in shape. University dons are a depressed breed, Landon. Research cuts, salary cuts, don't know why we stick it.'

His general grumbling continued for several minutes while he sorted out various papers, including some old maps of the Langton area. He had expected Arnold to arrive within the hour, to keep their appointment with Professor Agnew at Langton, but he was not prepared to put himself out: he had waited until Arnold actually arrived before he stirred himself.

'Thought it was a good idea to invite Agnew to join us,' Evesham said. 'He's been moody about the research grant, and suggested involving you, so I thought I'd kill two birds. Get him to come along, see how important the research is, and show him I'm cooperating, dragging you in.'

Even if the dragging in was done reluctantly, Arnold thought. But the charmless Mr Evesham seemed unaware of any undertones of displeasure in Arnold's bearing. Perhaps he considered Arnold's feelings as beneath his notice, even if he had begged a lift from him in the car.

They left Ogle some fifteen minutes later than Arnold had intended, so he was forced to take the A1 north rather than use the narrower, more winding roads he would have preferred. Arnold disliked the A1: it was a good road, and it provided splendid views as it ran north, but even so, there were much more interesting highways crossing the hills and fells of Northumberland. They reached out into tiny, half-forgotten villages, the kind that clung to their past and hardly seemed to recognize the existence of the twentieth century, faming communities that still fed on their roots and heritage.

'I've done some more work on Ailnoth,' Evesham said, raising his voice against the noise of the engine. 'Got some more papers, copied from the Bodleian.'

Arnold swung in behind a trundling caravan to allow an

urgent Jaguar to nose past him and accelerate away with a snarl. He checked his mirror carefully before pulling out to overtake the caravan himself. 'Did you discover anything new?'

'Very interesting,' Evesham bawled, his voice taking on a curiously high note. 'Seems he did some work at Winchester, on the King's Hall. Got a grant of timber for it. Six tree-trunks—*festa* in the manuscript. It was by way of a payment for building the *verina*, the window-frame of the hall.'

Arnold could not resist the comment. 'That might be a clerical mistake.'

'What?'

'*Verina*—window.'

'What the hell are you talking about?' Evesham asked irritably.

'I've come across a similar reading in an old manuscript— a building contract. The word was really *verna*—a windlass.'

'What the hell would he build a windlass in the Great Hall for?' Evesham demanded angrily.

But the seed had been sown. The don subsided unhappily, grumbling something under his breath, and leaving Arnold with the quiet, if childish, satisfaction of the thought that he had at least forced Evesham to reconsider his opinions and not regard them as sacrosanct.

At the first opportunity Arnold swung off the A1. He was heading along roads he had already travelled that week. Langton village lay only some five miles east of the Kilgour Estates although the village did not fall as part of the landholding of Patrick Yates. As they crossed the great ridge that ran up towards the Cheviots Arnold caught a glimpse of the head of the valley in which Kilgour House was situated, and almost as though Evesham read his thoughts, the Professor said, 'You ever come across that character Yates, of Kilgour?'

Surprised, Arnold nodded. 'I have, as a matter of fact. I

was up there during the week, dealing with a planning matter.'

'Watch the bastard. He's poison. He's a magistrate, you know, but I'd like to see the swine hanged.'

'What dealings have *you* had with him?' Arnold asked.

'Bastard.' Evesham sniffed, and was silent for a while. 'I was involved about two years ago with some investigative work on Kilgour land. Wild scrub country really, no value to anyone, grazed by a few sheep and that was about it. I had material evidence from Northumberland records of the 1830s that there'd been a pele tower in the area—you know, one of those defensive towers put up to hold back the marauding Scots.'

'I know.'

'Could've been about 1228 . . .' Evesham muttered an obscenity. 'I took a dig out there. All right, didn't go through all the formalities like getting Yates's permission, but he turned up one morning and tried to bawl me out. In front of students. They were helping with the dig. I gave him as good as I got. Lost my temper. I admit to a short rein. He went white at some of the things I said to him. He was oafing on about trespass and me being no better than a poacher, so I told him a few home truths too. The girls in the party quite liked the womanizing bit.' Evesham chuckled unpleasantly. 'You pick up rumours in the common room. We got a couple of senior profs who while their time away on the local bench. Yates, apparently, is an *active* bachelor —or used to be. I suggested those days were behind him. He changed from white to purple and then stomped off. You know what he did next?'

'What?'

'He blew the place up.'

Arnold swerved involuntarily. 'He *what*?'

'He blew the bloody pele foundations to smithereens.' Evesham's tone had changed: the malicious satisfaction was gone, to be replaced by a cold, edgy bitterness that Arnold found

intimidating in its commitment. 'He could have just ordered us off, closed access to us. We'd have been annoyed about that . . . but that wouldn't have been enough for that vengeful bastard. At the weekend, when we were off site for the degree ceremonies at the university, he went up there, bulldozed down to the foundations, stuck a load of gelignite or some bloody stuff into the hole and carved a great gouge out of the hillside. It must have cost him a bit to do it, but it gave him great satisfaction. I stormed up there, to his bloody mansion, and bawled at him. He was cool as ice. Just told me it was his hill, he could do with it as he wanted, and now there was nothing there for me to dig for, there was no reason why I should trespass again.'

Arnold could feel the old anger rising again in Alan Evesham as wounds never scarred over bled again. 'I shouted at him,' Evesham continued, 'telling him he'd destroyed part of our heritage, but he didn't even laugh at me! It was just contempt . . . I almost went for him, but he had a bloody big mastiff at his side at the time.' Evesham fell silent for a while, but Arnold caught a tremble in the man's hands, clasped firmly on his knees. 'You saw in my study, that mediæval pike?'

Arnold nodded. 'I did.'

'They used to use those pikes to stick heads on,' Evesham said coldly. 'As a warning, and as a punishment. That pike . . . it was just made for that bastard Yates's head. If I ever got the chance . . .'

Arnold was surprised at the over-reaction. He slowed as the car came over the hill and the lane narrowed. A farmer was ushering a small herd of cows across the roadway ahead of him, on their way to fresh pasture, so he stopped. Evesham was silent beside him, but there was a curious sound emerging from the man's throat. It was as though he were trying gently to clear his throat but the sound was a slow, continuous rumble, like a subdued growling. Arnold glanced at him. The man was oblivious: his eyes were on the cows ahead but Arnold was certain he did not see them. His eyes were fixed on a real past, now imagined; there might have been images of heads and pikes in that dream. Evesham's face had gained in colour, an unhealthy hue that matched the emotions he still clearly felt about the wanton destruction of a thirteenth-century pele tower.

Whatever had been said, and felt, and done in the brief relationship between Patrick Yates and Alan Evesham, it had left a suppurating sore on the Professor's emotions.

'We'll be at Langton soon,' Arnold offered.

The offer was rejected, and they drove the rest of the way in silence.

The village of Langton lay in a hollow. The cluster of cottages fronted a narrow village green bisected by a shallow stream in which five ducks paddled desultorily in the morning sunshine. At one edge of the village stood a converted farmhouse and barn, its modern reconstruction painfully insensitive to Arnold's eyes. On the rise beyond, a gravelled track led up to a yew hedge, past which could be seen the solid Norman tower of Langton church. As they drove down into the village Arnold's glance went to the crest of the hill: up there, behind the screening alder and birch, lay the remains of the controversial Langton Castle.

Parked outside the church were two cars, a dusty red Ford, and a battered old Buick that had seen long service abroad before it had ever been deposited in England. Arnold wondered at its history as he drove towards the church, and parked his car beside the low gritstone wall.

Evesham got out of the car and without a word walked down the path towards the entrance to the church. Arnold stood for a moment, looking about him, smelling the wind from the distant sea, glancing towards the line of the fells and thinking about days long gone in the Yorkshire dales of his youth. He turned, and followed Evesham. The path was ill-tended, weeds growing in the interstices between the ancient stones, and the nettlewort and couch grass were rampant. He paused by a leaning headstone: wind and rain had eroded the words commemorating a death in 1880. It was not so long, Arnold thought, before oblivion.

Some attempt at repairs had been undertaken in the north-east corner of the churchyard. There was a certain raggedness about the effort that suggested untrained hands, and there was certainly a great deal to be done if the churchyard were to be properly tidied.

The interior of the church was cool and dim. It was a small church, a narrow strip of faded carpet gracing the entrance and leading towards a table on which were displayed a number of ineffectual appeal pamphlets. The pews were old, badly varnished in places and ill cared for: Arnold smoothed the old oak with his hand and grieved silently for it.

On the east wall were two stained glass windows presented by long-gone families: at the transept, Arnold noted with a vague surprise, there was a stained glass window depicting the martyrdom of St Stephen, presented by the Edridge family. He had not been aware that the Edridges of Kilgour would have seen Langton as their local church.

The two men standing near the font were now turning to acknowledge Alan Evesham. Arnold walked unhurriedly down the church aisle towards them: he recognized Professor Agnew, dark-suited as always, bald pate gleaming dully in the dim light, his great elephantine ears with their pendulous lobes drawing attention from his sharp little eyes and the prim mouth that hid an innate generosity of mind and spirit well known to Arnold and probably to Evesham too, in spite of the military historian's complaints about cuts in research grants of late.

'Mr Landon,' Agnew announced, stretching out a hand in welcome. 'I am appreciative that you could make it. I'm aware we're trespassing upon your valuable personal time. So pleased you are able to come along and offer us assistance.'

Alan Evesham glowered sullenly, annoyed that it was being suggested openly that he required assistance.

'May I present you to the vicar?' Agnew intoned. 'Mr Landon—Mr Barnack, vicar of Langton.'

Barnack was thin, thirtyish and thickening about the waist. He had a wispy moustache that he seemed to wish to hide for its ineffectuality, his left hand stroking it gingerly as though he wished it had never come. He was dressed in corduroy trousers and a turtle-necked sweater as though to emphasize that Saturdays were not part of his working week and he really was putting himself out for this meeting. Arnold guessed that whatever the state of the research grant fund a generous contribution to Langton Church would be expected of, and given by, Professor Agnew.

He shook Barnack's hand: the grasp was limp, the skin damp. Barnack's eyes seemed oddly luminous in the dim light of the church, a deep-water creature unused to the sunlight on the hill. 'I'm pleased to meet you, Mr Landon,' he said unconvincingly.

Saturdays, Arnold thought, are Saturdays, after all.

'Mr Barnack hasn't been the incumbent here all that long,' Agnew said softly. 'We were discussing the state of the roof: his predecessor had made efforts, but not enough.'

Decidedly, a generous contribution would be expected.

'I see some work has been done in the churchyard,' Arnold offered.

'Community Project,' Barnack explained. 'There was some money left over, apparently, and the county sent a supervisor and a few young unemployed people to start tidying up. I'm not certain it was an immense success, and when the money ran out . . .'

'It's a start, anyway,' Arnold suggested, after a short, heavy silence.

'Well,' Evesham said snappishly, 'We didn't come up here to waste time. Shall we go into the vestry?'

Professor Agnew glanced at Arnold. There was nothing in

his expression that led Arnold to believe Agnew sympathized with him, but he suspected Agnew was grateful that Arnold was prepared to suffer Evesham's bad temper and worse manners at all. If not for too long.

Barnack led the way into the vestry. The room was narrow and cold. The old beech table was badly scarred at the edges; a thin cloth had been placed on its surface and a shaft of sunlight from the high window glanced down to illuminate the top volume of the three that had been placed on the cloth. There was a dark rich redness in the cover, deep under the encrusting dirt of age, and the faded leather at the corners had been badly worn, but the old records seemed to have been remarkably well preserved.

'They're not the original records, unfortunately,' the vicar was saying. 'These date from the sixteenth century. As far as I've been able to make out, there was a fire in the church about 1530. Records were damaged. An attempt was then made, over the following twenty years, to copy the fire-damaged material, but inevitably the work fell to several hands and the result is far from satisfactory.'

'That binding is older than 1530,' Arnold suggested.

'How do you know that?' Evesham asked sharply.

Arnold shrugged. 'I have a friend on the Quayside in Newcastle—antiquarian bookseller. He knows about such things. He's taught me a great deal. Those hinges—'

'Yes, yes, you're quite right,' Barnack said, glancing surreptitiously at his watch. 'It seems they did use older bindings, inserting new copies in with some original material. But that's as much as I know. Mr Evesham—'

'*Professor.*'

Barnack, slightly flustered by Evesham's correction, paused, glanced helplessly at Agnew for support, got none, and went on. 'Professor Evesham has already inspected these books with my permission. But I'm not sure what the purpose of this meeting this morning is. I'm here, I suppose, because two eminent gentlemen from the university have seen fit to visit the church here at Langton . . .' His voice died away, as his eyes sought out Arnold, concerned in some vague way that he might have upset his third visitor by not including him among the group of eminences, and perhaps worried he might have miscalculated by way of donation possibilities.

'Then let me explain,' Evesham butted in. 'I came here some months ago to follow up certain researches in military history at Langton Castle. I visited the church, checked the records, and found some interesting evidence that suggests a trace can be made upon the movements of a mediæval mason and military engineer called Ailnoth. Even to the extent of perhaps showing that he was buried here in Langton Church.'

Barnack shuffled his feet uneasily. 'I'm not sure . . .'

'The relevant entries are here, Agnew,' Evesham interrupted. He moved to the second book in the pile, dragged it out and for the next two minutes scanned through the heavy, fragile pages with their faded brown stains, seeking for the entries he required. 'Here they are . . .'

Agnew pored over them briefly, sucking at his lips thoughtfully. At last he turned to Arnold. 'Perhaps you'd like to take a look, Mr Landon?'

Arnold peered at the book entries as Agnew stepped aside. He was vaguely aware of the hovering presence of Alan Evesham but ignored it as much as he could: in moments he was taken up by the beauty and age of the old pages, the stained materials, the crabbed, almost indecipherable scrawl of long-dead scribes who had laboriously copied the births and deaths and folk memories of men and women who were now dust.

'That's the specific one there,' Evesham said impatiently, stabbing with his finger at an entry in the left-hand column. The man was nervous: his finger left a small, sweaty stain on the manuscript.

'Al . . . Iln . . . it's difficult to make out,' Arnold said.

'I read it as *Alnith*,' Evesham said quickly. 'It's dog Latin, of course, and not too well scribed. But it reads *Alnith the controller*—that's the meaning of *ordinantor*, just there— *Alnoth*, sorry *Alnith the controller interred September 5th 1187.*' Evesham's voice was shaky; his nervousness increasing. 'You see, Agnew, I think *Alnith the controller* was really Ailnoth the engineer.'

'The name's spelled differently,' Barnack interrupted.

Evesham glared at the vicar balefully. 'Read Shakespearean manuscripts. See how they didn't have common spellings even then, in the sixteenth century. Do you think they were particular in the twelfth?'

'But what's a controller?' Barnack responded. 'Is that the same as an engineer?'

Reluctance seeped into Evesham's tones. 'No. Not exactly, of course. But the thing is, Ailnoth the engineer was disgraced. My thesis is he fell out of favour as an engineer and architect and was forced to another kind of business— a supplier of plaster, stone and tiles. He came north in that capacity. I think he combined his craft as a mason and engineer with that of a building contractor.'

'And controller?' Barnack insisted stubbornly.

'He would perhaps have been employing a number of men to do the building work.'

'It sounds . . . tenuous,' Professor Agnew suggested softly.

'No more tenuous than a number of theories constantly put forward in the physics and classical departments this term,' Evesham replied heatedly. 'I was amazed, for instance that you saw fit to offer support to Armitage's project . . .'

Arnold's glance slipped away from the faded entry relating to Alnith the controller. He glanced along the lines above the entry, and turned back a page. There was something wrong. He leaned forward, peering closely at the entries as Evesham committed himself to unwise criticism of Agnew's decisions on research grant placings in the

university. In Arnold's experience you gained no credit for
your own work by the criticism of others, but that was
Evesham's problem, not his. He was becoming interested
in the little puzzle that was unfolding in front of him:
patiently, he worked back through the entries, turning the
pages. At last he raised his head. 'Ah. I see now.'

The quiet satisfaction in his tone caused the heat to die
between Evesham and Agnew. Professor Agnew turned his
head. 'What do you see, Mr Landon?'

'The entries are out of sequence.'

There was a short silence. 'What does that mean?' Barnack asked.

'They're not consecutive. You said earlier that some of
the records weren't originals—they were merely copies of
older, fire-damaged sheets. Well, it seems to me that when
the sixteenth-century scribe copied the entries and inserted
the more recent sheets in among the old, before the volume
was rebound in its old cover, he got some of the sheets mixed
up.'

'Did you pick this up?' Agnew inquired of Evesham as he
craned over Arnold's shoulder to take a look at the entries
himself.

'I . . . I'm not sure . . . well, I read the entries, I don't
think it really makes any difference about the order in which
they appear,' Evesham replied lamely.

'You'll have been searching for specifics, of course,'
Arnold suggested helpfully. 'I wasn't, of course. In such
situations things tend to leap out at you more easily.'

'Not very careful research,' Agnew rumbled in a doubtful
tone, 'if you don't even check upon entry sequence.'

'Time has been of the essence, you will recall,' Evesham
replied, his voice rising in anger. 'I was being pressed . . .
the research grant . . . and I don't see it makes much
difference—'

'I'm not so sure about that,' Arnold said.

Evesham glared fiercely at him, furious at the interruption, and at what he suspected was to be further criticism of his research abilities and techniques. 'I'm not accustomed to having amateurs,' he sneered, '*gifted* or not—'

'Why are you not so sure?' Agnew cut across him. 'What difference do you suggest it makes, Mr Landon?'

Arnold was silent for a little while, checking again the names, the dates of the entries, the difficult-to-decipher names and descriptions. 'Well, it's not for me to say, of course, for I have little experience in these matters. Even so, I find it interesting that so many people died within a few days of each other and were interred at this church.'

There was a short silence.

'I don't follow . . .' Evesham said, his anger dying, blanketed by his puzzlement. 'I didn't notice . . .'

'Because the entries were out of sequence, you didn't notice the sequence of interments. If you check, even quickly, as I did, you'll see that over perhaps a five-day period, according to the dates, there were something like eight interments. Rather a large number for a small parish like this one in the twelfth century.'

'A pestilence,' Barnack murmured. 'A famine . . . little children . . .'

'I don't think so. I can't read all the entries clearly, and I lack a classical education so I can't be sure of my translations. But I have picked up certain words in my own studies of the ancient building trades. Look, this entry . . . *Hugh*, buried on September 3rd, *Mapylton*, buried on the same day as the *Ilnith* entry, and *John Lobins*, interred on September 2nd. None of these were children.'

'Their ages are given?' Barnack asked.

Arnold shook his head. 'No. But that's probably because, as grown men, their ages were not known.'

'How do you know they were grown men?' Agnew asked, watching Arnold carefully.

'The dog Latin. I told you, I'm not skilled. But some

words ... this one here, a description of Mapylton, for instance. *Devysor*.'

'What's that mean?' Barnack asked.

Evesham cleared his throat. His tone was husky. 'It means a designer: a man who prepared the building designs from which masons carried out their work.'

'Master John Lobins, it seems,' Arnold added mildly, 'was the provider of *forme et molde*. I'm not clear what that means. But I do know what is meant by the term *dealbatores*, applied to *Hugh* and also to *Bennon*, interred the same day.'

'Let me see that,' Evesham said roughly and pushed his way past Agnew to pore over the book entries.

'*I've* had a classical education,' Professor Agnew said sombrely, 'but I've never come across the word *dealbator*.'

'There's little likelihood you would,' Arnold replied, 'other than by seeking out old building contracts. You see, when a building contract was drawn up, the masons responsible then had to draw together a working force. There were tilers and thatchers and carpenters—they were usually described as *helyers*. Then came the plumbers and glaziers, smiths and painters. Lower in the pecking order came the plasterers and pargetters. Perhaps lowest of all came those who supplied huts for the workmen who were building in stone and wood. The huts were made of wattle and daub. The men who built them tended also to be whitewashers. *Dealbatores*.'

'*Baldwin*,' Evesham gasped suddenly. '*Hottarius*.'

'A hodman,' Arnold said smugly. He was beginning to enjoy himself.

Alan Evesham moaned, a self-destructive, critical whine deep in his throat. 'Why didn't *I* see this?' he demanded. 'What the hell was I *thinking* of?'

There was a short silence, broken only by the harsh, frustrated rasping of Evesham's breath. Impervious to the presence of the others now, he feverishly scanned the pages of the records. Agnew watched him for several minutes, then turned gravely to Arnold. 'Do you think this is important?'

Arnold's eyes widened. He was no expert. He'd merely noticed something someone else had missed. 'Important . . . I'm not sure. Important to Professor Evesham? I suppose it . . . *could* be.'

Evesham's head half turned, reluctantly, away from the records. Arnold had an impression of one eye glinting hungrily in his direction. 'In what way,' Agnew continued, 'could this be important to Professor Evesham?'

Arnold considered the matter for a little while. 'I suppose . . . because he's trying to prove that Ailnoth the engineer is the *Alnith* here in the books at Langton. This could be helpful. The *Alnith* entry speaks only of the *ordinantor* or controller. But controller of what? The term was used of building works, certainly, but was it so used exclusively?'

'Go on.'

'Now the other entries are interesting because they speak of men who held particular jobs, descriptions certainly used in the building trade. This would serve to suggest that the ordinantor was one of the same group.'

Agnew frowned. 'The ice is thin—'

'But perhaps equally important is the fact of the dates of interment,' Arnold suggested.

'Why?'

'It suggests a local catastrophe.'

Evesham turned away from the records to stare at Arnold silently. Agnew glanced at him, permitted himself a wry smile, and looked back towards Arnold. 'It seems to me you already have the glimmerings of a theory.'

Arnold swallowed hard. He felt a quiver of excitement in his veins at the thought of the eminent Professor Agnew asking for instruction, and he was forced to admit the feeling of satisfaction that he now had Evesham's reluctant attention. The man was a boor; he needed taking down a peg or two. On the other hand, the ice was thin, As Agnew had already suggested . . .

'The Middle Ages was not the stay-at-home period that many people seem to think it was,' Arnold began. 'The fluidity of labour was really quite astonishing.'

'How do you mean?' Agnew asked, frowning.

'Stone buildings were rare. A small town would contain none but the church, or a nearby castle. The average town wouldn't provide sufficient employment for a considerable number of men in the building crafts: even modest building operations inevitably exhausted local supplies very quickly. That applied to skilled and unskilled labour. The result was considerable mobility of labour. For instance, a casual list of masons working in Windsor whose wages were in arrears in 1300 shows four each from London and Norfolk, and three from Lancashire, Shropshire and Hereford.'

'*Convocat latomos, architectos invitat,*' Evesham said hoarsely, '*cementarios et artis sculptoris . . .*'

'That, I believe,' Arnold said, 'was the Conqueror's command to build a great church for his abbey at Bury St Edmunds.'

Evesham's mouth snapped close like a steel trap.

'So workmen were drawn together for a building enterprise from some distances. It seems to me that the records we've been looking at suggest that some large building enterprise was certainly in train in this area in 1187. The people whose deaths are recorded here really tell us two things: first, that there was a group of people employed in the craft working in the area at this time; second—'

'They could have been local,' Barnack objected.

'I doubt it, for reasons I've mentioned. Hodsmen, a designer, a whitewasher, a controller . . . no, the talent would simply not have been here in Northumberland.'

'You were about to state the second point,' Agnew said.

'Second, they all seem to have died in a common catastrophe.'

'A building accident?' Evesham asked surlily.

'Who can tell?' Arnold replied. 'But grown men, dying

within days of each other, employed in the building trade
. . . a fire, perhaps, people dying of their burns over the
course of a few days—or a collapse of masonry, trapping
the men, so that they were interred as they were found. And
they would have been interred here at Langton wherever
they came from for the simple reason that transport would
not have been available to take them back to their home
villages. Not in time, at least, before putrefaction set in.'

'I'm still not certain how this supports Professor
Evesham's arguments about Ailnoth the engineer,' Agnew
said slowly.

'Neither am I,' Arnold said. He shrugged cheerfully. 'But
I must admit, that's not my problem. I'm only here to say
what I see and what I know. There's one thing, though—
the records would seem to demonstrate that there was
a man called Alnith—who might have been the Ailnoth
Professor Evesham seeks—buried at Langton; that there
was a building work of some consequence being carried on
at Langton in 1187; and if only a link could be found between
the Alnith and Ailnoth activities, the Professor has found
the basis for his thesis.'

'What kind of link?' Agnew asked cautiously.

'That's not for me to say,' Arnold replied.

Mr Barnack, vicar of Langton Church cleared his throat,
the possibility of a large donation looming ever closer.
'There is a local tradition, gentlemen. Perhaps I could
remind you of it.' He gazed around at them benignly. 'It
relates to the provenance of Langton Castle.'

2

The man who came walking up through the long grass of
the hill meadow, skirting the copse to strike out along the
path towards the castle ruins, was about fifty years of age.
He was tall and lean, moving with an easy stride that
suggested he was used to fell walking and would be fit for

his age. He wore a tweed jacket, and his trousers were stuffed into heavy boots: as he came forward he removed his battered hat to push back his thick grey hair before settling it back in place. His skin was weather-beaten, and as he came closer Arnold could see his eyes were brown, thoughtful, surrounded by the creasing caused by bright sunlight and searching fell winds.

At his heels moved a sheepdog, lean as its master, alert and careful.

'I thought I saw someone on the hill,' the man called out. 'Wondered what you might be up to.'

Mr Barnack made the introductions. 'Professor Agnew, Professor Evesham ... ah ... Mr ... er ... Landon ... This is Tom Malling. Stalwart of the church fabric; owner of the farm on which Langton Castle now stands.'

'I'll agree to the latter,' Malling said, smiling. 'I'm not sure what you base the former description on, though.'

'Your recent donations have been most welcome, Mr Malling, even though you don't attend.'

The vicar clearly never lost sight of his objectives.

'So what brings you gentlemen up to Langton?' Malling asked.

The vicar had already explained down below in the coolness of the church. There had been some dispute about the date when Langton Castle was first built; the dispute had dragged on for years. Waters had been considerably muddied during the 1830s when some enthusiastic amateurs had started a dig on the site. They had destroyed more evidence than they found, to support the thesis that the castle had been constructed as late as 1330. The learned articles they had then written had later been reproduced in part in the County History series: *that* accolade had given half-baked theories a certain credence, and it had proved remarkably difficult to unseat the argument, even though it was clear that while there certainly had been a castle built there in 1450, much of the 'original' work had in fact been constructed in 1720 by an

enthusiastic Lady Glynne-Stuyvesant whose passion had
been the creation of romantic ruins a little before the practice
became really fashionable. She had the money to do it: she
built them, knocked them down until they resembled ancient
ruins, and then had her portrait painted against the gloomy,
lowering backgrounds they presented.

Lady Glynne-Stuyvesant was not beloved by historians,
although there was no doubt she had considerably aroused
lay interest in ancient castles and even older abbeys.

'Ah,' Tom Malling said quietly. 'Lady Glynne-
Stuyvesant. Yes, she certainly did confuse things. Even
so, I think there's still some evidence that there was *something*
here in the fourteenth century.'

'You're interested in old buildings?' Arnold asked.

The brown eyes dwelled on him for a few moments,
summing him up. Malling smiled. 'Not really. I like looking
into some matters of antiquity, but really, it's just because
Langton Castle lies upon my land. I come up here sometimes
in the evening; it's a lonely place, and quiet, and you can
let your mind range. The past comes back to you then. It
even achieves a sort of reality for now, if you know what I
mean.'

Arnold did. He understood Tom Malling perfectly. From
where they stood now they had an unbroken view across
the hills of Northumberland, the fold of the land below them
allowing them to see for thirty miles or more. Today, with
the sunshine, there was a certain haziness, particularly out
towards the coast, and the scudding clouds, white and grey
against the sharp blue of the sky, seemed to accentuate the
distance and open up the horizon.

But with a mackerel evening sky, and the soft warmth of
an evening in high summer in Northumberland, Arnold
knew the atmosphere up here would be quite different.
The ruins of the castle would play their part of course,
as romantic ruins had always played their part for Lady
Glynne-Stuyvesant. But the backdrop of the hills would

change: they would shade darkly against the evening sky
lending an air of mystery. The cry of a wandering barn owl
would add to the solitude, where the lights of the village
below would be hidden by the slope, and under the deep
dark summer blue of the northern night sky memories would
take over, the ancient knowledge of the hill would stir,
uncurling itself slowly under the stars, until anyone sitting
up here would feel only the stilled hush of the meadow, hear
only the soft whisper of lives long ended, and recognize
again the importance to the present of what had occurred
in the past.

Tom Malling was staring at him.

The man seemed shaken, disturbed at something he had
seen in Arnold's face. It was as though Arnold's thoughts
had been communicated to him to strike some responsive
feelings deep inside Malling's own head. The confusion in
the farmer's eyes was caused by the shock of recognition
and by an unwillingness to accept how close another human
being could be to him, responding to his thoughts, feeling
as he felt. Arnold himself was vaguely disturbed: he and
this stranger were brothers under the skin, it seemed, and
it was not a feeling he could accept entirely. Both men
hardened a resistance that was reluctant, but real: both felt
a vulnerability they resented.

'Well,' Professor Agnew was saying, 'there's little enough
to go on here at the castle itself.'

The west wall was still standing to a height of some fifteen
feet, the stones pitted and scarred by time. The east side
had been clumsily rebuilt—possibly by the indefatigable
Lady Glynne-Stuyvesant, Arnold guessed, but the remain-
der of the castle had been levelled over the centuries. The
keep was a grassy mound: attempts at excavation had clearly
been made in the past but abandoned. It would probably
have been a wooden structure anyway, Arnold guessed,
inside the safety of the stone walls. Elsewhere, the perimeter
wall was visible only as footings, some of which had been

excavated, the rest appearing merely as craggy stones peeping through the rough, sheep-cropped turf.

'A romantic ruin,' Mr Barnack said cheerfully. 'But who knows what secrets it might reveal?'

Surprisingly, Professor Agnew, to Evesham's clearly expressed disgust, turned to Arnold. 'What do *you* feel about it?'

Taken aback, Arnold shook his head. 'I'm not sure. I mean, I'm not clear what I'm supposed to be looking for. The castle, well, it's been messed about with so much it seems to me a major dig would be required before you could ascertain with any degree of certainty whether it had really been erected in the time of Ailnoth. And even then, that doesn't prove that Ailnoth was involved.'

'But if we could prove that building works *were* being carried on,' Alan Evesham interrupted, 'we could argue the case for funding to carry out the dig. And it needn't be as expensive as all that: I'm sure we could pinpoint the *likely* position of the ancient works—'

'Expensive, extensive, that's all very well,' Agnew said, scratching his elephantine left ear, 'but you know the state of the budget.' Arnold thought he detected the beginning of impatience in Professor Agnew's tones. 'The faculty budget is limited. Government cuts . . .'

Arnold stepped away. This was nothing to do with him. He had the suspicion that although Agnew had his problems with his budgets he had also had problems in the past with Professor Evesham, and was not averse to getting his own back to some extent by withholding funds at this juncture. Although, Arnold concluded, there was a certain justification: the evidence for Ailnoth's presence in Northumberland was pretty slim, and he couldn't see that it was particularly important anyway.

Aware that Barnack was engaging Malling in earnest consultation, no doubt attempting to increase his benefactor's bounty, Arnold walked away along the crest of the hill.

Malling's dog watched him for a moment, then, after a brief hesitation, took a parallel course, watching Arnold as he would an errant sheep, ensuring it made no break from the flock. Amused, Arnold extended his hand welcomingly: the dog's ears flattened against its head and its belly dropped closer to the ground. It watched him, and he walked on, and it came closer.

The western wall of the castle had commanded a view in the old days that would have extended across to the Cumbrian fells. The ruins of Hadrian's Wall would have been a source for quarried material, no doubt. Below the west wall was a steep drop, although Arnold guessed from the line of the land that in earlier days the castle might have embraced the ridge some three hundred feet below. The shepherd's wall might well have an earlier history, for the ridge itself had a man-made look about it.

Something touched Arnold's leg. The sheepdog had decided he was trustworthy. Arnold sat down on a craggy rock and scratched the dog behind its ear. Below him a jay fluttered in the trees, scolding something in the scrubby undergrowth.

For a while he contemplated the horizon of the hills, allowing his mind to drift, to contemplate the past and recall the days when his father had shown him the countryside in the Yorkshire dales and explained to him the heritage that had been left to them, stone and wood and tree. But gradually something else began to intrude. Arnold had always admitted to curiosity, and it was now aroused, almost subconsciously, for although he was not concentrating, something was intruding, an annoyance, an excrescence upon his unconscious mind.

Something was out of place.

As soon as he became aware of the feeling he looked about him. Within a matter of seconds he knew what it was. His mind and eye had become attuned to nature; man-made structures intruded. And within the copse of trees below him there was certainly evidence of old activity.

He rose, the dog starting up swiftly beside him. Arnold descended the crag; the path was narrow but short, and he was quickly in the alder and young birch. The dog snuffled behind him as he pushed his way through the trees until he reached the mound, and the broken walls.

They were old, and they had served over the years as material for the walls on the slopes below. There was little to be seen as Arnold moved slowly around the ancient structure. In no place was it more than three feet high, and most of it had vanished altogether. Below the inner perimeter of the castle defences, it could well have suffered from siege.

'Landon!'

It was Alan Evesham. Arnold raised his hand in response.

'What are you doing down there?' Evesham shouted. 'There's nothing of any interest there!'

Not to you, perhaps, Arnold thought. 'I'm just poking around,' he satisfied himself by saying.

'Professor Agnew has to get back. He's offered me a lift. He suggests we meet again in the week, to discuss possibilities. I'll give you a ring, to let you know when.'

If I can make it, Arnold thought sourly. He turned away, just as the lean figure of Tom Malling appeared on the skyline.

He wandered around the perimeter of the building, struggling through the trees at some points. He grew confused, not certain whether he had lost the line of the foundations and he stopped, puzzled. The dog whimpered and he looked back: Tom Malling was descending the crag. The dog's body quivered, the tail swinging rhythmically. Tom Malling pushed his way through the trees to join Arnold.

'You seem to have made a friend of Sally.'

'She's friendly enough.'

'Not to all strangers. You seem to have . . . made an impact.'

Malling was frowning slightly, as though he was still

affected by the moments up above on the hill. He glanced around him. 'You've found the chapel, then.'

'Chapel?'

'That's right. When Langton Castle was restored by Lady Glynne-Stuyvesant they came across the outer perimeter of the castle. Much of it destroyed, of course. Farmers like me.'

'The needs of the land.'

'I suppose so. Anyway, the existence of the chapel here would suggest the castle was bigger than the good lady had at first realized. I think it took some of the wind out of her financial sails, too. Or so it's suggested in the County History.'

'Not the most impeccable source of accurate information.'

'Is that so?'

'I'm afraid it is. Enthusiastic Victorian historians had a tendency to indulge their imaginations and make situations fit their theories. To suggest this was a chapel, for instance . . .'

'You don't think it was?'

'Would you build your chapel outside the walls?' Arnold asked.

'Inside the *outer* walls,' Malling replied.

Arnold looked above them to the crag and shook his head doubtfully. 'I'm not so sure. Why build an outer wall down here? Professor Evesham might be able to tell us, since he's a military historian, but I would have thought that this area here would be fairly vulnerable to attack. It would have been well served for water—the spring over there which will have carved out that gully—and the area is levelled as though there have been gardens here . . . Yes, it may have been part of the outer grounds of the castle with the defensive inner wall surrounding the keep, but a chapel?'

'Maybe a chapel for the peasants out here, with another for the gentry inside?' Malling suggested.

Arnold smiled. 'It's possible But if this was a chapel for the poor, it was rather large, wasn't it?'

Malling looked around him, and nodded. 'I suppose so. I hadn't thought about it, really. Can't say I'm exactly into old buildings—though the farm itself is pretty old.' He stopped suddenly, and looked carefully at Arnold. 'From what they were saying up above you seem to know a lot about the way people used to build in the old days.'

'I'm interested.'

'And a lot about the way they lived?'

'I have certain limitations in that respect,' Arnold said vaguely, his attention beginning to wander from what Malling was saying to something he had seen in the walls to his left, shadowed by the trees. 'I suppose I know a fair bit about the building industry over the years, working as they did in wood at first, then stone . . . Excuse me . . .'

He edged away from the farmer and approached the ruined stone at the edge of the copse. He crouched down, staring closely at the stone, and he shook his head.

'What's the matter?' Malling asked, coming up close behind him.

'I'm not sure,' Arnold said hesitantly. 'It's just . . . odd, I suppose.'

'In what way?'

'Look at this here. It's brick.'

'*Brick?*' Malling leaned forward, inspected the thin piece of walling. 'Brick in a building this old?'

Arnold smiled. 'It was the Romans who introduced brick into England. They were more like tiles than modern bricks, of course, but their thinness enabled them to be very well burnt. That's the principal reason for their remarkable durability.'

'Are you saying that . . . brick there, it's Roman?'

Arnold straightened, frowning. 'I think so. But there's something odd about its colour, here. I can't just think . . .'

'But the Romans surely wouldn't have built a chapel here.'

'I'm not suggesting that. Remember, just as shepherds

raided the Wall for material for their pens, so it would be quite possible that others could have raided Chesters, for instance, to take brick to incorporate into their own later buildings. It was quite common, you see, for masons in Roman times and later, to use bricks for bonding courses. They inserted them at intervals into flint or stone rubble masonry.' He shook his head. 'But that doesn't entirely explain . . . I'm not sure.'

'So you know a lot about the masons of older times, then, Mr Landon . . . What are you doing about lunch?'

3

Arnold followed Malling's directions: the farm lay a half-mile across the fields but some three miles by the detour of the road which Arnold had to take by car. They parted on the hill; some fifteen minutes later Arnold drove along the winding lane that opened out into the track that dropped alarmingly down to the brook, the tiny bridge, and then the gateway to the farm.

The farmhouse itself nestled under the hill, protected by a bank of birch and horse chestnut, and the farmlands seemed well cared for and relatively prosperous, if somewhat given over, for EEC subsidy purposes, to the growing of rape. The farmhouse was typical of the area, bearing signs of an eighteenth-century structure built upon something rather older. As he grew nearer to the house he could in fact make out a brick-patterned sign that announced the building of the house in 1692.

Malling was waiting at the gate.

The garden through which Arnold passed was small and dilapidated. It seemed it had been laid out years ago, probably with flowerbeds, but they had deteriorated and were overgrown and weed-infested. Malling caught Arnold's glance. 'I have a woman comes in three times a week. She doesn't turn a hand to gardening.'

He led the way down the stone-flagged passageway into the kitchen. Clearly, Tom Malling lived a bachelor existence. There were few signs of a woman's hand. The curtains were feminine enough, but faded, and there was a general air of untidiness about the place which suggested to Arnold that the three-times-a-week hired help didn't turn a hand to clearing away, either.

Bread, cheese, an apple and a can of lager were offered and gratefully accepted. 'I hope you didn't expect a three course meal,' Malling said.

'This *is* three courses.'

'There's more lager.'

'I wouldn't mind a can,' Arnold said. 'But I also wouldn't mind paying a call first.'

'Top of the stairs.'

Arnold walked back down the passageway to the stairs and made his way up over the worn staircarpet. On the landing he paused, irresolutely, faced by two doors. He tried the first one and realized he had made a mistake. It was a bedroom. He paused, about to close the door, and then was struck by the fustiness of its atmosphere.

It was dimly lit, the curtains still drawn and it had a dusty stillness about it that suggested it had not been used for a long time. The bed was made up but, in marked contrast to the kitchen, everything was neatly placed. It was an unlived-in room, he felt, and something prickled at the back of his neck. There were three photographs on the chest of drawers that faced him. They were of the same woman, but he could make them out only dimly.

Softly he closed the door, and tried the door next to it. This time he was right: it was the bathroom.

Tom Malling was standing by the kitchen window when he returned, a can of lager in his hand. He turned as Arnold entered. 'I got another drink for you from the fridge.'

'Thank you.' Arnold sat down.

Malling watched him for a moment. 'This thing about

the bricks up at Langton Castle. You know a lot about such things?'

Arnold had the feeling the man really wanted to talk about something else, but was seeking a roundabout, less threatening approach. Though what the threat might be, Arnold had no idea.

'I know there are many misconceptions about bricks and their use.'

'This house, for instance,' Malling said, waving his hand. 'Can you tell me anything about it from the bricks used?'

Arnold nodded. 'I could. I have to admit, I'd be cheating if I didn't tell you I'd already seen the date of the house— 1692. But even if I hadn't I could have told you its date, roughly. It's an example of one of the later trodden bricks. They stopped using them at the turn of the century—few examples after 1710.'

'Trodden bricks?'

'A primitive method of manufacture. They dug out suitable earth. Trod it out on a piece of hard ground laid with straw. The treading of the clay was done in bare feet: they had to do it that way to make sure they got out all the pebbles, otherwise the clay would split or crack in the firing. They chopped up the clay in convenient sizes, laid them out to dry, prayed there'd be no rain and then they burnt the bricks.'

'I see.'

'Sizes of bricks weren't regulated until 1571 with the moulds they developed. These are certainly standard sizes.'

'Not like the ones up at Langton.'

The conversation was moving, but slowly, a stately galleon manœuvring through difficult, unknown waters. It wasn't Langton Castle Malling wanted to talk about.

'No, not like the ones at Langton. They are . . . well, a bit of a puzzle. You see, when the Romans left, brick-making died, in effect, in England. The tiles and bricks could still be cannibalized, of course, and that's maybe where the brick at Langton came from. But I can't be sure. There's something about it . . . I'll have to read some books again. There are plenty of examples of hard Roman brick being re-used, not least for the angles in church towers . . .' Arnold fell silent for a few moments, struck by an elusive thought. It was gone before he could hold on to it. 'Anyway, although there was plenty of great brick building in Italy, France and Germany in the twelfth century, like St Sernin at Toulouse, we've got very little in England. We built mainly in flint . . .'

'Hmmm.' Malling sipped at his lager. 'From what I gathered in the conversation at the castle, however, it's military history they're really on about.'

'Something like that.'

'So why are you brought in?'

Arnold hesitated, for some inexplicable reason unwilling to explain himself. 'I'm not sure, really.'

'I gathered it's because of your knowledge of the ancient building craft.'

'That's part of it.'

'So you know all about the masons, then, do you?'

'I'm not sure—'

'Professor Evesham, when he was arguing with Professor Agnew, he said something about the drawing together of the building crafts into Langton, and that you supported the argument—or had even advanced it.' Malling took another sip of lager, but it was almost as though he was calming himself, suppressing further some subdued excitement. 'So what was that all about?'

Arnold shrugged. 'Nothing very significant, really. Fairly common knowledge. A shortage of skilled and unskilled labour in mediæval times meant they had to bring together, from quite a wide area, the skilled people they needed to undertake a building programme of any size. In stone, anyway.'

'And that's what happened at Langton?'

'Of that, I'm not sure,' Arnold replied cautiously. 'It's a

possibility. The deaths in the area, the interments, they suggest—'

'If they *did* all come here to work on the castle—and that now seems something Professor Evesham will be clinging to, do you think they will have formed a secret society? A gild?'

Malling's eyes seemed to glitter feverishly suddenly. Arnold was held by the ferocity of the glance: it seemed *important* to Tom Malling that the fact should be determined. Arnold shook his head. 'I doubt it.'

'Why?'

'As far as I'm aware, it was really from the beginning of the thirteenth century that industry was organized on a system of craft gilds. It's true such gilds were strictly local—the fact that a man was a member of a craft fraternity in one town gave him no right to practise the craft in another.'

'But building workers . . . the *masons* . . . they were different.'

'Not so,' Arnold disputed. 'I admit that local gilds would be unsuitable for masons because they were on the move so much, from one part of England to another. That led to the formation of permanent gilds for some trades, but temporary associations—'

'The *lodges*,' Malling interrupted, almost sneering.

'That's right, associations centering upon the lodges or workshops where they were employed. But that wouldn't have happened here. We're talking of a gap of maybe a hundred years or more. But why are you interested?'

The banked-down fires in Malling's eyes died slowly. He took a long, careful sip at his can of lager. 'I'm not, really. I suppose I was just taken aback at the possibility that a craft gild of masons might have actually been established on my property.'

'It didn't happen.' Arnold hesitated. 'But what if it had —I mean, what difference does it make?'

'None, I suppose.' Malling managed a tight little smile. 'It's just that . . . well, I dislike masons—'

'You mean freemasonry.'

'Yes. When I look around me . . . there are evenings when I go up to the castle and just sit, staring out over the hills in the darkness. I think you know what I mean . . . feel what I've felt . . . This has been a great country but it has been brought to its knees by something rotten at its core. In my view that rotten thing is freemasonry. It claims to have Christian links but is anathema to the Christian Church; it claims to exist for good but is afraid to show its face in the light of day, clinging to secret practices; it argues that it is based upon ethical moral codes that have been developed over the centuries, but it is in reality a web of corruption and secret dealing, where every brother seeks to make the best advantage for himself and his colleague in the society. Freemasonry is corruption, Mr Landon.'

Arnold frowned, staring at the can of lager in front of him. He was unwilling to be drawn into this discussion, although he had the vague suspicion that this was why he had been invited to lunch with Malling. The man surprised him: the balanced, open-air farmer he had met on the hill had taken on a brooding vehemence accentuated by the unbalanced view he seemed to take of life and society, and the controlled ferocity with which he had spoken suggested banked fires of resentment inside him ready to rage uncontrollably at the slightest opportunity.

Arnold was also aware of a twinge of resentment: at Langton Castle both he and Malling had felt they had something in common. He now believed it had been a mistake. He had little in common with Malling, other than the realization of the depth and wealth of their heritage, summed up on a summer evening on the hill.

Defensively, Arnold said, 'I think that's somewhat exaggerating things. You may well be right, to some degree. I have no real opinion, or feeling about the matter. But you shouldn't confuse the mason's gilds with freemasonry.'

'I remember reading, Mr Landon, that no less an authority than Wycliffe once condemned the gilds.'

Arnold nodded. 'I can quote you. He denounced the new gilds, the *men of sutel craft*, because they conspired together so that no man of the craft should work for less than any other.'

'A trade union which became corrupted by power developed in secret.'

'I think you've still not understood the crucial break in the link between mediæval gilds and modern freemasonry. The travelling masons went to the lodges in the fifteenth century and made themselves known to the master in charge by a particular form of salutation.'

'A special handgrip.'

Arnold nodded. 'The secret handgrip is the only thing one can describe as a solid foundation for the erection of the vague and fantastic temple which later writers built to enshrine the mysteries of an occult freemasonry. Believe me, Mr Malling, as far as the available evidence goes there is simply nothing to show that modern philosophical freemasonry has its roots in the mediæval craft masonry. The first hint of "freemasonry" appears in a fifteenth-century rhymed treatise, but it contains no mystical peculiarities. Freemasonry is in fact an independent seventeenth-century growth. The mystical ritual wasn't really adopted until as late as 1773. The truth is, the whole thing was grafted on to the craft. It used its technical terms in a symbolic fashion. Nothing more.'

'But the gilds *were* secret. They were not to reveal what was done in the lodge,' Malling insisted.

'There was no doubt an *element* of secrecy about the craft,' Arnold admitted, 'and there is a superficial similarity also in the fact that skilled men possessed a knowledge of geometry at a time when all science, however elementary, savoured of magic. It's easy to understand how the gilds became surrounded by an air of mystery. But there is no *real* connection: the later body merely took over the words and symbols. There it ends.'

Tom Malling nodded, somewhat abstractedly. The glitter in his eyes had died, and he seemed calmer, almost relieved in some peculiar way by what Arnold had said. 'You may well be right. Freemasonry is evil . . . but the ancient craft gilds, from my understanding, had certain good things about them. The sworn masons, for instance . . .'

'You know about sworn masons?' Arnold asked in surprise.

Malling stared at him vaguely. 'I once read about Richard atte Chirche. It was in an old book, in the reference library . . .'

'The *Liber Albus*, perhaps.'

'It's possible.' Malling stared at his empty can of lager and nodded. 'Yes, they were responsible people. It's good to know that the connection between the crafts and the freemasons is tenuous, or even fraudulent . . .' He paused. 'It's a matter of little importance, I suppose, but I just had the feeling it would be ironic, feeling the way I do about the corrupt influences of the freemasons, that on my land there should have grown a gild to which freemasonry owed its origins.'

Arnold frowned. He watched Tom Malling warily. The comment suggested to him that the obsessions he had already detected in the farmer ran deeper than he had realized. Malling was a man given to over-reaction. The external person seemed controlled, balanced, equable in nature and friendly in temperament. But he was scarred inside by obsessive influences. Arnold remembered the bedroom upstairs, the fustiness of a room not used in years, the photographs of the woman in the dimness. And then there was his first impression of the house, with its old, untended garden, a flower garden of the kind a woman might have built and a man allowed to decay . . .

Impulsively he blurted out, 'You have a woman who comes in to clean, Mr Malling, but have you never married?'

There was a short silence. Malling continued to stare at the empty lager can. Then, silently, he rose and moved towards the door. Arnold rose also, feeling the blood drain from his cheeks, aware he had been guilty of a blatant and unwarranted intrusion into someone else's personal life. Malling led the way down the short passageway to the front door. He opened it and stepped out into the sunshine. He raised his head, looked at the sky, sniffed at the wind. 'It'll be a fine afternoon.'

'Yes,' Arnold agreed, subdued. 'Thanks for the lunch. I'd better be making my way back to the office now.'

There was a short silence. Somewhere up on the hill where Langton Castle stood rooks cawed raucously, disturbed by something or someone. Malling turned to look vaguely at Arnold, and something painful moved deep in his eyes, a long slow crawl of an unforgotten agony. 'I *did* marry,' he said.

Arnold made no reply, not knowing what to say, unhappy now that he'd even been so crass as to raise the subject.

'We lived in Cambridgeshire then,' Malling went on. 'Came north to this farm after we married. Isabel loved this land and so did I. We were happy. I thought that . . .' He grimaced suddenly, and his lips twisted as though there was a bitter taste on his tongue. 'She died . . .' He pondered the words, frowning, then shook his head, as though he rejected them as inaccurate. Arnold gained the impression that Malling was struggling within himself, forcing himself to accept a recollected reality rather than a myth. 'No . . . she committed suicide. It would be four years ago, now . . .'

Silence fell around them. The rooks were quiet, and the hills seemed to brood above the farmhouse, dwelling on the words Malling had uttered. Arnold began to understand. There were unspoken things between them, but he was now aware of what the empty bedroom with its old photographs might mean. The obsession with things of little importance to this farm, even though they might have wider social consequences, was an escape, a route Tom Malling took to avoid the painful personal things that affected him. To concentrate his venom and bitterness upon freemasonry meant that he could avoid turning inward to gnaw over the things that really hurt him, the loss of his wife, words that might have been said and perhaps never were, the sad detritus of regret that lay whispering like dried leaves in every man's mind when he contemplated the past and what the future might have held, had things turned out differently. Arnold thought of the vigils at Langton Castle.

'I'm sorry,' he said awkwardly. 'Life must be . . . lonely.'

Malling blinked. 'I manage,' he said crisply.

'I'm sorry, I didn't mean to imply . . .' Miserably, embarrassed, Arnold made things worse. 'It's just that I know neighbours can be no substitute for—'

'*Neighbours!*' Tom Malling almost spat out the word. 'Don't talk to me about neighbours! Or the Church. Mealymouthed words from the pulpit, explanations about holy ground being unsullied by suicides, sly sniggerings in the village. Hypocrisy and guilt, Mr Landon, these are the things which make up a village community. There is much evil in this world, and it needs extirpation. The ancient gilds had it right, perhaps.'

Arnold frowned. 'I don't follow—'

'The word neighbour,' Malling interrupted fiercely, changing tack, 'should mean friend, but when I look about me, in the village, and in the hills . . .' Malling half turned, looked out across the fells. Arnold stared with him, not certain what the farmer was looking at.

'Neighbours . . . There's at least one needs hanging,' Malling said in a soft, almost gentle tone, somehow the more chilling for its restraint. 'And one I'd quite cheerfully hang.'

But it was not until he was driving away from Langton

village that Arnold realized Tom Malling, when he spoke, had stared towards the head of the valley in which Kilgour House was situated.

CHAPTER 3

1

The Senior Planning Officer swivelled in his chair so that only his profile was presented to Arnold.

He was a large man, comfortably built, with a paunch that suggested it was pleasure rather than necessity that dictated his eating habits. This was in marked contrast to his predecessor, whose digestion was under permanent attack from his wife's cooking.

The new man was, like Arnold, a bachelor, however, and clearly in control of his gastronomic juices. He was rather less in control of his personality, which seemed to slip in and out of gear like a manic cuckoo clock. It was a matter for puzzled discussion in the office as to how he had managed to get this job: his interview must have taken place on a day when his star was in the ascendant. It was not that the office doubted his paper qualifications, or his experience for that matter: it was merely that he seemed to have been promoted beyond his capabilities in that, however good a planning officer he might have been, he seemed incapable of dealing with people.

Constitutionally incapable, Arnold considered: the man simply found himself uncomfortable when dealing with members of the human race. The profile was an example of the problem: it was not that the Senior Planning Officer had a Barrymore complex because someone had once told him he had a perfectly handsome, classical profile, it was merely that this way he did not need to meet Arnold's glance. The more serious symptom was that it was impossible to see him without an appointment, and when an appointment was made he was almost always out, called away on urgent business.

Communication was by memoranda: terse, grudging, and precise.

Consequently, it was with a feeling of surprise that Arnold found himself summoned to the presence. As the Senior Planning Officer stared nervously out of the window Arnold looked about him, noting the changes that had taken place in the room since its last occupancy. It was lighter, fresh wallpaper had been added of a kind unusual in the Morpeth offices, there were two framed Degas prints and a rather ineffectual watercolour of a Devon tor arranged on the wall behind the desk, and the curtains on the window were pastel shades with pretty flowers. And now that he had time to note more closely the Senior Planning Officer's appearance, Arnold became aware of the elegant grey suit and immaculate white shirt and blue tie, the carefully shaved nape of the neck, and the precise parting in the smooth greying hair. The Senior Planning Officer was a careful, fastidious man: Arnold wondered how he would manage when trouble came.

It would seem the Senior Planning Officer considered trouble had already come.

'Mr Landon,' he intoned in a modulated voice that had been developed against a shaving mirror, Arnold guessed, to check upon its weight, balance and moisture content. 'I've called you to my office to discuss a serious matter.'

Arnold believed it. So did the rest of the planning office.

The silence grew. Arnold was unwilling to break it. At last the Senior Planning Officer sighed and raised his profile a trifle. 'It's this Kilgour thing,' he said distastefully. 'There's been another letter.'

He gestured vaguely towards his desk. He showed an inch of cuff, precisely. Fascinated, Arnold was forced to drag his glance away towards the letter on the desk. 'Sir?'

'It's from that man Francis,' the Senior Planning Officer offered. 'He's threatening legal action against the department. Can he really do that, Mr Landon?'

'I'm not sure, sir. I mean, it's something that could better be answered by the Department of Administration.'

'This is a *planning* matter, London,' the Senior Planning Officer insisted sharply. 'There's no need to drag in the Administration people with their legal language. We must show we are capable of maintaining our own house in apple-pie order: no need to go running every time a problem arises. We must deal with it ourselves!'

What he really meant was *Arnold* must deal with it, of course. Arnold sighed. 'Of course. I merely meant, if it was a legal matter, it should be dealt—'

'This man is suing the owner of Kilgour House. That much is clear. But now he's saying that we should not treat the application from Mr Yates, or deal with it in any way, until the hearing of the lawsuit is completed. That could take months, Landon, years even. We all know,' he added gloomily, 'how dilatory lawyers can be. It's how they make their money.'

'I don't know how far the lawsuit has proceeded.'

'Then you need to find out, Landon, you need to find out,' the Senior Planning Officer said snappishly, clearly giving the impression he considered himself surrounded by an idiot clan. 'You're assigned to this application from Kilgour House: we certainly can't have the Francis fellow hauling the department into the courts. So forestall him, man. Find out what can be done.'

'I'm not sure how I can do that, sir.'

The Senior Planning Officer was faced with the same conundrum. He placed the tips of his elegant fingers together and a small wrinkle appeared at the side of his mouth as he began to whistle, gently and nervously. This interview had already gone on too long to suit his nervous disposition:

soon, he would begin to sweat. 'Well . . .' he murmured desperately, 'do what you can, man, do what you can. Go see this fellow. *Persuade* him.'

'Persuade him to do what, sir?'

The chair tilted irritably. 'Would you leave me now, Landon? I have another appointment.'

As he left the room Arnold noted that the appointments diary on the Senior Planning Officer's desk had a virgin, unsullied appearance. Nevertheless, Arnold had his instructions. He was to do what he could. He was to persuade the litigious Mr Francis.

'Persuade him to do what?' Hollywood Sanders sympathized. 'Pull back from his bloody action against Yates? No chance. He's virulent. Apart from that, it's none of our business, is it? Yates has put in a planning application. He's being sued by Francis. What's that got to do with us?'

'I suppose we could argue we have a *locus standi*,' Arnold suggested miserably. 'Right to appear in court as an interested party.'

'Try that on,' Sanders warned, 'and you'll have the Administration Department wallahs down on you like a ton of bricks. They got the lawyers; they like to do the court work.'

'But the Senior Planning Officer doesn't want them involved. It's a matter of departmental pride.'

'Bloody baronies, that's what we all work in. No one pulls together: each department jealously watching the others, buzzards over a piece of raw horsemeat.'

'It's an unusual way of looking at the public interest,' Arnold suggested.

Hollywood Sanders sniffed. 'Maybe so. But don't cross *our* Chief Buzzard for the sake of keeping your nose clean with Chief Buzzard Administration. Really want my advice, Arnold?'

'Please.'

'There's a new guy just joined us. Thorley. Green and fresh as a spring meadow. Hand the file to him.'

'The Senior Planning Officer—'

'Will never know. Until it's too late. And do you think he'd have the guts to bawl you out?'

Arnold was forced to admit he was tempted. But he shook his head. It would not be fair on young Thorley. 'I'll have to deal with it myself.'

'You're a nice guy, Arnold. *Stupid,* but nice.' Hollywood Sanders shook his head. 'You won't go far. But then, which of us will? Planning, like life, is a dangerous business—and one that none of us ever survives. Now isn't that a philosophical thought, Arnold?'

It was, but it didn't help Arnold to a solution.

The threatening letter from Mr Francis lay on his desk for several days. It was terse and to the point.

Dear Sir,

You will be aware that an action is pending between the writer and Mr Patrick Yates concerning the disputed ownership of the Kilgour Estates.

Should action be taken on the planning application submitted by the said Mr Yates, your department will be joined as a party to the action, and you will be held responsible for any works undertaken on the property to the detriment of the writer.

Yours faithfully,
R Francis

Arnold was not sure whether Francis had taken legal advice before writing the letter. It smacked of bluff, and a certain misunderstanding of the legalities involved. As far as the planning department was concerned, Patrick Yates was the duly registered owner of the estates and that was that, lawsuit or no lawsuit. On the other hand, the letter constituted notice, of a sort. Perhaps the best way out of the situation, Arnold concluded, was to do precisely what the

Senior Planning Officer had suggested. *Persuade* Mr Francis. To what course of action? That was another matter. Nevertheless, Arnold clung to the word *persuade* like a terrified parachutist. It might bring him safely to earth.

A visit to see, and talk to, the letter-writer was clearly necessary.

For the third time in two weeks Arnold took the road north from Morpeth towards Kilgour, Langton, and the sweeping rise of the Cheviot foothills.

The address on the letter had demanded a check on the map, and a chat with one of the older members of the planning department who knew the area well. Armed with detailed instructions Arnold set out from the office and looked for the coppiced hill above Langton that he had been warned about.

The sky was a shifting pattern of scudding clouds and the hills were clearly edged, the hint of rain in the air magnifying them slightly. The road was quiet and Arnold drove at a steady pace. When the coppice loomed up ahead he slowed, waiting for the turn-off: it was as well he had closely heeded the directions, otherwise he would have missed the narrow road that ran through the arched, deserted railway tunnel and branched left along the old track towards the cottage that lay half a mile on.

It was set under the overgrown hill that had once been a railway embankment. The cottage itself had started life as a tiny railway booking office: part of it had been demolished but the cottage itself had been renovated to some extent, though never finished. The roof was good, and the sitting-room and bedroom above seemed in sound order but the sagging stone to the right of the doorway in which the woman stood suggested that major structural repairs were required if the cottage was to remain habitable.

The woman was dressed to go out. She wore a light, belted raincoat. She was perhaps in her early forties, fair-haired, and her features were of a faded prettiness that had become marred by dissatisfaction. There was a petulance about her mouth that suggested to Arnold that she felt herself ill-used by the world, and the manner in which she used the cigarette in her left hand made him consider that anger and resentment would be one of the principal emotions that moved her.

As he stopped the car near the cottage she came forward. She was frowning, staring at him as though he did not measure up to her expectations, whatever they might have been.

'I was expecting a removals van,' she asserted with the belligerence of disappointment.

There seemed little Arnold could answer to the comment so he got out of the car awkwardly and said, 'This is Station Cottage?'

Her glance was sharp; it flicked over him like a paring knife, removed a slice for dissection and then discarded it. 'You didn't see a van on your way up here?'

'I'm sorry, I didn't.' Arnold hesitated. 'I'm actually looking for Mr Francis.'

It registered. The sharpness in her eyes was blunted for a moment, and then she looked at him again, warily. 'What do you want with him?'

'Is he here?'

'I'm *Mrs* Francis.'

They stood staring at each other as though preparing for conflict. Arnold could not understand the edge of tension that had already built up between them: she seemed resentful, and yet curious. He was unwilling to give her any information he didn't need to, but could not explain the feeling. It was as though he suspected she might use information as a sword, a method of attack.

'My name's Landon. I'm a planning officer at Morpeth.'

She was unimpressed. Her eyes said so.

'Your husband wrote to us,' Arnold tried again. 'I thought I'd better talk to him about it.'

'I wouldn't know what he'd write to you about,' she said, almost indifferently.

'It's about the lawsuit he has pending against Mr Patrick Yates.'

'*Christ!*' she said, and half turned away, thrusting the cigarette to her lips and drawing at it angrily.

'I take it he's not in at the moment,' Arnold suggested.

'Not at the moment, and not recently,' Mrs Francis said viciously. She stared at the cigarette for a moment, then dropped it, ground it out with her heel. Arnold was left with the impression she wished it was her husband's face. 'And I know sod all about what he's been writing you about. Not about that, and not about anything. Fact is, Mr Landon, I've had enough. The bastard walked out yesterday and it's taken him long enough to make a decision. *I* should have walked out on him years ago, and would have done if I'd had any sense. But I really thought when we came here things would change, that maybe we could get it together again, you know what I mean? Build our relationship, at the same time as we built this place together. *Build!* God, look at this place! I put my money into it, you know, and now the bastard's walked out! You sure you didn't see that bloody van?'

Arnold shook his head, embarrassed. 'I'm sorry, no. Er . . . the letter we had . . . it used Station Cottage as the address. Will Mr Francis be returning here?'

'When I'm gone?' She gave a harsh, barking sound that bore little resemblance to a laugh. 'Not bloody likely. It was my money, and that penniless bastard is getting nothing out of it. He's walked out and that's it. I'm closing down, moving out, and this goes on the market straight away. And he won't get his grubby fingers on a penny of it. So there's no chance he'll be getting back in here.'

The words she used about her husband bore little reflection of the image Arnold had of him at a distance: he had thought of him as the potential heir to a large estate, and this had clearly coloured his judgement. Unless that of Mrs Francis was completely soured. Perhaps something of his thoughts found echoes in her mind for she sneered suddenly, shaking her head. 'Planning officer, hey? He's been writing to you. And it's about that business over the lawsuit. Yes, you already said that, didn't you?' Her mouth was bitter, wry with the taste of resentment. 'That lawsuit, it's pie in the sky. Nephew of old Edridge he might have been, but he never cared a fig for the old man, any more than he cared for me. He married me because I could give him security; and he only tried to crawl back into Edridge's favour when he found that it would cost him if he didn't. He doesn't stand a cat in hell's chance in that lawsuit— and I hope he gets ripped to pieces by those shyster lawyers they employ in the courts. I want him to get shown up for the seedy bastard he really is.' She glared at him, thrusting her dislike of her husband into an overall hatred of all things male. 'I don't think I can help you, Mr Landon.'

'Thank you, Mrs Francis. I don't think you can. Unless you know where your husband can be contacted.'

'In hell, eventually. Until then, I couldn't care less.'

Arnold nodded and got back into his car. He reversed across the narrow lane with difficulty and manœuvred the car to return the way he had come. Mrs Francis watched sourly from the doorway of Station Cottage. As he slipped into first gear to drive away she called out to him, 'And if you see that bloody removals van, stir the lazy bastard to get up here!'

Arnold wondered what she had been like when the missing Mr Francis had first married her.

As he drove down the old railway track he considered it was likely he had had a wasted journey. He checked his watch. By the time he drove back to Morpeth the office would be closed. He had no idea where Francis had gone to, of course, but village life being what it was, it was quite possible that information would be available if he asked in the right area. He drove towards Langton village· Barnack

might be new, but vicars were usually recipients of information—and gossip.

The road looped over the hill past the coppice, and within
a mile or so he was back on the main road that ran into
Langton. Behind him was the valley where Kilgour lay; it
made Arnold think again of Tom Malling and something
crossed his mind briefly, a comment Malling had made.
There was something Arnold had found interesting, something he had meant to dwell upon, perhaps check up. The
thought danced away elusively: that happened to him more
and more these days, he thought gloomily. Advancing age;
the approach of senility.

There was something going on at Langton village.

The ruins of Langton Castle crowned the hill, and the
church nestled below, above the cluster of cottages and the
pub and the small village shops. To the left of the village
was an open meadow, and on it several marquees had been
erected. Several trestle tables were placed to the right of the
marquees and most of the population of the village seemed
to be scattered around the area. Arnold caught the flash of
sunlight on metal as the clouds above parted briefly and
sunshine flooded the village. Then the road dropped, he lost
sight of the meadow and he turned past the village shops to
climb up towards the church.

The vicarage was a dour, uncompromising building with
blackened stone and two blind windows on the north side,
one with a head of cusped ogee form. Arnold observed it as
he waited for an answer to the door bell. When the door
opened it was Mr Barnack himself who stood there.

'Ah, Mr Barnack . . . I wonder whether you can help
me.'

'Of course, Mr Landon. That's what I'm on earth for,'
Barnack said blandly. He brushed some crumbs from his
dingy-coloured sweater as he spoke and the slight bulge in
his cheek suggested to Arnold the vicar was half way through
a late lunch.

'I've just been up to Station Cottage to look for Mr Francis.'

'Oh yes.'

'He wasn't there.'

'Ah.'

'His wife told me he'd . . . left home. She didn't say *why* but I got the impression that the . . . er . . . domestic strife was of some long standing.'

'And you thought that perhaps information regarding this unhappy state of affairs might have reached my ears?'

'Something like that. I just wondered . . . would you know where I might locate Mr Francis?'

Barnack assumed an owlish look. Perhaps he thought it made him look wise; in fact, he merely appeared bemused by the sunlight. Heavily, he said, 'One does hear various pieces of information about local people, of course, but gossip . . .'

'I just want to know where he's moved to, so I can make contact. The fact is, he wrote to us, and the address given was Station Cottage, but—'

Barnack nodded sagely, accustomed to the vagaries and wanderings of his flock. 'He was not there. Yes, well, as I say, it is hardly my function to dispense gossip in the village. Equally, it *is* my function to render assistance where I am able. So, if I can satisfy one situation without offending the other I am happy to do so.'

Arnold waited.

'Of course,' Barnack continued smugly, 'while I am not really prepared to hazard a guess where Mr Francis might now be . . . ah . . . *living*, since I have no confirmation of the *fact*, I am certainly in a position to suggest to you where he *might* be this afternoon.'

Arnold sighed. 'And where might that be?'

'With the toxophilites,' Barnack intoned, making the group sound like a remote Christian sect.

'Archery?'

'The village is holding its fête this afternoon. An occasion for celebration which I always feel holds something vaguely pagan—in its roots, you know? However, all are gathered at Long Meadow this afternoon. You must have seen them as you entered the village. I suggest you go there, Mr Landon. It's more than possible Mr Francis will be present.'

'He's interested in archery?'

'Somewhere there,' Barnack said with a self-satisfied grin, 'I seem to detect a *non-sequitur*.' With every sign of enjoyment and anticipation he began to close the door. 'Let me simply add that he has *friends* who are interested and as for Mr Francis ... he does have a certain *macho* image to uphold ...'

Whatever the incumbent of Langton Church might feel about village fêtes and their possibly pagan origins—though Arnold suspected that Langton fête owed its conception to the 1930s rather than the 1300s—the villagers themselves seemed determined to enjoy the occasion. The entrance to Long Meadow was festooned with fluttering flags of all colours: a ruddy-faced farmer's daughter stood by a deal table at the entrance to the field collecting entrance money, and in the far end beyond the marquees a whistling and booming and cranking rattle pronounced the existence of a steam engine with its gathering of enthusiasts.

On the trestle tables that he had noticed there were scattered various field events, ranging from *Find the Lady* to jumble sales. A local schoolmaster sat in some rudimentary stocks for his pupils to send usually ill-directed tomatoes and wet sponges at him, and in one of the marquees a noisy game of bingo was inevitably under way.

The largest of the marquees was being used as a refreshment tent and several matrons stood at its entrance, sipping tea from paper cups. Children whooped around and from the loudspeakers slung among the bunting a recent pop song blared out, disregarded by all and sundry.

The archery enthusiasts were tucked away between the first and second marquees, with a demonstration area facing away from the main part of the fête, down towards the brook at the far end of Long Meadow. There were several barrels of beer nearby, and a dozen men partaking of refreshment. Arnold wondered about that, in view of the array of weapons present.

He was surprised by the weapons, as he drew near. He had perhaps expected to see the kinds of bows and arrows that were used in films and television plays, and from time to time in shop window displays. But as he looked around he realized this was a much more serious business than he had imagined. The weapons here on display were of a varied kind. There were some recognizable items that seemed to have been modelled on the old clothyards that were familiar to him from ancient manuscripts. On the other hand, there were modern varieties that owed more to science and technology than anything else. One glittering monster was being used for demonstration purposes: Arnold stood and watched for a few minutes as the muscular young man with the dark, curly hair and narrow lips flexed his muscles and brought the silently whirring aluminium cams at the bow tips into action. He was stocky, but well-built: his short sleeved shirt clung tightly to his powerful upper body and arms, and he clearly took pride in his gear and the bow he used. The leather guard on his arm, protecting the forearm against bowstring burns, was supple and gleaming, his green and brown camouflaged kit looked clean and new, and everything about him seemed to demonstrate sharpness and commitment.

Arnold didn't like his mouth: the sharpness and commitment were there too, and as he sent the broadhead arrow towards the target Arnold felt the man would have preferred a live target.

'About £350,' a woman's voice stated just behind him.

Arnold turned.

She was perhaps thirty years old, her dark hair cut short, her skin tanned by wind and sun, her clear eyes the palest blue imaginable. She was of medium height and slimly built, but the slimness was muscular, her hips and thighs powerful and strong, her breasts firm. She too wore a leather guard on her arm, and she carried a modern bow, although it was clearly not as expensive as the one wielded by the curly-haired man.

'Who is he?' Arnold asked.

'Nick Enwright,' she replied, hardly glancing at Arnold. 'Bit of a nutcase, really. I mean, £350! Mine cost me a hundred quid and it's good enough—and I'm committed. But Nick behaves as though he's in the bloody jungle. It's like he believes anything that moves is fair game and so he's got to have a machine that'll knock over whatever comes within range. He doesn't seem to realize we don't get too many elk, whitetail or mule deer around here. What he'd really like is black bear. But in Northumberland? And you don't see too many shark off the Farne Islands—and seals don't move fast enough to make fair game.'

'He actually goes hunting?'

The woman looked at him quickly, as though she felt she had been talking out of turn, exposing thoughts that should have remained unspoken. She looked Arnold over, perhaps aware of him for the first time. She showed in her glance that she thought him unworthy of anxiety and she smiled vaguely. 'Who knows? Better ask the magistrates.'

She moved away and Arnold watched her go. An attractive walk, an attractive body. Her features were a little hard, perhaps, and maybe she was putting too much effort into her athletic image, but he guessed she would be a determined, positive woman with a mind of her own.

Even if there was a hint of envy in her words and the way she looked at the man called Enwright.

Arnold moved on. Ranged along one of the trestle tables was a selection of magazines and books, competing with the table next to it which carried second-hand gear for the enthusiastic toxophilite. Arnold briefly scanned the cult magazines stuffed with information, advertisements for bows and arrows, leather guards, information about equipment and technical articles about drawstring weights and pulling power, cable guards, calibrations and stabilizers. When he saw articles about blood trails and multi-blade broadheads he gave up and moved on, to look at ex-Vietnam Camo jackets and bottles of doe-in-rut urine, 'guaranteed to lure bucks within shooting distance'.

'The lunatic fringe, Landon. It isn't what archery is all about.'

Arnold recognized the sharp tone before he turned. He was surprised momentarily, but then his surprise quickly evaporated. A meeting of this kind was not entirely illogical for a man with a passion for military history and an interest in mediæval weapons.

'Professor Evesham. Good afternoon.'

Alan Evesham was dressed in a light jacket and oatmeal-coloured trousers. He was certainly not prepared to undertake any shooting but the evil-looking crossbow he carried in his arms was probably not intended for actual use, but rather as part of a display.

'I've got a stack of stuff in the car,' Evesham confirmed. 'There's a mediæval section in the display in the marquee. Some interesting stuff there. I've got a few items which will surprise them.'

'You're not an archer, though?'

Evesham hesitated. 'I've done some shooting. I've even used this one a few times. And I am a member of the club, though I don't go in for some of the nonsenses of the real enthusiasts. Still, hardly imagined *you* were interested. Hidden depths, Landon.'

'I'm afraid I've misled you. I've no interest in archery.'

The veneer of vague cordiality that had overlain Evesham's manner slid away, its sheen rapidly disappearing at the Professor's realization that Arnold was here by chance. 'I see. Just been poking around at the castle, hey? Have you got anything new to help? I saw you wandering off around the chapel, but I can't imagine you'll find anything significant there.'

'I'm not sure you're correct in calling it a chapel. Surely, as a military historian, you'd assume the building lay in an indefensible position?'

'Outside the inner wall?' Evesham shrugged. 'Not unusual. Of course . . .' His voice died away as he pondered on the matter. Irritation took over; Arnold guessed it was occasioned by the thought that once again an amateur was trying to tell an expert what he should have known in the first place. 'Don't see what importance it can be anyway,' Evesham argued. 'The thing is, a building which postdates the period we're interested in can hardly be expected to reveal much in our search for Ailnoth.'

'There are Roman tiles in that structure.'

Evesham stared at him belligerently. 'So?'

'I . . . I'm not sure. But the matter needs investigating.'

'And that's what you've been up there for today? Waste of time.'

'Actually, I haven't been up to the castle at all today.'

'But you said—'

'No, Professor Evesham,' Arnold interrupted quietly, '*you* said. I've been looking for someone. I was told by Mr Barnack that he might possibly be here.'

'At the demonstration?' Evesham glowered about him. 'Most of the damned village is here, that's for sure. Who you looking for?'

'A Mr Francis, from Station Cottage.'

'Don't know him,' Evesham announced and walked brusquely away.

Irritated by Evesham's rudeness, Arnold strolled around the perimeter of the display. It was quite possible Francis was here, but there was no way Arnold would be able to discover him in this throng. Nor indeed did he feel he really wanted to be bothered any longer: he found the atmosphere in the Long Meadow vaguely disturbing. It was supposed to be a demonstration of toxophily, of weapons old and new. The object was to recruit to the club, clearly, and contests had been arranged for people at various stages in skills development, including a small school for children. But there were vague, almost indefinable overtones which Arnold found distasteful. The young man with the curly hair and the muscles was still flexing his powerful bow in front of an admiring audience, and at a small group to his left a tall man with a grey-flecked, neatly-trimmed beard was holding forth to a small audience about a safari he had undertaken in Kenya.

'The fact is, even the Wata, the legendary elephant hunters of the south, have to use deadly toxins. They can draw bows a white man couldn't even bend but arrow power alone is not enough to stop dangerous game. On my second safari I brought down a buffalo. I also got two antelope and a couple of guinea fowl. Of course, when I took the guinea fowl I abandoned the hollow tubes of light alloy: for that prey it's enough to use wooden arrows without sharp pointed tips. I mean, the impact of the arrow itself is enough to pierce small game . . .'

Bombast, Arnold thought, and strolled on.

He was not enjoying the afternoon. He really had better things to do than stand around listening to people who were not clear whether they were Crècy-orientated or Sherwood-Green fixated, artists or killers. Nor did he care generally for fêtes as a whole: clusters of people noisily determined to enjoy themselves tended to make him shrink away. The hills were clean and the air clear and he could have been walking above Rothbury Crags and seeing the hovering falcon rather than wasting his time here in Long Meadow, among the cacophony he disliked.

'I'm surprised to see *you* here, Mr Landon.'

Arnold was also surprised. 'Mr Malling!'

'I hadn't realized archery was one of your interests.'

'Nor I yours.'

Tom Malling wrinkled his nose, and glanced down at his dog, standing close to his heels. 'I'm not in the slightest bit interested in archery. These people . . . overgrown children or subconscious psychopaths . . . I'm not sure which.' He frowned. 'I must confess to a certain curiosity, of course. The past . . . fascinates me. I think we have that in common.'

'Buildings, not weapons,' Arnold suggested.

'For me, people, and the way they behave,' Malling countered. 'I suppose it's one reason why I always come to the fête. One has to support charities, of course . . . but when people get together on occasions like this something odd seems to happen. They behave in ways that are uncharacteristic.'

'I think I know what you mean,' Arnold replied, as he watched a stout lady, red in the face, trundling along in a three-legged race some fifty yards distant.

'Displays such as this bother me,' Malling said.

'I beg your pardon?' Arnold was confused.

'The archery. In other centuries, weapons such as the bow were used for war. This is different. It's an enthusiasm which borders on the unhealthy.'

'Why?'

'You can cause suffering with such weapons—even when they are of such modern manufacture. And that modernity, all this paraphernalia with these modern bows, it's as though it's caused by an obsession with death. In the old days things were different. Men tried to better their lot, control the evils that lurked among them, used weapons for functional purposes—'

'I think they still had archery meetings,' Arnold suggested, 'even in the fifteenth century.'

'Yes, to sharpen their skills! But not to play at death-dealing. Not to use weapons as instruments of mere pleasure.

No, it was a simpler society, one in which standards of behaviour were measured more carefully, and in which justice and punishment—though hardly administered—were not befogged by changing social attitudes and weakness, liberal viewpoints, and a social conscience. Everyone knew his place; they all knew what the punishment might be for transgression; and there were groups of men who were empowered to order society.'

The conversation bothered Arnold: Malling's voice had taken on a disturbing intensity. Arnold was not quite sure what the farmer was talking about and in an endeavour to avoid the embarrassment he was beginning to feel, he made things worse. 'In any case,' he said, 'it seems the world and his wife is here at Long Meadow.'

The short silence that fell between them was sharp. Arnold was aware of the rising colour in his face and he looked down at his feet. 'I'm sorry . . . I seem to . . .'

'Just what exactly are you doing here, Mr Landon?' Malling asked in a cool tone.

Arnold shrugged. 'Wild goose chase, I suppose. I needed to see a man called Francis. Lives in Station Cottage. Or did.'

'*Did?*'

'I met his wife. She was leaving. It seems Mr Francis has . . . has left her.'

'I see.' The words lingered in the air between them, almost like portents. Arnold glanced at Malling's face: the farmer's features were calm but something raged briefly in his eyes, perhaps a memory of disaster or of loss. The passion was abruptly replaced by coldness as Malling met Arnold's glance, then turned his head, looking around them at the scattering in Long Meadow.

'I think, Mr Landon, I might be able to help you. You say you want to meet Mr Francis. I think that'll be him, just over there.'

The coldness in Malling's tone was marked with contempt

and dislike. It found some echoes in Arnold's own feelings. Malling was pointing out the man with the grey-flecked beard who had been boasting of his successful slaughters in Kenya.

2

The man who was pursuing a legal action against Patrick Yates of Kilgour House was an individual very much in control of himself. He had a studied elegance which suggested he was aware of the attention he drew and battened upon it, encouraged it and honed it to his own advantage. His eyes were grey and crinkled in a friendly fashion as he spoke even though it was affectation that drew the veil of friendliness: there would be calculations behind the eyes that would not be for publication.

He was about forty years of age. He had spoken of his time in Africa: he must have been there for a number of years, since the mahogany of his skin owed little to an English sun. He had a wide mouth that hinted at a generosity Arnold guessed was spurious: there was something about the man that suggested he would always have an eye to the main chance, whether it was a business opportunity or a personal relationship.

As Arnold approached, the group he had been talking to was breaking up. Francis turned, became aware of Arnold's purposeful approach and half smiled.

'Mr Francis?' Arnold inquired.

'I am he.'

'My name's Landon.'

'I'm pleased to meet you.'

'I went up to Station Cottage but you weren't there.'

'No.' The grey eyes had hardened perceptibly, but the mouth still held the hint of a professional smile. 'I'm here. And you're looking for me, I presume. Are you a bill collector, Mr Landon?'

'Hardly that,' Arnold replied, shaking his head. 'I'm from the planning department at Morpeth.'

'I see.' Francis considered the information for a moment, while the smile faded. 'And what is it you want of me?'

'Well, we got your letter . . . I'm assigned to deal with the planning application from Patrick Yates, and I really wanted to talk to you, explain that our duties—'

'I'm not terribly concerned about your *duties*, Mr Landon,' Francis interrupted in a cold voice. 'I'm more concerned about my rights.'

'I understand that, but I'd like to explain our position to you.'

'And just what might that position be?' Francis drawled mockingly.

Arnold hesitated. 'The application from Mr Yates, it's one that we're called upon to process. Now of course, we have no legal interest in the dispute that you have with Mr Yates, and clearly we would have no argument to raise one way or the other—'

'But if you deal with the application,' Francis cut in, 'you would in my view be making a statement.'

'Surely, not so—'

'The statement that you believe Mr Yates is entitled to undertake developments on the land in question. But I contend he has no such rights. *I* contend that he obtained that land by fraud, by undue influence, and by chicanery of the worst kind. And anyone who supports his situation in any way whatsoever is likely to find himself involved in the same kind of legal action I'm bringing against Yates!' His voice had risen, the heat in his blood reflected in a growing anger as he dwelled upon real or imagined injustices. 'The fact is, Landon, Yates has tried to cheat me out of my inheritance. I don't intend standing around to let it happen. I'd see the bastard dead first. But I warn you: I'm suing Yates, and if you step across my path I'll drag your bloody council in as well. And that, I believe, must conclude our conversation.'

'Mr Francis, please—'

'We've nothing more to say to each other, my friend,' Francis hissed, and the cold menace in his tone caused Arnold to withdraw the restraining hand he had held out in protest. He stood there, watching Francis march angrily away across the field towards the marquee, and after a moment, feeling humiliated and angry at Francis's rude dismissal, he turned away to head back towards the entrance.

The girl he had noticed earlier was standing some twenty feet away, staring at him. She seemed troubled, and as Arnold walked past her she stepped forward. 'Excuse me . . .'

'Yes?'

She hesitated. She suddenly seemed younger than he had thought, uncertainty removing the jauntiness in her manner, and she smoothed the leather guard on her arm in a nervous reaction that belied her previously confident air. 'You were talking to Bob . . . He seemed upset.'

'He was certainly rude.'

'He can be that.'

'Yes, well, if you'll excuse me—'

'Please, a moment . . . What was he upset about?'

Arnold looked at her, took in again the short, attractively cut dark hair, and noted the squarish jaw that removed some of the femininity from her face, giving it a slightly masculine, over-positive look, and hesitated. 'I'm not sure I can tell you. It's his business . . . his reasons . . .'

'Not if it was about me,' she flashed.

Arnold observed her again, with curiosity. She seemed suddenly nervous and very vulnerable. 'I can't see what it has to do with you. I'm a planning officer, Miss . . .'

'Gregory,' she supplied. 'Wendy Gregory. I . . . I'm a PE teacher over at Broadwood,' she added inconsequentially. 'A planning officer . . . I thought . . .' She did not explain what she thought, but stared wordlessly for a few moments at Arnold.

'Yes, well, it was a pleasure to meet you,' Arnold said after the awkward silence, 'but I assure you, it was a planning matter and—'

'It's about Kilgour, then.'

Arnold shook his head helplessly, unwilling to discuss the matter.

'Why don't you help him?' she asked with a sudden passion. 'Why do you make things difficult? He's in the right, you know!'

'Miss Gregory, I'm in no position—'

'The trouble is, Yates is a magistrate, a wealthy man— even if it is Bob's money and land he's wealthy with—and it's always the same story isn't it? The Establishment, the clique, the society a man moves in, it'll serve to protect him, they all gang up on the outsider, the man who doesn't have the passwords, the *entrée*, the man who doesn't fit because his background isn't a cultivated one in the English scene! Oh, how I hate the *Establishment*!'

'Miss Gregory, I really don't know what you're talking about.'

'Then it's about time someone put you straight!' Miss Gregory's chin was set squarely as she glared at Arnold, determined to get her point across to him. 'I don't know how much you know about the background to the quarrel between Yates and Bob Francis, but believe me, it's not of Bob's making. All he wants—all he's ever wanted—is that which is his by right.'

'Miss Gregory—'

'I've no doubt the council at Morpeth will have heard one side of the story from Yates,' she sneered. 'After all, as a magistrate and an important figure in the county he'll have more than a few friends in the Establishment, Lord Lieutenant and all that jazz. But let's get at the facts!'

'I've already had a conversation with Mr Yates where he explained to me . . .'

'There you are!' Wendy Gregory exclaimed triumphantly.

'*He's* explained things, so that's all there is to it! But it's not the truth, don't you see? Yates has twisted and perverted the truth to suit himself: he's well practised at it because he's been doing it for twenty years!'

An altercation seemed to have started near the marquee. An argument had developed, someone shouting angrily and waving his arms about, surrounded by a small knot of people. For a few moments Arnold hoped that the determined Miss Gregory might be sidetracked by the noise but she had her pale blue eyes fixed on Arnold and was not to be distracted.

'He'll have told you how he came to Kilgour donkey's years ago and helped Charles Edridge turn the estate around. But did he happen to mention that he was a solicitor who had been struck off?'

Arnold hesitated. 'No, he didn't mention that.'

'I should think not! Because it has a bearing on the whole story. It explains so much, you see: the truth is that Yates was removed from the roll of solicitors twenty years ago, shortly after he qualified, in fact, because of falsifications in the client's accounts of his firm. I don't know the whole story but Bob dredged it out—it seems Yates had ideas above his station even in those days and wanted to cut a dash, live beyond his means. He got his sticky fingers in the till, got caught, but the firm didn't prosecute. They didn't want to have the scandal, and I guess they weren't too happy to have their own negligent supervision exposed, so they were satisfied with his being struck off. That's when he first came into contact with Charles Edridge.'

Arnold took a deep breath. 'Miss Gregory, I really must interrupt. I'm a planning officer. I wanted to see Mr Francis because he has written to us, threatening to draw us into his lawsuit. He has refused to discuss the matter and I don't see therefore that what you tell me is relevant—'

'If you listen, you'll understand!' Wendy Gregory flashed at him. 'It's because people haven't been prepared to listen that that bastard Yates has got away with things for so long!'

The noise at the marquee had risen, the argument spilling inside the tent, with someone running across towards the cars parked at the far end of the Long Meadow. Arnold's attention was dragged back to the insistent Miss Gregory.

'He wheedled his way into Charles Edridge's affections. Yes, I use the word advisedly: *affections*. Oh, it wouldn't have started like that, of course. A good companion, a pleasant guy to have around at house parties. But the fact is, Charles Edridge was a funny kind of bloke. My own theory is he was repressed as a child: dominant mother and all that. He went to Cambridge, grew up trying to be one of the smart set, went out to Kenya with his cousin, Bob's father, did a bit of farming there, but somehow, something was *wrong*. Bob's got some photographs taken on the French Riviera, the wealthy, smart set. Colonel Edridge is there, but standing so self-consciously, *pretending* to have a good time!'

Arnold eyed the angry young woman facing him. 'I'm not sure what you're trying to say,' he remarked, interested now in spite of himself.

'Look at those photographs and you'll see what I mean. He was *lonely*. He was in his late twenties, but he hadn't grown up. Maternally repressed, eager to show his manhood, wanting to be one of the boys, whatever the reasons deep down, in my view—and Bob's—basically he was a lonely unhappy man whose greatest problem was suppressed homosexual tendencies.'

'Are you saying . . .'

'Later events prove it,' Wendy Gregory said soberly. 'The guy was a closet gay. He didn't know it, or like it, and in those days it was a criminal situation to be in. But however hard he tried, in the end he had to admit he was homosexual.'

'Mr Yates told me that Colonel Edridge had married.'

Wendy Gregory made a humphing noise of contempt. 'What does that prove? He married a Swedish woman, but clearly she was unable to provide him with the security and affection he needed. The marriage failed, inevitably, because he was trying to live up to an image. And then Patrick Yates came on the scene.'

Arnold thought back to his visit to Kilgour House and his meeting with its owner. He shook his head. 'If you're trying to suggest that Yates . . . I have to say, there are some letters on the planning application file that would argue that Yates's inclinations are far from homosexual.'

Wendy Gregory smiled. There was no humour in he smile, and it gave her features an unpleasant cast. 'You don't understand much about men and women, Mr Landon. I thought I made it clear that Patrick Yates had an objective in life: to better himself, make himself rich, *get on*. And he's ruthless as hell: he'd do anything to get what he wanted. He cultivated Edridge, became his friend, made himself useful in managing the estate, but he did more than that. He became Edridge's lover. And don't look so pained. The fact is, I'm convinced Yates is bisexual: I *know* he can get turned on by a woman. There was one occasion . . .' A slow flush of mixed anger and embarrassment stained her cheek. 'Well, no matter . . . but I'm telling you he's got quite a reputation in the county. There've been quite a few women who've gone for his smooth charm—and who've been turned on by the insulting way he can treat a woman occasionally. More than one has got serious—there's been at least one divorce, and if rumour is true, there's even been a gas oven case. But that's been his *fun*, and his real inclination: using women for sexual enjoyment. But that never stopped him from developing the relationship with Charles Edridge that he did.'

'But why?'

'To make Edridge dependent upon him, bind him closer, *commit* him,' Wendy Gregory said calmly. 'What can be said by way of pillow talk is more likely to be taken to heart than a conversation in the morning room over sherry before lunch.'

The anger seemed to have subsided at the marquee. The knot of people had broken up. Arnold caught a glimpse of Alan Evesham marching back to the tent from the line of cars. His stiff-legged walk suggested his customary ill humour had worsened and he was keen to vent his spleen on someone. Arnold was grateful suddenly that Wendy Gregory had detained him.

'This is all very interesting, Miss Gregory, but I still don't see what bearing it has upon my own interest in the situation.'

'I'm trying to fill you in on the kind of man Yates *is*,' she insisted, 'so that all you people at Morpeth don't get the wrong idea about Bob Francis. He's been wronged, you see, and yet he doesn't seem to be able to get the message across to the people who matter.'

'I can't say *I* matter,' Arnold offered feebly, but escape was not that easy.

'You're *involved*, and it's important you know and *understand*. When Bob was small, he remembers, Colonel Edridge was a frequent visitor: he spent summers with Bob's father. But everything changed after Patrick Yates came on the scene. It soured. Yates began to extend his influence over Edridge: made himself indispensable around the estate first, and then began to pour the poison into the colonel's ear. There is no doubt that Bob was always regarded as Charles Edridge's heir, but Yates changed that, quite simply, by causing Edridge to believe that Bob was unworthy, and by *arranging* things in such a way that it seemed Bob's father was an enemy, rather than a friend.'

'Arranging things?'

Wendy Gregory smiled cynically. 'The short period Patrick Yates spent in the legal profession wasn't wasted. As I understand it from Bob, the estate needed a capital injection. There was a family trust of some kind, in which the capital was locked up. The Colonel couldn't touch it, but it seems Yates came up with the idea of breaking the trust, with the co-operation of Bob's father. The idea was that Colonel Edridge would actually draw upon the invested funds—there was a complaisant elderly trustee in the thing somewhere—and then Bob's father would bring an action against the trustee for breach. The idea was to get the thing formally aired, with a settlement being reached, a compromise being made out of court with a sum being handed over to Bob's father and the Colonel getting what he needed to sort out his problems financially.'

'But that's not what happened?' Arnold asked, intrigued.

'Exactly. The action came on, but somehow it wasn't the way it had been planned. It suddenly became *serious*. The lawyers weren't playing the game. The breach was being pursued. Bob's father couldn't understand it, but suddenly all communication between him and the Colonel ceased, no compromise was reached, he found himself as an aggrieved plaintiff—and he won.'

'I don't understand.'

'Neither did he. I mean, all Bob's father got out of it was a declaration. The trustee was found in breach of trust. There were costs of fifteen thousand quid, and the Colonel had to pay up. You'd have thought that would have damned Yates in Edridge's eyes, but the reverse happened. It was Bob's father who got cast as the grasping villain of the piece —and Patrick Yates as the supportive confidant of the Colonel. The whole business caused a serious rift in the family, and bound Yates even more closely to the Colonel —who was now getting on a bit, and needing Yates more than ever. It was a nasty business altogether—and Bob firmly believes it was all clearly planned, right from step one.'

The story had the sad ring of truth to Arnold. It was plausible enough, given the possible nature of Charles

Edridge. An isolated and distant man who had thrown himself into the social whirl of the upper set after university in a desperate attempt to find a place for himself and his personality; a man perhaps with no great gift for friendship who had married to nullify the intensity of his dangerous sexual needs. After the break-up of the marriage, the clear impossibility of producing an heir could well have pushed Edridge towards a close relationship with his cousin, with the idea and intention that the son, Robert Francis, would eventually succeed to the Kilgour Estates.

But had Patrick Yates really played Iago in real life? Had he manœuvred Edridge and Francis in an elaborate chess game where he would be the only eventual winner? And had the present owner in fact possessed the cold commitment to use sexual activity with Edridge to cement the relationship and eventually lay claim to the estates?

'No one in the family ever got to see Charles Edridge towards the end, you know,' Wendy Gregory asserted. 'He was kept locked away. There are stories in the village about the filthy rooms on the top storey where he lived, but that could just be malicious village gossip.' Wendy Gregory screwed up her pale blue eyes in thought. 'Difficult to determine, isn't it, between gossip and fact? But what I've told you is largely true. And it is true that no one saw Edridge for two years before he died. And the will left everything to Yates.'

'When did Mr Francis find out?' Arnold asked.

The woman shrugged, glanced around the meadow as though seeking confirmation from the man they spoke of. 'I'm not really sure. Several years, I'd guess. And Bob had adopted a . . . different lifestyle. He'd stayed on in Africa. Got into safaris, that sort of thing.' She grinned nervously. 'I think he saw himself as a cross between Hemingway and Gregory Peck in *Mogambo*, if you know what I mean. He was trying to write, got a few things published, but was out in the bush a lot. Bit isolated. Anyway, when he did get to hear about the estates, well, it was all a bit late. He was short of cash too, and . . . I understand there were problems with his wife . . . The upshot is, he was delayed returning, and when he did get back to England the lawyers told him it was all signed, sealed and difficult to upset. So, he took advice, moved into the cottage near here, got his thing together and took Yates to court. The law, of course, takes a hell of a time to get rolling. But it's finally on, at last.'

Arnold stared at the young woman. He nodded. 'I can understand all that. But why Mr Francis should want to drag us in . . .'

'He's touchy. You've got to understand,' she pleaded, 'he's had a rough time. He's become obsessed, the thing against Yates rules his head, he can't think of much else. Maybe he . . . over-reacts when he feels himself threatened, and the application that you're dealing with, well, it's another nail to shore up Yates's rights to the estate, you know what I mean?'

Arnold regarded Wendy Gregory carefully. 'And how do *you* feel about Mr Yates?'

She met his gaze boldly. 'He needs burying. The one satisfaction I have is what I once told him to his face. It was at the hunt ball. I was sixteen—just bloody sixteen, for God's sake, and he tried his charm on me. I laughed in his face. Then he tried to get a bit physical and I told him what I thought of him—old enough to be my father and coming it on with me. Like I said: the man needs *burying*.'

'I get the impression that . . . feeling is heightened by the way you feel Mr Francis has been treated.'

The pale blue eyes slipped away momentarily. Then her chin came up. 'You could say that. I think Bob deserves to nail that bastard Yates, and I hope he does. If I can help, I will.'

'Like talking to me?'

'It may help.'

'Mr Francis has your full support, then?'

For a moment she seemed about to say something and then her glance clouded, as though she detected something behind the question that she was unwilling to deal with, or admit. She stared at Arnold for a moment, and then without another word she turned and strode away, her muscular calves firm and strong, the line of her body stiff with something that could have been pride, or indignation, or determination.

Arnold would never know. But as he watched her walk away across the Long Meadow, stripping the leather guard from her arm, he wondered just how full her support for Bob Francis might be, and how far she would go in her furthering of his cause. It had led her to insisting that Arnold Landon have a full briefing of the story according to Bob Francis, merely on the basis that it *might* help Francis to have the planning office at least apprised of the 'facts', if that was what they were.

What was certain was that Francis was clearly capable of arousing a fierce loyalty in the breast of the young physical education teacher striding across the meadow. A loyalty that was in sharp contrast to the other image Arnold held in his mind: a woman in a raincoat, fading, disappointed and bitter, anxious to shed the last remnants of a relationship that had gone sour, and determined that the man who had left her should get nothing more from her as long as he lived.

CHAPTER 4

1

The following week remained hot and dry. Arnold spent the days working on some planning schedules that had been called for by the council, and his evenings tending his garden. At the weekend he drove out to Langton Castle, alone, and pottered around the ruin that Evesham had identified as the castle chapel. The glimmerings of some theories began to emerge in Arnold's mind, but the evidence was scant or even non-existent: and Arnold was aware of the dangers inherent in any such investigation, where enthusiasm for an idea caused the theorist to make facts fit those theories. He needed to do some reading, and more groundwork.

He found little time to dwell upon the planning application relating to Kilgour House. It was fairly straightforward, of course, apart from the objections, and he had arranged to meet several objectors in his office the following week. He did not set great store by the meeting: he had the feeling it would be unhelpful and difficult, because as far as he could see from the submissions they had little relevance to the planning application itself.

As for the character and lifestyle of Patrick Yates, that was none of his business. He admitted to being somewhat intrigued by Wendy Gregory's story, intrigued enough, indeed, to make some personal and discreet inquiries about Yates. He found responses wary. Yates had been elevated to the bench some years before and was reckoned a conscientious magistrate: the trouble was, it seemed, he was so conscientious that he sometimes went a bit over the top with some offences. Comments had appeared in the local press, suggesting that there were some people who seemed to want to make poaching a hanging offence, and one or two remarks had been made about Yates's sexual vitality, but Arnold had been disinclined to pursue them. Gossip of that kind was distasteful. Nevertheless, he did ponder upon the very real impact Patrick Yates seemed to make upon the women with whom he came into contact. His housekeeper, Pauline Callington, for instance: she had been a mixture of emotions, chief among which, Arnold suspected, was a cold rage that she had been treated as a servant by Yates in front of a stranger, when she clearly felt she deserved something better. A closer relationship, perhaps, than was normal, Arnold considered.

And then there was Wendy Gregory. There was no doubt she was in love with Bob Francis, and it was likely she was the cause of Francis leaving his wife. Idly, Arnold wondered whether Francis was now living with the physical education teacher with the pale blue eyes, though it was really none of his business. But gossip would be seething in the village, he had no doubt. As for her stories about the sexual predilections of the owner of Kilgour, well, Arnold was inclined to discount them. A sixteen-year-old girl could imagine things, and such memories would become enhanced by the passage of time, while other stories she had retailed or suggested seemed to Arnold to be the product of an overheated imagination, further fired by the breath of passion for Yates's enemy, Bob Francis. A bisexual who had led a woman to kill herself for love? It seemed unlikely to Arnold, not in this modern world. The older romantic years he himself dreamed of, well, perhaps it would have been different then . . .

Alan Evesham did not ring him during the week to fix another appointment, but that did not disturb Arnold. The odd scene at Long Meadow when Evesham had clearly been upset about something had demonstrated to Arnold, even if he was not earlier aware of it, that the man had a nasty temper that could explode if he was crossed. Arnold felt that if new theories came to light about the chapel at Langton Castle it was quite on the cards that Evesham would explode again, and Arnold was not keen to be around in that event.

Nevertheless, he pottered around at the site, inspecting the greenish-yellow tiles in the wall more closely and making an effort to trace accurately the line of the walls. The building was certainly larger than would normally have been expected of a castle chapel, and there were internal wall foundations that suggested to him a more complicated set of inner cells than would have been normal. Time and again, however, his mind drifted back to the bricks above the Roman tiles. He could not be certain, but there was something odd about their colour, something he could not quite place. The doubt niggled at him, teasing him, and became oddly overlaid by the remarks Tom Malling had made to him about freemasonry, and the older, secret gilds of the masons.

Once again, the elusive butterfly of thought alighted in his brain, a comment Malling had made, a name he had mentioned . . . This time, before the mental insect could take wing again Arnold had seized it, the name at least: Richard atte Chirche.

He could not recall the context in which it had been used. But it was of little importance anyway.

On the Monday morning the three men filed into his office to discuss the objections they had raised in respect of the Kilgour planning application. Arnold had suspected it was going to be a difficult meeting and had fortified himself with an early cup of coffee. They sat ranged before him, two elderly men dressed in faded jackets and trousers, a second-best finery that had seen better days, and a younger man, stocky, clad in a checked shirt that strained against his deep chest, jeans and smart leather boots. There was something familiar about him, but Arnold had no time to dwell upon it as introductions were furnished.

'I'm Saul Eldon,' the man with the bald head and sad eyes announced. 'I farm on the Kilgour Estate—Ash Farm.' He contemplated Arnold for several seconds, his hound's eyes gloomy, his lower lip drooping as though all his life he had suffered disappointment, and then he said, 'It was Mr Francis who told us it was best we came personally to talk to you about the estates and the application and all that. This is Mr Norwich . . .'

'Sam Norwich.' This man was different. He had allowed Eldon to take the lead as the oldest of the three but devils of anger danced in his eyes and his brown gnarled hands were clenched, not from nervousness, but from a barely controlled temper. It was not his present surroundings that bothered him, but what he saw as the injustices of years. He wanted action. He made Arnold nervous.

Arnold looked at the young man with the black curly hair. 'I'm Nick Enwright,' the man said, and Arnold recalled where he had seen him: at Long Meadow, drawing the bow of laminated graphite. The man's face was hard, his mouth set: he would be regarding this meeting as a waste of time. For him there would be other ways in which to solve a problem, and they wouldn't involve talking. Arnold swallowed, and turned back to Saul Eldon.

'I'm the planning officer dealing with the application in which you have an interest and to which you've raised objections. My name is Landon. I'm afraid my unpleasant duty is to tell you that I can't see anything in your submissions which gives grounds for raising the objections you do. I mean, there are no legal infringements mentioned, no problems that can be put before the planning committee in due course—'

'Mr Landon, we want *justice*,' Saul Eldon pleaded. Nick Enwright stirred, annoyed at the pleading, but remained silent as Saul Eldon continued. 'I've been on the Kilgour Estates for over twenty years, Mr Landon. You need to listen to me. When the Colonel ran the place himself we had certain agreements and he always honoured them, because he was a gentleman. He maintained all the fences around the woods, and the windbreaks. He let us take fallen timber for firewood. He paid half the cost of repainting the windows and doors of the cottages—'

'For God's sake, Saul,' the angry man beside him interrupted, 'them days is long gone.'

'Even so, Sam,' Eldon insisted wearily, 'it has to be said.'

'Things changed when Mr Yates took over the management of the farms,' Sam Norwich argued, his eyes narrowed angrily as he made his point. 'You've been out there, I believe. You've seen how some of the farms and cottages have been allowed to rot—and we know why. So that Yates can get more money after the tenants have gone. And he can raise more money on the vacant property, for himself.'

'I'm afraid there's nothing illegal in that,' Arnold suggested. 'And no breach of the planning regulations—'

'Just hold on there,' Norwich interrupted, almost spitting out the words. 'I could tell you about the way he treated the Beverlys: they came in on Bolton Farm, rebuilt part of the house, redecorated, farmed the land and they had three hundred good acres, dairy and arable. They worked their guts out. But Yates stopped paying for capital improvements, there were some bad years, the rents went up, the Beverlys couldn't pay and the bastard made them bankrupt so they had to leave the farm. Mrs Beverly does domestic work now up at Broadwood. It ain't right, Mr Landon, so don't talk to us about legal things!'

'But I have to. My powers are related to planning law—'

'*Planning!*' Norwich snorted indignantly. 'Tell him, Saul, tell him what fix planning's got you into!'

Saul Eldon scratched his bald pate reflectively and sadly. 'The roof of the house is leaking, but Mr Yates, he won't get it repaired. The rent's gone up, but there's been no improvements made for years. Then the inspector from the Health and Safety Executive, he came around. I don't know who called him in—'

'*Yates!*'

'—and he told me I wasn't to enter the Long Barn because it was too dangerous.'

'He did the same down with me,' Norwich said. 'There's three cottages on Back Field Farm, which is my holding. Only one can be lived in. I got a man there and he says it's squalid. He's leaving me. One of my barns was actually demolished after the inspector came around. He wouldn't even go inside: stood back and said it was too bloody dangerous.'

'And what about your other barn?' Nick Enwright interrupted, leaning forward, upper arm muscles rippling under his shirt. 'That bugger got burned down. You going to say it was an accident?'

Norwich glowered at the younger man. 'I don't know. It's still a useless shell, that I know, even though Yates got the insurance money two years ago.'

'The point is, Mr Landon,' Saul Eldon said, 'what's to be done to stop the bleeding away of the estate? Mr Yates has put in this planning application. It's all for improvements on the farms under his own control. But the tenancies, they're a different matter. Over the past twenty years, ever since Mr Yates got involved at Kilgour, things have gone from bad to worse. Tenants have been leaving steadily. When Mr Yates came there was fourteen farms tenanted at Kilgour. You know how many are tenanted now?'

'*Seven*,' Nick Enwright growled.

'And two of those is farmed by me,' Norwich added, 'and one other is nothing but a smallholding, if truth be said.'

'It's a desperate situation, Mr Landon.' Saul Eldon scratched at his bewildered pate. 'We don't know what to do. We've tried talking to Mr Yates. The Colonel now, he'd listen, discuss things. Mr Yates won't even talk. Sends messages.'

Like the Senior Planning Officer, Arnold thought sadly.

'It seems to us it's wrong, like, that this application should go through, and Mr Yates should spend all this money on improvements around the big house, when there's so much needs to be done—'

'And should be done, legally,' Norwich interrupted.

'—around the tenanted farms. So we want to register objections, Mr Landon. We want Mr Yates's application turned down. We want him to accept his responsibilities under the tenancies.'

Arnold shook his head. 'Gentlemen, sadly, I don't think I can help you. As far as I can see from your written submissions, there has been no breach of the Agricultural

Holdings Act 1948 and so there's nothing we can do. In all other respects, although your submissions would seem to suggest bad mismanagement of the estates, there's no grounds here for denying the application. Mr Yates is the legal owner. It's *his* income, *his* money to spend. He can spend it as he wishes, without reference to anyone. We can exercise planning control, but as far as I can see none of you is affected by the improvements: they are not detrimental to your properties or your enjoyment of them—'

'He should spend the money on the tenanted farms!' Sam Norwich almost shouted. 'But you ineffectual buggers here in County Hall will do nothing to stop him souring the land!'

'We have no power—'

'You have no guts, you mean!' Norwich stood up, clenching his fists. 'Come on, lads, we'll get no joy here. We'll have to sort this thing out for ourselves. I've always known it: it was a mistake coming to weak-kneed pussyfooters here in Morpeth! It's up to us; it's *always* been up to us!'

He turned and stalked towards the door, body rigid with anger. After a moment's hesitation Saul Eldon rose, more reluctantly, as though still hoping Arnold might have something positive to offer. Then he hurried out behind his fellow tenant-farmer.

Nick Enwright had risen too. He stood facing the desk behind which Arnold sat and he glared at Arnold as though aware of a violent course of action but not certain whether to pursue it. He wet his thick lips and tensed his fingers, as though itching to get them wrapped around the limb of a weapon of destruction, his powerful bow. 'I got a different problem, Mr Landon. Have you got a couple of minutes?'

Arnold contemplated the thick, strong fingers. He had a couple of minutes.

Enwright sat down again. He stared at his hands, as Arnold stared at him. He was in his late twenties, his hair was black and thick and curly and there was a sensual softness about his mouth that seemed out of character. The young man was clearly concerned to develop a 'macho' image: his preening at the Long Meadow display had demonstrated that, but Arnold wondered how much of that was based on insecurity. Then Enwright looked up and Arnold changed his mind. The young man's mouth might be soft, but it meant indulgence and selfishness, not sensuality, at least not of the sexual kind. He had brown eyes but they were of a remarkable coldness: there was something metronomic in his gaze, as though he was counting for effect. The silence grew between them as Arnold waited, a cold finger of anxiety touching the nape of his neck. He did not like Nick Enwright: the man had the coldness of a coffin about him.

'My father, he's in his late sixties now,' Enwright said. 'I work on the farm for him—Top Farm. It used to be good, Top Farm, but it's like the others now, pretty run down. But it's all I got.'

The farm, Arnold thought, and the bow he had used at Long Meadow.

'We got problems like the others,' Enwright continued, 'but I got a paper as well. Look at it.'

Arnold was unwilling to refuse the grubby document pushed across the desk towards him: he had no desire to displease the muscular young man facing him. It was an agreement: he read it quickly. Among other things it committed the estate to undertake repairs to the main walls and roofs of the farmhouse and buildings on notification by the tenant. Arnold looked up.

'Is it all right?' Enwright asked belligerently.

'It seems in order.'

'The bloody walls need repointing. There's beams and slates need replacing in the roof. The chimney stack is shored up and the whole house needs weatherproofing. I can't get Mr Yates to do anything.'

Arnold frowned. 'Your father holds the tenancy?'

'That's right.'

'Then if Mr Yates is in breach of this agreement, as you

say he is, my advice to you is, get your father to obtain a compulsory repairs notice from the District Council. They'll do it for you, I'm sure. After that, Mr Yates will *have* to remedy the defects.'

Enwright stared at Arnold with cold, glittering eyes. His lips moved back over his teeth as though he was imitating a snarling animal, and Arnold wondered briefly whether the young man was actually trying to give that impression. Perhaps he lived in a fantasy world, in which he postured, gave demonstrations which he himself observed from a distance, in another self.

'Mr Yates . . . he's got a down on me.'

'A down?'

'He's a magistrate.'

Arnold nodded, confused. 'So I understand.'

'My old man, he wants to hand the tenancy over to me in a year or so. He's been to ask Mr Yates, but he got a dusty answer. It's not right.'

'Your father wants to retire?' Arnold asked.

'Soon as he knows I got the tenancy, he'll pack up, live in the cottage. I'll look after him, he knows that. I can do that, Mr Landon.'

Arnold gnawed at his lower lip. Nick Enwright's head had lowered, hunching between his shoulders. Perhaps he now saw himself as a bull, ready to charge its enemy. Arnold frowned: he was getting fanciful, observing this young man's body movements. 'The law states that a tenant on retirement who wants to transfer the tenancy to his son is entitled to do so.'

'Mr Yates has got to do it?'

'He is under an obligation to do so.'

'And he's got to do the repairs?'

'He's contractually committed to it.'

'Then I got the bastard.' Abruptly, Nick Enwright rose to his feet. He towered over Arnold and dropped his elbows close to his sides, causing his pectoral muscles to bunch under the tight checked shirt. His eyes were glowing now, their dark depths alive with a malicious triumph. 'I been before him, you see. He put the boot in then, and I know he don't like me and wants to stop me taking over that tenancy. But now I know he can't, I've got the bastard. I'll make him eat dirt, this time. I'll shove his head in it. And if he don't do as I say . . .'

There was nothing sensual about Enwright's mouth now. It had thinned, and he was smiling, but it was the smile of a hunter, careless of life, sniffing for blood. A sudden image of death crossed Arnold's mind, and he asked, 'What did you appear before Mr Yates for?'

The glow in Enwright's eyes died. His glance dropped, and he frowned. He shook his head. 'It was nothing . . . they couldn't really prove much. He fined me, even though I knew he wanted to do something worse. It was just a pheasant . . . and a couple of salmon.'

He gave a curious ducking motion of the head and leered suddenly, his nostrils widening as though he savoured a lost odour, perhaps blood in the long summer grass, and then he walked out of the office.

Arnold sat still for several minutes. He was sweating. He could not explain what it was that bothered him, but something about Nick Enwright made his skin crawl. He clearly had built the body he was so proud of: the muscles were prepared, honed to a sharp fitness, and from the light way he moved on his feet he would be balanced, athletic out in the open.

Poaching. Just a pheasant, and some salmon. On the bench Patrick Yates was known to be hard. He would certainly have wanted to get his hands on Enwright; if the charge had been more serious, he would have done so.

Perhaps next time . . . In the meanwhile, Yates would be vindictive enough to deny the tenancy to the man who had faced him in the magistrates' court.

Arnold rose and walked across to the window. He felt hot and sticky and for some indefinable reason his heart was

still beating faster than normal, as though he was alarmed
by something. Like the presence of danger, or of evil.

Arnold's office window overlooked the car park. He looked
out. There was someone standing near the wall at the exit.
For a moment Arnold did not recognize him.

The man was standing in a tight, fixed pose. His legs
were braced, the muscles outlined rock-hard in the tight
jeans. His left arm was extended rigidly, his dark, curly-
haired head twisted, sighting along the line of his extended
arm. The right arm was bent, the right hand near his ear.
The whole of the man's body was immobile, tense, rigid
with a controlled power, as he played out a role, acted out
a fantasy in his head.

A deadly fantasy, in which a multi-bladed broadhead
arrow would be aimed at a target.

The head moved, the tension slackened and the man
turned to look back to the building he had just left a few
minutes earlier. Nick Enwright looked up at the windows.
He was smiling, the same smile Arnold had observed earlier.
He could not have been aware of Arnold's presence, watching, but he smiled up to the windows, hugging a secret,
cruel satisfaction to himself.

Then he turned and walked away with a smooth, swift
gait, a long athletic stride.

Arnold shivered and touched his neck. His skin was damp.
Someone should tell Patrick Yates that there were some
men you should not make your enemies.

2

The courtroom was low-ceilinged and through the mullioned
windows the morning sunlight glittered, dancing with dust
particles, reflecting off the polished surfaces of the recently
renovated tables. It was the first time Arnold had been in this
room: he was used to planning inquiries held in County Hall,
but the purpose-built courtrooms on the Ponteland road out

of Newcastle were unfamiliar locations as far as he was concerned. The courtroom was already beginning to fill up: Arnold took a seat, unobtrusively, near the back of the room and he was not surprised to recognize several of the people who entered after he had claimed his place. The two older men who had been to see him in his office entered shortly after he did, and nodded to him. The bald-headed tenant of Ash Farm, Saul Eldon, managed a gloomy smile, though his mournful hound's eyes remained sadly despairing of justice. Devils still danced in his companion's eyes, however: Sam Norwich still seemed to be simmering on the edge of explosion, and Arnold wondered whether the farmer ever did really calm down. Maybe he lived in a state of constant anger, a furious adrenalin keeping him active and snappish. He scowled in Arnold's direction, acknowledging his presence but tendering no polite greeting. He sat down grumpily, hunching himself forward, staring at his knees with his gnarled hands clasped tightly together in front of him.

Other men came in, generally middle-aged, lean of cheek, with the kind of skins that suggested a life in the open. Arnold guessed they would all have some connection with the Kilgour Estates, and had come to hear what the ultimate destination of the property might be, in terms of ownership. Their faces betrayed no feelings: unlike Sam Norwich, they were not willing to demonstrate their views openly. Perhaps they were being canny; perhaps they thought they had too much to lose if Patrick Yates succeeded and he saw disappointment in their eyes.

The landowner himself came in surrounded by a little flurry of people: his solicitor, a man Arnold vaguely remembered from Morpeth; the barrister whom Arnold had seen on the circuit from time to time; two clerks dancing attendance on the fussy solicitor clutching a bundle of papers, and, rather surprisingly, Pauline Callington. Yates had described her as his housekeeper, a term she had clearly resented; it was interesting to note she seemed to hold a sufficiently important place in his household to be accorded the privilege of a seat beside him in a hearing of such importance to his future. She seemed softer of features than Arnold remembered, and although her mouth was set rather grimly as the surroundings perhaps demanded, her pale blue dress emphasized her figure discreetly and she showed a great deal more femininity than when she had snapped her eyes at Arnold that day in Kilgour House.

Wendy Gregory came in alone. She stood hesitantly in the doorway for several seconds, and there was an odd strained set about her mouth that betrayed her nervousness. Patrick Yates raised his head and stared at her: Arnold was able from where he sat to catch a glimpse of the wolfish contempt in the man's glance as he stared at the woman. She was aware of Yates's scrutiny, and a slow flush coloured her cheeks, but she did not look at him. She hurried along the line of seats, and approached Arnold.

'Is there anyone sitting there?'

Arnold shook his head, and gestured to the seat beside him. Wendy Gregory slid into it, the stain in her face slowly subsiding. She appeared not to recognize Arnold; he suspected she was preoccupied with other things than being pleasant to brief acquaintances in whom she had no interest.

Arnold cleared his throat. 'It's one of the peculiarities of the English language,' he suggested.

She stared at him, recognition arriving in her glance, late and uncertain. 'What is?'

Her normally pale eyes were dark and confused, the lids heavy, and Arnold wondered, briefly and uncharacteristically, whether she would look like this in the dimness, when Bob Francis made love to her. He struggled to clear his thoughts, rearrange them. 'You asking me if anyone's sitting on an empty seat. If it's empty, logically, no one *can* be sitting there.'

Her eyelids flickered in incomprehension. He tried again. 'It's the same if you asked whether the seat was taken.' He tried a smile. 'If it *was* taken, it wouldn't still be there, would it?'

She withdrew slightly, as though he were infected with something contagious. 'I don't know what you're talking about.' Her tone was cold, and edged with finality.

Arnold grimaced to himself. It was the same with jokes. Usually, he forgot the punchline, or delivered it at the wrong point of time. He was not born to be a comedian, nor a lounge lizard, nor a salon habitué indulging in small talk and gossip.

Oddly, the thought quite cheered him up.

In any case, Wendy Gregory had forgotten his existence again. She had tensed. Bob Francis had entered the room, preceded by the hawkfaced barrister who was representing him. Arnold wondered how Francis could have afforded him: maybe it was his wife's money, for lawyers rarely took cases on the basis that they'd get paid only if they succeeded. Like doctors, their clients got buried or hanged too often to breed confidence. Or maybe it was Wendy Gregory who would be supporting Francis financially. He had glanced at her at last, and her body stirred as though she had been touched, the glance relaxing her, brief though it had been and non-committal, merely checking on the fact of her presence.

There was an usher at the door. He was trying to close it but someone outside was resisting. The door was pushed open and a young man slipped into the room. He made no attempt to sit down, in spite of the flapping hands of the usher. He stood against the wall, arms folded over his muscular chest. It was Nick Enwright.

The usher gave up, and Patrick Yates turned his head. His glance locked with Enwright's. His eyes were cold and unflinching, careless of Enwright's confident dislike. Arnold shook his head slowly: the enmity between these two men was open, and carried across this room even when other tensions could have taken precedence. There was a stir in the courtroom as the usher called them to attention. The judge was entering, to take his seat.

The audience finally subsided, with a buzz.

The hawkfaced barrister was called Wynne-Thomas and he spoke with just a trace of a Welsh accent that had been largely ground out of him by ambition and elocution lessons. He was summarizing the main issues in a final plea to the judge, Mr Justice Sykes, who had a reputation for severity as sharp as his cheekbones.

'In effect,' Wynne-Thomas was winding up, 'the argument for my client, Mr Robert Francis, is this. He had had every expectation of inheriting the Kilgour Estates. He had been on close and intimate terms with the late Colonel Edridge. They had corresponded affectionately. But from the moment that Mr Yates moved on to the estates as, eventually, manager, that relationship was systematically undermined, to such an extent that a rift developed in the family.'

Mr Justice Sykes raised his angular head and fixed Wynne-Thomas with an icy stare, calculated to encourage the barrister to brevity. Unabashed, Wynne-Thomas ploughed on.

'It is not my intention to dwell upon the manner in which Mr Yates has used the estates for his own benefit. It is not within my brief to show how he has systematically set out to take the best short-term financial advantage of them, even though that action might be motivated by the realization that he might be called upon in due course to account for the estates to my client. But it is the essence of Mr Francis's case that the destruction of the relationship between the deceased colonel and my client was part of a deliberate plot by Mr Yates to influence the Colonel. That influence took the form of innuendo, advising upon legal actions, the pouring of verbal poison into the susceptible old man's ear, and finally, guiding the hand that wrote Colonel Edridge's last will and testament.'

The judge sighed, leaned forward and scratched something out on the notes prepared in front of him. 'Mr Wynne-Thomas, will you be much longer?'

'I am almost finished, my lord,' replied the barrister, unruffled. 'But I would once again direct your lordship's attention to the background surrounding the making of the will. Mr Yates was in a position of influence, close personal influence, and he gave Colonel Edridge legal advice. There was no opportunity for other, independent legal advice. The Colonel was bedridden. Access to him was all but impossible. Mr Yates and his employees—for it was he who hired and fired, not Colonel Edridge—barred the way. The clerk who came to the house to witness the will played no part in its drawing up. And that will gave sole ownership and control of the Kilgour Estates to Patrick Yates. This, my lord—'

'You are now getting to the point, I trust?' Sykes queried, scratching the side of his nose with a lean, bony finger on which the nail seemed to curve like a claw.

'This is the contention of my client. The making of the will was bad in law. Colonel Edridge was subject to extreme undue influence. That influence was exerted over a period of years to such an extent that at the end of the time the bedridden colonel had no opportunity—or will—to form an independent judgement. He had been taken advantage of. The will should be set aside. The properties in question should then be allowed to fall in to their rightful owner under the proper law of succession as it applies to intestacy. We ask, your lordship, for justice for my client.'

Wynne-Thomas sat down abruptly. There was a brief stir in the courtroom. As Wendy Gregory clenched her fists beside him Arnold watched Wynne-Thomas with mild interest. The speech had contained elements of floridity, but had been delivered in a flat monotone that seemed to lack passion or commitment. Arnold was left with the view that Wynne-Thomas had been doing what he was paid for, and

no more. His heart had not seemed to be in the argument
he had presented. Possibly it was the inhibiting presence of
Sykes in front of him, and yet he had seemed to be largely
unmoved by the judge's interruptions or impatience.

Wendy Gregory muttered something under her breath.

'Your indulgence—'

Counsel for Patrick Yates was rising, but a brief gesture
from Mr Justice Yates stopped him half way and he remained in a half-crouching position like a wounded crow
trailing a black wing.

'No need, no need,' Mr Justice Sykes announced snappishly. He waved his bony finger dismissively and spread
out the papers in front of him with a bad-tempered frown.
'There are occasions,' he said, 'when one is called upon to
deal with matters of great moment in the courtroom. They
can be stimulating occasions. This is not one of them.'

There was a quiet hiss of breath from the woman sitting
beside Arnold.

'It seems to me,' the judge continued, 'the facts in this case
are relatively simple. Colonel Edridge intended—some years
ago—favouring Mr Francis with ownership by inheritance of
the Kilgour Estates. He changed his mind. He left them to
his friend and companion and estate manager, Mr Yates.
A holograph will was written—*in Colonel Edridge's own hand*.
That will was witnessed, by an independent witness. That
will was later proved. The person who benefited under the
will took possession of the estates and used them—under his
legal entitlement—as he wished. These are the *facts*.'

Wynne-Thomas was not looking at the judge. He was
beginning to collect his papers. Barristers were busy men:
they had many legal fish to fry.

'Facts are, of course, open to different interpretations.
After all this happened, Mr Robert Francis emerged from
whatever fastnesses had held him over the years to claim,
somewhat tardily, what he regarded as his inheritance. But
all had been done. All had been settled. The only course

open to him, if he was to overturn the situation, was to question either the facts or the interpretation . . .' Mr Justice Sykes shook his bony head sadly. 'Where something is argued, where a situation is to be resiled from by the law, it is necessary that certain proofs emerge. The burden of proof, in such cases as this, is known as the balance of probability: it was incumbent upon Mr Francis to show that, on the balance of probability, undue influence had been exercised. *Allegations* have been made . . . but where have been the proofs?'

The judge scowled at the papers in front of him, then favoured the whole courtroom with the same expression. 'Irrelevant considerations have been cast before us: they have wasted our time. We are not here to adjudicate upon the nature of Mr Yates's husbandry of the estates. The legality of the will itself has been tested in probate; that legality has not been seriously questioned in the hearing before us. We have heard no evidence that Colonel Edridge was of feeble mind—merely that he had reclusive tendencies. If he chose to spend his time largely with one companion only—Mr Yates—that was his business. It is hardly evidence of feeble-mindedness.'

From the manner in which Wendy Gregory wriggled on the seat beside him Arnold concluded that this was one point on which she certainly disagreed with the judge.

'Equally, there has been no firm, hard evidence of undue influence. Mr Yates was not acting as a solicitor, whatever his background might be. He did not draw up the will. It was holograph, properly witnessed. Where is the evidence of sustained undue influence? There is none. Mr Francis makes the allegation. But Mr Francis displays no *proofs*. Cases of this kind always raise the bodily temperatures of the people concerned: this heat can affect the logical movement of the mind. I confess to having seen no merit in the plaintiff's case at any point during these proceedings, and I conclude the case lacks merit. The motion for the setting aside of the will is accordingly dismissed. Mr Yates might have a case to answer in another court higher than this, but that is not our business. In law, he has *no* case to answer.'

'*Stupid old man!*'

The words burst from Wendy Gregory in a spurt of uncontrollable anger. Arnold started in his seat. The people around him froze. The judge's head came up; it was not certain he had heard the words themselves, but he had obviously been aware of the emotion that had sent them echoing around the courtroom. He stared at Arnold for several seconds, his blurred old eyes glinting viciously like a snake about to strike, then his glance slipped to Wendy Gregory. His snake's tongue touched his bluish, dry lips. 'Young woman, was that you?'

Wendy Gregory sat still, tightly wound up in her own terror.

'You have something to say?' snarled Sykes. 'Or is it merely a case of emotional, misplaced loyalty?'

He allowed an unpleasant smile to touch his old mouth, pleased at the fear he had instilled into the courtroom, and then, after a pause, he rose and made his way from the bench, trailing an embarrassed silence behind him.

When the door closed the courtroom broke into a confusion of sound as everyone tried to talk at once, to his neighbour, to his or her friend. Wendy Gregory remained silent. Bob Francis, seated at the front, was arguing vehemently with Wynne-Thomas who looked bored, shaking his head slowly, but positively. He stood up, and Arnold caught his words to Francis. '. . . I warned you, old boy, but you wouldn't take advice . . . I did my best . . .'

'He didn't,' Wendy Gregory muttered to herself. Her body was shaking with the release of tension. 'He *didn't!* He wasn't even trying.'

But he had never believed in the case, Arnold considered. Maybe it was Wendy Gregory's money that was paying the legal bills. Or maybe she was simply upset because the verdict had gone so harshly against Bob Francis and in favour of the man she hated, Patrick Yates.

The small group around Yates was breaking up from a brief flurry of self-congratulation. Patrick Yates himself seemed cool enough, though there was an unnatural brightness about his eyes, and a slight, self-satisfied smile marked his mouth as he glanced across the room towards the plaintiff. Francis caught the glance and went pale. Wynne-Thomas said something to him but, ignored, he shrugged and walked away. The crowd in the courtroom began to thin; Sam Norwich stumping grumpily away with a red face, suppressing his natural anger, Saul Eldon stoop-shouldering his way towards the doorway with his mouth down-turned and his glance on the floor. Arnold could not guess what they might have hoped for under the régime of Bob Francis: it might have been worse than they had bargained for, since there was nothing to suggest they would have fared better with a new owner. Francis was a globe-trotter who had come home only when money beckoned: he might have intended bleeding the estate in ways not dissimilar from Yates's. But the matter was hypothetical. They were stuck with Yates as their landlord.

Arnold began to make his way forward. At least *his* problems were largely resolved. With Francis defeated, there was nothing to prevent the smooth dealing with the planning application regarding Kilgour. The issues would be clear-cut: an application of planning law and practice, untrammelled by legal complications involving third parties, with or without *locus standi*.

He found himself unable to reach the door. Wendy Gregory and two or three other people barred the way. They stood, avid in their attitudes, listening to the exchanges that were arising between plaintiff and defendant.

'You're a damned fool,' Patrick Yates was sneering. 'You must have been advised right from the start that this action was a waste of time.'

Bob Francis stood facing him, his studied elegance now dissipated by the heat of his growing anger and disappointment. His mahogany skin had reddened, blood flushing in fury as he faced his enemy and the reality of his emotions was now displayed in the twist of his mouth, all hint of generosity gone as dislike and hatred for Patrick Yates scarred his features. 'You've cheated me, damn you, cheated me!'

Unlike Francis, Yates was in control of himself. He smiled cynically, holding his head erect, tilted slightly as he observed the younger man. 'Cheated? Not at all. You've cheated yourself. The fact is, Francis, you've been a damned fool in all of this. Had you come to me reasonably in the first place, everything might have been different.'

'Like hell it would!'

'I might have been persuaded of the justice of your case,' Yates drawled mockingly. 'I mean, out there in the bush . . . it was hardly your fault that you lost touch with Charles. You could certainly not be expected to behave in a familial way, at such a distance, with such problems of communication . . . I mean, it's not reasonable, is it? And you weren't to know that Charles and I would become such close friends—

'Too damned close, I hear!' Francis flashed.

Patrick Yates paused, still in control of himself but now cooler, more deliberate, a little of the mockery gone to be replaced with an edge of menace. 'And you weren't to know that Charles would forget you, ignore you . . .' As he shifted, turning slightly, Arnold caught a glimpse of Yates's housekeeper, Pauline Callington. She was standing at his elbow, watching Francis carefully. She put out a hand, touched Yates in a possessive, warning manner. Yates ignored her. 'But as I said, you're a damned fool. Always were. You should have come home years ago, fought for your inheritance then, looked after the old fool the way I did. And as for this action . . . it was always doomed to failure. Wynne-Thomas told you, right from the start. But who knows? If you'd come to me, pleaded with me, *begged* a little . . .'

The fury in Francis's features was naked now. Arnold was suddenly reminded that this man had lived in the bush, would know how to defend himself in the wild, and something of it showed in him now, in the menace of his mouth, the dangerous way in which he glared at Yates, leaning forward at the hips, almost as though he was ready to leap at the magistrate.

'If you think I'd ever beg from you, let alone from anyone . . .'

'But my dear boy, isn't that how you get by?' Yates inquired with a pleasant malice. Pauline Callington must have squeezed his arm suddenly, warningly, because he turned his head towards her for a moment, stared at her. He sneered. 'There are all sorts of people who beg in their own way. Women, particularly . . .'

Pauline Callington's glance hardened as she stared at Yates. Her hand dropped away, as though she had been stung by words meant as much for her as for Yates's main target.

'But from women,' Yates was continuing, 'one can expect it. One takes receipt of favours and expects to pay for them. But when a man—'

'Yates, I'll close your mouth. I'll close it for good!' Francis's mahogany skin was paling now, anger being replaced by the steel of determination.

'But surely I haven't got it wrong, have I?' Yates mocked him recklessly. 'I mean, as I understand it, you only married your wife for the money she had. And with that running out, and with the lawsuit here beckoning, you had to get cash elsewhere.' He paused, turned his head and slid a sly glance in the direction of Wendy Gregory. 'And you'll always find some stupid little slut who'll give all for love—and money as well!'

'Patrick . . .' Pauline Callington's tone was firm. She moved forward, slipping between him and Bob Francis. 'I think this has gone far enough. Time we went home.'

'My dear lady,' Yates soothed, 'if Francis can nurse his disappointment, surely I'm allowed to enjoy my victory?'

Wendy Gregory, standing in front of Arnold, was trembling violently. She was staring at Bob Francis, but he seemed unaware of her presence, unmoved even by the shaft Yates had aimed in her direction. He was beside himself with disappointment and fury, but his anger was channelled now, his whole body tense, like a predatory animal set to kill. Oddly, that tension gave him added control, and his mouth was like a piece of bent iron. He said nothing, glaring at Yates, and the magistrate, unmoved, sneered back. After a few moments Francis turned away, and stalked out of the courtroom. Wendy Gregory was shaking. She put out her hand, swaying. Arnold caught her by the arm. 'Are you all right?'

She seemed unaware of him and yet she leaned heavily, dizzily against his restraining arm. He guided her to a seat. Mercifully, they were at the back of the group and no one seemed to notice as she sank into the chair. Yates and his entourage were making their triumphant way out of the room in the wake of Bob Francis. Wendy Gregory's fingers gripped Arnold's wrist. She took a deep breath, and the fingers tightened. He was reminded her occupation was the teaching of physical education. She had strength and it was communicated to him as she gripped hard, seeking control. Her head turned, she stared at him, her eyelids blinking rapidly as though seeking for tears that should have come, or were being forced back. 'Do I know you?'

'Arnold Landon. We met at the archery club meeting the other day.'

She nodded, half-remembering, then other memories, more recent, clouded her glance. She released his wrist quickly. 'I'll be all right.'

'Are you sure—'

'Thank you, I'll be all right. I was dizzy for a moment . . . the heat of the room . . .'

Arnold hesitated, then stood up, reluctant to interfere

where his assistance was not required. Embarrassed, he mumbled, 'Well, if you're sure . . .'

'Quite sure,' she said in a quiet but firm voice, without looking up at him. Arnold nodded, and made his way slowly out through the doorway of the courtroom. When he glanced back she was still sitting there. She appeared to be crying.

The entrance to the courtroom lay at the top of a wide balustraded staircase. From the top of the stairs Arnold could look down the well to the ground floor. He paused, looking down: nearing the foot of the stairs was Yates, with Pauline Callington beside him.

Standing just inside the main doors was Nick Enwright.

In spite of himself Arnold stopped, and waited for the inevitable meeting. It was not curiosity so much as a reluctance to become involved in the scene that he guessed was about to occur. Patrick Yates had won his case and was in an elated frame of mind, but the young man waiting for him was clearly intent on disturbing that equanimity.

As Yates and the woman reached the bottom of the staircase Nick Enwright stepped forward.

'Mr Yates.'

The magistrate hesitated, then turned his head, muttered something to Pauline Callington.

'Mr Yates!'

Reluctantly Yates faced the young farmer. 'What do you want?' he asked curtly.

'You did well in there, *sir*.'

'What's that to do with you?'

'Nothing, like. Except it's good to see someone riding high before a fall.'

'What's that supposed to mean?'

Nick Enwright was grinning, unpleasantly. 'Just that you win some, you lose some.'

'You're talking in riddles, Enwright.'

'You won today, *sir*. But with my dad, well, it's going to be a different story.'

Yates paused, looked Enwright up and down contemptuously. 'Are you drunk?'

'Not at all. But I been taking advice.'

'Not before time,' Yates said curtly and tried to push past. Enwright barred his way. 'What the hell do you want?'

'I told you, I been taking advice. My old man's been hanging on at the farm tryin' to persuade you to let me have the tenancy so he can retire. *Now* I learn you can't do that, not in law you can't. There's an Act that says you got to hand over the tenancy to the son, if he wants it. My dad wants it, and I want it. He'll retire, I'll work the farm. And I'll do a bloody good job, Mr Yates, with or without your help. Believe it!'

Yates stared at the young man with open dislike. 'Enwright, you're a wastrel. You'd spend more time shooting game than you would in looking after the farm. There's no way I'll let you have that tenancy.'

'You can't stop it!'

'I can stop it,' Yates said viciously. 'I've got other plans for that farm—or at least for the capital I can raise with it in due course. As for your tenancy and your protected rights at law, you're misinformed, my friend. Yes, it's true the Act says the son is entitled to take on the tenancy after his father—but there's a proviso. It says *if he is suitable*. Are you *suitable*, Enwright? Do you think your claim would stand a cat in hell's chance against my word? Particularly when I can point out that you have a criminal record! Now get out of my way and stop bothering me, or I'll call the police on you!'

For one long moment Arnold thought Enwright was going to stand his ground. His muscles tensed and his fists were clenched. Then, swiftly, the tension died in him, he grinned wolfishly and stepped aside. Yates brushed past him, and Pauline Callington hurried behind. They walked through the open door and down the pathway to the main road.

They did not look back. If they had, they would have seen what Arnold observed. Nick Enwright stared after them for a few seconds, then suddenly he snapped into swift, polished movement, taking up precisely the same stance Arnold had seen him hold in the car park outside Arnold's office.

But this time, in his fantasy, the broadheaded arrow was directed at a human target.

3

Early the following week Arnold was somewhat surprised to receive an invitation from Professor Agnew to attend a morning sherry party he was giving in his department at Newcastle University. When he thought it over Arnold concluded it was by way of a thank-you for the work he had agreed to undertake with Professor Evesham, so he considered it would be churlish to refuse. He regarded himself as unsuited to the atmosphere of sherry parties—he preferred solitude on the wild hills—but he liked Agnew, so he decided to go.

When he entered the building the porter seemed to be reading the same newspaper he had been buried in the last time Arnold had visited the building. He did not look up as Arnold entered.

The room in which Professor Agnew was receiving his guests lay on the same floor as Evesham's workroom so Arnold knew more or less how to get there. He walked along the corridor until he came to Evesham's room; the door was open, and he hesitated at the entrance. The papers were scattered over the desk, and the display of arms was clearly visible, but there was no sign of Evesham himself. Feeling that he had escaped, Arnold hurried past and along the corridor to the elegant, tall-ceilinged room where Agnew was waiting. As he entered Agnew came forward, smiling, a welcoming hand extended, and Arnold realized he had not escaped for behind Agnew, at the edge of a small group of people, stood Alan Evesham, holding forth in some passion, waving his sherry glass to emphasize the points he was making.

'Mr Landon,' Agnew exclaimed. 'Delighted you could make it. The young lady will take your preference.' He beckoned to the nubile young secretary who was now doing duty as a sherry waitress. 'Dry, medium, sweet?'

'Medium, please.'

'Amontillado. Now then, introductions . . .'

There were several academics, a professor of engineering from Nottingham, two industrialists and the managing director of a shipping business on the Tyne. Two members of the boards of nationalized industries were introduced to him, along with a man from ICI, and Arnold was beginning to think he was in the wrong company and dazed with the rush of names and jobs and faces—most of which seemed to glaze over with lack of interest when they learned his occupation—when Agnew said, 'And of course, you know Tom Malling.'

The farmer shook Arnold's hand, and Agnew slipped away. Malling eyed Arnold for a few moments, then sipped ruefully at his glass. 'Not exactly my tipple.'

'Nor mine.'

'Prefer a straight Scotch myself.'

'I'm not a great drinker.'

'Well . . . I indulge a little too much, sometimes.' There was a reflective gleam in Malling's eyes for a few seconds, as though he considered loneliness and its solution, and then he shrugged and smiled vaguely. 'I'm not sure why I'm here, among this lot.'

'It's a feeling I've already had,' Arnold replied.

'What's your conclusion?'

Arnold looked around the room at the men in their business attire and the academics in their grey suits and considered the matter. 'I guess Professor Agnew is killing a couple of birds at the same time.'

'How do you mean?'

'The businessmen . . . he's out to strengthen his acquaintanceship with them. They like being called socially to the university. Flatters them. Academia is something they might aspire to later, when they've made enough money to afford it. Mastership of a college, that sort of thing.'

'We hardly fall into that category.'

'Ah no, but with us it's a matter of expressing gratitude in a discreet way. The academics here are present for a purpose, but we're makeweight, socially. Interesting, perhaps, as curiosities—a talking point later, over dinner. Not that Agnew would consciously do that.'

'No, he wouldn't.' Malling glanced around the room at their companions. 'I quite like old Agnew. That other fellow, though—Evesham—I dislike him. Rude sod.'

Arnold made no comment. After a while Malling looked at him thoughtfully and said, 'You and Evesham don't exactly see eye to eye either.'

'No?'

'He doesn't care for your involvement with his affairs. Up at Langton.'

'Is it that obvious?'

'He was like a bear with a sore backside.' Malling paused. 'But he's about to do the decent thing, it seems.'

Alan Evesham had broken away from the group he seemed to have been terrorizing with his erudition and his dangerously waving glass and was bearing down on Arnold and Tom Malling.

''Morning, gentlemen,' he said, unable even with such a greeting to avoid a hint of belligerence. 'Slumming, hey?'

There seemed little they could make by way of adequate reply. Evesham didn't need one. He clearly had imbibed several sherries, and his features were slightly flushed. He prodded Arnold in the chest with his forefinger, and a spot of sherry splashed on to Arnold's tie. 'You got any further with our friend?'

'Friend?'

'Bloody Ailnoth! Got no other friends in common, have we?'

Arnold wondered whether the boorish Professor Evesham could have any friends at all, but aloud he said, 'I'm afraid not. I've not really had time to—'

'Time, time, inclination more bloody likely! Can't guess why Agnew saddled me with you. I mean, what have you come up with?'

Arnold opened his mouth but the question had been rhetorical. Evesham continued, his eyes glittering with excitement and alcohol. 'Dammit, I'm certain Ailnoth is the guy buried up there at Langton, and if only Agnew would release the funds I could get on with my thesis and develop it properly. Not until some confirmation comes from *you*, he says. But I'm not turned on by gifted amateurs, Landon, you know that?'

'It hadn't escaped my attention,' Arnold replied bleakly.

'You've met Tom Malling, of course.'

'Yes, that's right, up at Langton Castle.' His eyes wandered around the room, and finally returned to his glass. 'You'll excuse me.' He walked away to replenish his glass, putting his arm around the flustered, unhappy secretary as she poured and taking the chance to whisper in her ear. She clearly disliked the experience.

Malling sighed. 'Not exactly the most sociable of men.'

Arnold was forced to agree.

'Are you going to be able to support his Ailnoth obsession?' Malling asked. 'Have you discovered any more?' When Arnold shook his head, Malling continued, 'And what about that chapel up at Langton? Have you had any further thoughts about that?'

Arnold hesitated. There was the puzzle about that chapel, but preoccupation with other things had caused him to thrust the problem to the back of his mind. He shrugged. 'I'll have to think more about it. There's *something* that puzzles me about it, the colour of the tiles, or maybe it's an association of ideas, I can't be sure. I just haven't had time . . .'

Malling nodded in sympathy. He was silent for a little

while, both men glancing around the room, noting the way interest groups seemed to have congealed in various corners, heads bobbing in earnest conversation. After a while, in a voice that seemed to struggle from him with difficulty, Malling said, 'You'll have heard about . . . about Yates, and Kilgour House.'

'The lawsuit, you mean?'

'That's right. Francis failed in his attempt to wrest Kilgour from that . . . that scoundrel Yates.'

'I was at the hearing. It seems Francis never really had a leg to stand on. Or so the judge seemed to think.'

Malling scowled, grimacing at his drink as though he found it suddenly distasteful. 'Six of one, though, isn't it?'

'How do you mean?'

'They are both . . . unpleasant men. *Scum.*'

The vehemence of the word seemed to shock Malling himself, even as he uttered it. Somewhat confused, he sipped his drink and shook his head. 'I mean, they're both arrogant men who are prepared to ride roughshod over the rights of other people, seize what they want out of life in spite of what it may cost their neighbours. Neither of them *deserved* to win that case. Both of them should be consigned to perdition. Maybe they will be one day.'

'I've yet to meet anyone who seems to have a good word to say for Yates,' Arnold muttered reluctantly. 'As for Francis, well, I can't say I know him particularly well. A fleeting conversation—'

'He's tarred with the same brush as Yates,' Malling interrupted passionately. 'The pity is, there's such a gap between law and justice. The two are not synonymous.'

'Were they ever?'

'They ordered these things better in the old days,' Malling mumbled.

'How do you mean?'

'The sworn masons—'

'Masons?' snapped the voice from just behind Arnold.

'You talking about masonry?' It was Alan Evesham, back with his glass topped up. 'Better be careful, my lad, ought to whisper in these hallowed halls if you have a go at the masons. Vested interests and all that.'

'We weren't actually discussing masons,' Arnold said stiffly. 'We were talking about the lawsuit involving Patrick Yates—'

'That bastard!' Evesham snarled, his face mottling with a swift anger. 'I heard he'd got away with it. Owner of Kilgour! Did I ever tell you about the dig and the way he—'

'You did.'

'I've often thought of ways of getting back at him,' Evesham brooded, his eyes hooding with malice. 'But when you get down to it, there's only one remedy for a bastard like that. Extermination.' He squinted at his glass, raised it to the light, then looked owlishly at Arnold. '*Extermination*. Treat him like the vermin he is.'

Looking back at the event a week later, Arnold still shuddered, not so much for himself as for Professor Agnew. Quite what the industrialists had thought when Evesham began to hold forth upon military history and emphasize the immoral role played in war by businessmen it was difficult to say. Agnew had tried to hush the man, but clearly Evesham was not used to protracted bouts of sherry-drinking and he would not be quietened. Arnold had shrunk into an embarrassed corner with Tom Malling, and it was not long before the farmer, introverted and silent, had offered his thanks and withdrawn. Arnold had followed him as soon as was decent, and as he walked past Evesham's room with its clutter he wondered whether the military historian would be sleeping it off there overnight. He certainly would not be fit to drive out to his cottage that afternoon.

Malling had questioned Arnold about Langton Castle and Arnold felt a little guilty that he had since done nothing to assist Evesham and Agnew in the way he had been asked. He wondered now whether Evesham stood any chance anyway of getting Agnew's support for the grant, after the way he had killed Agnew's party. Even so, his own curiosity had been whetted that day up at the old castle; the only problem was finding time to do anything about it. The workload he carried was heavy, there were two inquiries to prepare for and there was a heavy backlog of paperwork on his desk.

On the other hand, he was due for some leave.

He buckled down to clear his desk and deal with the demands building up there, and then, on the Friday, he left a note for the Senior Planning Officer, explaining he was taking a day's leave due to him. There was no point in seeking an interview, and as it happened an assent came to him within the hour.

He took the day off the following Monday.

It was a bright day, high clouds scudding across the blue sky with a fresh wind blowing in from the coast as Arnold drove inland and made his way towards the village and Langton Castle. The roads were deserted and he was able to enjoy the hedgerows and the fields. He was at peace with himself, he had secreted a half-bottle of wine with some sandwiches in the back of the car and he was looking forward to a day alone in the hills.

He parked near the church and made the ascent of the hill. Above Cheviot a dark cloud threatened, but here at Langton the sun was bright, the grass shining, and he climbed above the ancient walls until he could sit with his back against the crag and gaze down on what had been described as the old chapel.

The sun was warm on the back of his neck. He ate his sandwiches, drank his wine and ruminated, on the past, his own childhood in the Yorkshire dales, the ancient wildwood, the patches of shadow that crept across the green fields below him, the tramp of military feet on these hills since Roman times, and before.

His eyelids grew heavy and he dozed, but when he drifted back to the modern world he was still thinking about the crag and the chapel and the hill.

'Of course it's not a chapel,' he said aloud to himself.

Nor was it, of that he was now convinced. The line of the land was clear, if you just sat down and looked at it for long enough. Lady Glynne-Stuyvesant had a great deal to answer for with her amateurish meddling. Not so much for what she had done, but rather for the theories, half-baked and erroneous, that she had propagated.

The line of the crag had been the original line of the ancient castle wall. Forget its age, disregard the arguments, but concentrate upon the logic. Along that crag the ancients would have built an earthwork. Later, much later, there would have been erected wooden defences, but never to any great height, never of any consequence. The fall of the land and the steepness of the crag would have formed the defensive line itself.

And the chapel was no chapel. It had been on the outer perimeter of the ancient wall, a watchtower perhaps, a command post with an extensive view over the valley towards the dangerous northlands and the border, and back down beyond the valley where Kilgour House lay.

How old? Ancient. It was inevitable. Among that scrub and trees had once stood an old building, and it would have been built on again and again. But the likelihood would have been that the builders would never have dug deep, not after the first sound, rock-based foundations had been constructed for them. That would account for the old bricks. Why lift them from a solid foundation? Rather, re-use them and build upon them, century after century, until finally the castle lost its usefulness and the shepherds came in and broke down the walls for their own uses on the hills, and the scrub and the trees arrived, making their own insidious green shroud to hide the broken truth.

But there was something drifting in his mind, a piece of

information he could not slot into place, even though it was only half-remembered, half-digested.

He rose to his feet to gather up the empty bottle and the wrapping paper, and stood on the crag, looking across the fields, frowning. Somewhere in the distance a dog was barking excitedly: he could see it racing across the field, streaking home as he watched, but he barely thought of it as he puzzled, trying to trap the elusive words that tumbled somewhere in his brain, clicking together, but never into place.

Finally, annoyed with himself, he walked back down from the crag, realizing that further struggling would only be counter-productive. Forget about it, and it might return.

It was probably unimportant anyway: better to enjoy the day. He still had nothing to help Evesham, but at least he was out in the clean air of Northumberland.

Arnold did not pause in the village. He returned to his car and decided to drive back the long way, through the winding lanes and across the dipping roads over the hills, south first, and then east back towards Morpeth.

It was when he rounded the bend about a mile from the village that he saw the car in the ditch. The woman was standing helplessly near the offside wheel. It was Pauline Callington.

She was stiff, rather formal, and was unwilling to be grateful, but yes, she *was* in trouble. It would seem that something had gone wrong with the steering. She'd been shopping, was on her way back to Kilgour, when suddenly, on the bend, something had sheared, the steering was gone and the car swerved into the ditch. 'If you could give me a lift to Kilgour, Mr Landon,' she said firmly, 'that would be helpful. I can phone a breakdown service from there.' Arnold announced he would be only too pleased to help.

Reluctantly, Pauline Callington got into Arnold's car and Arnold set out for Kilgour. He tried to start a casual conversation but Yates's housekeeper seemed disinclined to talk to him. She sat stiffly, unwilling to be with him, forced by circumstance to be beholden to someone she regarded as below her notice.

Arnold was pleased when they finally turned into the driveway and headed towards the house.

They had passed the stables, where Arnold intended to turn the car, since he did not want to go up to the house and possibly meet Yates, when Pauline Callington's head jerked sideways and she hissed, a sharp intake of breath.

'*Stop!*'

Arnold applied the brakes. He stared at her; she was gazing back towards the old stables, but slowly she turned her head to look at him with blank, glazing eyes.

'What's the matter?' he asked.

She was silent for a few seconds and then she began to shake. Her mouth sagged in shock. 'There's something back there, beside the stable entrance.'

Arnold hesitated, stared at her. The hairs on the back of his neck moved, prickling. 'Wait here,' he said and got out of the car.

The sturdy entrance to the old stables loomed ahead of him, warm stone in the afternoon sunshine. Beside the gateway, half-concealed in the undergrowth, was an untidy bundle. For a moment Arnold thought it was a clump of old clothing, thrown down carelessly in the grass. Then he saw the leg, and the shape of the shoe.

Patrick Yates lay on his back, staring eyes glazed against the afternoon sunlight. His arms were thrown wide, in an attitude of crucifixion. His jacket was open at the chest, as though he had held it wide, to receive the gift of death.

In the centre of his chest was the bringer of the gift, standing proud and triumphant and deadly.

CHAPTER 5

1

When he was finally taken to Morpeth police station Arnold was treated quite well. A chubby young constable sat with him in the canteen while he ate the haddock and chips provided. Arnold was surprisingly hungry and ate the tasteless fish quickly. His mind was blank; it was as though he did not wish to think about what he had found at Kilgour, or the hysterical way in which Pauline Callington had behaved.

The tea was hot and very sweet. He did not normally take sugar, but he drank from the mug provided by the young policeman without demur.

The room they finally took him to was small, square and barely furnished with a table and two chairs. The big man who entered a few minutes later apologized for the starkness of the accommodation, and the graffiti on one wall.

'Normally, that shouldn't happen. I mean, we rarely leave anyone in here alone. In the interview rooms a copper usually stays with you. But for some reason . . . My name's Culpeper. Detective-Inspector.' He extended his hand; rather surprised by the old-worldly charm of the policeman's manner, Arnold shook hands.

Culpeper was in his mid-fifties, a large, broad-shouldered man with a comfortable face and a wistful mouth. The crowsfeet around his eyes suggested a kindliness more in keeping with helping old ladies across roads than with investigating murder incidents, though the precision of his neatly-parted, straight grey hair made Arnold feel this would be a man with a tidy mind and a tidy life, who would want his work to similarly conform.

'You've already been questioned, I know,' Culpeper said, 'and I've seen the statement you made. I thought, since I'm now taking over the investigation, it would be useful to have a chat with you, off the record, so to speak. You seem a fairly stable man, Mr Landon, not given to the kind of outbursts we've been faced with.'

Arnold's mind flickered back to the scene at Kilgour House when the police had arrived, and shuddered. Culpeper watched him carefully for several seconds, and then asked, 'Do you go along with what Mrs Callington was saying?'

'She was upset, overwrought, distraught—'

'That doesn't answer the question.'

'I . . . I haven't formed any view. I mean—'

'That was a crossbow bolt in his chest, did you know that?'

Arnold hesitated. 'I wasn't sure. I didn't touch it. I went into the house with Mrs Callington, kept her there until the police arrived.'

'And that's when she went over the top.'

Arnold nodded. It had been a curious response to the situation, odd in the sense that until the police arrived Pauling Callington had been completely in control of herself. Arnold had still been looking down at the corpse of Patrick Yates when the housekeeper had walked up to join him. She had stood there, stared, and then in a controlled, calm manner, she had suggested they had better call the police. Once the phone call had been made they had sat facing each other in the library; Pauline Callington had sat on the edge of her chair, hands in her lap, fingers laced, staring woodenly at the floor. No emotion had touched her; she had declined his suggestion of a drink. It was as though she was stunned, or allowing her mind to wander over the past. Or perhaps she had been gearing herself up to something.

'Did it seem a contrived reaction to you?' Culpeper asked softly.

Contrived. Arnold did not know. She had changed so radically once the police arrived. Her calmness had been shattered. He could not now decide whether there had been elements of the theatre in her collapse into hysteria; he did not know the woman, did not understand her psychological make-up, knew little about her relationship with the murdered man, so could not know why she had changed from an icy silence to a raging, threatening, accusatory passion.

Culpeper was watching him thoughtfully. 'Well?' he prompted.

'I . . . I really don't know.'

'But the allegations she made about this man Enwright, do you think they have any basis in fact?'

'She was hysterical, the pressure . . .'

Culpeper's eyes were hooded, but his voice was tinged with sadness, the gloom of disbelief in human nature. 'She has put it all in a statement, but it's disjointed, and . . . *spiteful*. She seems convinced Enwright killed Mr Yates. He has the motive . . .'

Arnold had heard her, at Kilgour, shouting at the police officers, telling them she *knew* Enwright had killed her employer. Enwright had hated Patrick Yates because of the farm tenancy situation, and because of Yates's attitude on the bench.

'There was tension between them that apparently came to a head after the courtroom hearing. You observed that, I understand, Mr Landon.'

Pauline Callington's eyes were sharper than Arnold had realized.

'And then there's Enwright's personal hobbies to take into account,' Culpeper continued softly. 'All this hunting gear, and the prowling in the woods, his use of a bow . . .'

'But not a crossbow,' Arnold demurred.

The hooded eyelids lifted, and Culpeper stared at Arnold with brown eyes soft as an autumn hillside. 'That's right.

Not a crossbow ... There's another thing, Mr Landon. That bolt wasn't *fired*.'

'How do you mean?'

'It was thrust in by hand. A violent thrust, and maybe a calculated one, or a lucky one. It came in at an upward angle, piercing the abdomen, looks like, and slicing into lung and heart. Not a lot of power needed, oddly enough. Track of the bolt, sliding in, a child could have done it.' The eyes narrowed suddenly, watching Arnold. 'Or a woman.'

Arnold made no reply.

'Who were Mr Yates's enemies, Mr Landon, apart from this man Enwright?'

'It seems ... it seems he was a very unpopular man,' Arnold managed.

'Would you count any females among those enemies?'

An image flashed across Arnold's mind, a woman in a courtroom crying, but a woman whose grip had tensed fiercely on his arm in distress, and whose muscled shoulder could flex a bow. A woman, also, who had good reason to hate Patrick Yates.

'Suppositions ...' he mumbled.

'Yes. But that's all we have to go on at the moment,' Culpeper said. 'Until we get hold of this man Enwright I'm not sure how far we can go, other than on general suppositions.'

'You can't find him?'

Culpeper grimaced. 'He's not at the farm. Disappeared. His father can't help us. Mrs Callington, of course, says she thinks she saw his Land-Rover headed towards Kilgour when she was travelling to the village; where he's got to since, we don't know. We'll find him, of course. And if it *was* his vehicle going towards the house ...'

Mrs Callington didn't say that when I was with her.'

Culpeper regarded him owlishly. 'It's in her statement. People think they remember all sorts of things *later*, when they've had time. Remember ... or *embroider*.' Culpeper sighed. 'Well, let's go over your own statement again, Mr Landon, and then we'll have to let you go home and take a rest, won't we?'

2

During the next few days Arnold was involved in a planning inquiry that engendered a considerable amount of heat from a group of conservationists in Northumberland. Normally, he would have followed their arguments with interest and a certain degree of sympathy, but on this occasion he found himself unable to concentrate on the matter in hand: rather, his thoughts drifted back constantly to the horror of the discovery at Kilgour. And inevitably, the interrogation by Detective-Inspector Culpeper had raised so many questions in his mind that he found himself listing the enemies of Patrick Yates in his mind, over and over again.

It was not his business, but he could not tear himself away from the contemplation of it.

On the Friday evening Arnold received a call from Alan Evesham. The history professor was brusque and to the point. He wanted to know whether Arnold had turned up anything on Ailnoth.

'I'm afraid not. I've been rather busy.'

There was a short silence. 'Yes . . . getting mixed up in murder, I hear.'

'I wouldn't have put it quite like that,' Arnold demurred.

'Don't suppose you would.' Evesham paused. 'I heard something odd about the murder weapon. There's been nothing in the papers, police keeping things close to their chests, but gossip has it the murder weapon was . . . mediæval.'

Arnold hesitated. 'It was a crossbow bolt,' he said, and waited.

There was a long silence. Something had happened to Alan Evesham's breathing. It had taken on a ragged edge.

'Well, yes, but it's none of our business, is it? Ailnoth's what we should be talking about. My time's up, just about, Landon. Agnew's called a meeting for week tomorrow. You'll be there, I trust. Even if you haven't turned anything up, you can give me some support at least.' Evesham uttered a short barking sound. 'Agnew seemes to have some respect for your . . . intuitive judgement.'

After he rang off, Arnold sat quietly in the darkening sitting-room of his bungalow. His recent obsession with thoughts of the death of Patrick Yates had been upsetting; perhaps he would be able to clear his mind if he returned to the problem facing Alan Evesham. It was healthier, and saner, to look at the death of a man six centuries ago than to project again and again the visions of murder that lay in his own mind.

He decided, the following morning, to go into Morpeth and visit the central library there. It was not as extensive as the City Library in Newcastle but it had a sound local history section, and quite a good collection on building history. There was still something that niggled at him about the chapel at Langton, but he needed to read, to browse, until perhaps the thought would clarify into something positive.

He found a seat in the reference library and sought out the books he needed. He sat down and was soon lost in the detail of mediæval building.

A century later the office of royal mason was filled by Henry Yevele. By 1356 he was sufficiently well established to be one of the masons concerned in drawing up the regulations for the masons' craft in London, and in 1365 he was master of the masons, controlling (ordinant) their work . . .

After a while, somewhat impatiently, Arnold set the volume aside. It was all very well reading in Arundel's *History of Building* but there were too many sidetracks, too much emphasis upon the lives of eminent builders in those early centuries, and not enough on the practical realities of wood and stone. For something told him it was there that he might find the answer that eluded him. He pushed Arundel aside, and directed his attention to the other volumes he had selected. He finally settled with Champney's monumental work, all sixteen hundred pages of it.

He delved into the history of brickmaking. Much of it was familiar. Men had made bricks, he knew, for six thousand years. Bricks were habitually found in the neighbourhood of flourishing Roman towns such as St Albans, the old Verulamium, and Colchester, or Camulodunum as the Romans had called it. But when the Romans left brickmaking ceased and did not flourish again for almost a millennium.

Arnold leaned back in his seat, thinking for a while, and then with a quickening pulse he turned to the back of the volume and began to check the index. It was several minutes before he found the section he wanted. He turned back to the main book text.

The first evidence of a brickmaking industry occurs in the early fourteenth century in Yorkshire, near Hull and Beverley. The trade of the port of Hull was principally with the Netherlands and the Baltic, where brickmaking flourished. The church of Holy Trinity at Hull provides a fine example of fourteenth-century brickwork. On the north side of the chancel the early brickwork stands revealed, in part red, in part blue, laid in broad mortar patterns . . .

Red in part, and then blue . . . The problem turned slowly in Arnold's mind, teasingly, glimmering with a half-seen light, beyond reach but there, positively and certainly. He read on, quickly, but the glow of excitement faded, as he realized he had missed the point he was looking for, the elusive, half-remembered reality. Excitement gave way to frustration and he gnawed at his lip. It was in this mood that he realized someone was speaking to him and he looked up from the book snappishly.

'What did you say?'

'I said good morning,' Tom Malling said uneasily.

Arnold cleared his throat. 'I'm sorry. I was . . . involved with this book, I wasn't aware . . .'

'I'm sorry, also, to disturb you,' Malling said. 'It's just that the librarian told me the book I wanted to consult was already being used, and that you had it over here. I came across, saw it was you, and wondered whether . . .'

'Book? Which book are you talking about?' Arnold asked, confused.

'Arundel.'

'*History of Building?* I didn't know you were interested in mediæval building.'

Malling shifted uneasily, shuffling his feet. 'I can't say I am. It's just that some things you said, when we talked . . . And I understand there are some things in the book . . .'

He half turned away, awkwardly, and Arnold stood up. 'Please, I'm sorry. I'm not using the book and it's most rude of me. Please take it.'

He handed the volume to Malling. The farmer took it almost reluctantly and then stood staring at Arnold, pale around the mouth. He held the book clutched to his chest but his mind was suddenly on other things. 'I . . . I hear it was you who . . . who found the body of . . . of . . .'

'Patrick Yates.' A slow flush coloured Arnold's uneasy cheeks. 'I'm afraid so.'

'What did he look like?'

Taken aback, Arnold thought for a moment. 'I don't understand—'

'Had he taken long to die?'

Arnold frowned and looked down at the book in front of him. He shook his head. 'I don't know. I don't think so. The impression I got from the policemen who spoke to me was that he had died fairly quickly. The shock . . .'

'I see.' Malling was silent for a while, still standing there, staring at Arnold. It took some moments before he was able to struggle out the next words. 'I understand they've now found the man they've been searching for.'

'Enwright?'

'Yes. It was on the news this morning: a man helping the police with inquiries. But local gossip has it he had gone to Aylesbury to look at a farmholding.'

'Oh yes?'

'Yates had many enemies.'

'So I understand.'

'Men . . . and women . . . You know that man Francis, don't you? There's a rumour that he . . . he might be involved, rather than Enwright.'

'I wouldn't know,' Arnold said rather sharply. Malling had the capacity to startle him, make him uneasy, and more than ever Arnold was resentful of the fact that he saw something of himself in the farmer, an echo of lost days, a view of the past . . .

'There's some would say that whoever killed Yates, it would be an Act of God, an ancient retribution, a visitation of justice upon the wicked,' Malling said slowly.

Arnold raised his eyebrows.

'It was murder.'

'Do judges commit murder when they consign a man to prison for life? Does the soldier commit murder when he kills?'

'The law—'

'The law is supposed to dispense justice, but when it does not, how is justice to be obtained?' Malling shook his head and snorted angrily. 'This man Yates was a man of property but his passions and appetites were evil. He deserved to die, so there are many who will merely applaud the fact of his death.'

'Applaud an act of murder?' Arnold questioned. 'I can't believe you really accept that.'

Malling's eyes were hooded as he clutched the volume of Arundel to his chest. 'I consider we have lost sight of the realities. I'm not a religious man, and I hate freemasonry and all such chicanery, but in this modern world we have lost the capacity to seek the truth, reach it, touch it, *bring it about*. In the world of our fathers things were differently ordered; there was an acceptance of the way in which things should be done, even among the subtle craft. Perhaps it's time we looked back to those days, and ordered our lives in the manner they did.'

Arnold was puzzled. 'I don't understand what you mean. The old, uncivilized times . . . we've outgrown the crudities of those periods. They can't be recalled.'

'You can say that, when you dream of stone and ancient woods?'

Nettled, uncomfortably aware that Tom Malling possessed an unwelcome insight into his emotions and needs, Arnold shook his head. 'We're talking about different things. I admire the skills of the past, and the methods—'

'But not the methods of dispensing justice?'

'The rope?'

'The justifiable killing.'

'Do you really believe it was right that Yates should die in that fashion?' Arnold demanded.

'He *deserved* to die,' Malling whispered drily.

It was suddenly more than Arnold could accept. 'Forgive me,' he said, 'I really must get on with my researches.'

Tom Malling straightened. He stared blankly at Arnold for several seconds, then nodded slowly. There was a veiled uncertainty in his eyes, as though he was puzzled by something, searching for words or actions which were now only half-understood and half-remembered. 'I'm sorry,' he mumbled. 'Thank you for . . . for the book.'

Arnold watched him covertly as he turned away and wandered towards a seat in the far corner of the room, uncertain of the direction he was taking. Arnold turned back to his own book and tried to concentrate but found it impossible to immerse himself in the text. He was annoyed: he had been working towards something, a theory about

Langton and Ailnoth, but now Malling had filled his mind with images of blood again. The teasing mediæval issue evaded him, and he could think only of Yates's body, half-hidden in the grass, sightless eyes glaring at the sky, the bolt standing upright in his chest.

When he looked up again Malling had gone. Arundel's *History of Building* was on the table. Arnold had the feeling it had not been opened, not consulted.

The newspapers carried a report the following day that a man was at Morpeth police headquarters helping them with their inquiries into the death of Patrick Yates. It did not name the individual concerned but Arnold had no doubt that it would be Nick Enwright.

When he arrived at the office he was met, inevitably, by colleagues who wanted to talk to him about it. Equally inevitably he did not want to discuss the matter. He simply wanted to forget all about Yates: the images were too clearly cut in his memory.

The Senior Planning Officer hovered at one stage, but reticence overcame curiosity and Arnold was grateful when the man went back to his office.

Hollywood Sanders was less reticent. 'It'll be him, all right. Take my word for it.'

'Who?'

'Enwright. He'll have done it. No smoke without fire. The cap fits, he'll have to wear it.'

'Are you talking about Yates's murder?'

'What else? This Enwright, he's a well-known poacher. Yates nailed the bugger on the bench. And there was this business about the tenancy he wouldn't give Enwright. The guy had all the motive in the world, and everyone knows he was a violent young sod. He'll be the one who planted that bolt in Yates. Crossbow fanatic, he is.'

'You're wrong,' Arnold suggested quietly. 'He doesn't use a crossbow, but a *longbow*.'

'Same thing, for God's sake,' Sanders said crossly. 'Crossbow, longbow, it's a bow, isn't it?'

'As I understand it, the man's been released.'

'Oh, they've let him go *for the moment*. That's the trouble with the law these days; weighted too much in favour of the guilty. Did things different in the old days, you know.'

There were echoes of Malling's views. Arnold grimaced. 'Thumbscrews and racks, you mean?'

'He won't get away with it,' Sanders announced, ignoring the jibe. 'Cock-and-bull story he's got about looking around Aylesbury for a farmholding because he knew he'd never get Top Farm from Yates. Besides, some reckon that fancy woman of Yates's, Pauline Callington—'

'His *housekeeper*.'

'Don't be such an *innocent*, Arnold,' Sanders jeered. 'I was saying, this Callington piece, she reckons she *saw* Enwright's Land-Rover headed for the house.'

'There are a lot of Land-Rovers in Northumberland. How would she recognize Enwright's?' Arnold asked.

'I just tell you what I hear,' Sanders grumbled. 'Why are you so bloody *sceptical*?'

Possibly because Arnold found himself unable to *believe* in Pauline Callington. He did not really doubt she had been Yates's mistress at some time; nor even that she probably loved him. It was likely, or otherwise she would hardly have accepted the indignities he heaped upon her in public. But he had seen her semi-hysterical, and could not make up his mind whether that hysteria had been deliberate. She insisted Enwright had killed Yates . . . but perhaps her own love had turned to something else—something violent—for which Enwright could be a convenient scapegoat . . .

And what of the rumour that Tom Malling had mentioned? Village gossip was suggesting that Francis might have been angry enough over the verdict given in court to have taken the law in his own hands. Years in the bush could make violence second nature to a man: Arnold could guess at the lurid imaginations that would be at work.

As for Malling himself, there was something odd about him that left Arnold uneasy. He certainly had the same kind of fascination for the past that Arnold had, but there was something about Malling's interest that raised the hairs on the nape of Arnold's neck.

Or was it merely that Arnold saw in Malling too close an image of himself, the solitary, introverted loner who had only the past for company?

Grimly Arnold shook himself free from such thoughts and concentrated upon his work. He had the second inquiry to prepare for, two further files had come down from the Senior Planning Officer—and he still had not managed to capture the elusive thought that hovered at the fringes of his mind concerning Ailnoth and Langton Castle.

3

Arnold went back to Langton again at the weekend to inspect the outer walls of the ancient castle. He looked again at the ancient bricks in the building and the words drifted back to him from the account in Champney . . . *part red, part blue* . . .

But that wasn't it. There was something else, some piece of information tucked away in the recesses of his mind that he was unable to tease forth.

He went to the meeting with Agnew and Evesham still struggling to seize the information he wanted.

Professor Agnew met his courteously and offered him a cup of coffee. Alan Evesham came in a little while later. He seemed bedraggled, a line of stubble on his chin, and Arnold gained the impression the military historian had not slept well for some time. Agnew inspected his colleague critically.

'You don't look well.'

'Been marking papers,' Evesham mumbled. 'And this damned grant . . . if you'd only see your way clear . . .'

'That's the purpose of this morning's meeting,' Agnew observed urbanely. 'But you really should not take things so much to heart. The examinations you've set were not formal tests ... they could have waited for term end. I understand it was your choice.'

'Keeping my mind off other things,' Evesham muttered, 'and keeping the minds of those young bastards on their work. Well, shall we start?'

Professor Agnew sniffed, shrugged and smiled vaguely in Arnold's direction. 'Of course. As far as I'm concerned, Professor Evesham, the support you're requesting must stand against a series of other demands made upon the research budget. I've now whittled down the submissions to a group I'm prepared to support because they seem to me to be a worthwhile series of projects which will add to our sum of knowledge. The difficulty I face over yours, as opposed to the ones I've mentioned, is that it seems to be based, essentially, upon a weak hypothesis.'

'Ailnoth—'

'The evidence you *suggest* is there is hardly of the kind that can be described as positive. If we are to back your research from our meagre funds we really must have something more concrete to go on. The Ailnoth you're interested in is hardly likely to be the *Alnith* of Langton. Unless Mr Landon is able to help us, therefore, it seems to me we've come to a dead end as far as argument is concerned.'

Evesham's lips suddenly writhed back from his teeth in a gesture of fury, perhaps brought on by tiredness, anxiety and frustration. 'Damn it, Agnew, does my project have to stand or fall on the word of an *amateur*?'

'When it has little else to stand on,' Agnew replied smoothly, 'what else is there?'

All three men were silent for a few moments. Evesham's dark, angry glance snapped across to Arnold. 'Well?'

Unhappily, Arnold shook his head. 'I fear I'm unable to help.'

'What the hell's that supposed to mean?'

'It's just that—'

There was a gentle tapping on the door. Its very gentleness prevented the outburst that Evesham was preparing in order to cut across Arnold's explanation. Agnew called out, and the door was opened gingerly. A young woman stood there, one of the secretarial staff. 'I beg your pardon, Professor Agnew. There's a . . . a Mr Culpeper here.'

The big, gentle frame of the policeman eased the door open. '*Detective-Inspector* Culpeper,' he said, smiling softly. 'Do you think I could have a word with Professor Evesham?'

Alan Evesham stared at the policeman with angry, red-rimmed eyes. 'We're in a meeting,' he snarled.

'It's important,' Culpeper said gently.

'So's this meeting.'

Culpeper smiled again. The smile was sad, but expectant. 'It's about a crossbow bolt.'

There was a silence in the room. The girl backed sideways, away from the door, and disappeared hastily along the corridor. Something had happened to Evesham's breathing; it had a ragged, distressed quality, an edge of panic. He stood up, tried to say something, but the words were strangled, incomprehensible.

Agnew frowned. 'Perhaps your room, Professor Evesham?'

Evesham nodded suddenly, and as Culpeper stood aside he marched out, to lead the way. Culpeper caught Arnold's glance, nodded in recognition, and walked after Evesham. Agnew stared at the floor.

Uneasily, Arnold looked about him. There seemed little point in continuing with this ill-starred meeting. He had nothing to offer these two academics anyway. It had always been a mistake: this was not his world, and he had been foolish to accept the suggestions that Agnew had made. 'I think it would be as well if I left now,' he said.

Agnew settled his troubled gaze on Arnold. 'I think so. If you have nothing to add . . .'

'I fear I just can't help. I'm sorry.'

Agnew nodded, preoccupied, and after a moment Arnold rose, shook hands with the Professor and walked out into the corridor. He walked its length, and the sunlight streamed in through the mullioned windows, casting patterns of light on the carpeted floor. At the far end of the corridor the handsome oak doors were open, leading to the stairs that would take him to the ground floor. He reached the doors, turned left, and then paused. On the wall beside him was a painting, of the Flemish school. Something stirred, in his mind, slow, turgid, the unsettling of a muddy thought.

The Flemish school. The drab figure in the tall hat stared sombrely at Arnold, the careful interior of the room picked out with precision, the stout matronly figure in the corner working at her sewing. Arnold stared at the painting, seeing it but not seeing, thinking, but with his thoughts beginning to whirl and rise and enter a confusion of facts and memories and suppositions. He closed his eyes and a red blackness descended on him as he squeezed his lids tight shut. Red . . . and black . . . *part red, part blue* . . .

Slowly, almost wonderingly, he turned and walked back along the corridor to Professor Agnew's room. The door was open: Agnew still sat dully in his chair, his brows creased with a vague, uncertain anxiety. He looked up as Arnold stood there.

'I think I can help after all,' Arnold announced.

Professor Agnew inspected his fingernails thoughtfully, observing them with a detached curiosity that suggested he had never seen them before. He chewed at his lower lip, nodding quietly to himself and then he sighed. 'Do you think you'd be able to . . . ah . . . give me chapter and verse for this?'

'I'd have to check the references, although I imagine one

of your research assistants could do it as well. I think the matter is well documented.'

'Hmmm. But how did this . . . theory return to you just now?'

'I was walking in the corridor,' Arnold explained. 'I saw a painting, of the Flemish school. It was a trigger. I'd been reading in Arundel and Champney, I'd read about the brickwork at Hull, part red, part blue, and I *knew* there was something I should remember. But the painting, the *Flemish* school, it reminded me that more came from Flanders than art.'

'Bricks.'

'Precisely. It is well documented that immigrants were entering England from the Low Countries well before the end of the twelfth century. The ships that brought them, it is believed, carried bricks as ballast. They were of a notable kind, not red and blue like the Hull bricks, but red, pink and orange—and especially cream and greenish-yellow. Very large quantities of these bricks were imported, because although they first came as ballast they soon became fashionable, and much sought-after.'

'But bricks are heavy, and roads were bad—'

'So local industry emerged again. And that's the point.'

'Ailnoth?'

Arnold nodded. 'Flemish bricks were fashionable—but expensive, so they were used only in those areas where there was trade with Flanders, and easy access to sea or river. Flemish bricks are therefore concentrated in the south of England—there was a shipment in 1278 of two hundred thousand for the Tower of London alone. But you don't find them in the north of England, generally. It just wasn't an economical proposition.'

'So what happened?'

Slowly Arnold said, 'I can't be sure, of course. It would need to be investigated. But let's put it like this, as a hypothesis. Flemish bricks were fashionable, but expensive.

A local product would need to be found to satisfy the demand. Local materials were eventually found and developed, in Suffolk. Little Wenham Hall is an example there —flints, lumps of yellowish solidified mud dug from the seashore, cream and greenish-yellow bricks.'

'So?'

'We have it on record that Ailnoth worked in Suffolk, in that area.'

'That doesn't prove anything.'

'Agreed.' Arnold hesitated. 'But the point is, if you look at what has been described as the chapel outside the existing line of Langton Castle you'll see something of considerable interest. The structure is ancient. It was actually once part of the outer wall, I'm convinced. And it is based on *Roman* tiles. But then trace up the original walls and you see something else. Old bricks, not as old as the Roman bricks, but old, twelfth-century old. And *greenish-yellow in colour*.'

'Flemish bricks?'

'No. They were never brought north because of the expense. I think they're the cheaper version, Suffolk made— and brought from Suffolk by a man, a building contractor, a supplier of materials who had come north from the Suffolk area—*maybe* after he had been barred as a master mason, *maybe* to offer skilled supervision on the site, well away from the scene of his disgrace, *maybe* knowing about the Suffolk bricks because he had worked there as a master mason—'

'*Maybe* Ailnoth,' Agnew murmured.

'And *maybe* buried at Langton, along with others who died in a building accident or a sudden plague.'

Interest glittered in Agnew's eyes. Warily he said, 'You think this supports Evesham's thesis?'

Arnold shook his head. 'I don't know. It's merely a small piece of evidence that *might* be regarded as supportive of his general hypothesis that Ailnoth and Alnith are one and the same. All I'm saying—'

'All you're saying is that this might be a sufficient piece

of evidence to suggest we should allow Evesham the funding to delve more deeply, investigate further.' Agnew smiled vaguely. 'Interesting . . . I get the impression that you are beginning to believe Professor Evesham's theory. He won't thank you for this, of course.'

Arnold smiled wryly, and shrugged. 'I haven't really done very much, and besides—'

The door burst open violently and Alan Evesham almost tumbled into the room. His hair was standing up spikily, and his hands were shaking in anger. He glared wildly at them both as though they were indulging in some kind of conspiracy against him. *'What the hell's going on?'* he demanded.

Arnold tried to say something but Agnew was rising to his feet. Arnold had never seen the Professor angry, but his normal urbanity was overtaken now by fury at the ill-mannered way in which Evesham had burst into his room.

'Evesham! How *dare* you thrust your way into my room in this way!'

'I want to know what the hell's going on,' Evesham bawled at the top of his voice. 'Someone's been into my room!'

'What on earth are you talking about?'

Evesham was almost beside himself with rage, but there was something else there in his voice which Arnold only picked up after a moment. It was panic. 'You've always said I shouldn't keep in my room what you regard as *clutter*, Agnew,' Evesham shouted hysterically. 'But no one gave you or any of your sucking-up colleagues permission to go into my room and remove items! I want to know what's happened, and I want to know who you got to do it!'

'Evesham, you'd better explain yourself,' Agnew said icily, 'and do it in a calm manner.'

There was a movement behind Evesham, and the young professor froze. Detective-Inspector Culpeper stood there, looking serious but calm. 'Perhaps I should explain,' he suggested.

Evesham's eyes were red-rimmed and wild. He looked sick.

'Please,' Agnew said.

Culpeper inclined his head gravely. 'I came to see Mr Evesham about his collection of mediæval weapons. We have been making inquiries among dealers in antiquities. The bolt that killed Mr Yates . . . there's a strong possibility that it was once in the possession of Mr Evesham.'

Alan Evesham made a gurgling sound.

'We can't be absolutely certain, of course,' Culpeper continued. 'But we can't check. It seems that the bolt Mr Evesham had has disappeared. It was stolen, he said, some time ago.'

'At the meet.' Evesham struggled out the words. 'Up at Langton—'

'And it seems that misfortunes do not visit Mr Evesham one at a time,' Culpeper observed. 'Not only the bolt seems to have been stolen—'

'Some sod's stolen the crossbow from my room as well!' Evesham declared passionately.

Culpeper caught Arnold's glance. He smiled thinly. Arnold gained the impression that the policeman did not like Alan Evesham. Nor did he believe him. The impression was strengthened when Culpeper said with a silky politeness, 'I think these are matters we can discuss further at police headquarters.'

Evesham opened his mouth to make an angry retort but stopped short as Agnew asked, 'Is that really necessary?'

Culpeper was not concerned with the reputation of the university. 'I am conducting a murder inquiry, Professor Agnew. The murder weapon was a crossbow bolt. Mr Evesham *had* one, but it mysteriously disappeared. He now tells me the crossbow itself has also disappeared. I cannot guess why this should be. But I think we can sort things out more easily if Mr Evesham comes to Morpeth to have a look at the bolt in our possession, to see if he can identify it. Then . . . then we can take a statement from him, which might help us clear up matters.'

'I thought you'd got hold of someone—'

'We have interviewed someone,' Culpeper interrupted. 'He has not been *eliminated* from our inquiries; at this stage he has not been able to help us a great deal. But we persist, and now . . .'

'I don't see how I can help,' Alan Evesham blustered.

'That remains to be seen, sir. But can we now go, so we can get it over with.'

'To Morpeth?' Evesham asked, reddening in the face.

'If you please,' Culpeper replied with a half-concealed edge of impatience in his tone.

Agnew was silent. Alan Evesham's face was white and there was an unmistakable panic in his eyes. 'This is preposterous!' he exclaimed.

'Maybe,' Culpeper replied sharply. 'Even so . . .'

Evesham shot one scared, angry glance in Agnew's direction and then hurried from the room. Culpeper nodded to Agnew and Arnold and then followed, closing the door quietly behind him.

Agnew inspected his fingernails, a slight flush staining his cheeks. Arnold sat still, unable to discard from his mind the outburst from Alan Evesham at the sherry party held by Professor Agnew. What were the words Evesham had used?

'Extermination. Treat him like the vermin he is.'

Startled, Arnold realized he had repeated the words aloud. Agnew was staring at him, open-mouthed. But it was not in surprise at hearing Arnold speak: rather, Arnold guessed, because the words Evesham had used on that occasion must have been heard by Agnew also, and had been in the Professor's mind now.

CHAPTER 6

1

On the Tuesday afternoon the Senior Planning Officer called Arnold to his office. Arnold thought at first the curiosity of the Senior Planning Officer had got the better of him, but when he was ushered into the presence he realized that his superior colleague was able to control such impulses. He was waved to a seat, and the Senior Planning Officer turned his chair so that he was not obliged to face Arnold. Staring out of the window, he said, 'There is now a difficulty over the Kilgour application.'

'I believe so, sir, yes.'

'What do you propose to do, Mr Landon?'

'Nothing immediately, sir. The death of Mr Yates means that the application will presumably not be proceeded with, at least not until the matter of the succession is settled.'

'Did Mr Yates leave any heirs?'

'I really can't say.'

'Is there a will?'

'Once again, sir, I don't know.'

The silence that fell suggested to Arnold that he *should* know. In a disgruntled tone, the Senior Planning Officer said, 'There's been a bad press.'

'Sir?'

'Councillor Stanley, the chairman of the planning committee, has been in to see me. Council elections are due soon. He's read a piece in the *Herald* and also something in the *Journal* which declares that Yates's attitudes were bad for the estates. He's also had a few letters, of the kind you already have on file. Fact is, Mr Landon, I am under a considerable degree of *political* pressure to have this planning application withdrawn.'

'I don't see how—'

'If there is no will, and if there are no heirs to the estate, what will happen to the land?' the Senior Planning Officer asked.

'It will be taken by the Crown as *bona vacantia*,' Arnold said.

'And matters will be taken out of our hands. The Crown Commissioners . . . Mr Landon, it seems to me action is necessary.'

'To do what?'

'We need to find out whether there are any heirs, or if there's a will. The local politicians want the application removed so things can simmer down. We can't really do that until we *know* there are likely to be no objections. But I'm under pressure for an early decision.'

'There's Mr Francis, of course,' Arnold suggested.

'I thought he'd fallen out of the reckoning,' the Senior Planning Officer said sharply.

'It depends,' Arnold said. 'The judgement given was that he has no right to the lands. Since they were legally owned by Patrick Yates they will go to Yates's heirs, not revert to Francis or others in Colonel Edridge's family. But that assumes the decision will stand. There is the possibility of an appeal—if Francis can afford it. And if that appeal were successful. Yates's death would become to that extent irrelevant. Francis would get the land.'

'Wouldn't that solve the problem?'

'I have a feeling,' Arnold said heavily, 'that Mr Francis could not be relied upon to behave towards the Kilgour Estates in a manner significantly different from Mr Yates. He's not really interested in the estates as such—only in what they can give him.'

'Oh dear . . . Mr Landon?'

'Yes, sir, I understand. I'd better make inquiries.'

At the least it would get him away from the suffocating gossip of the office, with its unhealthy concentration upon who might have murdered the unpopular magistrate, Patrick Yates of Kilgour.

He left Morpeth at eleven in the morning to drive into the Northumberland hills once again. He caught sight of the signpost to Ogle and wondered briefly about Alan Evesham. As far as he understood, the military historian had not been detained in police custody; he had made a statement and been allowed to leave. That he remained a prime suspect in the eyes of Detective-Inspector Culpeper, Arnold did not doubt. The story Professor Evesham had told was certainly odd, though Arnold did recall a disturbance at the archery meeting at Langton. There had been a display of weapons there; Evesham had been present; an altercation had arisen and the story was that the crossbow bolt had been stolen on that occasion. It was something Culpeper would no doubt now be checking.

As for the crossbow itself, that seemed a pointless theft which had little or nothing to do with the murder of Patrick Yates, since Culpeper had intimated the bolt had been *thrust* into Yates rather than fired at him. Was it a piece of embroidery by Evesham? The crossbow could certainly have been stolen from his room; the notoriously untidy clutter of that room had been open to all, since Evesham had been prone to leave the door wide open.

Nick Enwright had been at the Langton meeting, and so had Wendy Gregory.

Wendy Gregory.

There were two women Arnold had to meet today, and Miss Gregory was one of them. But first, he had a call to make at Kilgour House itself.

He arrived there shortly before one o'clock. The house had a closed-in, shuttered appearance, as though it found the attention devoted to it by the press of recent days unwelcome and it had drawn in upon itself. The driveway was churned with mud: Arnold had seen several photographs in the newspapers during the last two weeks, of the house, of Pauline Callington, face half-hidden by a raised newspaper, of the tenanted farms and their state of dilapidation. The articles had been openly critical of the dead man's management of Kilgour, and something of the old story—from the Francis side of things—had been published. It had led to the political pressure upon the Senior Planning Officer—and Arnold's visit now.

The door was answered by Pauline Callington herself.

Her face was pale, its lack of colour emphasized by the dark mourning dress she wore. Oddly, her hair was tied back with a bright red piece of chiffon, startling against the darkness of her dress. She wore no make-up and the tiny crowsfeet around her eyes were more than usually noticeable, while lines of discontent around her mouth and an apparent sagging of her jawline seemed to make her look older than he had realized earlier. She was still a handsome woman, nevertheless, and still a hard one.

'What do *you* want?'

Arnold hesitated. 'Do you think I could have a word with you?'

'About what?'

'About the future of Kilgour.'

Her mouth tightened, and something moved angrily in her eyes. The anger died, to be replaced by suspicion. 'Why should that concern you?'

'The planning application.'

She frowned, considered his explanation for several seconds, then with an obvious reluctance she stepped aside, gesturing to him to enter.

Arnold followed her as she led the way to the library. Dustsheets had already been draped over the furniture, with one exception. Near the window, overlooking the meadows beyond the house, stood a handsome carved oak chair. An eighteenth-century card table stood beside it. On the table was a whisky decanter, and a half-full glass of neat whisky. Pauline Callington sat in the chair, picked up the glass and stared at Arnold challengingly. 'Well?'

He could not be certain whether the challenge related to his presence there, or to his observation of the fact she had taken to Yates's whisky bottle. Either way, she had not offered him a seat. He was not expected to stay long. He had no desire to stay long. He found her a formidable woman.

'We're concerned about the future of Kilgour, or more specifically, the matter of the planning application,' Arnold said. 'To what extent, we need to know whether it's to remain on file, or whether it will be withdrawn or proceeded with by the heirs—'

'*Ha!*'

Arnold hesitated, watching her nervously as she finished the whisky and poured herself another. Her colour remained pale and she seemed unaffected by the alcohol but there was a cold glitter in her eye.

'Are there any heirs? To your knowledge, I mean?'

'Yates never married,' she said snappishly. 'He was an only child. There are no known living relatives. He was alone.'

Arnold hesitated. 'Was there a will?'

'A will?' The glitter grew sharper, ice under a winter sun, and her mouth became pinched, tight in its anger and frustration. 'Oh yes, there's a bloody will—or so he said! The *bastard*! I've contacted his solicitors, I've tried the banks, I've hunted high and low . . .' She took a long pull at her whisky, then put her head back against the carved wood of the chair. Her lips writhed back mirthlessly over her teeth. 'You see a wronged woman, my friend.'

'Wronged?'

She laughed now, but still it lacked warmth or real mirth. It was self-mockery and suppressed rage that came from her, and it made Arnold nervous. 'Don't misunderstand me,' she said, 'I knew what I was getting into. I knew Yates was a hard, calculating bastard with an overlay of charm that could bring women—and men—to his bed. The men, I can't vouch for them, though I heard enough about his relationship with old Edridge, but the women, oh yes, that I *can* vouch for! He had an eye, and if his success rate dropped in recent years that was only because he couldn't be bothered any longer. He had satisfaction here, sexually, and the added pleasure of making me squirm.'

'Mrs Callington—'

'Am I making you uneasy, Mr Landon?' She laughed on a high, brittle note. 'You knew I was his housekeeper—surely you guessed what everyone else knew? Of course I was his mistress, but the reason why I stayed on here as no one else did was that we *understood* each other. He knew I was as tough —and as calculating—as he was. He respected that. And it amused him to set it all up, and then make me squirm.'

Arnold asked, in spite of himself. 'Set what up?'

'The *arrangement*, of course! I stay here, service his needs —and some of them were peculiar, believe me—and then I'd get the estates when he died. He never thought he'd live long . . . He was right about that, at least, the bastard . . .'

Arnold had thought she had loved him. He had guessed it accounted for her acceptance of public and private humili- ations. Perhaps his thoughts were clear in his face for Pauline Callington stared at him contemptuously. 'It was an *arrange- ment*. I hated the bastard, but it was too late, I couldn't leave! He'd promised me.' Her right hand clenched suddenly in spasm and she put down her glass, her left hand trembling in passion. 'But I can't find that bloody will! He's cheated me. *Cheated* me!'

Arnold stared at her. Though the whisky had had no obvious physical effect, it had certainly loosened her tongue, for he doubted that she would have been so open with him otherwise. But the sudden thought struck him that there might yet be other secrets she would have to impart. Not to him, perhaps, but to Detective-Inspector Culpeper.

'When we found Yates dead,' he said slowly, 'you were calm. But when the police arrived, you were hysterical.'

She looked at him mockingly. 'Delayed shock.'

'You accused Nick Enwright of killing Yates.'

She raised her eyebrows and looked at him appraisingly. 'You've got a nerve. And you're no fool, either, are you, Landon? But there's just the two of us, so why don't we talk? Enwright? Obvious choice. The bastard wanted Yates dead—as much as I did. So why not set the police on to him? Stop him setting his gin-traps in the woods, and slicing those bloody arrows into the game. And draw attention away from me, too. Why not? I didn't want to sweat away in Morpeth HQ, did I? *I needed to find that bloody will!*'

'Are you saying—'

'*Saying?*' Her words slurred suddenly, as though the alcohol finally began to take effect. 'What the hell am I saying? Nothing! I couldn't stand that bastard with his groping hands and his funny ways! All right, he was attractive at the beginning, but he hooked me in the end with cheating lies and maybe I guessed it and didn't trust him and wanted him dead, but you'll never get me to say that outside this house! And if you think you'll ever be clever enough to get me to slip up . . .' She swung her arm in a sudden furious gesture, knocking the decanter to the floor and tipping over the card table. She stood up, staring at the whisky glass in her hand and then she threw that down too, and stood there breathing hard and furiously. The whisky in the decanter gurgled as it lapped on to the carpet, a steady stain spreading like blood on the dark red pile.

Pauline Callington raised her head and stared at Arnold, fully in control of herself again. The rage in her eyes had subsided; it was as though the last few minutes had never happened. 'I don't think there's anything more I have to say to you now, Mr Landon. Please leave.'

Arnold left. He got into his car and drove away. As he

pulled past the library windows he looked up. He caught a glimpse of her face as she stood there, looking out over the hills. He had the impression that she would not be seeing him, but what she had lost. Or what she had never really possessed.

2

Thoughtfully, Arnold made his way back towards the village.

He was in a confused state of mind. The attitudes that Pauline Callington had demonstrated to him were entirely unexpected. When Arnold had found the body of Patrick Yates she had seemed controlled. Her later hysteria in face of the police had seemed to him to be a matter of delayed shock. Now he knew that the hysteria had been deliberate —it had been the presentation of an unreal reaction. Pauline Callington had wanted to show to the police a feminine shock and horror of the kind they would have expected in an innocent woman. But its real purpose had been to divert attention, away from herself.

Did that mean she had something to hide? Arnold weighed the matter in his mind. It *could* have been a genuine attempt to avoid involvement, questioning, the pressure that would inevitably have been brought in a murder inquiry.

On the other hand, it could have been something more sinister.

He went over the sequence of events. Pauline Callington claimed she had left Patrick Yates to go shopping in Langton. He was alive when she left. Her car had broken down, she had obtained a lift from Arnold and it was he—the outsider—who had found the body in the shrubbery.

But was there not another scenario that was a possibility? They had only Pauline Callington's word for the series of events. There was the possibility that she had had a violent row with Yates. She *could* have become so incensed with the discovery of his true attitude towards her that she herself had killed him, in her violent passion. She was a formidable woman, on that point Arnold was clear. And he had no doubt she could have *planned*—and perhaps executed—the events thereafter.

If she *had* killed Yates in anger, she would have been cool enough and controlled enough to drive down to the village, perhaps *arrange* the car breakdown by damaging the steering linkage, and then to wait for someone—Arnold as it happened—to come along and provide her with an alibi.

Arnold frowned. It was possible. But when did she discover about the will . . . or lack of it? Before Yates's death, or after? And the car breakdown: she had claimed it was due to a steering fault, but had it been confirmed? Had the police checked? They'd made no suggestion that it had been tampered with, but . . .

Arnold shook his head. People bothered him in a way stone and wood did not. People gave him problems of emotional upset.

Of the kind he'd have to face, surely, with Wendy Gregory.

She and Francis were living together, of course. And if Francis was at her cottage and Arnold arrived asking about the future, there'd surely be a scene of some kind. He went over the kind of approaches he could make when he arrived there.

In the event, he was relieved: there was no answer to his knock at the cottage door. He waited for a while, uncertainly, and then he made his way out through the little white-painted wooden gate, got back into his car, and with a feeling of release drove up the hill past the church to the castle above the fields.

He would have to wait, of course. There was no point in returning to the office in Morpeth. He would wait an hour or two, then go back and see if they had returned. Meanwhile, he could fill in his time by doing a last check at Langton Castle.

The afternoon was overcast but warm, and a slanting sun sent rays of light through the clouds towards Cheviot. Arnold sat for a while above the outer walls of the castle and thought about the centuries it had seen, the men who had tramped its cold walls in the height of winter, the people who had prayed in the chapel, the lovers who had used the walls as shelter during warm summer nights.

Then he went down and looked again at the line of the scarp slope, and the ancient Roman tiles at the base of the copse-hidden structures, and at the cream and greenish-yellow bricks that had come from Suffolk hundreds of years ago.

Whether he was right or wrong was unimportant, he guessed, as far as Alan Evesham was concerned. The light of considered interest in Professor Agnew's eyes had convinced Arnold that there was now enough evidence to at least give some credibility to Evesham's claims, and there would be every possibility that Agnew would release finance to support Evesham's studies in Ailnoth and the buildings of the north. Always supposing Evesham did not have other priorities to deal with—like making it clear to the police that he had had nothing to do with the murder of Patrick Yates.

Suddenly Arnold felt weary. He climbed back up to the ridge and took the seat he had taken when he first looked down into the copse. The sun was warm on his face as he put his head back and closed his eyes. His thoughts began to drift: he remembered the sight of a sheepdog, racing across a field to greet its master, and the warmth of old stone under the summer sun; he lost his sense of the present and remembered the Old Wheat Barn,* unused for centuries but still retaining the marks of a genius, the ancient joints built by John of Wetherby; and then there was that bridge

* *A Gathering of Ghosts*

of mist he had crossed to go to an old manor house* where the secrets of centuries had lain hidden behind stone cellar walls, a passageway to the past. His thoughts were confused, blurring images of yesterday and last year, as the vagueness of sleep drifted over him and he dozed in the sunshine, dreaming of death, and his father, and the warm tints of coloured tiles in a wall.

He woke with a start. He stretched, then stared at his watch in disbelief.

It was almost five-fifteen.

He rose. His limbs were stiff. He looked about him for a few minutes, then reluctantly made his way back down to his car. He drove down to the village.

When he pulled up outside the cottage it still looked deserted. He opened the gate and entered the small front garden. He knocked at the door: the house echoed hollowly, as though it had been long since emptied and abandoned. Arnold was not certain whether he should wait any longer. He had not eaten since breakfast that morning and now his stomach was beginning to complain.

The best plan would be to go to the local pub in the village and get something to eat and drink. Pubs also dispensed information, if you were lucky.

The public house was called the Red Lion. The sign above the door stated that the licensee was one Sid Wright.

It was Mrs Wright who was serving behind the bar. She was a lean, pinched woman with a sharp nose and sharper eye. There was something about her mouth that suggested she disapproved of Arnold, and she certainly did not strike him as the chatty type so he retired with his drink, and the menu, to a corner of the room.

In a little while the lady of the house vanished into the back and the landlord himself stood behind the bar. He seemed to be of more promising material. He was large, a

* *Most Cunning Workmen*

tubular sixteen stone, and sported a pair of walrus whiskers that dragged attention away from the shiny nakedness of his skull. He wore a blue shirt and yellow sweater and he was sweating: dark stains appeared in the faded yellow of his armpits. Arnold wondered whether he'd been having a hard time in the back with his wife: working now in the bar he'd be likely to lose a few litres in perspiration.

Arnold went up and ordered a half of lager. He asked Sid Wright if he'd like a drink. The answer was a pint. It almost vanished at the first swallow.

Sid Wright cocked an inquisitive eye in his direction. 'Stranger around here?'

'More or less.'

'Passing through? Or Press?'

'Neither, really. On business.'

'What kind is that?'

Arnold hesitated. 'I've just called in at Wendy Gregory's cottage.'

'Oh aye.' Sid Wright leered. '*That* kind of business.'

'I was looking for Bob Francis.'

'He wor living there for a while, for sure.'

'*Was* living there?'

'Right. Moved out, few days since, now.' The tubular landlord leaned forward confidentially, elbows on the bar, and winked at Arnold with a conspiratorial left eye. 'Way of the world, if you know what I mean.'

'I don't understand.'

'Ah, you know how it is. Didn't you hear the story? Living up yonder he was, with his wife, but started this thing going with Miss Gregory. PE teacher, you know, 'andsome enough lass. His wife found out, and threw him out. So he came to live with Wendy Gregory. A few scenes in the village, Miss Gregory and Mrs Francis, but Bob Francis, well, he came out of it well enough. Talk is, he used some of Miss Gregory's money to support his claim for the Kilgour estates in the courts. Funny business, hey?'

'Funny?'

'Manner of speaking. I mean, his wife throws him out, he shacks up with Miss Gregory, he loses his claim against Yates, and then our friend and magistrate gets killed. Days after, seems like, things go sour between Miss Gregory and Francis, and then he walks out after a big row. *Talk* is, it's because she reckons he was only interested in her while she could help him, and since she can't raise cash for an appeal, he'll be moving on.'

So perhaps his visit to see Francis and Miss Gregory would no longer be necessary, Arnold thought. Francis could not afford an appeal; Wendy Gregory had no more money to give him, and they had in any case split up. Cheerfully, he asked what Mr Wright had on the menu.

'Homemade soup, Cumberland sausage.'

It sounded good, and Arnold discovered half an hour later that it was good. He dallied over the meal, since he had nothing pressing back at home outside Morpeth, and had two glasses of lager. A few people, obviously regulars, drifted in, and a young couple sat for a while, waiting for it to get dark, before slipping out for an evening walk.

At length the landlord came over to clear away Arnold's plates. 'Police were round this morning, you know.'

'Police?'

'They were looking for Bob Francis. I just been talking to Fred Singer, you know? He reckons he spoke to them this morning. They was making inquiries about this Francis feller. Fred, he says it's in connection with the murder of Patrick Yates.'

'I see.'

'They was back, late this afternoon. They asked Wendy Gregory about him, because seems like they can't get hold of Francis. He's skipped, like. Fred and Tom Malling was in the village when they left and Fred reckons she came out of her cottage very red in the face. I can guess what they said to her! I mean, the bloke she'd shacked up with, suspected of murder!'

'They're still looking for Francis?'

'Guess so.' Mr Wright stroked his expansive belly and considered the matter. 'My guess also is they won't be long making an arrest. I mean, where can he run to, like? Bad business, but not for trade. When the press came in like hordes last week we did quite well. A trial now, and that'd keep us through the winter.'

'What about Wendy Gregory?'

'Fred reckons she shot off in that red car of hers. Him and Tom had to move quick to get out of the way when she went around the corner.'

'Do you think she's gone to warn Francis, or to find him?'

The landlord shrugged, lifting his rotund frame with an effort. 'Shouldn't think so. Fred was saying she went off in the direction of Hampton. She's got an old mother there, about twenty miles off. Goes over regular, like. She'll have gone for a shoulder to cry on, but gossip in the village is she'll get no more than she deserves, comin' between man and wife. The old lady, her mother, she's a hard nut, I'm told, and she won't offer Miss Gregory much by way of sympathy. I reckon the parent-teacher association at the Broadwood school won't be none too pleased either: I think Miss Gregory will get a rough ride there, too. As for Francis —my bet is he's runnin' for cover. And backtrackin' like the fox he is, to hide his trail.'

It all seemed to remote now, for Arnold. He sipped his third lager and thought of Nick Enwright with his longbow and gin-traps, hunting at night, Alan Evesham with his crossbow and passion for mediæval weapons; Tom Malling expressing his dislike for the freemasons on the hill above Langton; Wendy Gregory, the third side of a triangle involving an errant husband and a bitter wife. And Bob Francis, possibly on the run from the police after wreaking his revenge on the man who had denied him what he regarded as his rightful inheritance. But Arnold need have no more to do with these people than he did with the embittered, frustrated woman who still searched the crannies of Kilgour House.

He finished his lager and ordered another, remembering again the man who had lain with his face upturned to the sky with the bolt planted solidly in his chest.

It was dusk before Arnold finally left the Red Lion. He sat in his car for several minutes, warm, generally content, and at peace with the thought that further action on his part with regard to the Kilgour Estates would be unnecessary. He started the car, let in the clutch and drove away from the village.

He hesitated at the crossroads, wondering whether to take the short cut home across the hills to the A1. He decided against it. The winding back roads were more pleasant. He had plenty of time. He was in a comfortable frame of mind.

Just four miles later, as his headlights picked out the red car abandoned at the roadside, his peace of mind was shattered. He slowed, then stopped. He got out of the car. It had been returning towards Langton, this vehicle half in the ditch. It was empty, but the windscreen had been shattered.

Arnold went back to his car and collected his torch. In the dim evening light he flicked it on, and shone it into the car. On the passenger seat was a short piece of old iron. It had been forged into the semblance of a crossbow bolt.

3

The car was lying with its nearside wheels in the ditch some forty yards from a bend. Beyond the car the hill rose: a straggling hedge led upwards to a swathe of trees lifting to the skyline, birch and alder and hornbeam. The incident must have happened shortly before Arnold had reached the spot: he could still hear the ticking noise of the cooling engine.

Irresolutely, Arnold stood with his torch swinging about across the field, the narrow beam losing its power as it lanced against the hill. Dusk had now changed to darkness as heavy clouds built up from the west, and Arnold felt he detected rain in the air as he raised his head and sniffed at the wind. He flashed his torch upwards to the trees, and thought he heard a swift thrashing sound. He paused, and next moment his worst fears were confirmed as he heard a cry.

It was the voice of a woman, high, scared and panic-torn. Almost without thinking, Arnold scrambled over the narrow hedge and began to run up towards the darkening trees.

His action was instinctive, and the blood pounded in his veins as he ran. The slope of the hill quickly made his legs ache, and he slowed as he neared the band of trees that led to the brow of the hill.

He stopped, breathing hard, and after a few moments raised his torch to send a slow sweep of light across the darkness of the trees. The leaves glittered back at him, he thought he caught the glint of an animal's eyes in the undergrowth, and irresolutely he moved forward, carefully, his heart pounding in his chest from the exertion of his run up the hill and the tension that affected him.

A rustling noise to his right made him swing around quickly: something scuttled through the undergrowth, disturbed by his approach. The hairs prickled on the back of his neck and his skin was abnormally sensitive, almost aching, as he swung the torch again.

'Please . . . !'

The call was desperate and cut off: he could not see the woman but he had caught the general direction and he ran forward, thrashing his way into the woods almost unthinkingly, not knowing why she hid among the trees, and not understanding the nature of the terror that affected her.

Twenty yards into the trees he stopped, and the silence of the wood swept around him like a suffocating blanket, with sky shut out under the canopy and a darkening moon losing its faded brilliance. He flashed the torch ahead of him in a long, slow sweep.

Then he saw her.

It was the whiteness of a nervous hand, half-raised, a signal against the darkness of the trees. She was kneeling or crouching down. He could not see her face, merely the gesturing hand, and he hurried forward, thrashing his way through nettles and scrub, the light dancing crazily in front of him until he reached the denser undergrowth where she was half hidden.

'What—'

'*For God's sake!*'

The woman grabbed at him, dragging him off balance, and with her free hand she struck at the flashlight, dashing it from his hand. He fell to one knee, pulled down by the urgency of her grip, and his knee burned as a thorn drilled its way into his kneecap.

'What on earth are you doing?' he demanded, groping for the flashlight. He picked it up, and for a quick moment the light played on the woman's face before she again grabbed at it, tearing it from his grasp.

It was Wendy Gregory, wild-eyed, hair in disarray, mouth open and panting and scared. The light flicked out. '*Do you want us killed?*' she hissed in terror.

She was lying on one hip, her back against the bole of a tree, glaring up at him in the darkness. He shook his head in puzzlement. 'What the hell's going on?'

'He's out there, with a bow!'

'A bow?' Arnold repeated stupidly.

'Enwright, for God's sake! He's trying to kill me! He's fixed things so that Bob is suspected for the murder of Yates, but he knows I'll never rest until I clear Bob, and so he waited for me in the roadway, until I returned from my mother's, and then he launched that crossbow bolt against me, smashed the car window—'

'But you can't be serious!'

'Serious, hell!' Wendy Gregory snarled. 'What do you think I'm lying here for? The car went into the ditch and I scrambled out. I saw him at the side of the roadway: he had the crossbow. At first, I could just make him out like a dark shadow, then I saw him raise the bow . . . I ran, just ran for cover, up the hill to these trees, but I heard him come after me, blundering about in the darkness and I lay low, then I saw your lights and when you stopped I called out . . . But for God's sake keep *down*! He knows where I am now, thanks to your lighting his way to us. We must keep quiet, keep down, and then we'll have to run for it!'

She was panic-stricken, almost incoherent, but there was something wrong, something that lurched incomprehensibly in Arnold's mind as she gasped out her terror. He could not see her face, but her grip was still fierce, strong and hard as it had been that day in the courtroom when a different kind of emotion had held her.

Arnold reached for the flashlight, took it from her. He hesitated, then depressed the switch. Nothing happened: the contact must have been damaged, or the bulb broken. Wendy Gregory's breath was harsh, painful in the silence of the woods. Arnold waited, and listened.

Someone was moving awkwardly through the trees some thirty yards away. Even as he realized it he heard a snapping sound, a metallic click and something came whirring noisily towards them, carving its deadly way through the scrub, until it clattered heavily against the tree behind them.

Suddenly, Arnold was convinced.

'Come on!' he shouted, grabbed Wendy Gregory by the elbow, and pulled her to her feet. They stood upright, and she was shaking violently. For a moment Arnold did not know which way to go, but realizing the trees still gave them protection of a kind they would lack in the open field, he plunged forward, away from the noise to their left, deeper into the trees, ascending the hill as the hunter behind them struggled to notch a fresh bolt into the mediæval weapon he held.

Low branches whipped at them as though trying to slow them, bar their progress, but Arnold, head down, half-dragged the crying woman through the scrub and undergrowth, deep into the bank of bracken that loomed up ahead of them below the brow of the hill. The going became steeper, and the bracken thicker so they were struggling, breath rasping in their chests as they toiled up to the ridge. There was a shout from behind them, fifty yards back, maybe further, compounded of rage and passion and then something whirred at them again, but across to their right, out of range and in the wrong line. Arnold glanced back and thought he saw movement, a man scrambling through the trees below them, but he could have been mistaken.

An iron band seemed to have clamped across Arnold's chest and he stopped, deep in the bracken, his legs almost giving up. Wendy Gregory pressed hard behind him, nearly causing him to fall. Her teeth were chattering and she pushed against him, younger, fitter, terrified. Arnold struggled on, clawing his way forward through the ferns and ahead of them the trees thinned on the brow of the hill, a dark skyline emerging, heavy with cloud, edged with pale moonlight.

The girl slipped, feet sliding in the earth below the ferns, and as she fell Arnold lost balance also, tumbling down, face scratched by stiff dead bracken. He shouted at her in spite of the tearing pain in his chest, dragged her to her feet and they lurched forward again, seeking the skyline, wanting the screen of the hilltop so they could run on, down in the darkness towards the haven of the distant village.

It was then that the scream cut across their panic.

It was a scream of pure agony. It pulsed against the hill, echoing through the trees, and it shocked them, brought them to a halt. It came again, like an animal in torment, and there was a thrashing, furious sound, a thudding noise and then a long wailing note, a human being in pain, the drawn-out tearing note of a man in excruciating agony.

Arnold could see the pale shape of Wendy Gregory's face, her mouth dark and open as it gasped for breath, the eyes shadowed sockets of fear, and he slipped his hand under his jacket, feeling for the thudding of his heart, heaving to catch his breath.

The wailing died, subsided to a series of short, moaning cries. Then the silence came back as it had been earlier, and the hill waited.

When the slow, shuffling, dragging sound came to them Arnold turned his back and dragged Wendy Gregory over the hill top.

The lights of the village twinkled, some three or four miles across the fields. Below them, to their right, the road swung pale under the fading light. Arnold hesitated. The woman was still shaking, her hand tightly grasping his, and she was still riven by panic. Gently, Arnold said, 'I think we're all right now.'

'Please, no, we must . . .'

'No, wait.'

They stood, and the trees behind them were quiet. A light breeze rose, ruffling Arnold's damp hair, and gradually his breathing slowed, the thunder in his chest subsiding. Wendy Gregory's own urgency began to ease. She leaned against him and he half-supported her as she began to cry, racking sobs that tore at her but oddly calmed her, for in a little while she stopped trembling and stood away from him.

'What happened?'

Arnold could not be sure, but he could guess. He stood there in the darkness of the hill and he thought about her panicked words earlier, and the scream among the trees. He thought of Alan Evesham and his cluttered room, and a dog streaking wildly across a field. He remembered the harsh proud iron in Patrick Yates's chest and what Yates and Bob Francis had had in common. And he thought of Ailnoth and times past and the men of subtle craft.

'I think it's all right, now, Miss Gregory,' he said. 'We can cut down to the road, and make our way back to my car.'

She was reluctant, but eventually trusting. She walked close to him as they descended the hill.

Half way down, they heard the coughing roar of an engine coming to life and the lights of a vehicle lit up the road, lurching off a side track to make its way back towards Langton.

'Yes,' Arnold said sadly. 'We're all right now.'

4

The Land-Rover stood in the yard, its door open. Arnold stood beside the door: the courtesy light was on and on the floor of the vehicle, below the driving seat, he could see the dark patch. He touched it: it was sticky. He wiped the blood from his fingers on the side of the vehicle, then turned and went up to the house.

The door at the main entrance was slightly ajar. He entered the silent house, moving carefully and quietly. The light groaning sound finally drew him to the sitting-room.

The man he was looking for lay stretched out in the sitting-room chair, his leg raised and resting on a pouffé. An attempt had been made to stop the flow of blood: a piece of wood had been twisted inside a strip of cloth to form a rough tourniquet. The attempt had not been successful: the cloth was badly stained, there was a pool of blood on the floor and spreading across the pouffé, and the man himself was ashen in colour, his eyelids flickering weakly as he watched Arnold come in. He opened his mouth to speak but Arnold ignored him, walking past him to pick up the phone and dial the emergency services for an ambulance.

Arnold had taken Wendy Gregory in the car to the Red Lion. While she had been attended to for shock and he had taken a stiff drink to calm his own nerves, the police had been called. Arnold had sat there with the whisky, and thought. When he had finished the drink and had regained control of himself he had left Miss Gregory in the publican's care and driven away from the village.

The man's eyes watched him for a little while as he sat down, waiting for the ambulance. At last the words struggled out. 'How did you know?'

'That it was you?' Arnold shrugged sadly. 'I didn't know, but I guessed. Miss Gregory . . . she thought it was Nick Enwright out there in the woods. But she talked of seeing you merely as a dark shadow, and she spoke of you *blundering* your way through the trees. Nick Enwright was an experienced hunter, used to working at night. He wouldn't have blundered about: he'd have moved silently and quickly. And then there's the clumsy business about the crossbow . . . Enwright would never have used such an old, inaccurate weapon. Not when he had an efficient method of destruction in his longbow.'

Arnold was silent for a while, watching the man. He tightened the tourniquet and the eyes flickered again. 'I feel nothing, It's numb.'

Arnold nodded. 'The ambulance will be here soon.'

'It would have been better to leave me, alone.'

Arnold understood. 'I couldn't do that. I thought things through, guessed it could possibly be you, and realized that where Enwright wouldn't have blundered into one of his own traps, *you* could have done.'

The man in the chair nodded sleepily. 'A gin-trap . . . it almost sliced through my leg.'

'I realized when you drove your Land-Rover away from where you'd had it parked that you'd be likely to go home. I couldn't just leave you to die . . . You see, I always felt we had some things in common, and in some ways thought alike. But I never really attached much to your statement that you thought Yates *deserved* to die. Then I wondered what Yates and Bob Francis and Wendy Gregory had in common, and I half-realized what would have been in your mind. It was Richard atte Chirche who was the key.'

'Richard atte Chirche . . .' The man's tone was drowsy.

'They ordered things so much better . . . justice . . .'

'But why now?' Arnold asked quietly. 'Why did you kill Yates after all these years?'

The man squirmed uncomfortably in the chair and moistened his dry lips. 'Years . . . so long ago . . . But for me it's never changed. I hated him. He used my wife, took her away from me, and then coldly discarded her. I loved her, it wouldn't have mattered, but she killed herself when she knew he didn't want her, and she realized how she had betrayed me. She was always here, you know, all the years after she died, she was still with me. I thought of her each day and waited for justice to catch up with Patrick Yates. But it never did, and one day I talked with you on the hill—'

'It couldn't have been I who made you—'

'No. But you made me think of the past, and how it can be as real—*more* real—than the present. And I talked with you of the sworn masons and Richard atte Chirche and I knew that justice would never come, that I had to take it in my own hands . . .'

'You stole the bolt from Evesham's collection at Long Meadow, the day of the archery meeting.'

Tom Malling sighed. 'It was on the spur of the moment. Perhaps I had blood in my mind then, but I can't remember . . . It was there, old, mediæval, an instrument of death. No one saw me, I just walked away . . .'

'And the crossbow?'

'That was later, the day we were at the university together. I walked past his room, saw the crossbow and I just walked in, dropped the weapon through the open window and collected it from the grass a few minutes later.' A wry smile touched his pained mouth. 'Though if I'd walked out past the porter with it, I don't think he'd have noticed.'

'But you didn't use the bow when you killed Yates.'

Malling's eyes were glazed. He thought for a while, silent, then he shook his head gently. 'I couldn't get the damn thing to work. But I was obsessed with it, using it as a sworn mason might have. But in the end, when I drove to Kilgour, he looked so surprised. The bolt . . . it went in so easily and all I could think of was of the ancient days, the men of subtle craft . . .'

Both men were silent for a while as Arnold observed the glitter of excitement in Tom Malling's eyes. When the light died again he said, 'I still don't understand why you tried to kill Wendy Gregory.'

'The bow,' Malling muttered. 'I worked on it, fashioned some bolts that would suit. I used it, in the fields . . .'

'What about Wendy Gregory?' Arnold persisted.

Malling stared at him for several seconds, uncomprehending. 'The woman . . . you don't understand . . . But she was no different, no better than Yates, in her own way! All those years ago Yates took my wife from me, treated her so badly that she put her head in a gas oven. He had to pay for that. But how was Wendy Gregory different? I stood in the street when the police came to her cottage, looking for that fool Francis. I saw her come out, angry and upset because her lover had walked out on her. But what of the marriage she had destroyed? What of the woman—the wife—Francis had left, for her? She broke that marriage as Yates broke mine, and she was no different from Yates, and I knew she had to die, ruining Mrs Francis's life . . .'

Hardly that, Arnold thought, as he remembered the hard, spiteful woman he had met at Station Cottage when he had first sought out Bob Francis. For Malling she had been the innocent partner in a game of seduction, a wronged wife with an errant husband. As he had been a wronged husband, with an errant wife.

'She came out, took her bright red car to go to her mother's. I saw her go; she almost ran us down. I had plenty of time. I went back to the farm. I got the crossbow and I drove along till I came to the side track. I waited. It was easy. When I saw her coming, in the dusk, I ran down to the road and I fired the bolt, smashed her windscreen. She ran for the trees . . .'

'Where's the weapon now?' Arnold asked quietly.

Malling shook his head. 'When I stepped on the gin-trap I dropped it, lost it. I had to . . . to tear myself free . . . the pain, and the blood . . . But I got back to the Land-Rover, and my leg was numb then . . .'

He had driven back the couple of miles, his blood soaking the floor of the Land-Rover. His attempt to murder Wendy Gregory had been clumsy: with the ancient weapon and the handmade bolts Malling had never really stood much chance of hitting her among the trees, in the darkness.

Arnold recalled how the bolts had flown wild in the darkness, wide of the target. It had been an ill-conceived, badly-prepared attempt to commit again a crime that itself had been badly planned, though lucky in its successful execution.

Arnold had been up at Langton hill that day when Patrick Yates had died. He had seen Malling's sheepdog racing back across the fields to greet its returning master. Arnold had seen the dog, but not the Land-Rover driving back to the farm. He could not have known that Malling was returning from murder, and yet the image of that dog had remained with him. He shuddered. Had his mind touched Malling's then, too?

'I'm tired,' Tom Malling said, and closed his eyes.

Outside, Arnold heard the clangour of the ambulance's warning siren.

It was several days before Arnold found time to go to the library, to seek out Arundel again. He had had to make a series of statements before Detective-Inspector Culpeper. He had had to explain himself to an anxious Senior Planning Officer. His immediate superior had been concerned to discover whether the planning problems really were over: Arnold considered they were. It seemed Pauline Callington had not found the will she sought and the chances of Bob Francis raising money seemed slim. He had turned up again, having gone to ground in Tees-side. Arnold suggested his cause was now a lost one and the Kilgour Estates would probably go to the Crown as *bona vacantia*.

Whether that would mean Nick Enwright would get his tenancy of Top Farm was questionable: there was a rumour that he was entering an agreement down south anyway, in the Aylesbury area. The other tenants of Kilgour were relatively happy, however: Arnold guessed they would be hopeful of receiving better treatment under the Crown Estates than they had under the régime of Patrick Yates.

'Not that it is any of our business,' the Senior Planning Officer suggested.

'No, sir,' Arnold agreed.

But Detective-Inspector Culpeper was still puzzled. It showed in his glance when he questioned Arnold, and when he read over Arnold's statement. He could understand Arnold's part in the events, but he was still unable to grasp the reality of Tom Malling's motivation. Revenge, yes, for the suicide of his wife, and a long, brooding resentment that finally banked up into a fire that killed Patrick Yates. But the pursuit of Wendy Gregory was another matter. 'He must be crazy,' he suggested.

It was a point of view. Arnold tried to explain about the past, about the way it could sometimes bear more reality than the present. He tried to tell Culpeper that there were days when he himself, high on a windy crag, could smell the heather the way the Romans had, and see a hawk soar as hawks had soared for a thousand years. On the fells of the border country there were ancient tracks, and on a frosty night, in the moonlit valleys, you could hear owls hoot the way they had called for centuries.

Culpeper could not understand how the past had become real for Tom Malling, real in all its crude solutions to a problem.

In the library, Arnold finally found the passage he had read long ago, and the passage Malling had wanted to re-read, that day he had spoken to Arnold in the library.

William Twyford and Richard atte Chirche with another mason were designated as official building inspectors in 1375. They were sworn to report nuisances and encroachments, to divide property, to issue bye-laws relating to party walls, and stillicides. In 1376 Richard atte Chirche was appointed 'sworn mason'. In this capacity he was given a status that can be described not only as judicial but also as executive, carrying out the sentences determined upon. The 'sworn masons' had become by this time adjudicators not merely of boundary and tenement disputes but as 'sercheours of wronges' and adjusters of the morals of the communities in which they held sway. As members of the gild they forced the following of ordinances; as men of the subtle craft they adjudicated upon craft disputes; but as 'sworn masons' they took upon themselves the powers of life and death, in a society where the law was uncertain, the king's justice distant, and the need for justice urgent and demanding. There is some evidence that executions actually took place, in cases of theft and adultery within the gild. Few cases were recorded by way of documentation; the sworn masons remained an esoteric branch of a secret gild, which died out in the fifteenth century . . .

Tom Malling had hated the masons but had drawn the distinction between the seventeenth-century shadow and the reality of the fourteenth-century need. His misunderstanding of that time, and its relationship to the present, had cost Patrick Yates his life.

He had not been a man of the subtle craft but he had taken on the cloak of the sworn mason. And in the end he had been unable to distinguish between the righting of wrongs, and murder.

THE END